Also by Samantha Chase

The Montgomery Brothers
Wait for Me / Trust in Me
Stay with Me / More of Me
Return to You
Meant for You
I'll Be There
Until There Was Us

The Shaughnessy Brothers
Made for Us
Love Walks In
Always My Girl
This Is Our Song
A Sky Full of Stars
Holiday Spice
Until I Loved You

Shaughnessy Brothers: Band on the Run
One More Kiss
One More Promise
One More Moment

Holiday Romance
The Christmas Cottage / Ever After
Mistletoe Between Friends / The Snowflake Inn

Novellas Now in Print
The Baby Arrangement / Baby, I'm Yours / Baby, Be Mine
In the Eye of the Storm / Catering to the CEO
Exclusive / A Touch of Heaven

Suddenly *Mine*

SAMANTHA CHASE

Cover designed by Dawn Adams/Sourcebooks, Inc.
Cover images © Cultura RM Exclusive/Christin Rose/marshalgonz/Getty Images

Published by Sourcebooks Casablanca, an imprint of Sourcebooks, Inc.
P.O. Box 4410, Naperville, Illinois 60567-4410
(630) 961-3900
Fax: (630) 961-2168
sourcebooks.com

Printed and bound in Canada.
MBP 10 9 8 7 6 5 4 3 2 1

Prologue

As far as cocktail parties went, this one was in pure Montgomery fashion. In a room filled with family, there was a lot of laughter, but there was also a lot of business talk.

Monica Montgomery rolled her eyes at that. It didn't matter how many parties she'd attended—and hosted—she still never understood the appeal of talking business when you were celebrating something wonderful! In this case, her niece Megan's engagement to Alex Rebat. Looking across the room, she saw them laughing and smiling as they spoke to the people around them, and it made her heart swell with pride.

"We did that," a giddy voice said from beside her.

Smiling, Monica looked at her sister-in-law Eliza and agreed. "We sure did. Now I can see why my husband loves playing matchmaker. It's a wonderful feeling to see the joy on the faces of a couple in love."

"And Megan and Alex certainly are," Eliza said with a happy sigh. "My baby girl is all grown up and I've never seen her look happier." She paused. "I only wish I could say the same for my sons."

Unfortunately, Monica was stumped on what to do with her wayward nephews. Neither Carter nor Christian seemed to have any interest in settling down. And that wasn't acceptable. There was a whole new generation of Montgomerys coming up in this world and she hoped her nephews would want to contribute to that.

"I have to admit," she began carefully, "Christian seems a little less…intense these days."

Beside her, Eliza nodded. "Believe it or not, he was dating someone."

"Really?" Monica asked excitedly.

"Pfft, don't get your hopes up. That relationship ended already, but it was nice to know that he was finally showing an interest in dating again."

"Any idea what finally changed his mind?"

Eliza shrugged. "Not a clue. My son doesn't share anything about his personal life, and for that I blame my husband."

This was new information. "Why? What does Joseph have to do with this?"

For a moment, Eliza looked extremely uncomfortable, managing to look everywhere except at Monica.

"Eliza?" Monica prompted.

With a weary shrug, Eliza responded, "Let's just say that my husband managed to interfere in a relationship Christian was involved in when he lived in London. Neither of them will say much about it and it was obviously ages ago, but…" Another sigh. "It's come up several times, and if I had to take a guess, I'd say my husband was a little less than compassionate."

"Oh no." Monica scanned the room and spotted Christian talking intently with his father. "Do you think we should go over there and break that up? Maybe they both need a reminder that this is a ballroom, not a conference room."

Eliza laughed softly. "It doesn't seem to matter."

"What about Carter? How's he doing these days? Dating anyone?"

"Carter seems to date a lot, but we never meet the girls and he only goes out with them once or twice." Shaking her head, she turned to Monica. "Here's the thing. I know exactly who Carter's going to marry, he just doesn't know it yet."

That was both cryptic and intriguing. "Really? And when did this happen?"

"When Carter was in the fourth grade."

Luckily, she hadn't taken a sip of her champagne or she would have been choking on it. "Um...excuse me?"

Nodding, Eliza explained. "I knew the moment my son had met his match, and they've known each other almost their entire lives. If I had my way, they'd be together right now."

"So why aren't they?"

"Neither of them is ready, but...soon. I hope she's still single."

"You don't know?"

"I've sort of lost track."

There was no way Monica was going to remind Eliza that there was a real possibility of the girl being unavailable. The last thing Monica wanted was to bring the mood down—after all, that would make her no better than her brother-in-law. Looking around the room, she spotted her husband and knew she was going to have a conversation with him later on in hopes of having him straighten his brother out and getting him to lay off of Christian.

Deciding to change the subject—sort of—Monica took a sip of her champagne and smiled at Eliza. "So, what are you doing with yourself these days? Anything exciting?"

"I've been working with Joseph's head of human resources lately and helping her with some new health incentives for employees."

"Really? I haven't heard anything about that," Monica said, intrigued. "Is this something that's only going to take place in New York, or do you think it will go company-wide?"

"I'm hoping for company-wide. They would have a corporate wellness nurse come to the office several times a month and do things like flu shots, blood pressure checks, and offer sessions on nutrition. It's in the beginning stages, but I'd like to think we can turn it into something all employees can benefit from."

"Color me impressed, Eliza," Monica said with a smile. "I had no idea you were doing any corporate work."

"Every once in a while, I like to get involved in something. This particular idea wasn't something I came up with myself—I heard about it while I was at my doctor's office. You know I had gone to school to become a nurse, but once we started having kids, I stopped working. Believe it or not, I've often toyed with the idea of going back to school and becoming an RN."

"I didn't realize that! That would be an awful lot of work, wouldn't it?"

Eliza agreed. "It would, and as much as I think I'd enjoy it, I enjoy our lives the way they are right now."

"I understand."

"Anyway, I mentioned the idea of the wellness program to Joseph and he liked it. We talked about it and he asked me to work with human resources to get it started."

"I'll have to ask William about it. It sounds wonderful!"

"Did I hear my name?"

Monica turned and smiled as her husband leaned in and kissed her on the cheek. "It's like you have some sort of radar, William," she teased.

"Sometimes I do," he teased in return. "What are you two lovely ladies talking about?"

Monica told him about the corporate wellness program. "Don't you think it's a wonderful idea?"

"Absolutely! We've been talking about it and were trying to figure out where to go with it next."

And then inspiration hit. With a sly look at Eliza, Monica turned to her husband. "I think it would be beneficial to go to San Diego next!"

Both William and Eliza looked at her in mild confusion.

"You do?" they said in unison.

"I do," she replied. "Just like it worked well to have Megan go and work with Christian's office because it's smaller, it might be nice to do the same with this program."

"Well, I suppose—" William said, but Monica was on a roll.

"And considering how Eliza has been working so diligently with Joseph's office, I think it would be a wonderful idea for her to share what she's done with Christian's human resources people."

"That does sound—"

"And," she barreled on, "I think I'd like to go with her and learn a little about it myself, and then I can talk to the people in your office, William. What do you think?"

"I…I, um…"

"I bet Eliza and I could go to San Diego directly from here and spend a week and get the ball rolling." She looked anxiously at Eliza for confirmation. "Don't you think?"

Eliza was still confused, but she rolled with it. "I agree. I think the sooner we get things going, the better." She smiled at William. "And I know Monica will be a fantastic asset."

William looked between the two of them, his eyes narrowing. "I guess I'll tell Robert and Joseph what's going on."

"Thank you, sweetheart," Monica said, squeezing her husband's arm. "I think this is going to be a wonderful thing for the company, and you know Eliza and I will do everything we can to make it succeed!"

"I know you will," he said sweetly. Then he kissed her again before going off to speak to his brothers.

It wasn't until he was across the room that Eliza stepped directly in front of Monica. "What was that all about?"

The wide-eyed expression on her sister-in-law's face was priceless. But Monica knew as soon as she explained herself—and her plan—Eliza would be on board.

Hooking her arm through Eliza's, she guided her toward the bar to freshen their drinks. "Just imagine all the possibilities a week in San Diego observing your son could do. Now that he's open to dating again, we just might find the perfect woman for him."

It took a minute, but Eliza's smile came slow and equally sly. "Why, Monica, you're a bit of a genius."

"Guilty as charged," she said with a grin. Raising her glass, she added, "Here's to a successful search!"

Chapter 1

"Don't these people have jobs?" Christian Montgomery murmured to himself as he sipped his morning coffee.

For a while now, he had taken to having his coffee out on his deck before going in to work. It was a chance to breathe in the fresh air and have some peace before the craziness of his day. People-watching had become his favorite hobby, and as odd as it sounded, he found it relaxing and therapeutic.

Scanning the sand, he smiled at the small circle of people doing yoga off to his left. Every day they were out there stretching and holding their poses, and it was almost hypnotic to watch. At times, he even found himself deep breathing along with them, as he imagined they were doing.

Not far from them was a trio of fishermen. Not once had Christian ever seen them catch anything, but they were out there religiously every morning—rain or shine. That was one hobby he had never had an interest in. It looked boring. Those guys were there before Christian came out on his deck, and he imagined they stayed out there long after he left for work. He could only hope they caught some fish eventually.

Then there were the surfers. They were also hypnotic to watch but offered a bit more excitement. There was no way he could even imagine himself doing what those people did, but it was cool as hell to watch. Some of them were amazing at it, while others sort of…well, they tried.

Which reminded him…

"Oh, this is glorious! I could totally get used to this!"

Great. His mother was awake and encroaching on his peaceful time.

Looking out at the waves crashing on the shore, he took another sip of his coffee before turning to look at his mother. "You're up early."

She took a long sip of her own steaming coffee before answering. "Well, as much as I complain about your father's snoring, it appears I can't sleep without him." With a serene smile, she added, "Besides, I was hoping to have a few minutes with you before you left for the office."

He'd been avoiding this sort of thing. After getting ambushed at Megan and Alex's engagement party with the news that his mother and aunt would be coming home with him, Christian had been doing his best to stay out of their way. But apparently, his reprieve was up.

He almost jumped at the feel of his mother's hand covering his. She looked so sweet, yet he had a feeling there was more to this trip to San Diego than starting some sort of wellness program.

"You work too hard," she said point-blank. "Monica and I tried waiting up for you, but we were both exhausted and couldn't stay up any longer. What time did you finally come home?"

"I don't know. Sometime around eleven."

She made a disapproving sound. "Were you working all that time or did you happen to have a date?"

It was a challenge not to roll his eyes. "I was working, Mom. I wouldn't have blown you and Aunt Monica off for a date."

"Well...you should," she argued lightly. "It wouldn't kill you to get out and date more."

"Mom..."

Placing her mug on the deck railing, she faced him. "Christian, you remind me so much of your father." Then she paused. "And that's not a compliment."

Okay, this was new.

"I don't know everything that happened in London and I don't want to know," she stated. "What I do know is that it's gone on long enough. You work too much, you spend far too much time alone, and I can't ignore it anymore."

Christian sighed wearily and drank the rest of his coffee before putting his mug beside hers.

"I get that you're disappointed in me—"

Her soft gasp stopped him.

"Christian, I could never be disappointed in you. Ever," she said vehemently. "But I look at you and I can see you're not happy." Reaching up, she cupped his cheek. "No mother wants to see her child unhappy. You need a life outside of work."

"That's not what Dad thinks," he mumbled.

"You know you don't have to do everything your father says, don't you?" Her words were soft and firm and when Christian looked at her, he saw a hint of a smirk on her face. "Your father is a very intelligent man, but not everything he says is the gospel truth.

As a matter of fact, I think it's safe to say that where anything outside of work is concerned, your father doesn't know what he's talking about."

Christian couldn't help but chuckle. "You're pretty feisty early in the morning," he teased.

She waved him off. "I'm feisty all the time, but no one seems to pay attention."

So many thoughts were racing through his mind. It was easy to stand here and say he didn't have to listen to his father—or anyone for that matter—but actually doing it without letting the guilt eat away at him was different. And it didn't matter how old he was or how independent he was; for some reason, his father could make him feel like an incompetent child with a few choice words.

"Christian," she went on, interrupting his thoughts. "If you're not happy in this career, you know you can change that, right? Just because you have the Montgomery name doesn't mean you have to work for the company."

"Everyone else does."

This time her smile was patient and loving and so completely a mom look. "Your brother doesn't, and for years your sister didn't."

"And now she does," he gently reminded.

"But she turned down the opportunity for a big promotion because she realized she wanted more out of her life. And from what I understand, you helped her realize that."

He felt himself blush. Clearing his throat, Christian turned and leaned on the railing. "Yeah, well… I hated the thought of Megan getting trapped like I am."

He realized a little too late what he'd just admitted.

"Sweetheart, you're not trapped," his mother said quietly, her hand covering his again. "If there's something you want to change, you should! Life is too short to stay in a place that makes you miserable."

"I wouldn't say I'm miserable—"

"But are you happy?" she quickly interrupted.

That question gave him pause. "Sometimes I think I am."

Beside him, she sighed. "Do you like living in San Diego?"

"What's not to like? I've got a great house right on the beach. The view alone makes it pretty spectacular."

"Christian, you've been living here for five years and this isn't even your house. If you like it here so much, why not find a place of your own and settle down?"

It was way too early in the morning for this conversation.

"Mom, Ryder and I have an agreement on the house. He's fine with me living here, and he knows if he wants to sell, I'm the first one who'll put an offer in."

"You're avoiding making any commitment here," she gently chided. "It's your cousin's house and your father's company, and I would love to see you pick something that's yours and enjoy it."

"*Bollocks*," he muttered, raking a hand through his hair.

With a small laugh, his mother scolded him. "No need for that language."

He almost laughed with her. After spending so many years living in London, Christian had picked up a lot of the lingo and every once in a while, it came out.

Usually when he was annoyed.

"Mom," he said with a huff of frustration. "This is not how I want to start the day—arguing with you about my life choices."

"I'm not arguing—"

"You are," he corrected.

"I'm concerned, Christian. There's a difference."

As much as he didn't doubt that, the truth was that he just wasn't in the mood for this particular discussion, so as a distraction, he hugged her. "And I love you for it." He placed a kiss on the top of her head. "Now, tell me how your search for a wellness provider is going."

If she knew why he was changing the subject, she kept it to herself. "I've been pleasantly surprised at how well things are falling into place. Patricia in human resources has been amazing!" She stepped out of his embrace and sat on the nearby chaise. "We're going to be holding more interviews—but it's a formality. Monica and I met the perfect applicant already."

"So then why keep interviewing?"

"This particular applicant we haven't formally interviewed yet, so we're covering our bases."

"Mom," he admonished. "That's not a great way to handle this."

"Oh, hush. Trust me on this one. I want to have backups, but I am confident that once we do the formal interview, everything will fall into place."

He studied his mother for a long moment and realized he didn't want to get too involved in this. Just admitting that to himself let him relax. With a smile, he said, "I do trust you. You've done great things with this program, so who am I to tell you how you should be doing things?"

"Thank you." She smiled proudly. "But the best part of the whole thing was how Patricia was able to secure office space that would require little to no work to modify."

He nodded, thankful for that little bit of news. The last thing he wanted was to deal with the headache of office renovations.

"Basically, you won't have to worry about a thing," she continued. "All you need to do is be pleasant and greet whoever we hire in a way that won't scare them away."

Christian laughed. "I'm hardly scary, Mom."

"You could smile more." She was about to say something else but instead glanced toward the house. "I promised your father I'd call him this morning, and you know he'll worry if I don't." Walking over, she gave him a quick kiss on the cheek before heading back inside.

The whoosh of relief at being alone came out before he knew it. As much as he loved his mother, she could be a bit exhausting.

Especially this early in the morning.

Turning his attention to the beach, a slow smile spread across his face. "There you are," he said quietly.

With a quick glance over his shoulder to make sure his mother wasn't coming back out, Christian immediately returned his attention to the shore. Every morning, dozens of surfers came out and started their days by riding the waves. When he'd first moved to San Diego and into his cousin Ryder's house, he'd been a bit annoyed at the constant sea of bodies practically right outside his door. It didn't take long for him to realize they weren't the least bit interested in him; they were here for the ocean. Nothing more, nothing less. And the longer he lived here, the more he appreciated all of the activity on the beach—particularly the surfing.

Surfing had never been something that interested him before, but one morning he'd come out on the deck with his cup of coffee and noticed one surfer in particular. Christian didn't know any of them personally, but had named them each based on what he'd observed. For instance, there was Surfer Dude—a young guy with sun-bleached blond hair and a tan who embodied exactly what Christian has always envisioned a surfer would look like. Then there was Older Surfer Dude, who was exactly as described. After that the names were a little more random: Tie-Dye Guy, Too-Tan Girl, and Burly Guy. They were the regulars, but if someone new caught his attention, he usually gave them a name while he watched them.

Seriously, this had been his greatest form of entertainment.

Then there was *her*.

No nickname would do her justice.

With long red hair pulled up into a ponytail and skin that was far too fair to be out in the sun for long, she stood out in a sea of blond surfers. From this distance, Christian couldn't be certain how tall she was, but if he had to guess, he'd say she was on the petite side. Dressed in long-sleeved black Lycra that encased an incredibly curvy body, she was completely captivating. Today's bikini bottoms were neon pink. Her legs were just as spectacular without the fabric as they were with. If he was a bolder guy, he'd head to the water and pretend he was a surfer to get a closer look at her and maybe introduce himself.

But…he wasn't.

And he couldn't.

Duty called.

But not before he watched her attempt at surfing awhile longer.

For all her gear and apparent enthusiasm, she wasn't a good surfer. Even without any real knowledge of the sport, Christian could tell she was a novice. He'd watched her stand and fall off her board more times than he cared to count, yet every time she fell, she got up and tried again.

He had to admire her perseverance.

And the way she looked soaking wet.

In his mind, he imagined being able to walk down to the water and right into it with her. He'd put his hands on her waist and help her onto her board. His touch would linger just a bit, and he knew his fingers would twitch with the need to feel her skin—to know if it was as soft as he imagined. In the suit she had on today, he could be bold and run a hand along her leg, skim her thigh before watching her swim into the current.

From there, he'd stay in the water to cool his own skin. He'd watch her catch a wave and ride it successfully until she was back at his side—exuberant at the thought of finally making it. She'd jump into his arms, wrap those magnificent legs around him, and kiss him.

Licking his lips, he could almost taste the salt, along with the softness of her. He almost groaned at the image.

From there he'd invite her up to the house and finally see how she looked without the Lycra.

No doubt it would be fantastic.

Behind him, he heard his mother and aunt laughing, and boy, didn't that kill the fantasy. Which was just as well—it wasn't as if he could do anything about it. There was no way he was going down to the beach or into the water or…inviting his surfer girl back to the house.

The thought was more than a little disappointing.

He had to get ready for work. Just like he always did. There hadn't been a day since he was fifteen that he hadn't been responsible or gone to the office. Even all through college, Christian had held a job with Montgomerys. Back then it was in his father's New York office, then later he'd jumped at the opportunity to move to London—partly for the change of scenery and partly to have a little independence. That hadn't gone quite as planned and now he was in San Diego, still making sure he never gave anyone a reason to question his dedication to the job.

Although…he was starting to question his own dedication. Lately, no matter how much he tried to tell himself otherwise, there was a growing discontent within himself. Maybe it was the job, or maybe it was just his life in general, he couldn't be sure. All Christian knew was that there were a lot of people counting on him and he couldn't sit on his deck looking out at the ocean all day. He had a full day of appointments, and no matter how badly he'd like to—for once—play hooky and enjoy a day for himself, he couldn't.

Joseph Montgomery wouldn't allow him to.

And whose fault is that?

Yeah, yeah, yeah. He knew he was responsible for

the position he was in now by refusing to stand up for himself early on and letting his father get away with calling the shots. They'd butted heads a lot—particularly in the past five years—but it didn't change anything. Every time they fought, Christian would cave out of respect to his father, because if nothing else, he was a good son. This was their pattern of behavior and it was too late to change the dynamic.

Or was it?

He caught sight of his surfer girl flying off her board and smiled. That made four times in the short time he'd been watching. She came up laughing—as she often did—and in that instant, he envied her. Did she ever feel discouraged? Did she ever break through the water after a fall and scream *bloody hell* and just want to give up? She was clearly failing and yet...she was still smiling and finding joy in it. How was that possible? If it were him and he was the one out there constantly falling off his board, he would have given up by now. Sometimes you had to admit defeat and realize there would be some skills you simply couldn't master. Didn't she realize that?

Now wasn't the time to find out, unfortunately. He had responsibilities and commitments and none of them made him feel joyful. If anything, he could already feel his body tensing up. It felt as if it began at the tip of his toes and was working its way up through his entire being—the muscles growing tighter until it felt constricting, like he couldn't breathe.

It wasn't the first time he'd felt that way, but it was happening with more and more frequency.

Rubbing a hand over his chest, Christian tried to calm

down and clear his mind. *Deep breaths*, he reminded himself. *Just take some deep breaths*.

And for several minutes he did. It helped. Sort of. Either way, he felt well enough to grab his coffee mug and give one last look at the beach before heading into the house and preparing for another full day of…nothingness.

Sophie Bennington breathed through the pain as she made her way out of the ocean and onto the shore. That last wave had hit her hard and she knew she'd be feeling the effects of it for the rest of the day.

"So not the day for this," she murmured, walking slowly to her stuff. It was still a bit surprising that she could leave her things in the sand and they'd go undisturbed, but right now she was thankful for it.

The beach wasn't particularly crowded—just folks like her who were interested in catching some waves before they had to head off to their real jobs and responsibilities.

She dropped her board on the sand and sat on her towel. She inhaled the fresh air before letting the breath out slowly. If it were up to her, she'd stay here all day and enjoy the sunshine and sounds of the waves crashing on the beach. Unfortunately, that was no longer an option.

Sure, she'd been pretty much doing that for the last several weeks—not that she spent entire days on the beach, but she also hadn't had any reason to rush off.

Not like today.

Today she had a job interview and almost broke out in a "Hallelujah" chorus over it. Moving to a new state on a whim had been completely out of her comfort zone, but a healthy savings account had meant that she didn't need to stress about finding a job right away. Part of her had felt like being a bit more rebellious and shirking some responsibility for a little while. But fun time was over, and her more practical side was coming out to remind her that she needed to find a job. She just hadn't realized it might take longer than she wanted.

But…she was feeling extremely optimistic about this interview and she had more than enough credentials and experience, and by all accounts, she should be a shoo-in.

"Don't go getting ahead of yourself," she quietly reminded herself. "Just because you think you're all that and a bag of chips doesn't mean everyone else will."

A girl could hope though, right?

All around her, people were moving and laughing and doing their thing, while Sophie contemplated the day ahead. It had been a long time since she'd gone on a job interview. Having lived her entire life in a small town, she had known everyone. Add to that having gone to college in the next town over and living at home, getting a job had been handled over Sunday dinner or at the potluck after church. Dealing with strangers was going to be a bit of a challenge.

"But I'm up for it," she said confidently. "I moved a thousand miles on my own. I can do this."

Daily pep talks were becoming the norm for her and she wasn't quite sure that was a good thing. Basically, she was talking to herself.

A lot.

Refusing to let herself believe she was going crazy, Sophie stood and stretched. The sky was definitely getting brighter, the morning clouds had moved on, and she noticed a mini mass exodus to the parking lot. That meant it had to be around eight o'clock. Her interview was at eleven, so she had plenty of time, but she had a feeling it was going to take every one of those hours and minutes to get her nerves under control.

With a final look at the ocean, she collected her things. She'd gotten it down to a science—towel rolled and put in her backpack, sunglasses on, flip-flops in her hand, and board under her arm. It only weighed ten pounds, but it was awkward as hell to maneuver; the board was close to seven feet long and she was barely five foot three, but she was stronger than she looked. Most people tended to underestimate her—in just about every way—based on her size. What they didn't know was that she had enough determination to do whatever she put her mind to and was willing to do the work to get it done.

Athletics came easy to her and at times, her size worked to her advantage. Where surfing was concerned, however, she had been encouraged to get a larger board until she gained some skill. Sophie had thought she'd be able to trade out for a smaller board by now, but that wasn't happening nearly as fast as she'd hoped.

"Soon," she said, making her way back to the parking lot. "I just need to practice a little more."

Or a lot, she corrected.

Walking across the lot, Sophie smiled at fellow

beach-goers and said a word of thanks to the kind gentleman holding the door open for her at the surf shop. Renting her board made a lot more sense than buying one outright—especially if she came to the conclusion that surfing wasn't her thing.

"How'd it go today, Soph?" Randy, the owner of the surf shop, asked. He was in his midthirties and had the look of the perpetual surfer—tan, shaggy hair, and puka-shell necklace included.

"I think I'm getting better," she said optimistically. "But that last wave knocked the wind out of me and the board hit me pretty hard as I flipped." Absently, she rubbed her hip. "No doubt I'll have a nice bruise to show for it by lunchtime."

"It goes with the territory," he said, taking the board from her and giving her a receipt. "Do you want to try a different board tomorrow? Maybe something a little lighter?"

"You said this was the size I should be using, since I'm a beginner," she reminded him. "And besides, I think I'm getting used to it. I need to work on my confidence and maybe my concentration."

He grinned at her. "You should have taken more than one lesson. And while I can appreciate your enthusiasm, it never hurts to get a little help with your technique."

Placing the receipt in her bag, she smiled. "I'll think about it. Right now I've got to go and get ready for my job interview."

His blue eyes widened. "Hey, that's great! Did you finally opt to go with an agency?"

"I did," she said, with just a touch of sadness. "They're sending me to meet with my first client company today.

It's not exactly what I had planned, but...I'm sure it's going to be great."

It was important to stay optimistic.

Over the past several weeks, she'd shared a little about her job search with pretty much anyone who would listen and prayed she'd get some recommendations. She'd begun to lose hope until she'd been talking to a couple of older ladies on the beach and they'd shared a lead on a potential position. That morning she had signed on with an agency and had mentioned the job opportunity to her contact. After some negotiation, Sophie had managed to secure the interview—even though there were others at the agency who had seniority over her.

"Fingers crossed," she said cheerily, walking toward the door. "If you don't see me tomorrow, that means I'm starting a new job!"

"Good luck, Soph! I'm sure you're going to do great!"

"Thanks, Ran!"

Pulling her keys out, she was in her car and on her way home in no time. Her studio apartment was only a mile from the beach, but traffic was already congesting the roads. It was nearing nine o'clock when she walked through her front door. Tossing her backpack on the sofa, Sophie immediately went to the refrigerator and poured herself a glass of orange juice. She was about to take a shower when her cell phone rang.

Taking the phone from her pack, she smiled and sighed at the same time.

"Hey, Nana," she said, kicking off her flip-flops. "How are you this morning?"

"Oh, you know me. Can't complain. How's California treating you? Ready to come home yet?"

They'd had this conversation several times a week since Sophie had moved away. "Nope. I'm enjoying the beach and the sunshine. I think I can see myself living here permanently."

"Now, Soph, you know California is one of the most expensive places in the country to live. Why would you put all that extra stress on yourself, especially when you know the cost of living is so much more reasonable here in Kansas."

"Not everything is about being cost-effective, Nana. Sometimes you have to leave your comfort zone to find what makes you happy. And worrying about the cost of living does not make me happy."

"I'm sure it won't—if you keep living there, the stress of it will make you downright miserable."

I walked right into that one, she thought.

"I don't think I'll be worrying for too much longer."

"Oh?"

"I have a job interview today!" she said excitedly.

Nana snorted softly.

"Oh, stop," she chided. "I think it's going to be perfect. It's exactly what I was looking for—practically as if the job was created just for me!"

"Probably a scam."

"Thanks for the vote of confidence."

For her entire life, Nana had been her biggest champion—always telling Sophie there wasn't anything she couldn't do. She was the only parent Sophie had ever known, and Sophie knew that right now, Nana was lashing out like this because she missed her.

At least, she hoped that was why.

A weary sigh came over the phone before Nana spoke

again. "I worry about you, that's all. This whole thing—you moving away in a show of defiance, well…it's hard for me. I thought you'd go and see that California wasn't for you and just come home."

Resting her head against the sofa cushion, Sophie let out her own sigh. "We've been over this. You know why I needed to do this."

"I know, I know. And…I hope you find what you're looking for, sweetheart. But I hate that you felt the need to do it so far away from me."

For a moment, her heart hurt. "It was time for a change. I couldn't stay there knowing—"

"I know," Nana quickly said, and Sophie was thankful they weren't going into details again. She couldn't handle that right now. Not when she needed to focus on positive things.

"I went surfing again this morning," she said, abruptly changing the subject.

"And? How did you do?" Nana asked, with her first hint of encouragement.

"Still not getting far, but I'm having fun!"

"That's my girl." She paused. "Tell me about this job you're interviewing for. Is it really what you're looking for, or are you settling because you need to find a job? Because if you're going to settle, you know I can help you out financially until you find the right one."

It would be easy to accept the financial help. And right now, with her bank account balance dwindling, a little padding wouldn't hurt. But she'd sworn to herself that she'd make it on her own no matter what. She wasn't broke, and today's meeting was a done deal.

They were going to be her first clients, and once she proved herself to the agency, no doubt she'd get a few more assignments.

"I'm fine, Nana. I promise. I have a good feeling about today." For the next several minutes, she talked about the position and all it would entail, and she could barely contain her excitement. By the time she was done explaining, Sophie was almost breathless. "So now I have to shower and find something to wear and do something with my hair so I don't look crazy—"

"Your hair is beautiful. If you use one of those silver clips I gave you, it will be perfect." Nana was silent for a moment before adding, "You're perfect. And don't you ever forget it."

And just like that, Sophie relaxed.

To most people, she might come off as being confident, but sometimes she needed a few words of encouragement from the one person who loved her.

"Thanks, Nana."

"Go and show these people why they'd be lucky to have you! And promise you'll call me later and tell me all about it."

Smiling, Sophie replied, "I will."

Ending the call and placing the phone on the cushion next to her, she wondered why life wasn't always as simple as it used to be. There had been a time when she never would have considered leaving her hometown. She knew everyone, and everyone knew her. Life was uncomplicated.

Until it wasn't.

Secrets had a way of ruining everything.

"So not the time to be thinking about this," she

murmured, forcing herself to stand up and grab another glass of juice.

One of the reasons Sophie had hopped in her car and driven a thousand-plus miles for a change of scenery was to help her forget. The other was to start over—as someone nobody knew, and people could choose to either love her or hate her for herself, not because of her family history.

So far, it had been working.

Sometimes, however, her mind was her own worst enemy.

"Not now and not today," she stated firmly, drinking her juice and walking determinedly toward the bathroom. "I have to kick butt on this interview, so only happy thoughts!" With that, she turned on her shower and then immediately reached over and turned on her iPod, cranking up some of her most motivating music.

Under the spray, she sang—badly—at the top of her lungs while she washed her hair. One song led to another and by the time she shut the water off, she'd gone through at least a half dozen of them. Clearing her throat, she realized she may have been a little overzealous in her singing.

"Not smart, Soph. Definitely not smart."

Opting to *listen* to the rest of the playlist, she went about carefully applying her makeup before starting the lengthy process of drying her hair. How many times had she considered cutting her long tresses, only to back out at the last minute? It was a love-hate relationship, basically—she loved how it looked when it was styled and behaving but hated it every time she had to dry and style it.

Studying her reflection as she combed through the wet tangles, she said, "Clearly, I have issues."

Issues or not, she finished getting herself ready—hair, makeup, and a kickass outfit of a jade-green pencil skirt that matched her eyes and a white blouse. It was simple but crisp and professional, and when she walked out her front door a little later, she felt like she could take on the world!

Two days later, Christian came home early and went searching for his mother, stopping in the doorway to the guestroom. "You're leaving?"

Eliza looked up from her suitcase and gave him a small smile. "We had planned to stay another couple of days, but Uncle William called to tell your aunt that Gina is having early contractions."

"Wait—isn't she only, like, six months along?"

"Exactly. That's why your aunt is so frantic about getting home. William tried to assure her that he had everything under control and he'd call her if they were going to admit Gina to the hospital, but"—she let out a soft laugh—"you know how your aunt is about her grandchildren. She's been there for the birth of each and every one of them. All six."

"You don't think Gina's going to deliver the baby this soon, do you?"

His mother moved around the room collecting her things. "I doubt it. But Monica wants to be there to help Mac and Gina with whatever they need. No doubt they'll need a hand taking care of their son. He's only three and if Gina has to go on bedrest, or if the baby does come prematurely, someone will need to be with her full-time." She sighed. "That's the sort of thing grandmothers do."

Christian wanted to roll his eyes at the longing he heard in his mother's voice. There was no doubt that his cousins were procreating like wild and it was putting a lot of pressure on the rest of the Montgomerys, but normally his mother wasn't so obvious about it.

"Megan and Alex will be pregnant before you know it," he said optimistically, even pasting a smile on his face for good measure.

She waved him off and resumed her packing. "I hope you're right, but that still leaves me hopelessly behind. This baby will make her seventh grandchild. And your aunt Janice and uncle Robert are coming up right behind them. And what have I got?" she asked, but Christian had a feeling she wasn't exactly speaking directly to him.

"Mom..."

"Sure, your sister and Alex are anxious to start a family, but what about you and your brother, huh?" Still not looking at him, she tossed the last of her items into her suitcase. "Neither of you will even consider settling down, so I'll have to be content to be Great-Aunt Eliza, watching everyone else have grandchildren while I'm forced to play with...with...Snickerdoodle!"

"Snickerdoodle?"

Snapping her suitcase shut, she spun to face him. "The dog I'm going to have to get—one of those yappy little things that I can fit in my purse and carry around like a baby. That is my future, Christian."

With a soft laugh of his own, he stepped into the room and wrapped his arms around his mother, hugging her close. "Let's not go there just yet," he said with amusement. "For all you know, Megan will have twins or something."

"You know she's not pregnant yet, right?" Eliza asked flatly.

Nodding, he said, "I know. But I'm hopeful."

"Twins don't even run in our family. Alex's either."

"And you know this…how?"

"I was a little inquisitive when I met his parents," she murmured. "Not one set of twins on either side. So you see, I don't have a choice but to put all of my hopes and dreams in Snickerdoodle."

He kissed her on the top of her head and took a step back. "Maybe you can run this whole speech by Carter before you go getting a dog carrier, huh? For all you know, this may be the exact thing he needs to light a fire under him to pick a girl."

Swatting him away, Eliza breezed out of the room as she called out to see if his aunt was done packing.

Feeling more than a little exhausted, he sat on the corner of the guest bed and relaxed. While he had to admit that this visit was a little more like a whirlwind than the comfortable exchange they usually enjoyed, he was still sorry to see his mom leaving so soon.

Rising from the bed, he walked out of the room and down the hall, where he found his mother and aunt straightening up the second guest room.

"You know you don't have to do that, right?" he asked, leaning against the doorjamb. "I have a cleaning service that comes in once a week. They'll take care of all this."

"Nonsense," Aunt Monica replied, putting the last of

her things into her suitcase. "I couldn't leave without cleaning up a bit. It's bad manners."

This time he did roll his eyes, but he laughed too. "Did you talk to the people in human resources? Do they know you're both leaving?"

"I did," his mother responded. "And we hired a corporate health aide today, so things are right on track. Your people have access to all of the training materials we created and they know where to reach me if they have any questions."

He wanted to feel relieved, or at least a little excited, but his mother's voice was a little…stilted.

"Are you happy with this new hire?"

Both women shrugged and murmured "yes" and "sure," but neither sounded overly enthused.

"Okay, out with it. What's wrong with this person? Are they not fully qualified? Do you think we need to keep interviewing?"

"No, no, no," his mother said, waving him off. "It's nothing like that."

"Then what's the problem?"

Aunt Monica took the lead on this one. "Honestly, we found the perfect person, but—"

"But what?"

"She didn't show up for our first meeting," Eliza replied. "She called, and there was a perfectly good explanation, but…"

He waited her out for another minute.

"Monica and I had hoped to have the time to get to know her a little bit more, that's all. It's not a big deal or anything, but it was something we had both wanted to do. Then our schedules were filled with calls for some of the other Montgomery offices and working with your human resources team, so we didn't have time to reschedule."

Christian knew this was his mother's baby and had to ask... "Okay, well... I get why Aunt Monica is leaving, but why don't you stay, Mom? You just got here, and I'm sure there's more you can do. Maybe you can reschedule the appointment and have the time to get to know her more." Although for the life of him, he had no idea why this was even an issue, but whatever. "And on top of that, I'd like for you stay a little longer."

And just like that, his mother's face transformed from neutral to positively beaming. She stepped forward and cupped his cheek. "That is quite possibly the nicest thing you've said to me in a long time."

Damn. And it really wasn't all that nice, he thought.

"I'm just saying that you don't have to go," he clarified. "I know I haven't been home as much as I had hoped, but I promise to make the time so we can have our meals together if you stay—breakfast out on the deck, I'll take you to lunch, and then we'll come home and make dinner together. What do you say?"

"I say that you are an incredibly sweet son," Eliza said. "And if I hadn't already talked to your father, I'd consider staying. But as soon as I mentioned coming home, he went into the helpless man mode and whined about how much he didn't know what he was doing and that he needed me at home. So..."

"Honestly, men can be such babies," Aunt Monica said, securing her luggage and placing it on the floor. "No offense, Christian."

"None taken," he said, smiling. He looked at the two

of them—while he normally preferred his privacy, it had been nice having them here. "So what time is your flight? What time do we need to leave?"

They exchanged looks. "Um… We figured you'd be busy," his mother explained, "so we called for a car service to pick us up."

As if on cue, a horn beeped.

He looked at his mother in disbelief. "Seriously? You didn't think to ask me to drive you to the airport? And for that matter, why didn't you tell me any of this while we were all at the office? Was I supposed to come home and find a note saying you'd left?"

Basically, he had no idea what time his mother and aunt had come to the office or when they'd left—their schedule wasn't something he was overly concerned about. But today he had forced himself to leave the office early so he could take them both to dinner. If he hadn't come home when he did, they'd both be gone.

"Now who's being dramatic?" Eliza asked.

"Well? Isn't that what you were going to do?" he demanded.

With a murmured "excuse me," his aunt carefully made her way out of the room to tell the driver they'd be right out.

"To tell you the truth, Christian, I figured you wouldn't mind," his mother stated firmly, her spine stiffening as she spoke. "I know you work long hours, but you haven't particularly gone out of your way to be here since we arrived, so I thought it would be best if we simply left." She crossed her arms over her middle and waited for his response.

He raked a hand through his hair. "Okay, fine. I know

I wasn't a good host, but still, Mom, you could have given me a heads-up about leaving."

She seemed to soften a little. "It all happened so fast. One minute we were making plans to go walking on the beach, and the next Monica got the call about Mac and Gina and she immediately started making plans to fly out. I thought it best if I left too."

How could he argue with that? It was all logical, and it made sense for them to go—especially if their work here was done.

"I hate that you're taking a car to the airport. What kind of son does that make me?" he grumbled.

Immediately, his mother was hugging him and laughing softly. "A smart one. Now you won't get stuck in traffic like we're going to be."

Christian thought of all he could be doing at the office, and as if she'd read his mind, his mother poked one long finger into his chest. "But since you're not going to be stuck in traffic, take tonight and do something relaxing. Something fun! Something that doesn't require you to be in a suit and tie behind a desk!"

And with that, she gave him a loud, smacking kiss on the cheek. "Now come on and help us get all this luggage out to the car. We don't want to miss our flight."

Fifteen minutes later, they were gone and Christian was out on his deck staring at the ocean—much like he had started his day. The only difference was that now he had taken off his tie, unbuttoned a couple of buttons on his shirt, and was taking a sip of his beer.

"This won't do," he murmured and set the bottle down, then walked into the house. Five minutes later, he'd changed into a pair of shorts and a T-shirt. Most people didn't realize that he enjoyed relaxing at home and didn't spend the bulk of his time wearing a shirt and tie. With a satisfied grin, he picked up his beer and scanned tonight's crowd of surfers.

As he leaned on the railing, Christian felt himself relax. It was still pretty hot out and for a minute, he contemplated changing into a pair of swim trunks and going in the water. Normally, at this time of day he was still at the office, but now that he was home, it was possible to indulge a bit.

"When in Rome," he said. Straightening, he spotted a familiar red ponytail, and his desire to head down to the water had little to do with swimming and everything to do with getting a closer look at the woman who'd been intriguing him for weeks.

She was paddling out on her board, and he watched in fascination as she went through the entire ritual of waiting for the perfect wave, getting up on her knees, and eventually standing. Christian held his breath as he watched her find her balance and silently cheered her on as she straightened. For a second, he could have sworn he heard her joyful laugh, but that simply wasn't possible. Still, it kept him smiling.

To her left, another surfer was quickly approaching—a big, burly guy with long hair and tattoos—and even though Christian didn't know much about the sport, something seemed a bit dodgy. He was fairly certain that you weren't supposed to crowd each other like that. Helplessly, he stood rooted to the spot as the second surfer got closer and closer, until they collided. The redhead went flying one way, the burly guy in the opposite direction.

Burly guy surfaced. She didn't.

Chapter 2

Before he knew it, Christian had leaped over the railing and was sprinting to the beach. From his perch on the deck, he'd felt like he was much closer, but no matter how fast he ran, he didn't seem to be getting any nearer.

She surfaced and was swimming toward the shore, with the burly guy berating her the entire time. Rage filled him as he listened to the wanker hurl insults as if she had been the one to collide with him. Not sure of what he should do, Christian stood and waited. The two of them were walking out of the water not ten feet away and his fists clenched as the dialogue became clearer.

"You don't belong here!" Burly Guy yelled. "You could kill someone if you don't pay attention to the surfers around you! Why don't you go to one of the resorts and take lessons, or better yet, give up! You've been at this for weeks and you're nothing but a nuisance!"

To her credit, his surfer girl didn't yell—hell, she didn't even argue. All she said was "Thanks for the advice." Then, with her head held high, she walked the rest of the way out of the water and started toward the parking lot, awkwardly carrying her board.

"Hey!" Burly Guy yelled again, storming after her. "You better listen to me! I'll be sure to tell Randy that you're a danger to everyone out here and he shouldn't rent to you anymore."

That had her stopping in her tracks. Slamming her board into the sand, she unfastened the band from around her ankle, straightened, and turned, and Christian could almost feel the frustration vibrating off her. And then she completely unleashed on him.

"You know what?" she said firmly. "You are nothing but a bully! In case you hadn't noticed, I was up and on my board first. And you know how I know? Because I *was* paying attention and I saw you come out after I already chose my wave. And considering you were behind me, *you* should have been the one to back off!"

"Now, you listen," Burly Guy snarled, but she held up a hand and cut him off.

"No, *you* listen!" she stated, her voice growing a little louder. "I have every right to be here. There's an entire ocean for all of us to use and you don't get to tell me where I can and can't surf. And if you so much as even *think* of talking to Randy about me, you will be sorry!"

Burly Guy stood there, slack-jawed, for a moment. Just when he looked like he was about to respond, someone yelled out, "Ollie! C'mon, man, let's go!" And just like that, Burly Guy turned to walk away.

"Ollie?" the redhead repeated with amusement. "Seriously, your name is Ollie? Is that why you're so mean—because you got stuck with a ridiculous name?"

The guy glared at her and, if Christian wasn't mistaken, growled. "Watch where you surf," he snapped and then turned and stormed off.

"Right back at ya!" she called after him.

Laughing softly, Christian stood and watched to see what she would do next. He figured she'd grab her board and…then he wasn't sure. Her options were to either return to the water or head to the surf shop. Much to his surprise, she let out a shaky breath and sank to the sand.

And even more to his surprise, he walked over and sat beside her.

She looked at him with wide emerald eyes and gave a soft gasp, but said nothing.

"You were pretty brave," he said, resting his arms on his bent knees. "Bloody brilliant, actually. That guy was pretty intimidating."

Beside him, she relaxed a little. "Yeah, well...he was completely in the wrong. It's been a crappy couple of days and he was the perfect outlet for my frustration."

Christian nodded, unsure of what to say.

"I've seen him around here almost every day and he's a jerk to everyone," she went on. "No one ever talks back to him, they simply stay out of his way after he's done berating them."

He looked at her and found he was seriously impressed.

She shrugged and looked out at the waves. "People like him are the worst. They bully, they belittle, and most of the time, they have no idea what they're even talking about. If I had been in the wrong, I probably would have apologized profusely and followed the herd and simply gotten out of his way." She paused. "But I knew I was right. I'm very aware of my surroundings and I knew he was coming in behind me even as I was heading out, but I thought he'd wait and let me catch my wave." Then she muttered a curse.

And it was completely adorable. He couldn't help but laugh softly.

She glared at him and he saw he'd seriously offended her.

"Sorry," he murmured. "I just… I guess I misjudged the situation."

Tilting her head, she studied him for a moment. "Why would you say that?"

Great. How was he supposed to explain that he'd been watching her and came down here to try to rescue her without sounding like some sort of creep?

Swallowing hard, Christian looked away from her and figured he'd rather be honest than lie to her. "I saw the two of you collide and then he surfaced before you, but he didn't look like he was too concerned about where you were. So…"

"So you came to help me?" she asked, her voice a little uncertain, wary.

Nodding, he looked at her. "I thought I was acting heroic, but then you rose from the water like a bit of a badass." He laughed softly. "So clearly you did not need my assistance."

With a small smile, her eyes scanned his face and then she looked away again. "Yeah, well…there's a first time for everything."

Now he was the one who was curious. "Why would you say that?"

She must have caught on to his using her own words on her, because she laughed. "Let's just say that normally I'm a bit of a pushover. I don't like confrontation and I'd much rather turn the other cheek. But like I said…"

"Crappy couple of days, huh?"

She smiled. "Big time. I was supposed to start a new job. I had my first meeting scheduled the other day," she explained. "But I had a flat tire and by the time I got it fixed, I was a mess and had to change my clothes and was late heading to the appointment. There was an accident on the freeway and by the time I arrived, the people I was supposed to meet with had gone for the day."

"Damn," he said. "That is a crappy day."

"I know, right?"

"They didn't fire you before you even started, did they?"

She shook her head. "No, but it makes for a lousy first impression. I wouldn't blame them if they did fire me. It's my first job here and..." She sighed.

"Is this a job that you want or a job that you need?"

"Need," she said wearily. "I moved here a little over a month ago and have been job hunting while living off my savings—which are now dwindling." She muttered a curse again. "I know I'm perfect for the job."

"Maybe you can reach out to them tomorrow," he suggested. "Just because you missed your appointment doesn't necessarily mean they won't see you again or let you reschedule."

"I know, I know. Like I said, it just makes for a lousy first impression," she said miserably, resting her chin on her hands. "I think the universe hates me."

"Yeah, I know that feeling well," he murmured, and they fell into a companionable silence while the waves crashed on the shore in front of them. There was so much more he wanted to say to her, but no matter how hard he tried, nothing came out. In his mind, he'd imagined all the things he'd ask when he finally met her and now here they were sitting side by side in the sand and he couldn't utter a word.

Brilliant, Christian. Bloody brilliant…

Finally, she stood. Christian had no idea how much time had passed, but he had no choice but to stand with her. Brushing sand from his shorts, he straightened and looked at her with a smile. She was almost a foot shorter than him and for the first time tonight, he took in her long-sleeved top and bikini bottoms.

Curvy, he thought.

Her green eyes looked sad and he wished there was something he could say to make that look go away.

"Thanks for wanting to rescue me," she said, leaning against her board.

"Sorry you're having a bad week."

Nodding, she thanked him again. "So, um… I guess I should go. It's getting late and I need to bring the board back to the shop." Lifting it, she shifted it in her arms and took a step back. "Have a good night."

"Wait!" he said, a little frantic. There was no way he could let her walk away without at least finding out her name. "I—I realized I never introduced myself. I'm Christian." He held out a hand and almost sighed with relief when she accepted it. He wrapped her much smaller hand in his.

"It's nice to meet you, Christian," she said. "I'm Sophie."

Sophie. Studying her for a moment, Christian realized the name fit. "Do you mind if I walk with you?"

She shrugged. "No problem."

Before she could object, he took the board from her. She hesitated for only a moment and then they walked together—slowly—toward the parking lot.

"So tell me about this job."

Another shrug. "It's a nursing job," she said. "Corporate. Back home I worked in a small doctor's office and it made me crazy. I love being a nurse, but I like the idea of not going to the same place every day."

"And this job offered multiple locations?"

Shaking her head, she explained. "No, it didn't. But the hours were flexible, so I could work for several companies and mix things up a bit. It's through an agency and they're going to be my first clients. You know, sort of like a test to see how well I do before my bosses will assign me to more companies."

Wait… This all sounded mildly familiar, but what were the odds of this being the same thing his mother and aunt had come here to start?

"I don't think I've ever heard of a corporate nurse," he said, fishing for more clarity. "Is it like having a nurse's office in school?"

Beside him, she laughed, and it was rich and husky and a little bit sexy. "I don't think I would put it quite like that, but…yes. Essentially, I would have set days that I go in to a particular corporate office where I would do things like do blood-pressure checks, administer flu shots, routine physicals, that sort of thing. It's not particularly challenging, but I'm a people person and I think it's hard for the average employee to take time to see a doctor about maintaining their health. This way, we're bringing the doctor—or…me—to them."

He nodded as they climbed the steps leading to the parking lot.

"Either way, it would have been a great way to get started and see if this is what I want to do."

"You're not sure?" he asked.

"I moved to San Diego in search of something new—new surroundings, new job. So far all I've accomplished is the surroundings. I can't believe a job can be so elusive." Then she gave him a lopsided grin. "At least, I think it's elusive."

He chuckled. "You're not sure?"

"I haven't exactly been consistent with the job search."

"I would think there'd be a big demand for nurses," he said. "I mean, the sheer number of medical centers and doctor's offices I see around here would lead me to believe that."

"Oh, I'm sure there are plenty of jobs, but I'm a little…shall we say, picky about where I want to work."

He admired her honesty. Maybe if he had held out for the job that he really wanted he'd be a little happier right now.

"Nothing wrong with that," he finally said.

"Sure, it all sounds like a good thing until you're facing the possibility of rolling your change to buy groceries."

Christian stopped in his tracks and stared at her. "Sophie, then maybe you need to take something else on temporarily. It might not be ideal, but it's better than going broke."

Her laugh was a little more boisterous this time and when she studied him, her smile was warm and friendly. "I'm being a little dramatic. It's not that bad yet, I promise. And besides, I think you've encouraged me."

"I have?"

She nodded. "I think I'm not going to let this get me down. I'm going back to that office tomorrow and I'm going to demand to talk to someone in human resources and have that meeting. I know I am more than qualified for that job and I at least deserve the chance to be interviewed and to start with a clean slate!"

"Well, I didn't quite say you should do that..."

"No, no, I know," she clarified. "I'm just saying that I have to at least try. Maybe this wasn't the job for me, but I should at least get the opportunity to sit down with them and start the position knowing I'm taking it seriously, right?"

"I suppose." Honestly, if he were the one she was supposed to meet with and she hadn't shown, he wouldn't have given her a second chance. That was not the way it went in the corporate world, but he wasn't going to say that to her and risk making her feel worse than she already did about her circumstances.

"Anyway, I should go." Taking the board from him, she smiled again. "Thanks for carrying it, and thanks again for trying to help."

"I'm glad you didn't need it," he said, almost bashfully.

They stood facing one another until it got a little awkward.

"Well... Good night, Christian. I hope to see you around."

He gave a small wave as she turned to walk away.

And yeah, he hoped he'd see her around soon too.

And not just from the privacy of his deck.

The next day, Christian was having his own crappy day.

For starters, he didn't feel well. Everything was... off. He was a little warm, a little jittery, more than a little tired, and his concentration was shit. Maybe he was coming down with something. No matter how long he looked at the reports in front of him, nothing was making sense. In an hour, he was supposed to meet with a new client he'd been courting for months and he needed to get himself together.

"Focus, dammit," he muttered, taking a long drink of his coffee. Probably not the best option considering he was already jittery, but he hoped it would wake him up a little too.

After he'd watched Sophie walk away, he'd gone home and found that he was at a loss for something to do. With his mother and aunt gone, there almost wasn't a need for him to be home. Going back to the office seemed a bit ridiculous, so he'd forced himself to make a real meal for dinner instead of opting for takeout, and then he'd sat and watched TV until well after midnight.

Then sleep had eluded him.

He'd tossed and turned and done more than his share of cursing, but nothing had seemed to make his brain shut down enough for him to relax and go to sleep. He was edgy and uncomfortable—and no matter how great his Sleep Number bed usually was, last night there was no perfect setting to help him.

Sometime after two, he'd risen and—feeling more than a little desperate for sleep—made himself a cup of chamomile tea. It wasn't something he normally drank, but he always kept some in the house for his mother's visits because she enjoyed it. More than once she'd mentioned how it always helped her sleep, so he figured he'd try it.

Didn't work.

By three, he'd gone out on the deck, sat on one of the chaises, closed his eyes, and listened to the sound of the waves.

That worked until he realized there was no way he could sleep out on the deck. So, half-delirious from exhaustion, he'd opened the French doors that led to the far end of the deck. Part of him was a little ill at ease about sleeping with the doors open, but desperate times called for desperate measures, and as he crawled into bed at three thirty with the sound of the waves lulling him, all thoughts of security were forgotten.

Unfortunately, his alarm had gone off at six thirty and three hours of sleep was not enough to get him through this day. If he could get through the meeting with the Davenports, he could go home after that. No doubt he'd be able to sleep tonight without any trouble. Looking at his watch, he saw it was already eleven and his meeting was at one.

"Christian?" his assistant Erin called from the doorway.

Looking up, Christian scowled. "What is it, Erin?"

"Patricia from HR is here and she'd like to speak with you."

With a shake of his head, he responded, "I don't have time right now. Tell her we'll have to talk later this afternoon."

He wasn't about to admit that he was already planning on leaving as soon as his meeting was over. No one needed to know that. And basically, there were very few things that he needed to handle directly with his HR department, so no doubt if it was really all that important, she could reach out to someone else.

Figuring that was that, he was surprised when he looked up and saw Erin still standing in the same spot. "Problem?"

She took one hesitant step into the room, and that was his first clue that something was up. Erin had been working with him for over two years now and she was an extremely confident person who knew when he didn't want to be bothered. To see her looking less than such had him more than a little curious.

When she was in front of his desk, she said, "It seems that there's a problem with the program your mother and aunt were here about and Patricia can't get either of them on the phone. She's a little anxious about it and I think it would be best to talk to her now rather than later."

Bloody hell.

"Erin," he began evenly, "I am a little swamped here going over the file for the Davenports. Surely I'm not the only person who can talk to her about this. Can't she reach out to someone at my father's office who's in charge?"

"I thought of that too, but it seems like the issue is… unique to, well, here."

Okay, now he was even more curious. Tossing the file aside, he let out a loud groan of frustration. "Tell her to make it quick."

Smiling at him, Erin said, "I will. Thanks."

As she walked out of the office, Christian raked a hand through his hair, his chest tightening. The last thing he needed was another distraction this morning. Why didn't people understand he had a job to do and that it wasn't possible for him to put out everyone else's fires? Although if he were honest, he wasn't getting a whole lot done on the Davenport file anyway. Maybe this little meeting with Patricia would be enough to break him out of whatever was bothering him and get his head focused like it needed to be.

"Thank you so much for meeting with me, Mr. Montgomery," Patricia said as she walked into the room. She was an older woman—in her sixties—with a sleek blond bob, dressed in a classic Chanel-style suit. Christian often noticed how she was a throwback to another time—a time when employees put a little extra effort into how they dressed for work. He appreciated her effort, admired it. And normally she was the first with a smile, but right now she looked more than a little uncomfortable.

Motioning for her to have a seat, he relaxed in his chair. "What can I do for you, Patricia?"

Sitting primly, she folded her hands in her lap before she started to speak. "As you know, your mother and aunt entrusted me with their new corporate health program."

He nodded as she went on to describe all of the work they'd accomplished this week. Holding up a hand to stop her, he asked, "I thought everything was in place? My mother mentioned that you had hired someone."

"Oh, we did," she said. "The agency they're using assigned a nurse to us and she was supposed to meet with your mother and aunt and..." She paused for a moment. "Well, she's here today for an orientation."

"Patricia, I don't see what—"

"Christian?" Erin's voice came across the intercom.

He picked up the phone. "Yes, Erin?"

"The Davenport people are here," she said quietly.

"What?" he cried, panic gripping him by the throat. Jumping up from his chair, it suddenly felt as if he couldn't breathe. "They're two hours early, Erin! Did you remind them of their appointment time?"

"I—I did, sir. But they are insisting they see you earlier. It seems they met with Brannigans this morning and now they're anxious to talk to you."

"*Brannigans?* They met with Brannigans?" The tightening in his chest grew to almost painful proportions.

"Mr. Montgomery," Patricia said, concern lacing her tone. "Are you all right?"

Brannigans was an investment firm like Montgomerys. They were their direct competition and Christian was more than a little concerned that not only had the Davenports openly admitted they'd gone to them, but that they'd come here to comparison shop!

Wiping sweat from his brow, he ignored Patricia's question and said to Erin, "Set them up in the conference room and tell them I'll be in shortly."

"Are you sure?"

"Offer them coffee, something to drink, whatever we can to tide them over while I get everything together," he went on. "We can do this, but I'm not going to jump through their hoops and run in there."

Christian heard her small sigh. "Yes, sir."

Hanging up the phone, he turned to Patricia. "This will have to wait," he said, but he was breathless and his head was spinning. Reaching for the desk to steady himself, he took a moment to try to catch his breath. Doing his best to focus, he looked at Patricia and noticed the stricken look on her face right before she ran from the room.

At least…he thought she ran. Everything was starting to look a bit wonky, tilted. Christian did his best to focus on his office door, but it seemed to be getting farther and farther away. Slowly, he made his way around the desk and the pain in his chest got sharper. Gasping painfully, he almost dropped to his knees.

This is it, he thought. *This job has officially killed me. Why didn't I listen to everyone who'd been warning me to take it easy? Why didn't I quit when I wanted to? Way back when I left London?*

Off in the distance, he could hear voices, but they were muffled. A million thoughts raced through his head—why hadn't he taken that vacation to Hawaii last year? Why were his only trips for either business or family events? And lastly, why hadn't he asked Sophie out last night?

The pain in his chest started to subside, but everything else was still off. Blinking several times, he saw people entering his office. It took a couple of tries to focus, but then he saw Erin and Patricia—both of them encouraged him to sit. Nodding, he agreed and let them lead him over to the leather sofa against his far wall. Erin immediately loosened his tie, and even though his first instinct was to swat her hand away, he simply didn't have the energy to do so.

He was tired.

So, so tired.

"Miss Bennington! In here!" Patricia called out.

He had no idea who that was and right now, he didn't care.

Resting his head against the sofa cushions, Christian closed his eyes and tried to take a deep breath but found that he couldn't.

"I've called 911," someone said. He didn't recognize the voice, but then again, everyone still sounded muffled.

He could feel people moving around, but he was just too tired to open his eyes and see what all the fuss was about. Maybe if he could lie down for a little while, he'd feel better.

The touch of someone's hand on his temple startled him, but still he didn't open his eyes. The hand felt cool against his skin, and it went from his temple to the pulse at his neck and then finally to his wrist.

"Does anyone have an aspirin?" that same voice asked, and now he wondered who it belonged to. Just as he was about to ask, he felt a little pressure on his bottom lip as he was instructed to "chew this." He assumed it was the aspirin and simply complied.

"Paramedics will be here in five," Erin called out.

Okay, he was starting to recognize voices again and—strangely enough—the pressure in his chest was easing. He took one breath, then another, and found it a lot easier than it had been moments ago. It took a bit of an effort, but he wanted to sit up a little straighter. As soon as he moved, however, there was a hand on his shoulder encouraging him to sit still.

Now he opened his eyes, and the first thing Christian noticed was the crowd of concerned faces—besides Erin and Patricia, there were several of his junior executives staring at him. Frowning because he hated being the center of attention like this, he was about to speak when he was encouraged to relax.

That voice.

He knew that voice.

Turning his head, his gaze locked on a pair of serious and concerned green eyes.

Sophie.

What? How? Why? So many questions and no one would let him speak.

"Your heart rate is going up again," Sophie said softly, keeping her fingers on his wrist. "It's vital for you to relax, Christian. The paramedics are on their way."

"I don't need the paramedics," he finally said. "I'm fine now."

The look she gave him showed that she didn't believe him even the littlest bit. "You're pale and your skin is clammy. Your pulse is jumpy and you almost passed out."

Um...yeah. He didn't need the laundry list; he'd lived it.

"I'm fine," he repeated, feeling a little of his strength return. Looking over at Erin, he said, "Cancel the paramedics."

She turned her head as if she hadn't heard him.

Traitor.

Since his loyal assistant wasn't feeling particularly like listening to him, he faced Sophie. "Look, you're right. I had a bad moment there. I didn't sleep well last night and I guess it caught up with me. As a medical professional, you know paramedics don't appreciate being called to a scene when there's nothing wrong, so really, just...cancel them. Tell them I'm fine. And since you're a nurse, they'll believe you!"

If he thought his reasoning would win her over, he was sadly mistaken.

Christian heard the flutter of activity coming closer to the office and knew that everyone who worked for him was going to watch him getting wheeled out on a stretcher, and that was unacceptable. Sophie went to stand, but he frantically grasped her hand and pulled her in close.

"I do *not* want to leave here on a stretcher," he ground out.

With a simple nod, she stood and walked over to greet the paramedics, and then—in a move that surprised him—she addressed everyone else in the room.

"We need to make room for the paramedics to come in!" she called out. "So unless you are a medical professional, you need to leave the office. I'm sure that"—she looked over at Erin and asked her name before continuing—"I'm sure Erin will update all of you as soon as we have more information. Thank you for understanding!"

As the paramedics moved toward him, everyone else quickly filed out of the room.

Before he knew it, they were checking his vitals and talking to him, and it was a little overwhelming. Sophie came over and gave them the rundown of what she'd observed as well as the vitals she had taken before they arrived. He wanted to be annoyed at her high-handedness, but honestly, right now he was grateful not to have to think so much.

"Mr. Montgomery, we're going to need to take you in for a cardiac evaluation," one of the paramedics stated, and Christian immediately looked to Sophie for help.

She cleared her throat and said, "Um, is there any way we can let Mr. Montgomery walk out of the building?"

"Seriously?" the second paramedic asked. "He may have had a heart attack. We need to get him in the bus as soon as possible and get him to the ER." Then he looked at Christian. "Sorry, Bud. We need to do this now."

They helped him to his feet and onto the stretcher, but at least he wasn't fully reclined. They gave him oxygen and secured him, and once again, his eyes went to Sophie's.

"I'll be right behind you," she said, taking his hand and walking alongside him out to the ambulance.

It was a good thing she was trained to work well under pressure, because when Sophie had walked into Christian's office and seen the condition he was in, she almost cried. Why? She honestly couldn't say. Maybe it was because he had been so nice to her the night before or maybe she was reacting to witnessing someone she knew in true distress.

Okay, so...technically, she didn't really *know* Christian. He was simply an acquaintance.

A really nice acquaintance.

But still, she was a nurse and dealing with someone in the midst of a medical crisis should have her ready to leap into action. Back home when she'd worked for Doc Kelly, the most they ever saw was the flu or the occasional broken bone. And during her clinicals, she'd been able to detach herself. But seeing Christian looking so helpless had affected her in a way she'd never experienced before.

At the hospital, she wasn't allowed to go to the examination with him, but within minutes she had been brought to him because he kept asking for her.

And while that should have been weird—they'd only met the night before—it wasn't. If anything, she wanted to be there for him.

As soon as Sophie stepped into the room, she was at his side and he'd taken her hand in his—and she liked that he was a toucher. She sat with him as he was given a complete cardiac workup, and with each test they performed, she explained it and answered any questions he had.

"Is there anyone you want me to call? Your parents? Siblings? The office? Your girlfriend?" she asked, her eyes not meeting his.

Sure, she was totally fishing on that last one, but she couldn't help but be curious.

After walking away from Christian yesterday, she had called herself every kind of idiot for not asking him if he wanted to have coffee or something. At the time, she was in her wetsuit and it wasn't as if she could have gone anyplace right then and there, but they could have made plans for later on. It was exactly the thing Sophie'd been telling herself she needed to do more of, yet when a sexy guy—who was clearly a good guy, too—essentially landed at her feet, she wished him a good night and walked away.

All night and all morning she'd been hoping to run into him again.

She just hadn't thought it would be while he was having a heart attack.

"I'd prefer to wait until we get a final diagnosis," Christian said, interrupting her thoughts. "No need to get anyone upset if they don't need to be."

Typical man.

Nodding, Sophie noted that he hadn't given her an answer on the whole girlfriend thing. She looked at their joined hands and hoped he wasn't the type of guy who would hold hands with one woman while dating another. Then she wanted to smack herself in the head, because it wasn't as if he was holding her hand in a romantic way—he was looking for a little comfort while going through a scary experience.

They sat quietly as the medical team walked out of the room. No doubt the doctors would look over all of the test results and confirm whether or not what had happened to Christian was a heart attack. She hoped it wasn't. He was far too young for that sort of thing.

He was calm right now. Relaxed. And with his eyes closed, Sophie allowed herself to take a minute to study him. Dark brown hair that was looking a little haphazard right now, a strong jaw, and the kind of face that made a woman sigh with appreciation. He was tall—easily six feet—and even though he was in a hospital gown right now, she remembered from last night that he had an impressive physique. Christian was tan, but not overly so. He didn't look like someone who spent a lot of time at the beach. But more than anything, she couldn't help but admire his lean muscles—she had to stop herself from reaching over and stroking a bicep.

That would be wrong, right?

Sophie spoke after a minute. “Can I ask you something?”

“Sure.”

“If no one had been in your office with you, would you have called for help?”

Without hesitation, he replied, “No.”

“Wow,” she said.

“My turn. Can I ask you something?” He turned his head toward her and opened his eyes, and she was instantly struck by how blue they were. Had she noticed that last night?

“Sure.”

“What were you doing at my office?” Both his tone and his expression were serious, and at first Sophie wasn’t sure what to say.

“Remember the job I told you about yesterday?”

He acknowledged her question.

“It was with your company,” she said.

One dark brow quirked, and she thought it was sexy as hell.

Clearing her throat—and her mind—she continued. “I had no idea it was your company. Honestly, I didn’t give much thought to whose company it was. I met a couple of nice ladies on the beach a few days ago. They were sitting in the sand watching the surfers and when I came out of the water, they struck up a conversation with me.” She shrugged. “One thing led to another and I was telling them about my job search and the agency I had signed with and they told me they had the perfect job for me. All I had to do was apply.”

He looked at her quizzically.

“Well, I told them they needed to go through the

agency—I didn't want it to seem like I was poaching jobs from them. So they called and specifically requested me, and after a little negotiating, the agency agreed to send me."

"And…these ladies, they were willing to just hire you after seeing you on the beach?"

Nodding, she went on. "It's true. I was out surfing Monday morning and there they were, sitting on the sand. They applauded when I got out of the water. I thought they were teasing me at first. Then they explained that they were impressed with my determination."

It was Christian's turn to nod.

"Last night you encouraged me to make sure things got started on the right foot, and…that's what I did. I went to the office—your office—and asked to speak to someone in human resources. Patricia agreed to meet with me, and it was the best interview I ever had!" she gushed. "When we were done, she asked me to wait out in the reception area and that's when she went to talk to you. Only I didn't know it was you she was going to talk to. I wouldn't have tried to use that to my advantage, I swear."

He laughed. "Sophie, I didn't think that at all. It seemed like such a wild coincidence that you were there, that's all."

She sagged with relief. "Well, I'm glad I was there. I mean, I know I didn't do much and your staff seemed to have it all under control, but I'd like to think that I would have been heroic in saving you. You know, if you needed it."

It made her feel good to see that he was feeling a little bit better.

"Sort of like someone running to the beach to save a drowning person who wasn't drowning?" he teased.

"Exactly!" They were both smiling and chuckling when the cardiologist came in.

"How are you feeling, Mr. Montgomery?" he asked. Sophie looked at his badge and saw his name was Dr. Asher. He was looking over the chart in his hand and barely glanced at Christian.

"I'm feeling much better," Christian said. "I don't have any pain or any of the symptoms I had earlier, and really, I don't think it was a heart attack. I was exhausted from lack of sleep. I'm hoping you'll cut me loose so I can return to work."

Sophie gasped, hating that after all he'd suffered, he wanted to go back to work!

Tucking the chart under his arm, Dr. Asher looked at Christian. "You're partly correct. You did not have a heart attack."

"I knew it!" Christian said victoriously.

"However," Dr. Asher quickly added, "your blood pressure is high. We're going to need to monitor that."

"O-kay… So, I can go, right?"

"Wait," Sophie jumped in. "If Christian didn't have a heart attack, what caused all of those symptoms?" Honestly, she already had that figured out, but she didn't want to say anything until the doctor confirmed her suspicions.

"Anxiety attack," Dr. Asher stated. "You mentioned earlier how much you work and what was going on when the attack hit. You also mentioned that you've felt that tightness in your chest before, correct?"

Christian gave a curt nod and she knew he wasn't

being one hundred percent honest with the doctor. Taking his hand in hers, she tugged gently until he looked at her. "Christian, it's important that you tell Dr. Asher how often this has been happening. You may have dodged a bullet this time, but there's no guarantee this won't lead to a heart attack in the future if you don't get your anxiety under control."

"I don't have anxiety!" he yelled, and the monitors began to beep like crazy.

When both she and Dr. Asher gave him stern looks, Christian at least had the good sense to seem apologetic.

"Mr. Montgomery, your girlfriend is right. You need to tell me exactly what's been happening and what leads to you having these chest pains. I've already consulted with your primary physician and you'll need to do a follow-up with him tomorrow." He reached into his lab coat pocket and pulled out a piece of paper. "He's agreed to see you first thing tomorrow morning to discuss some treatment options with you."

"Treatment options?" Christian repeated incredulously. "What treatment options? It was an anxiety attack! I'll try to relax a bit and I should be fine." When he went to sit up, Sophie gently grasped his shoulder to stop him. The annoyed glare he shot her had her instantly releasing him.

"I'm afraid there's a little more to it than just... relaxing," Dr. Asher explained. "You need to take this seriously, Mr. Montgomery. You're far too young to be heading for a heart attack. I'm sure your doctor will prescribe something for your blood pressure—some diet modifications and exercise—and he'll most likely recommend that you reduce your work hours."

"That's impossible!" Christian cried out with frustration. "Do you think I enjoy working so many hours? Don't you think if I could cut back that I would?"

"I don't know you well enough to make that observation," Dr. Asher said evenly. "Either way, you need to get proactive about your health or you'll be seeing a lot more of me, and fairly soon." He turned to Sophie. "His discharge papers are ready. Make sure he gets to his appointment with his physician in the morning."

"I'm right here!" Christian snapped. "I don't need the two of you talking about me as if I'm not even here!"

When Dr. Asher started to speak again, Sophie cut him off. "I've got this. Thank you for everything, Dr. Asher."

He wished them both a good day before leaving the room. Once he was gone, Christian tried to rise from the bed.

"Whoa," she said to him, once more grasping his shoulder to stop him. "Aren't you forgetting something?"

"What?" he asked irritably.

"For starters, you're still hooked up to all of these machines, and secondly—you're not wearing any pants."

It was adorable to see him blush.

"Oh."

"Yeah, oh," she mimicked with a grin. "Give me a minute and I'll find a nurse to come and disconnect you. I'll wait out in the lobby and take you home."

"I need to go to the office," he stated.

"Okay. Be right back." There was no way she was taking him to work, but she wasn't going to tell him that right now. What Christian needed most was to stay calm, and arguing with him wouldn't help with that.

After she talked to one of the nurses, Sophie walked to the hospital lobby and pulled out her phone. Thankfully she had Montgomerys' number from when she'd called that morning to see about getting another shot at her interview. She figured she'd get Christian's assistant to give her some clues as to how she could get him home without causing him too much stress.

Miracles could happen, right?

Chapter 3

Christian opened his eyes when Sophie put her car in park. It took a minute for his brain to realize what he was seeing.

"This isn't my office, Sophie." They were parked in the lot by the surf shop.

"I know," she said lightly.

"So why are we at the surf shop?"

"Well, we're not *at* the surf shop, exactly. I remember you saying that you lived near here. I have no idea which house specifically."

He wanted to argue, but he didn't want to be sitting in the parking lot, so he gave her the address and quickly directed her to turn at the first block to the right and six houses down. Once they were in his driveway and Sophie made to get out of the car, he stopped her.

"You said you were taking me to my office."

"Um…no. You said you needed to go to the office. Two totally different things."

This time he didn't stop her from getting out of the car. Instead, he climbed out and met her at the hood. "You know I can take myself there, right?"

She gave him a patient smile. "I'm sure you could—even though your car's still at the office. It would be easy for you to call for an Uber. But then you'd have to worry about the late afternoon traffic, because, let's face it, you'll want to go inside and shower and change your clothes to wash that hospital smell off you. By the time you get done with that you're going to want something to eat, because, again, let's face it, you must be hungry. I know I am." She paused and lifted a shoulder. "I'll stop at the grocery store and grab a salad or something like that and eat all by myself at my apartment. Like I usually do."

He didn't say a word.

"What about you? Do you usually eat alone? It's boring, isn't it? Do you cook, or do you do a lot of take-out? What do you think you'll have for lunch?"

He'd heard enough. Raking a hand through his hair, he said, "You're not going to let this go, are you, love." It wasn't a question.

However, he did notice how her eyes went a little wide at his statement and it reminded him that Sophie had no idea he'd spent so much time living across the pond.

England, dammit! he silently reminded himself.

"You mean reminding you how you need to take the day off and have something healthy to eat while you relax? That would be no," she said with a hint of sass.

He liked sass.

Apparently.

"Look, you don't understand. I have a lot of responsibilities and—" He stopped when his phone rang. Looking at the screen, he saw it was Erin calling. With a muttered curse—of the American variety and not British—he answered, walking up the steps to the front door and going inside. Even without turning around, he knew Sophie would follow.

"Erin, how is everything? Did you reschedule with the Davenports? Were they upset?"

She laughed. "Funny, that's what I was calling to ask

you. Not about the Davenports, but about your health," she said dryly. "How are you feeling?"

Christian gave her a quick rundown of what had transpired at the hospital, and he figured she'd be on his side where coming back to work was concerned.

He was wrong.

"You need to take this seriously, Christian," she said firmly. "My father-in-law had a heart attack when he was forty-two and it nearly killed him. His doctors said his high blood pressure and his insane work schedule were largely to blame—especially since there was no history of heart disease in the family."

That's when Christian realized there was no history of heart disease in his family either.

Dammit.

"I have an appointment with my physician first thing in the morning. I'll be in as soon as I'm done," he said, tossing his keys on the kitchen counter.

"That won't be necessary. I cleared your schedule through the end of next week," Erin said sweetly.

"You did *what*? Why? What gave you the right to do that?" he demanded.

"I can't take all of the credit," she went on, unfazed. "After you left, I gathered everyone around for an impromptu meeting and reassigned as much of your work as I possibly could and then went about moving all of your appointments out. Everyone was greatly concerned about you, of course."

"What about the Davenports? Even knowing that they went to see the Brannigans, you *still* rescheduled with them? There's no way they'll wait another week to talk with me!"

"Not true. David Marcum sat with them—along with me—and we gave them a general outline of what you had prepared for them and they were pleased," she said proudly. "Honestly, I almost think we could've signed a contract with them today if we'd pushed a little."

"Erin! This is beyond crazy! You had no right to step in like that! David had no right to step in like that! I'm going to have to talk to him and—"

"I asked him to step in, and you know what? He's been dying for a little more responsibility around here. Everyone has. You hoard all the clients and then complain about how no one is pulling their weight! Christian, you have to realize that you're not the only one capable of handling the accounts. You have a fantastic group of executives here who are tired of twiddling their thumbs while you work eighty hours a week."

He sat at the kitchen table and sighed. "Erin, this is how I do things—"

"Well, you're doing them wrong," she snapped. "And I hate to do this to you, but…I called your father and I called Ryder."

His chest instantly seized in pain and he gasped. Sophie was immediately at his side and he did his best not to meet her gaze—unwilling to let her see too clearly what was going on.

"Why…would you…do that?" he asked through clenched teeth.

"Because I knew this conversation was going to happen. I knew you were going to make light of what happened today, and I also knew if someone didn't step in, you'd end up back in the hospital. You put way too much stress on yourself, Christian."

"And you're adding to it right now!" he barked. "You had no right to call my father! And on top of that, why Ryder?"

"Your father because, well...he's your father. And Ryder because he used to run this place." She paused. "It's a week, Christian. Okay, ten days including the weekend. Take the time and rest. And until you get the clearance from your doctor, you're not allowed in the office."

Another chest pain.

"I'm allowed anywhere I damn well please! It's my company!" he countered.

"Not for the next ten days. If you come into the office, your father will be called and then he'll show up here and take over. Is that what you want?"

Immediately his mind flashed back to London and how his father had ruined everything for him. There was no way he would allow that to happen again.

He wanted to throttle his assistant more than anything in the world right now. But he also couldn't help but be seriously impressed with her leadership skills and how she had managed to work quickly and efficiently—even if it meant screwing him over a bit in the process.

"Fine. Ten days," he muttered.

"And don't worry. Everything is under control here."

He hung up and slid his phone away from him. Eyes shut, head tilted, he did his best to breathe deeply and try to will away the pain in his chest.

Without him realizing she'd done it at first, Sophie had her hand on his wrist and was taking his pulse. Then she felt his forehead.

Lucky him. He had his own personal nurse whether he wanted one or not.

And right now, he didn't.

"You know you're just proving everyone right, don't you?" she asked, gently releasing his wrist.

It was pointless to pretend he didn't know what she was talking about. "Yeah, well, old habits die hard."

She gave him an amused look and walked over to pour him a glass of water. Placing it on the table, she sat. "From what I heard, you have a ten-day break, correct?"

He nodded.

"No doubt your doctor is going to agree that it's for the best. He may recommend an even longer break."

"Not gonna happen," he argued lightly.

"Okay, fine. So let's say you get him to agree to the ten days. You should take advantage of the time and relax, Christian. Catch up on some sleep, sit on the beach, and get some sun. I wouldn't recommend trying anything new, because the point of this break is to let go of this anxiety."

"I hate that word."

Reaching out, she placed a hand over his and gently squeezed. "I'm sure you do. And for what it's worth, I'm sorry that you're dealing with this."

He considered her. Yesterday, when he'd finally seen her up close, she was makeup-free and she'd been beautiful. She had a small patch of freckles on the bridge of her nose and cheeks, and her hair—even up in a ponytail—looked long and luxurious.

The woman sitting beside him was breathtaking. Her hair was longer than he'd imagined and more fiery in color, with a riotous mass of curls. Her emerald eyes were wide, with the longest lashes, which looked natural. And her lips? Well…last night they had been mildly tempting, but today, painted with a red that almost matched her hair, she was a combination of Irish rose and temptress.

Which was probably the last thing he needed right now.

Knowing he could sit there and look at her until it bordered on inappropriate, he turned his hand over and squeezed hers. "Thanks. Unfortunately, there's no one to blame for this but me. I did this to myself."

"What do you mean?"

The first thing that hit him was that Sophie didn't move her hand away. Here they were, virtually strangers, yet he'd reached out to her for comfort more times today than he could count. Wasn't that odd? A little uncharacteristic of him?

"Christian?" she prompted.

"Oh…uh, I mean that I've turned into a bit of a workaholic who clearly has some issues with control," he said with a self-deprecating laugh. "Erin pretty much told me that my staff has been looking for more responsibility and I've been hoarding the work."

"Yikes," she said with a small laugh. "You must really hoard, because most employees don't go looking for more work."

That had him laughing with her. "It was a little bit of a surprise for me to hear. No one's said a word about it to me."

He now realized why that was—he'd never made himself available to listen.

Sure, he'd known that most of the staff wasn't

happy with the way he was doing things, but Christian always figured it was simply because he wasn't doing everything the same way his predecessor—his cousin Ryder—had. So he'd always blown off any comments and chalked it up to people just not liking change.

But basically, it would seem it was *him* they didn't like.

And with good reason.

The thing was, he hadn't always been this way. Back in London—at the office he had launched—Christian had a great relationship with everyone on staff. He could remember sitting in the open office space and working together as equals. Not once had he shut anyone down or thought twice about sharing the workload. Unfortunately, while he had thought he was doing a great job and being an amazing boss, he was being lied to and taken advantage of by the people he'd trusted the most.

And damn, that sting of betrayal still hurt.

"Hey," Sophie said gently. "Where'd you go?"

Blinking, he focused on her. "What?"

She smiled and her gaze seemed to see right through him. "You went off somewhere in your own head. You okay?"

Why deny it? With a shrug, he said, "Right now? Not so much. A lot has happened today."

She nodded with understanding and slowly pulled her hand from his. "I should probably go so you can rest. You mentioned several times today how you hadn't slept well. Maybe now that you're home and know that you don't have anything pressing to do, you'll be able to relax and get some sleep."

"Maybe." The thing was, he wasn't tired anymore. "You mentioned something about lunch," he said, hoping he sounded interested enough for her to want to stick around. Her smile was slow and a little shy and Christian had to admit, he liked the light flush on her cheeks.

"I did," she agreed. "Would you like me to go and get something, or do you have something here we can make and maybe eat out on the deck?"

If there was one thing he tended to do, it was keep a fully stocked refrigerator. At least, fully stocked with the makings for sandwiches and quick meals. "I'm sure we can find something here we can have," he said, standing. "I'm not much of a cook, but I enjoy eating."

Grinning, she joined him by the refrigerator. "Okay, let's see what we can do!"

Then something happened that hadn't happened in a long time.

He was relaxing.

Seriously relaxing.

As in, he could feel the tension easing from his body in a way it never had before.

And why? Because he was standing in his kitchen making sandwiches with a beautiful woman. Together they worked to put a simple meal together and the entire time, Sophie talked about her move to San Diego from her hometown in Kansas. She mentioned the culture shock of going from the Midwest to living on the coast and how she couldn't believe how much higher the cost of living was in California.

"How much did you research before you decided to move?" he asked, piling his sandwich high with thinly sliced turkey breast.

"I'll admit, not nearly enough. All I knew was that I wanted to see the ocean and live as close to it as I could." Moving around him, Sophie took out the makings of a salad to share. "You know, most of what you have here in your refrigerator is pretty healthy. The cold cuts are going to be a big no-no for you since they're so high in sodium, but considering it was all we had to work with, I think this one last time should be okay."

Frowning, Christian stared hard at his sandwich. "One last time? Seriously? What am I supposed to eat for lunch?"

Sophie's husky laugh wrapped around him as she closed the refrigerator door with her hip. "Ooh…lots of good things—salads, fruit, lean proteins. You have far more options than you realize!"

"And no sandwiches," he said hesitantly. "Like forever or temporarily or…"

"I'm beginning to think you have some sort of sandwich fetish."

"No!" he quickly said, realizing that he sounded a wee bit like a crazy person about food. "It's just that they're so easy to make and all that other stuff sounds like I'm going to have to put in more of an effort than I'm used to."

Patting his hand before she took their plates, she said, "I'm sure you'll adjust."

Leaning against the granite countertop, Christian watched the sway of her hips as she carried their lunch out to the deck.

Never had he so looked forward to a meal.

"I don't know about this."

"You're making a big deal out of nothing."

Sophie eyed Christian warily. "Like it or not, Christian, you had a pretty intense health scare today. You may not think that you're tired, but trust me, you are."

He quirked that dark brow at her again and she was finding it sexier each time. "And you know this...how?"

Sighing dramatically, she explained to him all the ways an event like what he'd experienced today—topped with the exhaustion from lack of sleep—was currently harming his body without him realizing it.

"Basically, you think you're fine, but your motor skills aren't as sharp as they need to be, and I can't in good conscience allow you to drive your car home from the office. I can't."

They were still sitting on the deck even though they had finished lunch over an hour ago. There was a light breeze coming off the water, and they had been so engrossed in their conversation that neither seemed to consider cleaning up and going inside. Now that they were talking about Christian's well-being, however, Sophie suddenly felt bad about monopolizing his time when he should be sleeping.

Standing up, she started clearing the table.

"I hate to break it to you, but I can call for an Uber to take me to pick up my car as soon as you leave," he said, causing her to halt.

"Christian, you have to trust me on this," she said firmly. She felt like she was dealing with a petulant child. "You're already complaining about missing ten days of work, do you want to add to that when you crash your car because you fell asleep behind the wheel?"

With a snort, Christian stood and gathered the remainder of their lunch mess. "You may not believe this, but I've never had an accident. Ever. And I've driven home from the office on far less sleep than I had last night, after far more stressful days. I can practically do the drive with my eyes closed." Clearly, he thought he had gotten the best of her because he gave a cocky grin and walked into the house.

"Surely you can call your assistant and someone can drive the car here to you," she suggested as she followed him into the kitchen.

"No one has the keys," he said.

Darn. She hadn't thought of that.

As they worked together to clean up the kitchen, she racked her brain for a solution that wouldn't involve Christian driving today. She wasn't stupid—she knew he needed his car tomorrow morning to get to the doctor, but that didn't mean he had to be the one to get it. Maybe there was someone else they could call to go with her, and Christian could wait here and—

"I can hear you thinking from here," Christian said with a laugh. "You need to let this go. I have already left my comfort zone in a dozen different ways today by letting so many people tell me what to do. This is one thing I'm not going to be swayed on."

She didn't know him all that well yet, but she was coming to realize that Christian Montgomery (a) didn't like to accept help, and (b) pretty much liked to be in control at all times.

Typical man.

Wiping the countertop, she looked at him. "How about this, you call an Uber—"

"Thank you," he said sweetly. "That's what I said I was going to do."

"Not finished," she responded just as sweetly. "You call for an Uber and I go with you and drive your car home, with you in the passenger seat."

Now he looked at her as if she were crazy.

"What? What's wrong with that?" she asked.

His initial response was part growl, part laughter. "What is it with you? Look, I appreciate everything you've done today. I was relieved not to be at the hospital alone. But I'm not your responsibility, Sophie. You've done far too much already and…and…"

"And?" she prompted, even though she had a feeling he was ready to show her the door.

His shoulders sagged and his expression went from amusement to neutral in the blink of an eye. "I'm not comfortable with having someone do so much for me. I'm not trying to be ungrateful, I swear. It's just…"

One of the things Sophie prided herself in was her ability to be compassionate and know when someone had been pushed to their limit. Never did she want to be the kind of person who overstayed their welcome or went where they didn't belong.

And obviously, she didn't belong here.

With a curt nod, she looked around for her purse and went to pick it up. Taking her keys out, she turned to Christian and forced herself to smile. "I'm sorry."

His eyes went wide. "You're sorry?"

"I've been bulldozing you all afternoon, and that wasn't very nice of me. You needed a ride home—or…to your office—and I did what I thought was best rather than taking your feelings into consideration. So, I'm sorry."

Feeling the first sting of tears, she slid her sunglasses on before Christian could see that she was about to cry. With a smile she hoped looked sincere, she said, "I hope you feel better, Christian. And maybe I'll see you around."

"Sophie, I..."

But she wasn't listening. She couldn't.

Instead, she quickly made her way to the front door and was out before Christian could stop her. It was doubtful that he'd chase after her, and still she made herself practically run to her car. She was out of the driveway and down the street before her first tear fell.

"Dammit," she murmured, wiping the moisture from her cheeks. And the weird thing was she had no idea why she was crying. Why was she so upset? It wasn't like she was surprised by the turn of events. She'd known she was going to have to leave his house eventually, so...

"I just hate that he wanted me to leave," she admitted out loud. It would have been one thing for her to call it a day and for them to part ways when they were both smiling and laughing and maybe making plans to see one another again. It was quite another to see how badly he wanted her to go and how he really didn't want her help.

As she drove away, she tried to do the one thing that she always did—be optimistic.

Only...it wasn't so easy this time.

Christian Montgomery was a good man; she'd known this from their initial meeting the night before. And even today, as she'd stood by his side while ER doctors poked and prodded him, he had shown a vulnerable side. Back at his home, she'd seen yet another side of him—he could be funny and charming. But at the end of the day, he clearly preferred being alone.

And that made her sad.

Sophie knew she was alone right now and it was her choice—her temporary choice. Moving to San Diego had meant leaving all of her friends and family behind while she chose to move to a new place sight unseen: she'd driven into the city and stayed at a hotel while she looked for a place to live. That was what she'd wanted to do—see the city first before committing to a place to live. And while she didn't regret it, her end goal was to meet people, make friends, and have the kind of life she always wanted—one that was filled with people who knew and liked her for herself, not because they felt sorry for her or for—

She muttered a curse. "Stop it," she reminded herself.

Negative thoughts popped into her head at the oddest of times and she knew she couldn't let them gain a foothold.

Easier said than done.

Glancing at the dashboard clock, she noted it was a little after four. She could go home and change and be at the beach within the hour. Maybe a couple of hours in the water would be the best way to clear her mind. At least, that had always been how it worked since she'd decided to try surfing.

With her mind made up, she felt a little lighter. Happier. Yes, the thought of catching some waves—and maybe having a little more success than last night—seemed like the perfect way to end the day.

At her apartment, Sophie quickly stripped and changed into her suit. The weather and the water were still warm enough that she didn't need a full wetsuit—something she knew would change in the next month or so. But for now, she was more than happy to slip on bikini bottoms and the long-sleeved top. Switching her belongings from her small purse to a canvas satchel, she slid on a pair of flip-flops and set off.

There was a little more traffic as she made her way back to the beach, but she didn't mind. She could see the ocean and knew it wouldn't be long until her only concern was finding the perfect wave.

If only finding her perfect life could be that simple.

And what was worse was having second thoughts about going to her usual surfing spot because it was so close to Christian's house. She didn't want him to think she was coming to check on him or that she was making an excuse to see him again. That would be awkward. But on the other hand, the thought of finding another surfing spot and another surf shop wasn't the least bit appealing.

"I guess I can deal with him thinking I'm a weirdo," she murmured as she pulled up to the surf shop.

After getting her board and making small talk with Randy, Sophie finally walked onto the sand and kept her focus on the water—refusing to look to her left toward the row of houses.

The water was a little cool tonight, but she wasn't deterred. Over to her right, she spotted Ollie and opted to move a little farther down the shore to make sure there was no repeat of last night.

And that put her almost in front of Christian's house.

Unable to stop, she allowed herself one glance over her shoulder and saw that the house was dark. Sighing with relief, she turned back toward the water. Hopefully, he was sleeping and not out picking up his car, or worse, not—

"Stop it," she told herself. "He's a grown man and he's not your responsibility."

It was one thing to say it and another to believe it.

With her board at her side, Sophie forced herself to clear her mind of any and all thoughts of Christian Montgomery. Tilting her head back, she closed her eyes, took a deep breath, and let it out slowly. She did it another three times and when she opened her eyes and looked at the ocean, the only thing she felt was peace.

Walking out into the water, she listened to the sound of the waves and smiled as she spotted a young family whose toddler was running away from the water every time the waves came ashore. The child's squeal of laughter was contagious, and she stood mesmerized for several moments as she watched the scene.

A particularly high wave hit her midthigh and brought her out of her reverie and back to the present. There were waves to catch—and tonight she was determined to stay on her board. Today she'd gone after what she wanted where the job interview was concerned, and even though it didn't seem to have done any good, it had felt great not to back down from the challenge.

Just like right now.

Climbing onto her board, she paddled out a little farther than she normally did and was rewarded with a wave that seemed to be coming especially for her. And as she made her way into position, a wide smile on her face, she couldn't help but hope that this was a sign that things were finally going to go her way.

~

For four days, Christian had spent his time doing two things—wandering around his house and fielding phone calls from his family.

Both were making him crazy.

Here he was—at seven o'clock on Monday morning—and he was wide awake with nothing to do. As much as he'd love to disobey the doctor's orders, he'd been scared straight enough to know that wasn't the thing to do. His blood pressure was better than it had been in the emergency room, but not by much, and he knew if he didn't make some drastic changes in his life, being bored was going to be the least of his problems.

His mother was worried sick and had cried because she wasn't there with him, and offered to fly back. His father offered to come and take over the day-to-day operations at Montgomerys while he was incapacitated. Christian turned them both down.

Fast.

Then his sister had called and offered to come and stay with him, using the excuse of being able to work with his IT department again on some updates. If he were more of a selfish person, he would have taken her up on the offer, because he knew he could trust Megan to keep an eye on things at the office without trying to take over. And he'd enjoyed having her there back in the spring.

The biggest surprise had been when his brother had called and offered to come and cook a month's worth of meals for him. Christian had laughed it off because even though Carter was one of the biggest celebrity chefs around, he couldn't imagine him coming to San Diego and being happy preparing boring meals for one person. Once they had gotten that whole pretense out of the way, they had eased into some great conversation—something they didn't indulge in too often mainly because they were both workaholics.

"Maybe you should let Mom come," Carter had said. "I know she was just there, but you know she's worried sick about you now. She called me and cried, dude. Like seriously cried."

"Oh, geez."

"You know Mom's not the overly emotional type, so for her to be like this, you know it's real."

"I'm not incapacitated, Carter," Christian had argued. "I don't need a babysitter. What I need is to figure out how to change a lifetime of bad work habits."

A snort of derision was his brother's response.

"What? What was that?"

"You and I both know you don't have bad work habits, Christian. What you have is years of Dad badgering you about being the model employee—the model CEO. He wanted you to be the golden child of Montgomerys and in the process he sucked the life out of you!"

Okay...yikes, he thought. This was something they definitely hadn't talked about before.

"I wouldn't say he sucked the life out of me—"

"Tell me something," Carter interrupted. "Can you honestly say you love what you do? That sitting behind a desk, reading figures, and planning other people's finances makes you happy? That you're passionate about it?"

"Not everyone is passionate about their jobs, Carter."

"I am."

"Yeah, well… You're lucky. And we can't compare the two. Your job allows you to travel and create new things while meeting new people in festive environments. That's not how the majority of careers are."

Carter let out a loud huff of frustration. "You're avoiding the question. Do you still get excited about meeting with new clients?"

"It's interesting," he reasoned.

"Oh my gosh, can you please just give me a straight answer? Yes or no, dude? It's not that difficult!"

"Okay, fine!" he'd shouted. "No, no I don't get excited about meeting new clients, I'm not happy at my job, and yes, a little of the life has been sucked out of me while I try to please Dad. But this is all I know! This is all I've ever been *allowed* to know! So while you got a free pass to go off and do what you want to do, remember it's not like that for everyone."

"Christian…"

"I hated you for that." he went on. "You had the balls to stand up for yourself and I never even knew that was an option. And every time I even *dare* to comment on how I need a break or how exhausted I am, I end up being guilted because I feel that way! Do you have any idea what that's like?"

His heart had raced and he had trembled all over because he'd finally said the words out loud to his brother that he'd always been afraid to say.

"Geez, Chris, I had no idea," Carter said gruffly. "I mean, I knew Dad was hard on you, but…I had no idea you felt that way about me."

Shit. The last thing he'd wanted to do was make his

brother feel bad. Christian knew what it was like to have someone do that to you, and he never wanted to be accused of being like their father in that respect.

"I don't hate you, Carter," Christian finally said, his voice sounding rough to his own ears. "I just wish I could have had the choice."

"But you do! You are not obligated to stay in a job—a career—where it's killing you."

"It's not that easy—"

"Yes, it is! Seriously, you think you're the first Montgomery to break out of the family rut? The only reason you're even in San Diego is because Ryder needed a break! And you know what? He never went back. He made a life for himself in North Carolina not working sixty hours a week. James ran away from being part of it, and Zach moved as far away as he could and he's always run his division on his own terms. You remember how often he would travel and go off on those crazy extreme-sport adventures?"

"That almost killed him? Um…yeah."

"Not the point," Carter reasoned. "I'm saying that the only one killing himself over this company is you."

Yeah. That was becoming more and more obvious. All of his cousins were married and had kids and weren't working for months—years!—on end with no vacations. He was the last Montgomery working for the company who was doing that. Even his father and uncles took time to get away from the office, so…why wasn't he?

"I know this was a crappy time to bring this up," Carter said, interrupting his thoughts, "but I thought it was important to talk about it. A heart attack at your age isn't anything to take lightly."

"It wasn't a heart attack."

"It's a precursor to one, and you know it." With a sigh, his brother went on. "Look, I know you're taking a week off, but...why not two? If you don't want me to come there, why don't you come and see me? Right now, I'm in New Orleans, but I can take a couple of days off and we can hang out and relax and do a little sightseeing. The last time you came here, you were in and gone in less than twelve hours."

"You kept changing the date of the restaurant opening," Christian argued lightly. "I did what I could."

"Mom and Dad stayed for five days. They ate, they played tourist. All I'm saying is if the old man can do it, then so can you."

While he understood what his brother was saying, he still hated being compared to his father.

"Look, I'm gonna say one more thing and then I'll drop this. I swear."

It was Christian's turn to sigh. "Fine."

"Maybe let them come and see you. Talk to Dad face-to-face and tell him you're going to start delegating more and taking some time for yourself. This would be the perfect time for you to do it, because he's not going to want to upset you and risk sending you back to the hospital."

Logical? Yes.

Happening? No.

It wasn't like he didn't appreciate their concern. He did. But he knew that having them both stay with him would only add to his stress. Because no matter how much his parents promised to behave, his mother would no doubt hover and make him crazy and his father would just...well, be himself, and that would definitely make Christian crazy. There was no way he could deal with them right now. The most important thing to do for himself was try to figure out how to make these lifestyle modifications he needed without losing his mind.

Baby steps. One thing at a time.

Changing his diet was easy enough. Getting more exercise wasn't going to be an issue either. Cutting back on his work hours? Um...yeah. That one was going to prove to be the most challenging. Even thinking about it right now had his muscles tensing up and it took a real effort to make himself focus on something else.

His conversation with his brother had been eye-opening, and while Christian had refused the offer to go to New Orleans, Carter had promised to call and check in on him—he was already looking forward to it. Over the years, they had drifted apart—mainly for the reasons Christian had stated earlier, and he hated his brother's independence. Loved his brother, hated how he was living the life Christian only dreamed of.

Something to think about at another time.

Grabbing his coffee mug—because cutting coffee out of his diet was not going to happen—he walked out onto the deck and sat down. This was something that really did relax him, and he had to admit, it was nice to be able to stay out here and linger rather than rushing inside to get ready for work.

Except...every time he came out here, he looked for Sophie.

He was still kicking himself for the way they'd ended things when she was here. It wasn't his intention to make her feel bad or for her to leave the way she had. But in that moment, he was feeling a little overwhelmed and he knew he hadn't handled things well. And in the process, he'd hurt her feelings. While he wanted to apologize to her, he wasn't sure how.

Sure, he could've gone to the water every time he saw her, but every time he was about to step off the deck, he chickened out. Partly because he wasn't really sure what to say, and partly because he was afraid he had misread the situation and maybe she was only interested in him as…you know, a patient.

And man, would that suck.

Then there was the possibility of calling her, only he didn't have her number. They hadn't exchanged them when she was here and—

Wait a minute, he thought. She had interviewed at Montgomerys—or rather, the agency she worked for had sent her to Montgomerys—and no doubt she'd filled out an application, so really, he could call the office and ask Patricia for that information. It would simply be a matter of him calling to thank her for her help—at least, that's what he'd tell Patricia.

With a nod of approval at this idea, Christian smiled and felt a little bit better about the situation as a whole. Calling her would mean he wouldn't have to see the expression on her face if she was really only interested in him because of the whole anxiety attack thing—he could apologize and not have this hanging over his head and consuming his thoughts any longer.

With a big exhale of relief, he relaxed in his seat and took a sip of coffee. The thought of another day sitting around the house was beyond unappealing, but what else was there to do? His doctor had recommended finding a low-stress hobby like reading, but that wasn't something he envisioned himself doing for hours at a time. No, he needed to get out of the house so he wouldn't be tempted to check his emails or watch the stock market or anything related to the financial world.

Oddly enough, that got him thinking about Sophie again. When they'd been talking over lunch, she had shared with him that she'd decided to take up surfing as a distraction of sorts. It wasn't as if she'd been dreaming of being a surfer her whole life or anything, but once she arrived in town she figured it was a great way to meet people and learn something new.

Christian really didn't want to surf, but there were other things he could try—other sports or activities. Standing up, he leaned on the railing and looked out at the morning crowd. Most of them were surfers, but there was also a group who did yoga on the beach, and there was a constant stream of joggers.

Now that he thought about it, he'd been on the track team in high school and college, so maybe it was something he could ease back into.

Out of the corner of his eye he spotted a sassy red ponytail and the curvy woman it belonged to. He needed to do something about this obvious attraction he had for her. That meant he had to talk to her and apologize for his behavior and then feel her out about seeing her again.

As usual, she didn't look in his direction, so for the next hour, Christian was content to watch her try to master the sport of surfing.

Which—oddly enough—was both entertaining and arousing.

Chapter 4

Hanging up her phone, Sophie wasn't sure if she should leap with joy or be offended.

Patricia from Montgomerys had called to thank her for her assistance during Christian's health crisis and then not only gave her a schedule for next week but also told her that they had reached out to the agency she worked for and put them in touch with several other offices in his building.

And recommended Sophie for all of them.

All. Of. Them.

Getting more jobs wasn't what bothered her. It was the reason for why or how she happened to get the job that was bugging her.

"I don't understand," she'd said to Patricia. "I haven't even started working for you yet. Why would you reach out and recommend me to other businesses?"

"After you came in and we had a chance to talk, I realized you truly are the perfect fit for the position—something that both Mrs. Montgomerys had said you would be."

"Wait—who?"

"Mrs. Eliza Montgomery and Mrs. Monica Montgomery," Patricia explained. "They said they had met you on the beach and had invited you to interview for the position."

"So…they're both related to Christian?"

"Eliza is his mom," Patricia said pleasantly. "She was excited about you coming in—and I hate to say it, but she was also disappointed when she missed getting to meet with you again."

With a bit of annoyance, Sophie replied, "I explained what happened. Believe me, if I could have gotten there…"

"Oh, I know, I know," Patricia said. "And believe me, I'm so sorry you had to deal with that. But I think it was a blessing in disguise."

"How so?"

"If you had gotten the job earlier, you wouldn't have been here when Mr. Montgomery fell ill. I believe your being here made all the difference."

Normally, Sophie wouldn't mind taking the credit for saving someone, but other than trying to keep Christian calm, there wasn't anything anyone could have done to help—or hinder—Christian's prognosis.

"That's sweet of you to say, but it was the fast action of your staff that helped. I merely stood by and tried to keep him calm while we waited for the paramedics."

"You're too modest," Patricia said. "Anyway, after talking to you, and meeting you personally, I can already tell that you're very good at your job. I talk to a lot of the other human resources managers here in the building and when I told them about all that you did for Christian, they all wanted to meet you. But Christian was the one who insisted on calling and singing your praises to your bosses and then sharing the information with the other companies in the building."

"This was Christian's idea?" she asked incredulously.

"Oh…um, well, yes. He feels incredibly thankful to you for all you did."

"I see."

Sophie wasn't stupid—she'd accept any and all the jobs she might get through this. That was a no-brainer. But knowing that Christian had more than likely orchestrated it bothered her. Was he doing it simply because he was thankful, or was it because he'd acted like a jerk when he'd refused to let her help him?

Unfortunately, she didn't know him well enough to be sure.

With no other choice—because she would make herself crazy sitting here thinking about it—she took a shower and got ready, bracing herself to go knock on Christian Montgomery's door.

Did she take a little extra time in the shower and use her favorite scented soap?

Yes.

Did she spend a little extra time on her makeup?

Yes.

And did she curse more than once while she styled her hair because it was way too long and took forever to make look good?

Again, yes.

But as she looked at her reflection when she was done, all Sophie could say was "Damn, girl! You look good!"

With all of the extra attention she'd already given herself, choosing something to wear was a bit more challenging. Obviously, he knew she wasn't working, so showing up on his doorstep dressed up would look ridiculous. However, showing up in a pair of cutoffs and a T-shirt seemed wrong. It wasn't as if she had an extensive wardrobe to begin with, but right now it sure as heck felt that way!

Deciding on a pair of faded denim capris and a bold blue halter top, she felt casually sassy. That was a thing, right?

Slipping on a pair of flip-flops, she grabbed her purse and was out the door, feeling much calmer than she had an hour ago. The drive took less than fifteen minutes, and as Sophie parked in his driveway, she took a moment to give herself a small pep talk.

"The good thing is that you have a job," she said quietly. "It shouldn't matter why you have the job, the fact is that you have one." She paused. "And while it would be great if he apologized for coming off as being ungrateful last week, you need to remember that he'd had a traumatic day and maybe it wasn't about you at all."

Sighing, she flipped down her visor and checked her reflection in the mirror, fixing her lipstick. When she was done, she flipped it back up and continued her talk.

"If he recommended me for these jobs because he feels sorry for me, then I am completely within my rights to tell him that I'm offended. I don't need charity. However, if he did it based on my experience, then I'll be polite and say thank you." She took a steadying breath and thought about how she was going to feel when she saw him back at the office after he went back to work. "He needs to know that I'm going to be checking up on him and his health more than anyone else in the company—especially in the beginning—since I know his history. Like it or not."

No doubt he wouldn't like that one bit, but those were her terms and she wasn't going to be budged.

At least, she hoped she wasn't.

With one deep, cleansing breath, Sophie climbed from her car, fidgeted with her hair, and made her way up the front steps. Ringing the bell, she wondered how Christian was going to react to her showing up unannounced.

Although, really, how else could she show up? It wasn't as if she had his phone number.

When the front door opened, she almost forgot how to breathe.

His hair was a bit of a mess and it looked like he hadn't shaved in a few days. But it looked good on him. Really good. His blue eyes sparkled with surprise and she swallowed hard, trying not to sigh dreamily.

Then she glanced down.

Big mistake.

Dressed in a pair of black athletic shorts and nothing else, Christian Montgomery was like some sleek, athletic god.

She'd recognized that he had a fit physique before, but seeing him standing before her practically naked confirmed it.

And then some.

"Sophie, hey," he said, smiling as he leaned against the doorframe. "What brings you here?"

Right now, she was having a hard time forming words. Never before had she seen such a perfect male specimen and her fingers nearly twitched with the need to reach out and touch his flat stomach, and then maybe scratch their way up to tangle in his hair. She bet he smelled really good too.

"Sophie?"

Oh. Right. He'd asked her a question.

"Um… I wanted to talk to you," she said, her voice trembling a little—and not from nerves over what she wanted to say, but from the sight of him.

Maybe she should go…

Stepping aside, Christian motioned for her to come in, and with no other choice, she walked into his house.

Swallowing hard, she walked in front of him and looked around. She'd admired the house when she was here before, but at the time, her main concern had been Christian and his well-being. Now she could see just how beautiful the space was—high ceilings, exposed beams, colors that were cool and soothing in shades of tan and blue, and a wall of windows facing the ocean.

Not a bad way to live, she mused.

"Can I get you something to drink?" he asked, coming to stand beside her.

Part of her was afraid to turn and look at him because…well, she didn't want to do anything stupid.

Like drool.

"No, thank you," she said, keeping her focus on the stacked-stone fireplace. There was a massive television mounted on the wall above the mantel. She'd never seen a TV that big before. Stepping closer, she studied it.

Behind her, Christian laughed softly. "Yeah, I know. It's a bit on the big side, right?"

"It's practically a movie screen," she said, looking over her shoulder and smiling at him.

Again, big mistake.

He returned the smile.

Her heart quite literally skipped a beat.

Christian moved closer to sit on one of the sofas before motioning for her to take a seat as well. "So… you wanted to talk to me?"

Right now? Not really. There were some other things she'd like to be doing with him, but she noticed him looking at her expectantly, and that forced her to push all sexy thoughts of him aside.

With her purse on the sofa beside her, Sophie sat primly, hands folded in her lap. "First, how are you feeling?"

His smile faltered a little. "I'm doing okay. I'm bored out of my mind, but I'm being respectful of my doctor's orders and not calling into the office or even checking emails. It's a lot harder than I thought it would be. But on the plus side, I've been sleeping well and I've made some modifications to my diet that I'm not hating, so… all in all, I'm all right."

"Good. That's good." He was watching her, and Sophie fought the urge to squirm under his appraisal.

Christian leaned forward, resting his elbows on his knees. "Was there something more?"

Why was she hesitating?

Oh, right. Because half-naked Christian Montgomery was very distracting!

She cleared her throat and did her best to focus on… his forehead. "Okay, so here's the thing—I got a call from Patricia today." She waited for him to react, but he didn't. "She called to give me my schedule."

Still no reaction.

With a huff, she went on. "Then she told me how

you'd called my bosses and recommended me to be hired by other companies in the building! I appreciate your confidence in me, but..."

"But?" he prompted.

"You don't even know me, Christian," she blurted out. "For all you know, I'm terrible at my job! I could be...lazy or have no bedside manner! Maybe I stink at taking blood pressures or—or make people cry when I give them a flu shot. I mean, you don't have any idea!" She was breathless by the time she finished and sagged against the sofa cushions.

Without a word, Christian rose and walked to the kitchen. The entire space was open so the living room, dining room, and kitchen formed one large space and she was able to watch him pour her a glass of water. He handed it to her.

"Thank you."

He sat on the sofa opposite hers. "First of all, you and I both know you're excellent at your job. Anyone who was there with you that day in my office will attest to that."

Blushing, she said, "We don't know that."

He gave a small smile. "I disagree. And on top of that, from everything Patricia told me, you were the one my mother and aunt wanted to hire. The position was never going to anyone else."

She took a sip of the water and placed it on the coffee table on top of a coaster. "And what about the other companies?"

"Everyone in the building talks, Sophie. We're not the only ones looking to incorporate this kind of health program. We were just the first to do it. And now that we have, it didn't seem like a big deal to recommend your agency and you to them."

"But I haven't even started with your company yet."

He simply shrugged. "Why are you arguing with me about this? You said so yourself, this was the perfect job for you."

And it was. She knew that. But… "I feel like I may get any future jobs under false pretenses, or…something like that."

Still amused, Christian relaxed and slung one arm along the top of the cushion. "No false pretenses, Sophie. You are more than qualified for the job and any others you may get. Patricia was talking to me about that when…well, you know."

Nodding, she countered, "It's not like I don't appreciate this—because I do—but I don't want the recommendations because you feel obligated or something."

"Believe it or not, this has more to do with how much my mother and aunt loved you and raved about you."

Her eyes narrowed as she tried to gauge whether or not she believed him. "Where are they, anyway? Do they live nearby?"

"My parents live in New York and my aunt and her family are in North Carolina."

She looked at him quizzically. "But…they were here, right? I met them on the beach?"

He nodded.

"Do they visit often?"

He shrugged. "No. They were here to start up the whole corporate health thing. I guess I'm still surprised that they met you and how everything sort of worked out the way that it did."

"At first I thought they were just being nice, but then I realized they were chatty by nature," Sophie said, smiling.

"That pretty much is a perfect description of them."

"Anyway, I wasn't sure how to end the conversation so I could get back into the water, and ended up sitting with them for a while and sharing my life story." She chuckled. "I don't even know how that happened."

"Because they're crafty like that," he said. "Trust me. They have a gift for drawing things out of people that they wouldn't normally share."

"That sounds a little ominous."

Christian went on. "It's sort of a family trait—at least in my parents' generation. I used to think it was only my uncle William, but it turns out Aunt Monica is just as crafty—and she's clearly teaching my mom."

Sophie placed her now-empty glass of water on the coffee table. "That sounds like there's a story there."

"Let's just say my uncle is known as the family matchmaker. He found wives for his three sons—my cousins—and once they were all married off, he moved on to his nieces and nephews. We thought he was done at one point, and it seems my aunt got the matchmaking bug. She claims responsibility for my sister Megan and her fiancé Alex getting together."

"And you don't believe that?"

Christian shook his head. "My sister and Alex met at my cousin Zach's wedding and hooked up there. Then they didn't see one another again for almost two years."

"How did they meet up again after all that time?" she asked, loving to hear about people falling in love.

"Megan moved to Oregon to work for Zach, and Alex

is one of Zach's best friends. So really, it was only a matter of time before they reconnected. I don't see how my mother or my aunt think they had anything to do with it."

"I'm sure in their own way they helped."

He gave a little snort. "To hear them tell it, they're responsible for Megan moving across the country and going to work for Zach."

"And you don't believe that either?"

"No one tells anyone who they have to hire in this company," he said matter-of-factly. "Zach wouldn't hire Megan just because his aunts told him to."

She gave him a hard glare at the irony of what he'd just said.

"What?" he asked, brow furrowed.

"And yet here you are hiring me because your mom and aunt told you to," she stated, crossing her arms over her chest.

"It's not the same thing, Sophie. Not at all. They hired your agency and requested you. I have nothing to do with any of this. Trust me."

"Really?" she asked sarcastically.

Leaning forward, he met her gaze. "Look, they are different situations. We are adding something new to the company and needed to hire someone. They were in charge of hiring that person. It's not like they called me and said 'Hey, you have to hire Sophie and find a position for her.' So you see, two completely different things."

Maybe.

She still felt like the two situations were very similar, but she'd be willing to let it go for now.

"I'd like to believe you."

He let out a sigh of frustration. "Are you always this argumentative? Because I've got to tell you, it's exhausting."

"Sorry," she murmured. "And honestly, I'm not. I usually have better manners than this. I've never argued—even lightly—with anyone, especially not someone I work with!" And that's when it hit her: she was going to be working with him. What was she thinking, coming here and arguing with him like this?

Standing quickly, she grabbed her purse and stepped toward the door. "I should go," she said, suddenly feeling awkward and uncomfortable. "I'm glad you're feeling better, and I'm sure I'll see you at the office next week."

Moving nervously, she made her way to the door.

Christian's hand on her arm stopped her. When she turned, she saw confusion in his deep blue eyes.

"Hey," he said softly. "What's going on?"

"I—I just remembered someplace I need to be," she lied and immediately felt guilty for that too.

His eyes scanned her face, but his hand gently curled around her arm. "Really? Just like that? Without looking at your watch or anything, you suddenly remember that you have somewhere else to be?"

She bit her lip before saying, "Uh-huh."

A slow smile played at Christian's lips. "Where?"

"Where?"

"Mm-hmm. Where do you have to be?"

Why couldn't he just let her go? Why was he questioning her like this? "What—" she croaked and then cleared her throat. "What difference does it make? I needed to clear things up and I did, so..."

"So?"

She rolled her eyes. The man was infuriating.

And sexy.

That last one hit her when she went to move and somehow ended up even closer to his bare chest.

Licking him would definitely be wrong, right? And more than likely a little inappropriate.

It didn't stop her from wanting to do it, though.

"Sophie?"

Her eyes traveled up until they met his and she let out a slow exhale.

"Why are you leaving?"

"I…I told you."

"I'm glad you came by," he said, and it took her by surprise.

"You are?"

Nodding, he maneuvered them until they were moving back toward the sofas. "I felt bad about the other day. About my behavior. You were…well, you were the only person who was there for me and I was a little less than gracious about it. I'm sorry."

Her eyes went wide. "You're…you're sorry?"

He nodded again. "I never thanked you for all you did. Somehow, all I managed to focus on was what you wouldn't do for me rather than all that you actually did. That was terribly selfish of me, so I'm sorry."

Her heart fluttered at his words and she felt herself blush. "In your defense, you weren't feeling well and had enough to deal with without me adding to your stress."

"Somehow I don't think what you did was stressful, Sophie."

Swallowing hard, she found it hard to look away from him. "Really?"

"Really," he said gruffly, his gaze heating, and in that moment, she wasn't sure what exactly was happening.

"Christian," she said softly, "I…I was glad I could help."

"Me too."

Was it her imagination or had he moved closer?

They stood like that—locked in one another's gazes—while Sophie tried to figure out what to do. Should she move away or even closer?

"I have to ask you something," he said, his voice low. He didn't wait for her to respond. "Are you really mad at me, you know, because of the recommendations?"

She whispered, "No."

Mesmerized by the heated look in his eyes, she wondered why he'd ask her something like that. Had she gone too far and been too argumentative with him?

"Sophie?" Now it was Christian's voice that was a mere whisper as he closed the distance between them.

"Hmm?"

"I'd really like to kiss you."

Her heart beat like wild in her chest at his words. Smiling shyly, all she could think to say was "Okay."

The word was barely out of her mouth before Christian's lips claimed hers.

It wasn't the taste of the ocean on her lips, like he'd fantasized about so many times.

It was better.

Sweeter.

And far more addictive.

Christian's arms banded around Sophie as he pulled

her closer and groaned with pleasure at the feel of her soft curves pressing against his bare chest.

Yeah, he'd gone out for a jog earlier and should have pulled a shirt on before answering his door, but he hadn't. And now he was glad for that decision, because seeing how Sophie had been watching him—all but staring at him—had made his decision to be bold and kiss her easier.

It was good to know this wasn't a one-sided attraction.

Her soft moan as she wrapped her arms around him was a highly erotic sound. Christian took the kiss deeper—thrilled and more turned on than he'd thought possible as her tongue touched his. It had been a long time since he'd felt this strongly about a woman and he couldn't remember a time when he'd been this aroused by a simple kiss.

Okay, so it wasn't quite so simple. It was hot and wet and sexy, and he shifted them so he could sit on the sofa and cradle her in his lap. Sophie moved with him and when they were in their new position, she hummed with approval.

They were in his home. It was completely private. And some primitive part of him wanted to take this further. Christian felt like he'd been waiting forever for her, even though he hadn't known her for even a week.

It was crazy and impulsive, but he couldn't stop this feeling no matter how hard he tried.

Which, to be honest, wasn't much. He was too wrapped up in all the sensations—how soft her lips were, how sexy she sounded, how incredibly responsive she was to him.

With his hands gently skimming up and down her spine, he had to focus so he wouldn't lose the thin grip he had on his control. The halter top left most of her back bare and the softness of her skin was driving him crazy.

And for a man who thrived on always being in control, it was an odd feeling.

One hand reached up to anchor into her hair—which felt just as silky as he'd imagined—and slowed them both down. He sipped at her lips, angled his head, and trailed kisses up her cheek and then back again. When he finally lifted his head, they were both breathless. Sophie rested her head on his shoulder, and for the life of him, he didn't know what that meant or what he should say.

Technically, he had stated his intentions and she could have said no.

But she seemed as into it as he was, so hopefully she wasn't upset.

"We shouldn't have done that," she said, her voice barely a whisper.

Those five little words hit him hard. Tucking a finger under her chin, he gently forced her to look at him. His eyes scanned her face and it took every ounce of strength he had not to dive in for another kiss—no matter what she said. Her lips were so red and wet, her cheeks were flushed, and she was still breathing a little hard.

She was sexy as hell and he could feel himself trembling with the need to stay in control.

"Why?" he whispered.

Sophie swallowed hard. "We're going to be working together, Christian. This isn't appropriate, and..." She scrambled off his lap and sat beside him. "It shouldn't have happened."

He felt completely gobsmacked and had no idea how to respond to what she was saying.

"You have to understand," she said. "It would look really bad for me to be messing around with you as soon as I start this job. People will look at me like that was how I got the position."

Raking a hand through his hair, Christian let out a frustrated breath. "Sophie, no one is going to think that. And what happened here had nothing whatsoever to do with work or your job or...any of that." There was no way not to say what came next. "The truth is, I've sort of been...aware of you for a while now."

Putting a little more space between them, she looked at him nervously. "Um, what?"

"I've seen you out surfing," he clarified.

"You mean—that night when you thought I was drowning," she stated slowly.

But Christian shook his head. "Before that." Sighing loudly, he stood. "Every morning I have a cup of coffee out on my deck. I started doing it a while ago and I found it was a nice way to start my day." He looked straight at her. "It wasn't like I was purposely looking for you, but...you kind of stand out."

"Stand out?"

Nervously, he touched a strand of her fiery hair. "A redhead in a sea of blonds," he said, almost mesmerized by the feel of her. "Every morning, if you were out there in the ocean, I saw you. I didn't stay out there the entire time and it wasn't like seeing you was the only reason I was out there," he quickly explained. "But it was normally while I finished my coffee. So many times I tried to convince myself to go down to the beach and introduce myself."

"Then why didn't you?" she asked, her voice softer and a little less nervous now.

He shrugged. “Cowardice, I guess. There never seemed to be the right time to go about doing it.”

“Until you thought I was drowning?” she asked with amusement, and Christian saw the first hint of a smile playing at her lips.

He smiled back and felt his cheeks heat. “Well, yeah. Like I said, cowardice.”

Sophie reached up and captured the hand that was still playing with her hair and squeezed it. “I don’t think it’s cowardice at all. I think in the same position I would have felt the same way.”

“Really?”

“This move has forced me out of my comfort zone. Back in Kansas, I knew everyone in town, so I never experienced the awkwardness of meeting someone new. Even when I went to college, it was local, and I knew so many of my classmates that even when I met someone new, we had friends in common.” She paused. “Moving here sight-unseen meant everyone was a stranger. I had to get over my insecurities and break out of my comfort zone and force myself to talk to people.”

“It’s the opposite for me. I’ve always been at ease meeting new people, and I’ve never hesitated to introduce myself to a beautiful woman,” he said with a lopsided grin. “You were the first woman who made me pause.”

“Why?”

Hesitating because the admission was a little embarrassing, Christian considered his words. “My life is a mess—you know, in case you haven’t noticed.”

“It’s not that bad.”

“Besides being a workaholic, I have…well, I have

trust issues. Pretty much with everyone, but particularly with women."

"Someone hurt you," she said tenderly, squeezing the hand she was still holding.

It was pointless to deny it. Other than his sister, Megan, no one knew the extent of why he was so uptight about the way he currently ran his life. But he felt that it was important for him to share with Sophie, because he had a feeling she could help him change—to break out of this rut he was in and maybe start living again.

"I used to be the head of the Montgomerys office in London," he began, looking at their hands rather than directly at her. "It was a dream come true, because it got me away from everyone. I'd been working for my father since I was a teen and I was thrilled to be far enough away that I could start making a name for myself. About two years after I'd started, my father started taking trips over to see how things were going."

"Just for the sake of checking, or because he thought something was wrong?" she asked, and Christian was thankful that she wasn't going to let him get too deep into his own head on this.

"The first time was to oversee a deal that we had been working on together remotely. I felt good about all of it and it was important to me for him to see me as an equal."

"That makes sense."

"Anyway, businesswise, I was fine. He couldn't find anything wrong with the way I was running the office." He paused and let out a long breath. "I was involved with someone—she was my assistant, actually—and he got all over me about how unprofessional I was and how I was jeopardizing the company reputation."

He immediately noticed the look of unease on her face. Essentially, he was proving her earlier comments correct. "Did he leave, or did you end the relationship?"

"At first, it was little comments to me on his daily phone calls, but I kept telling him I had everything under control." Then he shook his head. "Anyway, he started coming around more and more and staying for longer periods of time and things became strained with Poppy."

"Poppy?" she asked with a small smile. "That's a very English name."

"It's a ridiculous name," he murmured. "Anyway, things were getting tense between us and Dad was always there, and then he went and hired a new assistant for me and transferred Poppy to work with my VP, Greyson."

"How was that his place?" she asked with disbelief. "It was your office!"

"My father isn't big on boundaries. In his mind, any office of mine was an office of his." Thinking back, it still made him mad. "Unfortunately, I was working on a major deal—one of the biggest financial deals of my career. I knew if I could stay focused on contract negotiations and making the client happy, it would be the ultimate victory for me. The deal I had worked for my entire life. And I thought if I could prove to him that I could handle an account of this magnitude, he'd back off. And to be honest, moving Poppy took one distraction off my plate."

"She…she was keeping you from your work?"

Christian shook his head. "No, but the constant badgering from my father was."

"What happened next?"

"I closed the deal and made a lot of money for Montgomerys," he said, his voice void of emotion.

"Oh. Well, that's a good thing, right? That should have made your father happy."

"You would think."

"Christian. We don't have to talk about this. Although… I don't understand why you're telling me all of this."

"I'm getting to the reason," he said, and knew he had to finish the story so she would understand him a little better. That maybe she'd see why he was so stressed out and maybe she'd be able to help him.

With a steadying breath, he continued. "I closed the deal on a Friday. Dad called and asked me to meet him at the office on Saturday morning. I thought it was odd, because we had planned on meeting for lunch, but he insisted I come to the office first." He shook his head at the memory. "I arrived first. I thought no one was in the office at first—but Poppy and Greyson were."

She looked at him oddly.

"And they certainly weren't working," he said with a mirthless laugh.

Gasping, she said, "I'm so sorry. How horrible for you to find out like that!"

"Turns out the two of them had been carrying on for a while. Long before my father moved her over to work for Grey," he said. "Somehow, Dad found out about it. As I was standing there screaming at the two of them and demanding to know how they could do this to me, in strolls dear old Dad to say 'I told you so.'"

Her eyes went wide. "No!"

"Unfortunately, yes."

"But…how could he know when you didn't?"

Christian shrugged. "Apparently he's very observant.

Claims he noticed some lingering looks and caught them whispering with one another a few times in a way that seemed more than a little cozy, so he hired a private investigator. When he knew he had the proof…well, there we all were."

"That's awful! He didn't think there was another way to break the news to you?" she asked with a hint of disgust. "I swear, some men have no right to be fathers."

"What?"

She looked surprised. "Nothing," she said quickly. "It's nothing. So what did you do?"

"I fired them both, told Dad to leave, and then spent the better part of a month getting the company in order because I wanted out. Luckily, that was around the time my cousin Ryder—who owns this house and used to run the office here—was looking for someone to take over temporarily so he could take a break. It just worked out that he was happier elsewhere and I had no place else to go."

"Wow, Christian. Just…wow. I can see why you struggle with stress, but don't you see you'd be courting the same kind of trouble if we were to get involved? I don't want to be the cause of stress in your life."

But he shook his head as she spoke. "You're the reason I feel like I'm ready to stop this destructive pattern of behavior," he explained. "I want to get to know you, Sophie. When I'm around you, I feel better—lighter, happier. I'm done letting other people dictate my life for me."

"I don't know what to say to that," she said carefully. "I think it's great that you want to make this change, Christian, but…are you sure it's me you're looking to spend time with, or am I someone you want to use to get back at your father?"

That thought hadn't even crossed his mind, but now that it was out there, it was all he could think about.

As if sensing his thoughts, she said, "Besides, I think you need to focus on getting better first."

"Oh," he said, feeling completely dejected. It was probably for the best, but he couldn't help but want to argue. This wasn't about his father. This was about her—them—and he wasn't sure how to go about convincing Sophie of that.

"I really would like to get to know you better, too," she said, sounding optimistic. When he looked at her face, her smile was sincere and beautiful. It gave him hope. "I'd like it if we could maybe… If we could be friends. Or is that weird? I mean, are you friends with your employees?"

"You're not my employee, Sophie. You're like—a subcontractor or something. And besides, I don't interact with any of my employees any more than I have to," he said, hating not only the way that sounded but the look of disappointment on her face.

"Oh."

"But"—he did his best to sound lighter and as optimistic as she had—"I think, with your help, that it's time for that to change."

Chapter 5

BEING FRIENDS WAS A GOOD THING.

In theory.

But a week later, Sophie was having doubts.

A knock on her makeshift office door made her look up to see the main reason for her doubts standing in the doorway.

"Hey," he said, a sexy grin on his face. "I promised my doctor I'd come in for a blood pressure check before my meeting with the staff today and again after."

Nodding, Sophie motioned for him to have a seat. Patricia had set up space for her to use as a medical room. She had her own desk, a couple of chairs for the employees to use while they were with her, and an assortment of equipment for her to use—a scale, an electronic blood pressure machine, a laptop, and a supply cabinet for her to stock the basics like Band-Aids, gauze, tongue depressors, and the like.

"How are you feeling?" she asked, going for casual. With every other Montgomery employee she'd met with this week, she'd been a completely pleasant professional. One glance at Christian, however, and she felt like a giddy schoolgirl.

Damn the man and his incredibly good looks.

And let's not forget that kiss.

Yeah, she'd been trying to pretend that kissing Christian wasn't a big deal, but it totally was. If anything, she'd been playing the scene over and over in her mind since it happened. She probably could have made herself think of something else, but ever since he had proclaimed that he was looking for her help in learning to be friends with people again, they'd been spending time together.

A lot of time together.

Like seeing each other every day time.

"You know," he said, interrupting her thoughts, "I'm feeling pretty good. I was glad to go to work on Monday, and making it a short day wasn't nearly as painful as I thought it would be."

Sophie had encouraged him to work only a half day that day and was surprised that he'd listened.

He sat and made himself comfortable, slouching a little in the chair and loosening his shirt cuffs. "Yesterday was a little bit longer of a day but—as I mentioned—I was more than ready to leave at four."

She nodded, because they had talked about that while they'd jogged on the beach.

Yes, she'd skipped her evening surf in exchange for jogging.

Hopefully, today she'd get the courage to tell him she wasn't enjoying jogging the way she enjoyed surfing.

"But how are you feeling about this meeting today? Are you anxious? Stressed? Any overall negative feelings that are causing you distress?" she asked, reaching for his wrist to take his pulse.

"Nope," he responded, still smiling. "I met with Erin this morning about how I planned on delegating the workload around here and I feel good about it. And if everyone's as on board with taking on more work as she claims, then I have to believe they'll be able to handle it."

She smiled at him. "Good for you! So what are you going to do with all of your free time?"

Closing his eyes, Christian chuckled. "I haven't given it much thought. I'm not even sure how much time we're talking about. All I know is that I am determined to try to make these changes by cutting my hours."

Sliding the pressure cuff up his arm, she teased, "Oh, come on. You sounded a lot more confident last night while we were jogging. You mentioned taking a vacation and going to spend some time with your brother in New Orleans. What happened to that?" With her stethoscope in place, she added, "I need you to be still and relax for a moment." Then she hit the button on the electronic machine and listened to his heartbeat.

When the machine beeped a minute later, she removed her stethoscope before taking the cuff from his arm. Turning, she made a note in his chart. "That's much better than the last time I checked it for you."

"The last time you checked my blood pressure, we thought I was having a heart attack, so..."

With a light laugh, she leaned against her desk and faced him. "I'm glad it wasn't that."

"You and me both." He was still seated and was looking at Sophie with mild amusement.

"What are you thinking right now?" It was a question she was asking him more and more. Usually, she was making sure he wasn't thinking about work—something she knew stressed him out. But right now, she was honestly curious about what was on his mind.

"Have you ever been to New Orleans?" he asked, his gaze steady on hers.

"Me? No. Up until I moved here, I'd never been anywhere but Kansas." Shrugging, she crossed her arms over her middle. Never traveling wasn't something that had ever bothered her before, but for some reason, admitting it to Christian now had her feeling a little self-conscious.

"I've only been there once myself," he said conversationally. "It was for Carter's restaurant opening. I flew in, ate, and pretty much flew home." He paused. "I hadn't given it much thought until he and I spoke last week. Now I think I should go."

"But...?" She could tell there was more to what he was saying.

"I don't know. I think Carter's as much of a workaholic as I am, except in a different environment. I know the restaurant keeps him busy, he's looking at opening in other locations, and I hate the thought of being in the way."

"He invited you, didn't he?"

"He did, but maybe he was trying to be nice."

"Maybe he wants to see you," she countered.

He laughed again. "So you think I should go."

"Absolutely! The chance to hang out with your brother, eat some amazing food, and get away for a few days? Um, yes, Christian. This is kind of a no-brainer."

"Maybe for you," he murmured.

"For most people," she said, doing her best to sound at least a little firm.

He came to his feet and straightened his sleeves, refastened his cuffs. "Enough about me, how's your day going?"

"Can't complain, Boss," she said with a sassy

grin. Actually, calling him boss was nothing more than a reminder to herself to keep things professional. Touching Christian—even in a professional way for medical reasons—had her own pulse skittering all over the place. That was something that had never happened to her before—and certainly never with a patient.

"You know I'm not really your boss, right?" he asked, stepping in closer. The grin on his face told her he knew exactly what he was doing. He was teasing her—something he seemed to enjoy doing. And she had to admit, she enjoyed it just a little bit too.

"Are you the head of this company?" she asked, trying to keep a straight face.

"I am." He took another step closer.

"Well, then..."

Christian was right behind her when she turned again. Her soft gasp of surprise seemed to please him.

"Can I ask you something?" he asked, his voice low and a little gruff.

She nodded.

"Would you be interested in going to New Orleans with me?"

Everything in her wanted to say yes—so much so that she almost blurted it out giddily. But common sense prevailed and she took a step back. "Thank you, but I can't."

"Can't?" he repeated with a hint of disbelief.

"I'm on call with the staffing agency, Christian. You know that. This is only part-time, and I've been unemployed long enough. I can't take off for a weekend. It's not the responsible thing to do."

"Are you always so responsible, Sophie?" he asked, coming closer.

Clearing her throat, she moved aside, hitting her legs on a filing cabinet. “I—I am. I have to be,” she stammered nervously. “Besides, I don’t think it’s appropriate for us to be going away together for a weekend.”

He looked at her quizzically. “Why not?”

“Christian, we’ve been over this. Whether you want to admit it or not, it wouldn’t look right for me to go to New Orleans—or anywhere, for that matter—with you.”

“I’m still confused here, Soph. You’re saying that we—as friends—can hang out together, but we can only hang out here in San Diego. Do I have that right?”

When worded like that, it did sound flimsy.

“What if I moved away? Are you saying we couldn’t be friends anymore? Or what if you were the one to move? Does this mean I couldn’t come visit you?”

She knew he was teasing—saw it in his eyes—but she refused to give in and laugh. “Yes. That’s exactly what I’m saying.”

His blue eyes went wide right before he started laughing. Heartily. It was something he was doing with more frequency and it always made her smile.

“C’mon, Sophie. What’s the harm in going and hanging out with my brother? You’d get to visit someplace you’ve never been before, eat at one of the best restaurants in the country, and make sure I don’t stress out.”

“Nice try, Montgomery,” she said firmly. “I think you’re trying to avoid being alone with your brother. What I don’t understand is why.”

“I’m not trying to avoid spending time with Carter. I wouldn’t be going to New Orleans if I was.”

“Then why ask me to go with you?” she countered.

"How about because I enjoy spending time with you? Or that I thought you might enjoy it? Take your pick."

It was so damn tempting.

Christian was charming and she didn't doubt his words.

It was she who couldn't be trusted.

Every day had become a struggle to keep her distance—to simply treat him as a friend when all she wanted to do was grab him and kiss him and never stop.

Which—as she stood here looking at that lopsided grin and mussed-up hair—she wanted to do right now too.

Forcing herself to look away, Sophie busied herself straightening her desk. "I appreciate the offer, but I really can't." She looked at her watch and then glanced at Christian. "Isn't it almost time for your meeting?"

His smile fell a little, but he gave her a curt nod. "It is. I'll come by afterward for you to get another check and then I'll call the results in to my physician."

"I can do it for you," she offered. "It's not a big deal."

Sliding his hands into his trouser pockets, he gave her another small smile. "Thanks, but I think I can handle it." Turning, he walked to the door, looked over his shoulder, and said, "See you later."

Waiting a full minute after he left, Sophie slumped at her desk.

How did people do this? How did they hide their feelings—push them aside no matter how much it hurt? She'd known and had been involved with enough men to know the difference between a friend and someone who meant a lot more.

And Christian definitely fell into the *meant a lot more* category.

It was weird how fast it had hit her. When he sat next to her that night on the sand, she remembered thinking that he was the type of man she'd always wanted—kind, compassionate, handsome. He was all those things and so much more. Unfortunately, with his history with his ex in London and the overall situation with his father, they had too many strikes against them.

Her desk phone rang and she answered it. "Yes?"

"Hey, Sophie, it's Patricia. Do you have time to go over some new forms we want the employees to fill out?"

Looking at her watch again, she knew she didn't have anyone else coming in for at least thirty minutes. "Sure. Your office or mine?"

~

"I hate jogging."

Christian came to a halt on the sand and turned to see Sophie bent at the waist, breathing hard. She waved him on as she shook her head, her long ponytail swinging from side to side. "Um...what?"

Angling her head, she glared at him. "I hate this. The jogging. It's totally not my thing." Then she let out a loud breath. "There. I said it."

When he was beside her, he crouched to get eye-level with her. "If you wanted to stop, you just had to say so. I know I picked up the pace there, but you shouldn't feel like you have to keep up."

She shoved him and he fell back on his ass, and couldn't help but laugh. When she went to straighten, he grabbed her hand and tugged her on the sand beside him. "Christian!" she cried. "Dammit, now there's going to be sand everywhere."

"It's a beach. Of course there's sand everywhere."

"Seriously?" she deadpanned. "I meant on my clothes."

"Ah. Gotcha," he said. "So what's going on?"

She grimaced as she tried to get comfortable. "I'm not a runner. I thought I could be, but I can't."

"Oh. Okay." He paused. "Then why did you keep agreeing to come with me?"

She shrugged. "I don't know. I thought I wasn't giving it a fair shot. My surfing isn't improving, so I thought maybe this would be something different to try. Turns out I hate it."

"Hate's a bit of a strong word," he countered. "I mean, maybe—"

"No. Trust me. I hate it."

Message received. If her words weren't strong enough, the vehemence behind them and the scowl on her face were.

"O-kay," he responded slowly. "So do you want to head back to the house?"

"Only if we can walk," she said, coming to her feet. Without looking at him, Sophie began walking away. Christian quickly scrambled to his feet and went after her, grasping her shoulder and forcing her to face him.

"Hey. What's going on? Are you mad at me?"

Her shoulders sagged and her brow furrowed. "No. Why would you even ask that?"

"Soph, you got up and started walking away, what was I supposed to think?"

"Maybe that I was heading back to your house?"

As much as he wanted to take her at her word, something was up. Her tone and her stance were both defensive, and if there was one thing he was learning about Sophie, it was that she rarely acted this way. She was always smiling and encouraging. When she went to move out of his grasp, Christian held firm. When she tugged a second time, she growled with frustration.

"What?" she cried. "What is your problem?"

"My problem?" he parroted, loudly. "Sweetheart, that's a question for you. You can't possibly be this upset over jogging."

"Who says I'm upset?" she asked, her voice dripping with sarcasm.

Christian leaned in until they were almost nose-to-nose. "You're acting awful dodgy, Soph."

"Dodgy? You're calling me *dodgy*?" she asked incredulously and then pulled back. "Wait. What's dodgy?"

He laughed. "Sorry, love. Every once in a while, some lingo I picked up while I lived in London slips out. I have no idea why."

"Are you insulting me?"

His eyes went wide. "You know what, you are acting dodgy. Which—for the record—means you're acting suspiciously. Now, I don't know about you, but I can stand out here all night and wait you out. I've got nothing else to do, since we're not jogging. So you can either spill it and tell me what's got you all twisted up or we can stand here until the tide comes in. Your choice."

And for a moment, he thought she was going to opt to wait for the tide to come in.

Thankfully, she started to speak.

"Fine. I—" She stopped and sighed. "I hated having to confess about jogging."

Seriously? That was it?

"Back home, I never would have said anything. I would have just kept doing it and hating every second of it. Since I moved, I made the decision not to do that anymore. After all, there's no reason for me to do things I don't like, right?"

"Well, no, but—"

"I believe in honesty," she went on, as if Christian hadn't said a word. "And I expect it in return."

"O-kay."

When she looked up at him, her green eyes were wide and sad. "Why are you here, Christian?"

Not sure where this was going, he replied, "Because we said we were going jogging."

Shaking her head, Sophie reworded her question. "I mean, why are you here with me?"

Now he was confused. "Same answer. I don't understand where—"

"Gah!" she cried and pulled out of his grasp. She paced a few feet away and returned. "You're out here jogging because your doctor encouraged you to get out and get some exercise, right?"

He nodded.

"And you're out here because you left work at a reasonable hour and this was a way to pass the time, right?"

He nodded again.

If anything, her expression grew even sadder. "You don't need me to jog with you, Christian. I'm sure you have other friends you could have called to do this with you if you really didn't want to run alone."

His mouth opened and closed, because he didn't have a clue how to respond to it. He did have friends—not a lot, but there were certainly guys he could call to go for a run with him. But if truth be told, he didn't want to run with them. He enjoyed the time he and Sophie spent together, and he'd been hoping that the more time they spent around each other, the more she'd see that they could be more than friends.

So far, that hadn't happened.

Now it sounded as if she wasn't even interested in being his friend.

So he had to speak up, and hopefully wipe that sad look off her face.

"Look, I could call a buddy or two to jog with me, but I've enjoyed spending time with you. I thought you felt the same way. But if I read something that wasn't there—if you were only being nice because of the whole anxiety attack thing—then...you should know that you're not obligated to be here. And there's certainly no pressure for us to be friends."

"Christian..."

"I'm sorry if I'm monopolizing your time," he said quietly. "I'm sorry if I made you feel like turning down my offer of friendship wasn't an option. That was never my intention."

"Now I'm confused," she said.

Sinking both of his hands into his hair and tugging with frustration, he went on. "I don't want to be a charity case, Sophie. Clearly, it's been far too long since I've tried to be friends with a woman and I suck at it. I thought it was what you wanted and—"

"It is!"

He shook his head. "No. It's really not. The look on your face says otherwise." With a weary sigh, Christian turned and started toward his house. "I should've just kept my damn distance. This is why I work so much—because dealing with relationships on any level is awkward as hell."

Sophie fell in step beside him—almost jogging to keep up with his much longer stride. "Okay, I think we're having two different conversations, because I never said I didn't want to be friends. I just don't want to jog."

Snorting with disbelief, he kept walking.

"For the love of it," she snapped, grabbing his arm. "Will you slow down? I already told you I hate jogging and you're making me jog to keep up!"

When he stopped abruptly, they collided. Christian reached out to steady her before she fell over and then instantly released her. Touching Sophie was so not what he needed right now. He looked at her expectantly, although the last thing he wanted was to hear her make excuses for why he'd misread the situation.

"I don't understand what's happening right now," she said, and Christian could hear a slight tremble in her voice. "I don't think it's fair that you're mad at me for being honest."

Damn. She had him there. Just because he hadn't wanted to hear her admission didn't mean he had the right to be upset with her.

At least not to her face.

"Believe me, I'm all about people being honest too, Sophie. I've had more than enough of people keeping secrets and lying to my face," he said, hating how harsh he sounded. "I wasted a lot of time on relationships where way too much was happening behind my back. I'm not interested in going there again."

Frowning, she stood silent for a moment. "I don't think my not wanting to jog really compares to your girlfriend cheating on you," she murmured.

And again, she was right. He was making way more out of this than he should. Unsure of what to do with himself, he took a few steps away and then faced her again. "Why don't we just call it a day, okay? And… I guess I'll see you around at the office." This time when he started to walk away, she didn't stop him, and he wasn't sure if that made him happy or pissed him off more.

It didn't matter. He'd wait until he was home to growl or throw something—probably both at the same time.

It shouldn't be this hard, he thought. It shouldn't be this difficult to get his life back on track. Hell, maybe he'd waited too long to take these first steps, but…he'd thought it would be easier. He'd met a woman who he found attractive and he thought she felt the same. Their kiss had been amazing, and the fact that she worked for Montgomerys—part-time—really wasn't an issue.

Obviously, he was wrong.

Well, maybe not wrong, but he'd certainly misread the whole thing, saw things that weren't there, and now he felt like a complete idiot.

His anger and frustration growing with each step, he decided to just say "screw it" and took off at a jog for the remainder of the way. No doubt Sophie wouldn't even try to catch up, so really, why was he prolonging the misery? The sooner he was back in his house, the sooner he could freely vent his frustration and get it out of his system.

Maybe.

It didn't take long until he was taking the stairs to the deck two at a time and then he was opening the door and inside where the air conditioning almost burned his heated skin. With a shiver, he tossed his keys on the kitchen counter and went to grab a bottle of water. Drinking the entire contents without taking a breath, he slammed the bottle beside his keys.

Not sure of what to do first, Christian kicked off his sneakers and was about to peel off his shirt when a loud knock on the deck doors took him by surprise.

Sophie.

Muttering a curse, he walked over and slid open the door. He didn't say a word. Didn't get a chance to.

"My whole life people lied to me," she said, her breath ragged. "My friends, my family, the entire town."

Christian moved nearer, but she held up a hand to stop him.

"I was raised by my grandmother. My Nana," she corrected, before taking a steadying breath. "My parents died when I was two."

"God, Sophie, I'm sorry," he said softly, wanting nothing more than to wrap her in his arms at her sad admission.

"They were killed in a car accident," she went on. "It was a winter night. The roads were slick and the car skidded on some ice and went off into an embankment. That's what I'd always been told."

Her voice was oddly void of emotion and a chill went down Christian's spine.

"Four months ago, I was at work in Doc Kelly's office when I had to get a medical history for a new patient—older guy, late fifties. I was taking his information when he mentioned how he'd grown up in the area, moved away, and recently moved back. He was making small talk and I smiled." She paused. "He kept looking at me oddly and asked if I had grown up locally. I said yes."

By now, she was shaking, so without asking, Christian gently grasped her arm and led her into the house and to a chair at his kitchen table. Silently, he grabbed a bottle of water and placed it in front of her.

"Thank you," she said before taking a long sip. Slowly, she put the cap on the bottle and set it on the table. "Anyway, he kept staring at me until it got uncomfortable. I was about to leave the room to ask if one of the other nurses could finish for me when he asked if I was related to Laura Colby." She paused and met his gaze. "That was my mom."

Christian sat beside her, his mind swirling with questions, but he knew he needed to let her finish.

"I told him she was my mother and he shook his head and said he was so sorry to hear about her death. I'm used to people offering their condolences, so I didn't think anything of it. Then he…he said…it turned the whole town upside down when it happened." She played with the water bottle. "I thought that was an odd statement, because it was a car accident. I didn't think there was anything so shocking about that to put the town in a tizzy, but I kept that to myself."

With a nod, he waited.

"Then he looked at me and said, 'We really thought he'd get the death penalty. We all knew Laura was too good for him, that he had a problem, but no one thought she'd be the one he killed.' And I had no idea what he was talking about. Any time I'd ever heard about the accident, it was how their car went off the road in the rain. The way he made it sound was like he was talking about somebody else."

With a shaky breath, Sophie took another drink of water before continuing.

"Doc Kelly came in then, and I excused myself and ran out of the room. Right out of the office. I drove home and for the life of me, I still don't remember doing that. All I know is I was suddenly in the living room and looking at Nana and demanding to know what this man was talking about."

Christian's heart beat like wild in his chest as a sense of dread washed over him.

"Sophie, you don't... I mean, it's okay if you don't want to—"

"My father killed my mother," she said flatly. "He was an alcoholic—had a history of DUIs. That night—the night of the accident—he was drunk and my mother tried to stop him from driving." She blinked away tears, took another sip of her water before looking at him again.

"Sophie..."

"He not only killed her but a couple they hit head-on, as well." She let out a mirthless laugh. "Amazingly, he walked away without a scratch."

He had no words.

"Nana never wanted me to know what really happened. Small town and all, she was able to get word around that she would prefer if I thought both my parents died in a car accident—you know, choosing to omit the fact that my father was the cause of it. Everyone went along with it—my whole life, all my friends, neighbors, coworkers—anyone who knew the real story went along with the lie." Tears ran down her cheek freely now. "They all lied to me. That's why it's so important to me to tell the truth—no matter what." She swallowed hard.

"Once the cat was out of the bag, I was pretty much hell on wheels around town. I talked to everyone—accused everyone of keeping the truth from me. I went online and researched the case, but considering it happened twenty-five years ago and there wasn't really an internet then, there wasn't much for me to find."

"I can't even begin to imagine how you must have felt."

"He's serving a life sentence," she said shakily. "And I get to be the daughter of the town drunk. The guy who killed three innocent people because he loved alcohol more than anything else."

"I'm sure nobody thinks that."

"Nana says the same thing, but..." She shrugged. "I'll never know. I don't want to know. My whole life, everything I thought I knew, it's all just... I hate it."

Muttering a curse, he wanted to kick himself for making her talk about this—for making her even think about things she clearly wanted to forget. As he studied Sophie's face, he saw she was pale and shivering. He instantly stood and pulled her to her feet, wrapping her in his arms.

"I'm so sorry, Sophie," he said softly, placing a kiss on the top of her head. "I'm so sorry you had to go through all of that." He thought that might help her relax, but she shoved at his chest, taking him by surprise.

With a steadying breath, she straightened her spine. "That's why I need to be honest with you, Christian."

"It's okay," he said. "I get it. Really." After her horrific story, the last thing he wanted was to have her hammer the point home about how she felt—or didn't feel—about him.

"No, you don't," she stated, her voice stronger than it was a moment ago. "The thing is—I don't want to be just your friend. When I'm with you...I laugh. I smile. And while I've made some friends since I moved here, and I go out and have fun with them, it's not the same. You make me...you make me happy, Christian. And I understand all of your reasons why you want to avoid anything more with me. I get it. After everything your dad did and the way you were betrayed by a woman you worked with and were involved with, I understand. I do." She paused and let out a slow breath. "But here's the thing. I'm not her. I would never do something like that to you or to anyone. That's why—that's why I shared my story with you. I wanted you to know why I'm practically honest to a fault. Lying—even a little white lie—doesn't sit well with me anymore."

"Sophie..."

"But I also expect the same in return," she went on. "And I think you and I have that in common. We've both been hurt by other people's lies. Their motivation may have been different, but ultimately, we were hurt by them. Do you understand what I'm trying to say?"

He was almost too afraid to hope.

"I think so," he said carefully, second-guessing his instincts and afraid to do or say the wrong thing.

Sophie took one step toward him, then another. "I don't think you do. So I guess I'll have to show you."

And just like that, her arms were around him and she was up on her tiptoes and pressing her lips to his.

Leaving her comfort zone was totally becoming her thing.

Pressed up against Christian, Sophie poured everything she had into the kiss. It was crazy and a little impulsive, but after sharing what she had with him, she needed to chase those dark thoughts away.

And kissing Christian was the perfect distraction.

He didn't question it and—if anything—he seemed just as on board with it as she was.

Not that she was surprised. Their last kiss had been incredibly hot and she hadn't been able to push it from her mind; hopefully, he hadn't either.

Her hands raked up into his hair as his arms banded tighter around her waist. She loved how warm and hard his entire body was. Admiring his physique was one thing; getting up close and personal with it like this was another.

One kiss led to another and another until she was almost dizzy. She didn't want to move, didn't want anything to break the spell they were currently under, and he must have felt the same because they stayed right there in the kitchen. There was no moving to the sofa or even a chair. Purring, she rubbed against him and smiled against his lips when he groaned deep in his throat.

It was the sexiest sound she'd ever heard.

Part of her still couldn't believe she was doing this—being the aggressor like she was. The old Sophie—pre-California Sophie—never would have followed a man home and kissed him. She went on nice dates to dinner or to a movie and waited for her date to kiss her.

And not one of those kisses could even compare to the way Christian was kissing her now.

Her skin was heated, her breath was ragged, and as much as she hated to stop, she needed a moment to breathe. Moving her head to the side didn't deter him at all. He simply kissed her cheek, the column of her throat, and oh boy, did that feel good! Licking and nipping and rubbing his stubbled jaw against her own soft skin was like sensory overload.

Whispering his name, she swallowed hard and waited for him to lift his head and look at her. His eyes were as dazed as hers must be and she loved their slumberous look. He was the handsomest man she had ever met, and it seemed crazy that she was locked in his arms like this.

"So, um… What I was trying to tell you earlier," she said, her voice quite low, "was that I wanted to be more than friends with you."

A slow, sexy grin spread across his face as he leaned in to rest his forehead against hers. "That's good, because I really want to be more than friends with you too."

Relief washed over her, as well as pure joy, and she couldn't hide her smile.

"I know things may be a little weird at times," she said, "and with your history of—"

His finger on her lips instantly silenced her. "We're not going to go there. No looking back, okay? The situations are completely different, and even though I can't explain it, I just know it. In my heart I know that what we have is going to be better." He placed a gentle kiss on the tip of her nose before continuing. “From the first time I saw you, I felt a connection to you. It was like I looked up and there you were.”

His words warmed her heart. “I’m glad you found me.”

“Me too.”

Taking a step nearer, Christian gently wrapped his hand around hers and led her into the living room, where they sat on the couch. His arm went around her, tucking her in close beside him. If it were up to her, they could stay like this all night. Well, maybe order some takeout, because she was hungry and hadn’t eaten dinner yet, but other than that, she could stay right here and be happy.

“You’re the bravest woman I’ve ever met,” he said. She looked up at him quizzically. “You moved away from the only place you’ve ever known and you did it all on your own. You’re trying new things, starting new jobs, and it sounds like you’re finding a new you.”

“It was something I felt like I had to do,” she admitted. “I could have gone my whole life living in the same town, working at the same job, and doing all the same things. I probably would have been happy doing it too. But in one instant, everything changed and became tainted.”

He nodded, and Sophie knew he understood exactly what she meant.

“Nana was so upset that I wanted to leave. But I felt betrayed by her the most. Although now that I’ve had time alone to think about it, I know it couldn’t have been easy for her. After all, my mom was her only child and she lost her. On top of that, she’d had to take on raising a toddler. So I’m learning to let go of some of my anger, but it’s not easy.”

"I can't imagine it would be," he said, kissing her softly on her temple. "Do you speak to her at all?"

"Almost every day. That was one habit I couldn't break—even when I was at my angriest. Then I realized she was angry too. If I had stayed, we probably would have spent a lot of time arguing, so I think it was the right decision for me to move." She shrugged. "She hates it, though. Every day she comes up with a new reason why this isn't the place for me and I know she'd be happier if I moved home."

Sophie felt him stiffen.

"Would you?" he asked, his voice gruff. "Would you consider moving back?"

"I don't know. If something happened and I had to go back, then I would. But there's nothing there for me anymore. I can't remember things without this new cloud over them."

"There's got to be at least some good memories for you."

"In time, maybe. But right now, even thinking about things I did with my friends or any of my accomplishments at school, I either obsess about how my teachers knew my real story when I didn't, or I get angry at all the things my mom missed out on because of my father." She shook her head; her voice trembled. "He destroyed everything, and for what?"

Christian pulled her impossibly close to him as the dam broke loose and she began to cry. The only other person she had cried in front of had been her grandmother, and somehow, this felt even more intense, more emotional.

He whispered kind words to her—soft words, caring words—and for a few minutes, she let him say them as he held her. It was important to share this story with him so he knew her—really knew her. If anything, he was going to be the first person to understand this new woman she was becoming—warts and all.

And hopefully, he would like that woman.

Tilting her head, she looked up at him. She didn't wear a lot of makeup, but no doubt what little she had on was smeared all over her face. "Feel free to run for the hills," she said, trying to make light of the situation. "I'd completely understand."

But the look on his face was so tender, so caring that it said more than any words ever could. Cupping her cheek, he caressed it with his thumb. "I'm not going anywhere," he said solemnly. "Thank you for sharing that with me. I know it wasn't easy and I'd imagine no matter how much time passes, it's still painful to talk about. I'm humbled that you wanted to share it with me."

"I...I thought it was important for you to know where I'm coming from. Why I'm here and why honesty means so much to me."

"I'll never lie to you," he promised. "Because I feel the same way about it. You don't have to worry."

Feeling more than a little exhausted, she hugged him.

Then her stomach rumbled.

Loudly.

With a chuckle, Christian tucked a finger under her chin and nudged her to look up at him. "How about we order some takeout, eat out on the deck, and watch the sunset?"

It sounded glorious, but she was feeling like a hot mess at the moment and really wanted to clean up, which was what she said to him.

"I should probably go home and freshen up. I can be back in about an hour."

He grasped her shoulders and pointed toward the stairs that led to the second floor. "There's a shower right upstairs and everything you need to freshen up."

"Christian," she said with a soft laugh, "my makeup is all gone, no doubt my clothes stink from the run—"

Placing a finger over her lips, he stopped her again. "First of all, you don't need any makeup. You're beautiful. And secondly, my sister keeps a small stash of clothes here for when she comes to town on business. I know she's got at least a couple of pairs of yoga pants and T-shirts up there that she wouldn't mind you borrowing."

It was so tempting...

"I don't know... I wouldn't be gone all that long."

This time he silenced her with a kiss. "Rush-hour traffic. Why put yourself through that?" Another kiss. "Besides, I kind of like the fact that you're here with me. You can go shower and change, I'll order dinner and open a bottle of wine for us. What do you say?"

He kissed her again and it was quite possibly the deepest, wettest, sexiest kiss in the history of kisses.

She was dazed, dazzled, and more than a little turned on.

And when Christian lifted his head, all she could do was give him a breathless "Yes." After that, she was ushered into a bathroom that was almost as big as her apartment. Not wanting to sound like some kind of country bumpkin, Sophie simply nodded as Christian showed her where everything was.

"You can use the robe hanging on the door and go

into the guest room and rummage through Megan's things when you're done."

"Are you sure she won't mind? I feel a little weird borrowing a stranger's clothes."

Amused, he leaned against the vanity and shook his head. "Trust me, my sister won't mind one bit, and there's nothing weird about it. Anything else you need?"

Just to the left of him was the doorway that led to the master bedroom. They'd walked through it to get to this wonderland of a bathroom, but she hadn't done more than simply glance at it. Now all she could see was a massive bed and French doors that opened to overlook the beach.

Would it be wrong to be bold and say *to hell with taking a shower, take me to bed*?

"I think I've got everything," she said instead and almost hated that she couldn't be that bold.

Soon.

Maybe.

Hopefully.

"I'm thinking Chinese for dinner. Any requests?"

"Nothing too spicy. Other than that, I'm good."

With a nod, he left the room, closing the door behind him, and all the air seemed to leave Sophie's lungs. Slowly, she spun around and looked at the space, still a little speechless. She had no idea that people really lived like this—with such luxury—and it shamed her to think about her own tiny apartment and how she could never invite Christian over to see it. She would be mortified for him to see how she lived.

"Not going to focus on that right now," she murmured, walking over to the shower and turning on the water. Four different jets sprayed along with a massive shower head. Christian had pulled out a couple of towels for her, so all she had to do was strip and enjoy the most decadent shower of her life.

Twenty minutes later, she had her hair wrapped in a towel turban-style and was wearing Christian's robe. It was the softest material and felt like she was wrapped in a cloud! It was also about four sizes too large and she had to roll up the sleeves several times so she could see her hands. Now all she had to do was go to the guest room and find something to wear.

Opening the bathroom door, she nearly screamed when she found Christian standing there, poised to knock. "Ohmygod!" she cried, her hand going over her heart.

She'd clearly scared him too because he jumped back, mirroring her pose. "Sorry," he said after a moment. "I was just coming up to let you know that dinner will be here in about fifteen minutes." Then he started to laugh and Sophie immediately joined in. "I never realized how scary knocking on a door could be!"

"Me either!" Leaning against the door jamb, she looked at him and couldn't help but smile. The man she had met two weeks ago was attractive in a reserved kind of way. But the man standing before her was so much more. He had a great laugh, a sexy smile, and more than anything, a kind heart.

"You're looking pretty serious over there," he said, taking a step closer. "Everything okay?"

"I was just standing here thinking about all the changes in you in the past couple of weeks. Smiling looks good on you." She meant it to be a light compliment, but his expression went serious as he moved in even closer. With her head tilted back to look at him, she tried to figure out what he was thinking.

"The biggest change is you," he said, his voice low and deep and rich. Caressing her cheek, he studied her face. "You make me smile, Sophie."

Unable to help herself, she placed her hand on his chest. Right now, it would be so easy to lean in and kiss him and then move them over to his bed. But tonight wasn't the night for that.

As if reading her mind, Christian reached for the tie on her robe and gave a light tug. "You have no idea how much I'd like to unwrap you." His voice was rough even though his touch was gentle.

"Do you?" she asked with wonder. It still boggled her mind that this man was attracted to her and wanted her.

He pressed in close until she was against the jamb. "You are pure temptation. And knowing that you're here in my bedroom wearing my robe is sexier than I imagined it would be."

Part of her wanted to argue that there was nothing sexy about her, but the look on his face made her believe him.

They stayed locked like that and Sophie silently willed him to take the decision away from her—to tug on the robe and peel it from her body. But he didn't. He didn't kiss her; his touch stayed chaste. Finally, he let out a long breath and leaned his forehead against hers.

"Go get dressed," he said after a moment. "I'll meet you downstairs."

And when he turned and walked out of the room, Sophie wanted to kick herself for not being bolder.

Chapter 6

"You're frowning. There's no frowning in NOLA."

If anything, Christian's frown deepened. Then he cursed as his brother smacked him upside the head. "What the hell?"

"I warned you and you didn't stop," Carter said with a satisfied grin as he lifted his drink. "If you were planning on moping around, why bother coming all this way?"

Good question, Christian thought.

For a little over two weeks, he hadn't been able to stop smiling. Why? Because of Sophie. They'd spent every day together and it was hard to remember what it was like before she came into his life. The night she'd showered at his house had been a game-changer. For starters, he'd never known the extent of his self-control until he stood with Sophie pressed up against him wearing nothing but his robe. Walking away from her and not giving in to what he wanted to do had been one of his most difficult challenges ever.

There hadn't been another situation like that—thankfully—but the image of her fresh from the shower was never far from his mind.

Since that night, however, he'd been doing something he hadn't done in a long time: living.

"Okay, now you're getting that goofy look on your face," Carter said with a snort. "Seriously, what is going on with you?"

Honestly, he'd been afraid to tell anyone about his relationship with Sophie. It wasn't that he was ashamed of it or that he wanted to keep it a secret, but...old habits die hard. Part of him wasn't prepared to let anyone in on this new phase of his life, and part of him didn't want to hear anyone trying to compare this relationship with Sophie to the one he had in London with Poppy.

"So who is she?" his brother asked, and Christian cursed as he turned his neck so quickly that it cracked.

"What?"

"Please, there's only one reason a guy gets that look on his face and it's because of a woman. And besides that, there have been no less than three women making eyes at you from the bar and you haven't even noticed. So? Who is she?"

In that moment, Christian knew if there was one person he could trust not to share this information with his family—and mainly their father—it was Carter.

Relaxing in their booth, Christian shared how he'd first seen Sophie on the beach, how he'd tried to save her from drowning though she hadn't needed it, and finally how she'd been the one to show up the day he had the anxiety attack.

"Holy shit," Carter said, leaning forward and smiling from ear to ear. "So she saw you pretty much at your worst and you still pursued her?"

Damn. He hadn't thought of it like that, but...yeah. With a careless shrug, he went on. "She stayed with me at the hospital and drove me home—refusing to take me to the office to get my car. That pissed me off."

"She's smart. No doubt you would have gone in to

the office and made an excuse to stay and ended up back in the hospital. Good for her."

Frowning, he glared at his brother. "Anyway, I acted like a jerk and sent her home."

A smirk and a nod were Carter's only response.

"A few days later she came by to check on me and…I kissed her."

"Good for you! Took you long enough."

"Long enough? I'd just met her!"

"Chris, you'd been watching her surf for like, what? A month? You should have introduced yourself way sooner, but I get why you didn't." He took another sip of his Crown and ginger. "And can I say how cool it is that she's a surfer?"

Christian laughed. "I wouldn't exactly call Sophie a surfer. She's trying really hard but has yet to master it. What she needs is lessons, but she's determined to learn on her own. I'm impressed that she's still trying."

"Have you gone out there with her?"

Christian grinned and took a pull of his beer. "I gave it a try and I have to admit, it's a lot harder than I thought it would be."

"So you face-planted too?"

"More times than I care to admit."

"Good for you!"

Putting his bottle on the table, he asked, "Why is that good?"

"Because you're finally doing something other than sitting in your office playing with facts and figures and finances! You're too damn young to be living like an old man, for crying out loud. If this woman has managed to get you out of the house and doing something without wearing a three-piece suit, then I am all for it!"

"I'm not living like an old man."

"Please, it was getting harder and harder to tell you and Dad apart."

And just like that, all the good things Christian had been feeling went away. His back stiffened along with his expression. And just when he was about to snap at his brother for making the comparison, Carter held up a hand to stop him.

"Getting mad at me doesn't change things, bro. When are you going to realize that his grooming you into a mini version of himself is killing you? I would have thought having a heart attack would have taken care of that."

"It wasn't a heart attack."

"Pretty damn close," Carter countered.

"Look, I get what you're saying, but…it's not that easy. As it is, the last thing I want to do is tell him about Sophie."

"Why?"

"Because she works with me and—"

"Wait, wait, wait—she works with you? When were you going to mention that?" Then he paused. "Oh, wait. That's why she was at the office the day you had the attack, right?"

Nodding, Christian explained. "Oddly enough, she ended up getting the position Mom and Aunt Monica created. It's a long story how that all happened but that's why she was there and now it's why things have the potential to be awkward."

"That will only happen if you let it," Carter said,

raising his glass to him. "You have the power to shut the old man down. And the way I see it—and don't get all pissy on me—seems like Dad did you a favor with Poppy in the end. Granted, he could have gone about it in a different way, but who knows how much time you would have wasted on that woman."

"He's just so arrogant," he said, realizing that Carter's words didn't piss him off. "I think that's what bothered me more than the whole cheating thing. It was his attitude afterward—like somehow it was my fault that it happened, and it had some reflection on my position in the company."

Carter gave a mirthless laugh. "That's because he's obsessed with the damn company. I swear, why couldn't he be more like Uncle William? Even Uncle Robert—who we all know is a hard-ass—was a better role model to his kids. Why is Dad the lone lunatic?"

Christian's laugh was sincere. "That's a good way to describe him."

"It's totally true. I don't know how you've dealt with it all these years. I know I couldn't have done it. One of us wouldn't be here right now, I can tell you that."

It was no secret that their father had been shocked when Carter decided to go to culinary school instead of business school. And even after becoming an enormously popular celebrity chef, Carter had taken more than his share of grief from their father about his choice of careers. It was only after his brother had opened his second restaurant that things had calmed down. Still, there wasn't a doubt in Christian's mind that out of the two of them, Carter was far more vocal about standing up for himself.

Although…maybe that was all about to change.

He paused and considered his next words. "Okay, here's the thing—and you need to think on this rather than just talking off the top of your head."

"Sounds ominous."

"How do I change things?" Christian asked, desperate for some real advice. "I mean, it's one thing to say that I have to tell him to back off, but you and I both know he doesn't listen to me."

Carter studied him hard for a long moment. "Before I answer, I have a question for you."

"Go for it."

"Are you planning on staying in San Diego? At Montgomerys? Or are you looking to do something else?"

"As much as I'd like to say move on to something else, the truth is that I don't know. I enjoy what I do. Or at least, I used to. Honestly, I don't know anything else. This has been my life practically since I was fifteen."

Nodding, Carter picked up his drink and finished it. "You do realize that we have a large extended family—most of whom work for the company—and manage to have lives outside of the office, right? And that now includes our baby sister."

"I'm aware."

"So what makes you think you can't do it?"

"Habit," he replied honestly. "Sure, I can say I'm going to cut back my hours, delegate more, but how soon until I revert to type?"

"Who says you will?"

"Again, habit."

"You never had a reason *not* to revert to type before.

Maybe Sophie is the motivation you need to make that happen." He paused. "Is this serious? This relationship?"

"It's too soon to tell," Christian murmured.

"Bullshit," Carter countered. "Have you slept with her yet?"

Christian's eyes narrowed at the question and he felt a rage toward his brother. "That's none of your damn business," he growled.

"So that's a no, then," Carter said, unfazed.

Christian would like to deny it, but he couldn't. He was taking things slow with Sophie—something else he'd never done before—and while there was no denying a little bit of frustration, he knew the wait would be worth it.

"You've been dating for…what, a month?"

"Two weeks."

Carter gave him a mildly amused look. "Aww, how sweet."

Unable to help himself, he laughed. "Screw you."

"Anyway, I'm saying that it's been more like a month, because—let's face it—it seems the two of you clicked from the night on the beach when you saved her when she didn't need to be saved."

He said, "I guess."

"So what are you waiting for?"

"It's been a long time since I've been seriously involved with anyone. I don't want to mess it up."

"How could you possibly do that? Just because you haven't dated doesn't mean you don't know how, Christian."

There was no way to explain it, because he wasn't quite so sure what his logic was either. Sophie seemed to be happy with the way things were going and he certainly didn't want to rock the boat by moving too fast for her.

"And on top of that," Carter went on, "what are you doing here in New Orleans with me when you could be home with Sophie?" Then he stopped. "Ah…now I see why you'd be afraid to mess things up. You already did by being here instead of there."

He made a vicious curse, but Christian knew his brother was right. Instead of sitting in a swanky bar drinking with Carter, he should be taking Sophie out someplace nice. So far everything they'd done had been more on the casual side, but didn't she deserve to be wined and dined? Didn't she deserve more than takeout on his deck after they'd gone jogging or surfing?

Man, he really was bad at this.

Finishing his beer, he slammed the bottle on the table and looked at his brother. "Okay, since we've already established how I've messed this up, how about telling me how to fix it. All of it."

Carter's smile grew to devious proportions. "Brother, I thought you'd never ask."

"Sophie, you can't afford to do things like this! How are you going to pay your rent if you act this impetuous? I thought I raised you better than that."

Laughing at Nana's theatrics, Sophie made herself comfortable on her sofa and admired her newly pedicured toes. Wiggling them, the smiled. "It's not like I do this sort of thing all the time—or ever. But this seemed like a special occasion and I wanted to do something to make myself feel…you know, pretty."

With a snort, Nana went on. "You don't need a coat of nail polish that's been painted on by strangers in some overpriced salon to make you pretty. You're a beautiful girl, and if this…this…Christian person can't see that, then maybe you should break up with him and come home."

It always came back to this—Nana telling her to give up and come home. She hadn't fallen for it yet and she didn't plan to any time soon.

Or ever.

"Nana, I think it's time you accepted the fact that I like it here. I've signed on with an agency that will send me to different companies, so I'll be working full-time. It's a great rotation, the commute is easy, and the money is more than I thought I'd make. You should be happy for me instead of constantly looking for the negative and encouraging me to give up."

Her heart was pounding like wild as she said her piece, but she couldn't let this pattern of behavior continue. It wasn't helping their relationship at all—if anything, it was making Sophie feel less and less optimistic about fully repairing it.

"You know I worry about you," Nana said meekly. Any minute now she'd start to cough and talk about how poorly she'd been feeling.

"I know you do. And I know you only want what's best for me. But you have to accept that what's best for me right now is living and working in California and dating a nice man who wants to take me out on a fancy date," she said happily. Even thinking about dressing up and going out with Christian tonight had her feeling giddy.

When he had suggested going out to one of the fanciest restaurants in town, she had balked at the idea. But she was finding that Christian could be very persuasive when he wanted to be.

Cough, cough, cough.

Here we go, Sophie thought.

"Did I tell you that I had an appointment with Doc Kelly on Friday?" Nana said, suddenly sounding breathless. "He said...he said that my blood pressure was low and that I was looking a little jaundiced. Recommended that I should start thinking about an assisted living facility."

"Really? Did he tell you which one you should consider? You know, Jeanie at the front desk would be the one to help you with your applications. She's great at that."

"Oh!" Nana cried with annoyance. "You know darn well that I don't want to go into an assisted living facility! And I certainly wouldn't ask Jeanie to help me." She snorted with disgust. "Do you know that woman actually takes Zumba classes?"

"And what's wrong with Zumba?"

"She's almost fifty years old, Sophie! It's ridiculous!"

Laughing out loud, Sophie sat forward and took a minute to catch her breath. "I have to go and get ready. Christian's picking me up in an hour and I need to finish up."

A small huff was Nana's only response.

"I'll call you on Sunday like always. And don't eat too much peanut brittle at mahjong tonight."

Another small huff.

"Nana?"

"Hmm?"

"I love you," Sophie said with a small smile, even though her grandmother couldn't see it. "And I miss you."

"I love you too," she said quietly. "And I hope you have a good time tonight."

Her smile brightened. "Thank you!"

"Hope you don't get food poisoning. You know how these restaurants are who don't cook their fish all the way—"

"Okay, that's it. I'm hanging up," Sophie said, partly amused, partly annoyed. "I'll talk to you on Sunday." As she hung up the phone, she felt mildly exhausted. Leaning against the sofa cushions, she considered what to do first.

Her nails looked great, she'd showered earlier and had put on enough lotion so that—theoretically—she should slide off any surface she sat on, and her dress was hanging on the bathroom door just waiting to be slipped on. Fixing her hair and makeup was the next order of business, but first she stared at the new dress she'd purchased especially for tonight—a strapless jade-green silk sheath. It was plain and yet...elegant. She felt a little like a cliché wearing a green dress with her red hair, but once she'd stepped into the boutique and spotted it, the salesgirl had all but gushed about how it was perfect for her.

And it was.

Never in her life had she owned something that made her feel so sexy.

So did the fact that she couldn't wear a bra with it.

A slow smile played at her lips as she wondered if Christian would find that out for himself tonight. She hoped so. Like, seriously hoped so. While she loved that they were taking things slow, part of her wished he wasn't such a gentleman. Ever since her little foray at throwing herself at him three weeks ago, she hadn't been quite as bold.

"Maybe I'll have to be tonight," she murmured happily as the thought stuck.

Yes. Tonight would totally be the night her boldness returned. Jumping to her feet, she walked right over to the dress and touched the soft fabric. The salesgirl had also encouraged her to buy some new lingerie—and that included the lacy thong in the same color as the dress.

Feeling a little empowered and knowing she now had a mission, Sophie immediately began getting ready. She envisioned the look on Christian's face when he saw her and if it was even half as hot as the way it looked in her mind, she just might ask him to skip their reservation and stay in.

When he'd suggested going out to dinner—someplace special, he'd said—she got the impression he thought she wasn't enjoying their meals at his house. Was he kidding? The view of the beach was amazing! And it was so convenient, since most of the activities they'd been doing were beach-related: the jogging, surfing, and lately, just walking and talking as they made their way up and down the beach.

How she had managed to live her entire life without being near the ocean was a mystery to her, because she couldn't imagine ever living anyplace else.

And there was no way she was ever going to admit that to her grandmother.

Her phone beeped with an incoming text. As she walked across the room to grab it, she knew it was going to be from Christian.

> Can't wait to see you. Any chance I can pick you up earlier?

She laughed. And then something hit her—maybe tonight wasn't about her being bold. Maybe tonight was about her coming to his rescue.

Christian had been hurt on many levels—and not just by his father, but by his ex. The one time they'd talked about his situation, it was obvious that even though the whole thing had happened years ago, it still affected him today. He'd been living his life based on that one event—cutting himself off from friends, family, and relationships. Wasn't it time for that to stop?

Sophie agreed to a new time and went to get herself ready with nothing but seduction in mind.

By the end of the night, she was going to do everything possible to put all of Christian's ghosts to rest.

Her sexy dress and matching thong were going to be her own Wonder Woman costume.

Looking at her reflection in the mirror, she gave herself a satisfied smile. "Let's do this."

It took a lot to surprise Christian these days.

And tonight, he was most definitely surprised.

Sophie had transformed from tempting girl-next-door

to a goddess. The green silk she was wearing left little to the imagination even though it flowed past her knees. It delicately hugged her curves, and ever since she'd opened the door to him, he'd been tempted to do the same.

And if he didn't know any better, he'd swear the little minx was trying to make him crazy.

Her lips were painted a deep crimson, her eyes looked almost exotic with the way she'd applied her makeup, and her hair was...well, let's just say all he'd been imagining all night was fisting his hand into it and holding her to him while he kissed her until she was breathless.

Shifting in his seat to ease the tightness in his trousers, Christian forced himself to think of something other than getting Sophie alone and out of her dress.

"You look beautiful tonight," he said and then wanted to smack himself, because that was not helping him get the image of her out of his mind.

Blushing, she reached over and gently caressed the back of his hand. "Thank you."

Yeah, she was definitely trying to make him crazy, because her newly painted nails were lightly scratching his skin and that brought images of them doing that down his back.

Another slight shift to alleviate some pressure...

Time for another tactic.

"How did your day go with the agency?" he asked.

Her entire face lit up with pure delight as she told him about how she had taken on a rotation with other companies like his. There was so much excitement in her voice and it was easy to see how much she loved what she did and how much starting this new career meant to her.

It left him thinking about his conversation with his

brother the previous weekend. Christian knew he didn't have the kind of passion for his job anymore that Sophie did, but was there something else out there that he could be passionate about? Was it possible?

Her hand stopped and gently squeezed his. "Hey," she said softly, "you okay?"

Clearing his mind, he said, "Uh-huh. Why do you ask?"

"You sort of got this far away look in your eyes while I was talking." She laughed softly. "Or maybe I was boring you with tales of short commutes to work and my love of colorful scrubs to wear."

Turning his hand to clasp hers, he smiled. "You weren't boring me at all. If anything, you amaze me with your enthusiasm for your job."

With wide eyes, she squeaked, "Really?"

"You do. I don't think I ever had that. I was passionate about my job—but in a way that was more about drive than joy. When I listen to you speak about your work, it's clear that it makes you happy." He paused. "And that got me wondering if there was anything out there that I would feel that way about."

"Are you thinking about changing careers?"

He shrugged. "I don't know. It's crossed my mind more times than not, but I wouldn't even know where to begin."

Sophie studied him for a moment. "Can I ask you something?"

"Anything."

"Is this about wanting to change jobs because you want to, or because you want to escape dealing with your father?"

Ouch.

Okay, this was so not the conversation he wanted to have.

"The way you're frowning tells me I've touched a nerve," she said carefully, but she wasn't deterred. "All I'm saying is—don't let anyone take away your joy. Whether it's joy you find in a career, a hobby, or...a person. I'm struggling with that right now with my grandmother. She's trying to convince me to give up living here and go home. I'm not giving in, but it's a constant struggle with her. Any time I share any news, she comes back with a negative comment and tells me I should just quit and move home." She shook her head. "Not happening."

The thought of Sophie leaving San Diego—and him—hit Christian harder than he was prepared for. Squeezing her hand, he pushed his own anxiety aside and said, "You know it's just because she misses you, right?"

They fell into a companionable silence and when their dinner was served, they switched to talking about their meal rather than their lives. Christian was happy for the reprieve. He had wanted tonight to be a time for them to enjoy each other's company; he hadn't expected things to go to such a depressing topic.

There was no way he was telling Carter about this. No doubt his brother would totally get on him for blowing it.

Again.

Once their plates were cleared away, their waiter asked if they wanted to order dessert. Sophie placed an order with a sweet smile, but before the waiter could walk away she asked, "Would it be possible to get those to go?" Then she shot Christian a sexy look that had him imagining all kinds of scenarios, like feeding her dessert out on his deck.

In his bathtub.

In his bed.

The waiter looked at him and Christian nodded. "Whatever the lady would like, box it."

Sophie let out a happy little sound and damn if he didn't want to hear it again all night long.

Her hand was doing that scratching thing. "You didn't have anything else planned for after dinner, did you?" she asked softly.

He had thought about going dancing, but they could do that at home too.

He replied, "I was going to see where the night took us."

Leaning in close, she wet her bottom lip, her eyes looking intently at him. "The night is going to take us back to your house, hopefully, where we'll eat our dessert. Later."

Could a man really be this lucky?

He'd done nothing but fumble through this relationship and yet she was still here with him, wanting him.

"That sounds like a good plan," he said, closing the distance between them and kissing her softly on the lips. Her name was a mere whisper when he lifted his head.

She let out a soft moan that sounded way too sexy for the middle of a restaurant. "I got a little pampered today, bought this dress—and what's under it—with you in mind."

Was it warm in here? Because it suddenly felt very

warm. He was damn near sweating. Where the hell was that waiter with their dessert?

Her lips were nearly on his when she added, "I can't wait for you to see what I'm wearing—and what I'm not."

He all but fell out of his chair in his hurry to flag the waiter down. "Check, please!"

After that, Christian felt like he was all thumbs. Their dessert arrived and he paid the check and felt like he was almost dragging Sophie from their table out to his car. She didn't seem to mind. Instead, she was laughing and walking just as quickly as he was. The drive back to his house seemed to take an eternity. Why was everyone in San Diego out on the road right now? It seemed like the entire population was taking the same route as them and he had to stop from growling with frustration.

The entire time he drove, Sophie's hand was draped on his thigh and doing that same scratchy thing she'd done to his hand over dinner.

It was amazing his trembling hands weren't causing them to go off the road.

When they finally—*finally!*—pulled into his driveway, he felt more on edge than ever before. It was only a couple of short steps to get into the house, yet he'd be more than happy to take her right there in the car.

I can do this. I can control myself for a few more minutes.

That's what he kept telling himself, but he was strung so tight right now that if her hand kept doing what it was doing a little north of its current spot, there wasn't a doubt in his mind that he would pounce.

And for someone who was always so in control of his emotions, Christian realized how unlike him it was to even think of doing such a thing.

Sophie moved closer and made a sexy little humming sound. "Dinner was fantastic," she said, but her voice sounded different—it was breathless and husky.

Turning, Christian looked at her face and was instantly aware of the fact that she seemed just as on edge as he was. A slow smile played at his lips. "It was," he agreed, his own voice sounding foreign to him. "But I have a feeling that dessert is going to be even better."

With another little hum, she delicately licked her lips. "I'm betting on it."

Why were they prolonging the wait? Leaning in close to her—close enough to feel her breath on his lips—he said, "Hungry?"

This time when she licked her lips, her tongue touched his lips. "Starving."

"Sophie?" His voice was a near-growl now.

"Hmm?"

"Get out of the car."

Her smile was triumphant. "I thought you'd never ask."

What happened next could only be described as two people giddily tripping over one another in their haste to get to the front door. When Christian unlocked it, they stumbled inside, quickly closing the door behind them. The bag with their dessert fell to the floor when Sophie wrapped herself around him and nearly brought him to his knees with her kiss.

Images of other places he wanted to feel her mouth instantly came to mind, and Christian knew that if he didn't at least try to slow things down, their first time would be right here in the entryway.

The thought was a little enticing, but he instantly pushed it aside.

After seeing Sophie in his robe, in his bedroom, he'd done nothing but envision her sprawled on his bed and dammit, he was going to get them there.

Soon.

Now.

Scooping her up into his arms, Christian quickly strode to his room as she continued to kiss him—his jaw, his neck—anyplace she could reach, her lips tasted. Placing her on the bed, he took a minute to simply marvel at her being there.

"I've been thinking about this," he gruffly admitted. "Ever since you showered here."

"Can I let you in on a little secret?"

He nodded.

"I wanted you to pull open the belt of the robe that night and look at me," she said softly, seductively. "I almost did it myself, but..."

He nearly swallowed his tongue at her admission. "But?"

Shyly, she said, "I thought I had been bold enough for one day. I thought if the time was right, we'd both know it."

"Damn."

Her face was the perfect combination of angel and vixen.

And he couldn't imagine wanting her more.

Placing one knee on the bed, Christian leaned toward her. One hand skimmed up her leg—loving the softness of her calf, the back of her knee, her thigh…

"Can I tell you another secret?" she asked, squirming ever so slightly under his touch.

"You can tell me everything."

"I thought about this all day. This. You and me. Everything I did to get ready for tonight was for this exact moment."

Her admission touched him in a way he had never experienced before. They had talked about why she felt it was important to be honest and he believed her. There were times, however, when words were just part of the seduction—the bedroom talk. And he knew this wasn't one of those times. Sophie was telling him exactly what she meant for no other reason than to be truthful.

And it was a complete turn-on.

It was on the tip of his tongue to ask her what exactly she did, but he had a feeling he was already enjoying it.

Stepping back, Christian slipped off her sandals and noticed the bright coral paint on her toes. Lifting her foot, he kissed her ankle.

And she hummed with pleasure.

Slowly, his hands retraced his earlier path—skimming up her calf and lifting her leg so he could kiss the sensitive spot behind her knee.

Her hum became a low moan.

Feeling bold, Christian leaned in closer and kissed a path up her thigh, sliding the green silk of her dress up as he went. He opened his eyes in time to see the tiny panties that matched her dress and hissed at the sight of them. He brought his gaze up to meet hers.

"For me?" he asked, his voice low and gravelly.

Biting her lip, Sophie nodded, and all Christian could think of was how damn lucky he was.

His hand shook as he touched her intimately, his finger gently caressing the thin material. "How attached are you to them?"

Sophie's smile grew. "They're yours to do with as you want."

It was like waving a red flag in front of a bull. He knew what he was going to do with them and as his hands grasped the fabric and tugged, he smiled triumphantly as they tore away from her body. Holding the scraps in his hand, he looked down at Sophie. "A thong?"

She nodded again. "I thought you might like it."

"Now I'm sorry I didn't take the time to strip you properly."

Another sexy hum. "I bought more. If you're lucky, you'll have other opportunities."

He loved the way she thought.

"Sweetheart, I do believe that Lucky is about to become my middle name."

Sleepily, Sophie tiptoed across the room and into the bathroom. Closing the door behind her, she felt along the wall for the light switch and squinted when the entire room lit up. There was a large mirror over the vanity and it was hard not to look at herself—naked, squinty, with bedhead and all.

Not her best look. However…

"I look glowy," Sophie said with a satisfied grin. Leaning closer to the bathroom mirror, she confirmed it. "Yup. Definitely glowy."

On the other side of the door, Christian was still asleep. The sun wasn't even up yet and she had needed to pee, but after a quick glance in the mirror at her disheveled state, she knew she needed a closer look. With her hair a riotous mess, her lips a little swollen, and some delicious aches all over her body, there was no doubt she was a woman who had spent an amazing night being thoroughly loved.

The happy little sigh couldn't be contained and once she'd finished in the bathroom and slowly padded back to the bed, Christian instantly reached for her.

He didn't say a word—simply guided her back beside him and held her close. He was warm and hard, and Sophie couldn't get enough of being pressed up against him like this. Their legs tangled together, his arms wrapped around her, and then his lips sought hers.

"I missed you," he murmured against her lips before settling her in against his side.

Sophie couldn't stop herself from smiling. "I was only gone for a minute."

But he shook his head. "It felt much longer."

Kissing his chest, she rested her hand over his heart and immediately relaxed. "Go back to sleep. It's way too early for either of us to be awake."

"Mmm..."

It was obvious that he was nearly asleep and she didn't mind. It was barely four in the morning and she could definitely use a little more sleep herself. Her mind, however, was going a mile a minute with thoughts of their night—the conversation, the dinner, the drive home, and ultimately the dessert. It had taken several hours to get to it, but it was well worth the wait. She never knew eating could be such an erotic experience. Between licking the frosting off each other's fingers—among other places—and feeding one another, there was no way she would be able to look at a simple slice of cake the same way ever again.

She placed a feather-light kiss on his chest as she snuggled closer. The French doors that led out to the deck were open and she could hear the sound of the waves crashing on the shore, mixed with the soft sound of Christian's breathing. Both were soothing to her and Sophie had to wonder how she had gotten so lucky—how the darkest and lowest point in her life had led her directly to this place.

And to falling in love with Christian Montgomery.

Never one who took romantic relationships lightly, Sophie used to laugh at her girlfriends who always had crushes or who seemed to fall in love at the drop of a hat. She preferred to get to know someone and get a feel for who he was on multiple levels before deciding if she could connect with and—eventually—get romantically involved with him. And everything she had learned about Christian in the past month made her feelings deeper and deeper, to the point that it almost scared her. Mainly because it had happened so soon.

And partly because everything about him was so incredibly different from anything she'd ever known.

Take his home—Sophie had grown up in a small rural town. The home she and her grandmother shared was a modest two-bedroom house with one bathroom. The roof leaked, the exterior needed paint, and their appliances didn't match. But it was filled with a lot of memories—there were framed pictures all over the house that told the story of her life. Whereas Christian's home looked as if a designer had decorated it and it was void of any personalization. It didn't matter how beautiful the space was, every time she came here it made her sad to think of him living someplace so cold.

She had to wonder what his family was like. From everything he'd shared about his father, she already didn't like him. But his mother and aunt had been so sweet and friendly that it confused her to imagine those two personalities in one family. As for her own family—meaning her grandmother—they were who they were, and even though right now she wasn't feeling her closest to Nana, Sophie always felt loved.

Or at least she had.

Yawning, Sophie forced herself to stop thinking about the negative. Too many wonderful things had happened to her in the past twelve hours to ruin them with tainted memories. She was in bed with a wonderful man, in a beautiful room, and very satisfied. That was what she needed to focus on.

That and…maybe being a little bold and being the one to wake Christian up this time. Any time they had dozed earlier, it had been Christian waking her up because he wanted her again. This time, she wanted to be the one to slowly tease him to wakefulness.

Her hand gently rubbed his chest and he hummed softly in his sleep. Next, she shifted so she could lift up on one elbow and look at him a bit. Leaning forward, Sophie began to kiss all the spots her hand had just touched. Earlier, she had found how much Christian loved to have her kiss his chest. And while she rained gentle kisses on him, she moved her hand lower—over his abs and then lower still.

Hiding a smile, Sophie could tell Christian was waking up.

As she continued to touch and taste him, his hand slowly skimmed up her spine and tangled into her hair, tugging.

She really loved when he did that.

"Mmm… I thought you told me to go back to sleep," he said, his voice soft and sleepy.

"I did," she said breathlessly between kisses. "But then I started thinking about all the ways you woke me up over the course of the night and wanted to try that out for myself." Lifting her head, she met his gaze in the moonlight shining through the open doors. "You don't mind, do you?"

If anything, his hand fisted tighter in her hair. "I will never complain about your hands and mouth on my body," he said fiercely.

Sliding over him and straddling his lap, she ran her hands up his chest. "We'll have to sleep eventually," she teased as her nails scratched their way back down.

Christian hissed at her touch, releasing her hair only to grasp her hips. "But not yet," he said, guiding her lips to his.

The next time Sophie opened her eyes, the sun was shining and the room was completely bright. Stretching, she realized that she was alone in the bed. Slowly she sat up, clutching the sheet to her chest and marveling at the view through the glass doors.

"That is one heck of a view to wake up to every morning," she said softly.

"Yes, it is."

Gasping, she turned and saw Christian standing in the doorway with a tray in his hands. He walked over and placed it on the bedside table before leaning in and kissing her thoroughly. "And I wasn't referring to the beach."

She blushed and tried to duck her head to hide it. But Christian tucked a finger under her chin and gently forced her to look at him. "When I woke up a little while ago, you were sleeping so peacefully and all I could think of was how beautiful you looked."

Self-consciously, she ran a hand over her hair. "I'm a bit of a mess."

He sat beside her, caressing her cheek. "You're beautiful."

Part of her wanted to deny it—mainly because accepting compliments always made her feel a little uncomfortable—but when she looked into his eyes, she knew he meant what he was saying.

Glancing over at the tray, she asked, "What have we got here?"

Christian reached for it. "I made you some coffee and a little something to eat."

Her heart squeezed at his thoughtfulness. There was a bowl of fruit with strawberries, pineapple, and cantaloupe, along with a cup of yogurt. "You're going to spoil me."

Then he kissed her cheek. "You deserve to be spoiled."

Oh boy, she thought. A girl could easily get used to this.

"Aren't you going to eat anything?"

He shrugged. "I had my coffee. That's normally all I have for breakfast."

Grabbing her mug, she took a sip of the steamy beverage and sighed with delight. "Oh, that's good." But then she had to put on her nurse's cap. "You know that's not healthy for you, right? You need to be taking better care of your diet."

"And yet you let me eat all that cake last night," he teased, and she seriously blushed thinking about those escapades again. Taking her hand in his, he said, "I love that you're concerned, and if it helps, the coffee was decaf."

"Christian..."

"And I did have some of the fruit while I was cutting it up."

Unable to help herself, she chuckled. It was hard to be stern when he looked so relaxed and deliciously adorable. When he wasn't in work mode, Christian had some seriously boyish good looks—a wonderful smile and a great laugh. She wished there was a way for him to stay more like this.

"You're looking pretty serious right now," he commented.

Now wasn't the time to bring up work or health issues. Now was the time to bask in the afterglow of a fantastic night. So rather than risk it, she went for something she knew would distract them both.

"Just wondering how playful we can get with fruit and yogurt," she said with a sexy grin. And before she knew it, Christian was on his feet and stripping his shirt off over his head.

"Let's find out!"

Chapter 7

The following week was busy for them both. The agency Sophie had signed with kept her very busy and she was only needed at Montgomerys for two days. Christian knew eventually it would go to only once a week or less, but right now while they were getting everything in place, he was more than happy to have her there as often as they could.

If anyone happened to notice how often he went to get his blood pressure checked, they didn't say a word. Although he figured Erin was a little suspicious, because after his fourth trip to Sophie's office, she simply smirked when he walked by.

It was fine. He didn't care. It felt good to have a reason to get up and leave his office, and even better every time he saw Sophie. She made his day brighter, gave him something to look forward to. If he could, he'd find a way to keep her employed with him full-time, so he could get up and go see her whenever he wanted to.

Realistically, that wasn't going to happen. Overall, Montgomerys was a huge company, but his branch of it wasn't. And there was no way he was going to push for an expansion just for the sake of having Sophie close to him every day. Instead, he was going in the opposite direction—for himself. Not that he'd shared that with anyone.

Several things were becoming abundantly clear for

him—he wasn't happy at his job and hadn't been for a long time. On top of that, he wasn't sure what it was that he wanted to do. If he didn't stay here doing what he'd done for far too long, what else was there? He wasn't trained for anything else, nor had he ever had the opportunity to figure out if there was anything else he might have been good at. Leaving Montgomerys only to go work for another company while doing the same thing wasn't the answer.

But he didn't know what was.

Today was the first day that he was staying until five. It wasn't something he had particularly planned, but he had a late afternoon meeting that had ended only thirty minutes earlier and by the time he finished making his notes, he'd be leaving with the rest of the staff. Hopefully he hadn't missed Sophie leaving. He wanted to take her to dinner tonight here in town at a sushi place she'd been curious about. His plan had been to take her to dinner and then home with him. Having her in his bed was becoming addictive. Just the thought of—

The ringing of his cell phone broke into his thoughts and he grimaced when he saw his father's name on the screen. Letting it go to voicemail was an option, but his father was fairly persistent and would keep calling until Christian talked to him.

Letting out a long breath, he swiped the screen. "Hey, Dad. What's up?"

"Christian," Joseph Montgomery said formally. "How are you feeling?"

Relaxing , Christian sat back in his chair. "I'm doing well. I haven't had any issues in weeks."

"Excellent! That means you'll be resuming all of your regular hours and responsibilities?"

Pinching the bridge of his nose, Christian silently counted to ten before answering. "I have resumed all of my responsibilities. I have a wonderful staff and nothing is falling behind, if that's what you're asking."

"And your hours? You've practically been putting in part-time hours. That's not how a leader should be presenting himself to his employees."

So many thoughts and retorts swirled in his brain, but Christian knew he had to be careful with what he said or things would escalate quickly.

"Dad, I appreciate your concern. I do. Everything is fine here. I've been in touch with every single one of our offices and no one is complaining or even talking about my hours."

"Maybe not to you."

"Has anyone said anything to you?" he asked with a snap, feeling as if he was losing the battle with his patience.

"Your uncles and I were talking about how the younger generation doesn't seem to take their positions seriously anymore," his father replied. "I don't mind when we're talking about your cousins, but I don't like it being said about my own children."

Sighing, Christian made a mental note to call his uncle William. He was the one who really was the head of the entire company, and if he was concerned about Christian's hours, then he'd give it some thought. But for now, he'd deal with his father blowing off steam and spouting out things that he had no right or reason to.

"I heard that Mac is taking some time off," Christian said conversationally.

"Yes," Joseph said wearily. "The doctor's put Gina on bedrest and Mac wants to be home with her. It's crazy, if you ask me. Monica is there helping out, and so is Gina's mother. What could Mac possibly have to do there?"

"He's concerned about his wife, Dad. There's nothing wrong with that."

All Joseph did was make a noncommittal sound.

"And I was talking to Ryder yesterday and he mentioned that he and Casey are going on a two-week European vacation with Summer and Ethan."

"A frivolous trip, if you ask me."

"I wasn't," Christian stated.

"I don't appreciate your tone. I see where you're trying to go with this—pointing out all the ways your cousins are shirking their responsibilities to justify doing it yourself. Well, I don't care what they're doing. I'm concerned with what *you're* doing."

"Maybe you should be a little less concerned. After all, I'm a grown man who happens to run a very successful business."

"A business you have thanks to me," his father argued.

Here we go, he thought.

"Yes, I have this job because of you, but maybe you could back off a bit and appreciate all that I've done," Christian argued. "Maybe—just once—instead of calling to criticize, you could offer a little praise. How about that?"

"You're not that needy, are you?" Joseph asked with more than a hint of condescension.

"It's not needy. It's something a normal father would do for his son."

A sound by the door caught his attention and Christian looked up to see Erin walking hesitantly into the room with a stack of contracts she had prepared for him. With a sympathetic smile, she placed them on his desk and then pointed to her watch, mouthing "good night" to him.

"Constantly seeking praise and approval is a sign of neediness," Joseph went on. "Doing your job well and representing the company in a way that is fitting to your role as a leader should be all that you need, Christian. I think this little episode of yours was a cry for attention and made you weak."

"Weak?" he cried. "Dad, I thought I was having a heart attack! My blood pressure was at an unhealthy level! This wasn't some sort of stunt for attention!" Huffing with frustration, he raked a hand through his hair.

Erin slowly tiptoed backward toward the door and silently asked if he needed anything. She gave him a final look before walking out of the office, closing the door behind her. If he was smart, he would have asked her to buzz in with a fake emergency of some kind, but *that* would be weak. And there was no way in hell he was going to ever show that to his father. Especially not after this conversation.

"You're being more argumentative lately and I won't stand for it! I'm your father and you will treat me with respect!"

"Respect is something you earn, Dad," Christian replied sharply. "It doesn't matter to me if you're my father or not, you have done nothing to earn my respect. You've bulldozed me my entire life and I'm done with this! Either you learn to back off, or don't bother calling me. Are we clear?" His heart was pounding like mad in his chest and he felt a little breathless. Panic was starting to set in that maybe this little outburst wasn't the smartest thing for him to do.

Silence.

Christian waited what felt like an eternity before clearing his throat. "I need to go. I'll talk to you soon." And without waiting for a response, he hung up the phone and carefully placed it on his desk. His heart was still racing and he felt himself shaking, but surprisingly, he also felt relieved. He had said the words that he'd been dying to say for ages and lightning didn't strike him. Granted, there was no telling what kind of fallout was going to occur from this, but it sure as hell felt good to finally get some things off his chest.

Taking several deep breaths, he started to feel like he was almost normal. A soft knock on his door made him look up. "Come in."

Sophie peeked around the door and smiled at him. "Hey! You ready to go?"

Yeah, he was definitely feeling better. Funny how just the sight of her did that for him. "More than you know."

She stepped into the office and shut the door behind her. Today was her second day of the week on-site and she was dressed in electric-blue scrubs and a pair of tennis shoes, with her hair pulled back in a ponytail. There was a stethoscope draped around her neck and she had the blood pressure cuff in one hand and her tablet in the other. He eyed her warily.

"You doing okay?" she asked, coming to stand next to his chair.

Laughing, he asked, "Why? What have you heard?"

She laughed with him. "A little birdy told me you were a wee bit agitated, so I thought I'd come up and check on you."

For a minute he wasn't sure if he should throttle his assistant or give her a raise.

"They did, huh?"

Nodding, Sophie rested her hip on his desk. "Want to talk about it?"

That was a no-brainer. "Not particularly."

She studied him for a moment before turning a little more professional on him. Holding up the cuff, she asked, "Mind if we get a check?"

Shrugging, he replied, "Sure."

Shifting in his chair, Christian let Sophie do her thing. Once she was done, she typed things on her tablet. Without a word, he got up and crossed the room. Looking out into the reception area, he noted that everyone was indeed gone, and closed the door. When he turned around, Sophie was still typing. Slowly he walked toward her, loosening his tie as he went. When he was standing behind her, he leaned in and placed a gentle kiss on the back of her neck.

"Your numbers were a little high," she said distractedly. "You sure you're feeling okay?"

He placed another kiss on her neck, then another, until she finally put her tablet down and rested both hands on his desk.

"I know what would make me feel better," he whispered hotly against her ear.

"Christian..."

"There's no one on the other side of that door. Everyone's gone for the day." He paused and licked the sensitive spot behind her ear, smiling as she shivered. "It's just you and me."

Arching her back, she pressed her bottom against him—there was no way she could miss his arousal. Bending forward until his chest was pressed against her back, he pleaded his case a little more. "I figure we could spend some time making me relax and then I could spend a lot of time thanking you. It will be so good. I promise."

His hands moved up the front of her—cupping her breasts—and he had her panting and moving beneath him. He whispered her name, gently bit her earlobe.

"We shouldn't," she said breathlessly, but the way her body was responding to him told Christian that she wasn't really fighting him on it.

"We totally should," he replied, slipping his hands under her top and moving the lace of her bra aside.

"Christian...maybe...oh, you have the most perfect hands," she panted.

Gently, he squeezed her breasts, kissed her throat. "And you have the most perfect breasts."

Then she was done protesting.

She was done talking.

And he was more than ready to follow through on what he'd promised.

"Okay, I feel like you're not getting it."

"This is a lot more work than I was anticipating."

"We've done this before."

"Yeah, but I wasn't really paying attention to the details. I was more interested in getting my hands on you in your wetsuit."

They were standing in the ocean and Sophie splashed water at him playfully. "Seriously? I was so proud of myself for trying to be a good teacher!"

He grinned bashfully. "I thought it would be easier than it was and that I wouldn't need so much instruction." Then he took a steadying breath and gripped his board. "Let's start again."

"Are you sure you're going to listen this time?"

Nodding, he said, "I will. I promise."

"Fine. Here's some things that you need to know." For five minutes she rambled on with as much technical advice as she could give.

"How about we just go swimming?" he asked, but Sophie ignored him.

Smiling, she looked at him. "So? Are you ready?"

Christian shook his head. "Not even a little."

"Randy told me I should practice on the beach at first."

"Surfing on the beach? Really? That sounds a little crazy."

"It's not and you're not practicing surfing, per se, on the sand. You're going to practice going from a prone position to standing. If you can master jumping into position on land, it makes it a little bit easier to do it on the board on the water."

"Somehow I doubt that."

She sighed. "I told you we didn't have to do this. You already tried it a couple of times and didn't enjoy it. Why try again?"

"Because it's something you enjoy and that makes me want to try." She thought it was very sweet that he wanted to do this for her, but she knew his heart wasn't in it. And honestly, it was taking some of the fun out of it for her as well.

Moving around her board, she came to stand in front of him. "Let's make a deal."

"I'm listening…"

"I love that you want us to do things together, but obviously we don't have the same interests or the same skills. Surfing is something I do and I enjoy it. You enjoy jogging. How about you go for a jog while I surf? Or maybe you swim while I surf?"

His blue eyes narrowed. "I feel like you're trying to get rid of me here."

"Well…"

"Okay, okay, I get it. I know I'm not really into it, but…I don't know. I have no idea what I *am* into because I've never been allowed to explore that."

"Ever?"

"I played sports in high school, but…that was high school. I'm not looking to play football or baseball. I need to find some hobbies and interests as an adult and I have no idea where to even begin. So yeah, I'm sort of hopping on your interests and hoping something sticks."

He was even sweeter when he was vulnerable like this. Reaching up, she cupped his cheek. "Christian, not all interests have to involve doing something physical. Maybe we can try going to an art gallery or a museum. We can play board games or have our own little book club." She paused. "Ooo! Or maybe we can go to a vineyard and do a tour and a wine tasting! That could be fun!"

Why hadn't she thought of these things before? All this time she was killing herself trying to learn a new skill when there were so many other opportunities open to her. California was filled with places she'd never seen before; wouldn't it be great to explore them together?

"I know you grew up in New York and lived in London, but have you traveled around California since you moved here?"

Shaking his head, he said, "No. Never seemed to have the time. Or the desire."

"Why?"

He shrugged. "I don't know. I'm not big on playing tourist."

Her enthusiasm instantly waned. "Oh."

Stepping in closer to her, he added, "But I'd be willing to give it a shot. It was never appealing before because I didn't have anyone to go exploring with."

Her eyes widened as her smile grew. "Really? You'd do that for me?"

Laughing, he said, "It's got to be easier than jumping up on a moving board on the water."

Splashing him one more time, she grabbed her board and moved away. "You never know. I might want to take up skiing or hiking or—paragliding!" Thinking she had made her point, Sophie walked out of the water and stood her board up in the sand. In the blink of an eye, Christian was doing the same.

"For your information, I happen to be an excellent skier, I'm pretty sure I can hike, considering I was a Boy Scout and did a lot of camping, and paragliding sounds like a great way to see a lot of places at once."

She hadn't expected him to agree quite so easily, but

now that he had, she was excited to get started. "So, maybe this weekend we can look into doing something like that?"

"Paragliding?"

"Anything!" she said with a laugh, reaching for his hand. "It just occurred to me that it can be just as exciting to see new places as it is to learn new things. Growing up in a small town and never traveling anywhere means that there is so much I have to see. There's a whole country's worth of sights that I would love to see in person, rather than on TV or in a book!"

There wasn't much enthusiasm from him on that one.

"Did you travel a lot as a kid?"

"Sure," he said casually. "We had family in North Carolina and we used to go see them frequently, and we spent a lot of time in upstate New York and out on Long Island to see family as well. We vacationed in Florida, Hawaii, Mexico, and Europe. It was going to Europe for the first time that gave me the idea of opening a branch of Montgomerys there."

She studied him for a long moment. "You really loved it there, didn't you?"

Wordlessly, he nodded.

"Have you ever considered returning? Not to work there, but to visit?"

"Hell no."

"Why not?"

"Too many bad memories."

She looked at him oddly. "So replace them with good ones."

"It's not that easy."

"Why not? I mean, I have a lot of bad memories

about where I lived, but that doesn't mean that I'm never going back. Maybe putting so much time and energy into avoiding going to London—or Europe—isn't productive. Or healthy. If that is a place that gave you joy, why deprive yourself of it?"

At first he didn't say anything—he simply paced a few feet away and stared out at the water. She could practically feel the frustration vibrating off his body and couldn't understand why he felt that way. It seemed simple—go back to London and do the things or see the people he missed. How was that a bad thing?

"Christian?"

He turned to look at her, but gone was the lightness that had been there only moments ago. "What do you think is going to happen when you visit your grandmother?" he asked, surprising her.

"What do you mean?"

Now he fully faced her. "I mean will you suddenly be able to walk around town and not think of all the people who you say betrayed you? Will you be able to not think about how hurt you were before you left? Can you have a conversation with former teachers or even your friends and not have it bother you anymore that they knew the truth about your mother's death?"

"I really can't say how it will feel or how I'll react," she said, hating the slight tremble in her voice. "All I know is that I'll return someday. It's not an option. Do I want to live there?" She shrugged. "I don't know. But I'll see my grandmother and I guess I'll find out then." She paused and noted how he didn't seem to have anything to say to her response. "But I do know this—I'm not afraid to go back. Clearly you are."

And with that, Sophie picked up her board and walked toward the surf shop. It took a full minute before she heard Christian behind her.

"Hey!" he demanded when he caught up. "What's going on?"

For the life of her, she didn't know why she was so wound up or how they had gone from playing in the ocean to snapping at one another.

Oh yeah, he had been a bit of a jerk.

Stopping abruptly, she spun around to face him. "You know what? I'm tired and it would be best if I went home." When she turned to walk away, Christian grabbed her arm. There wasn't a doubt in her mind that daggers were practically shooting from her eyes when she looked at him.

At the moment, he didn't look all that happy either.

He hung his head. "Look, I…I get what you were saying, okay? I felt a little attacked and I lashed out. I didn't mean anything by it. The whole London thing is a phase of my life that I need to just…leave in the past. It's better that way."

"No, it's not. You're not dealing with it. You've never dealt with it," she argued. "And until you do—until you come to grips with what happened there and your father—it's always going to be a sore point with you."

"Geez, Sophie, cut me some slack here," he countered. "Not everything can be gotten over. Sometimes bad things happen and people don't get over them. It's not a crime."

Pulling her arm free, she glared at him. "It is when it stops you from living your life. It is when one single word pushes you back to a place in time and makes you lash out at people for no reason. And it is when you're too afraid to do something about it." Picking up her board again, she walked away.

She returned her board to Randy.

She got in her car and drove home.

And she walked through her front door and felt more miserable than she had in a long time.

After a long shower, she slipped a simple T-shirt-style nightie on and padded to the kitchen to find something to snack on. She and Christian had had a late lunch and had planned on making something for dinner after their surf.

Best laid plans and all…

"Ice cream," she murmured when she pulled open her freezer. A crappy night gave her permission to eat ice cream for dinner, she reasoned. Taking out the pint of triple-chocolate fudge, she slammed the freezer door shut and reached for a spoon. Walking across the room, she glared at her sofa—which also doubled as her bed. At least it was the pull-out kind, but right now, she resented even having to put in that kind of effort.

Muttering a curse, she put the ice cream down and made quick work of opening the bed. Because along with giving herself permission to eat ice cream for dinner, she was allowing herself to eat it in bed too.

"You're a real rule-breaker, Soph," she grumbled, scooping up the pint and spoon again.

Within minutes, she was under the blankets, dealing with brain freeze and watching a rerun of *The Big Bang Theory*.

"Living the dream."

She laughed a bit, but mostly she felt like crying.

Today had been a near-perfect day. When Erin had come to find her to let her know that Christian was having a bit of a crisis, Sophie had practically sprinted to his office. Their lovemaking had been sexy and wild, and it had made her feel a little illicit and decadent at the same time. After they had cleaned up, he had taken her to lunch at her favorite café, around the block from the office. They'd laughed and talked about current events and what they'd planned for the night. Ironically, they never talked about what had initially upset him.

She knew Christian was capable of sharing things with her, so this was something he clearly didn't want to share. And that was fine. Really.

Okay, it bothered her a little bit. After all they'd shared with one another, what could be so bad that he would prefer to keep it to himself?

She'd let it go to focus on their plans for tonight, and then those had been shot to hell too. Why? Because there were still things he didn't want to talk about.

And the worst part? Sophie had told him from the get-go how important honesty was to her. Technically, Christian wasn't lying to her. He wasn't even being dishonest. He was simply keeping things to himself. And he was honest about being upset by them, but not about what they were.

"Men," she muttered.

With her ice cream finished, she forced herself to crawl out of bed and put the pint in the trash and her spoon in the dishwasher. Pouring herself a glass of water, she was halfway back to the bed when a knock at the door had her jumping and spilling the liquid on the floor.

"Dammit!" Putting the glass on the nearest surface, she stormed back to the kitchen for paper towels. Another knock startled her again.

"Sophie?"

Christian.

Being childish wasn't who Sophie was and no matter how annoyed she was with him, she would still open the door and let him in.

Which she did.

Holding on to the doorknob, Sophie leaned against it and simply stared at him.

"Hey," he said quietly, waiting for her to speak.

But she didn't.

Okay, maybe she was acting a little childish.

"Can I come in? Please?"

Moving aside, she motioned for him to step inside. She closed the door behind them and continued cleaning up the water spill.

"I should have called first."

She shrugged and finished wiping up the floor. When she stood and went to throw the towels out, Christian stepped in front of her.

"Hey. I'm sorry," he said. His expression looked sad, pained. "I took something out on you and I shouldn't have and then I got pissed because you were pissed. You had every right to be annoyed with me and—and I don't know what else to say other than I'm sorry."

Well, she did appreciate that he admitted he was wrong, and as much as she wanted to push him on what had set him off earlier, right now it didn't matter.

"I'm sorry too," she said. Turning from him, she threw out the paper towels and shut off the kitchen light. When she faced him again, he didn't look any happier.

"We never had dinner."

With another small shrug, she said, "I had ice cream."

Laughing softly, he reached for her and slowly pulled her into his embrace. "Yeah, I had a bag of pretzels. What a pair we make, huh?"

And right then she realized the answer to that was a wholehearted *yes*. They certainly did.

"Want me to get takeout?" he asked, looking at her.

"I'm not really hungry," she said quietly. "I was just sitting in bed watching some TV."

Christian looked around and seemed to stop short when he realized that her bed was also her sofa. He'd only been to her apartment twice and neither time had been for long. No doubt it was a little bit of a shock compared to where he lived.

"Want some company?" he asked, looking at her again. Then he looked over at the television. "I love this show."

"You do?"

He nodded.

Stepping out of his arms, Sophie walked over to the bed and pulled back the blankets and smiled. "I'd love some company."

He stripped down to his boxers and climbed into bed next to her. It was only a queen-size bed and the mattress was thin, but he didn't say a word, didn't complain. He simply reached for her and tucked her in beside him as they settled in to watch something that gave them a laugh.

They needed that right now more than anything.

"Good morning."

Christian knew before Sophie even spoke that she was awake. He had been gently raking his hands through her hair for several minutes and knew it was only a matter of time before she woke up.

"Good morning," he said, placing a kiss on the top of her head.

"Did you sleep okay?"

It wasn't the most comfortable bed in the world—or long enough for his frame—but...

"I did," he said, kissing her again. "And you?"

"Me too."

They stayed like that for several minutes and Christian realized this was a first for him—spending the night at a woman's house, in her bed, without sex. It should have felt weird or at least foreign, but instead it felt...nice. Comfortable. Somehow the act of holding Sophie all night while they slept felt far more intimate than making love to her.

He wasn't a fool—they might have been able to crawl into bed, watch TV, and pretend that everything was all right, but he knew why she was upset and he wanted to make things right.

"I had an argument with my father yesterday," he said quietly. "It was mostly the same old, same old, but then he threw in that the anxiety attack was a way to get attention—*his* attention—and how it made me look weak." Swallowing hard, he waited for her to gasp in shock or offer him sympathy.

Instead, she sat up beside him and he could see a hint

of fire in her eyes. "Seriously? He thought that was for attention? Does he need the hospital report? Or...or... for your doctor to call and explain to him how wrong he is? Because that can easily happen!"

This, he wasn't prepared for.

It was one thing for his siblings to come to his defense, but no one else ever had.

"Sophie, I don't think—"

But she wasn't listening; she jumped from the bed, her long hair flying around her like a fiery halo. "I am so tired of people like that—questioning someone's health or doubting it! How could he not know his own son? And on top of that, what kind of egomaniac says that sort of thing out loud?"

With a huff, she stomped off to the kitchen and from his position in bed, he watched in fascination as she continued to mutter and curse on his behalf while making coffee. Two minutes ago he was fine with the whole staying the night without sex, but right now, sex was the only thing on his mind, because her temper and defense of him was way more of a turn-on than he ever imagined.

He kicked off the blankets and swung his legs over the side of the bed.

"I mean, does the man have any idea how scary an episode like that can be?" she ranted, pulling mugs down from the cabinet. "Or how many people think it's anxiety when it's really a heart attack?"

Standing and stretching, Christian continued to watch her.

"Ignoring symptoms like that can be detrimental and life-threatening," she stated, her back still to him as she put milk and sugar out on the counter. "I bet he wouldn't take it so lightly if it happened to him!"

If he was a betting man, Christian figured his father wouldn't last five minutes in an argument with Sophie on this topic. With a grin, he quietly made his way across the room.

Spinning toward him while brandishing a spoon, she snapped, "Does he even realize how much stress *he* creates?"

As much as he was enjoying himself, he knew he had to put a stop to it. Technically, Christian agreed with everything she was saying, but he was done thinking about his father and letting him ruin his mood. Closing the distance between them, Christian wrapped his arms around Sophie's waist and rested his forehead against hers.

"It's kind of hot how you're defending me," he said, softly, teasingly.

She instantly relaxed in his embrace. "Well, someone has to do it."

He pulled her closer. "You were pretty fierce there for a minute."

"I don't see this sort of thing very often, but I've seen it enough that it makes me mad. So many people don't get the medical help they need because closed-minded people try to tell them they're imagining their symptoms or that they're being dramatic." She paused and looked up at him. "Don't ever let anyone try to talk you out of how you're feeling. You know your body better than anyone else."

And that sentence was the perfect segue out of the topic of his father and his health.

Moving against her, he huskily said, "I think you're getting to know it pretty well too."

Luckily, she took the hint, because he was done focusing on the negative in his life. At least for right now. She gave him a sexy smile. "I agree."

The rich aroma of coffee filled the air, but he wasn't in the mood for that—he was in the mood for her. Everything else could wait. He was about to lower his head to kiss her when her phone rang—an odd little tune that rapped "Nana's on the phone… Nana's calling you…"

With a whispered apology, Sophie stepped away to answer the call. With nothing else to do, Christian poured them each a cup of coffee and went to sit back down on the bed. He wished he could give her some privacy, but in the small studio space, there wasn't any place for him to go other than the bathroom.

So he sipped his coffee and then reached down to where he'd dropped his pants the night before, pulling his phone from the pocket and checking his email. Surprise, surprise, there were three from his father—all asking for reports on clients that had nothing to do with him.

Delete.

Delete.

Delete.

Closing out of email, he opted to look at his texts—less chance of getting aggravated that way. Scrolling down, he saw one from his brother and grinned.

New Restaurant a go! Opted for Montauk!

Christian's eyes widened as he read. That was news. Last he had heard, Carter was going to be doing two new locations for his restaurants—one in New York and one in Florida. Even though Carter hadn't said where specifically in New York he was looking, Christian had automatically assumed he meant Manhattan. Montauk was literally at the end of Long Island—the very tip of it—and as far from the thriving metropolis of the city as could be!

He took another sip of his coffee before tapping out a response.

> Didn't realize you were thinking that far away from the city.

His phone instantly rang and he looked to see Sophie standing in the corner of her kitchen talking intently to her grandmother.

That can't be good, he thought. His phone rang again and he saw Carter's name on the screen and quickly answered.

"Hey, what's up?"

"So you don't like the Montauk location?" Carter immediately asked instead of exchanging pleasantries.

Laughing quietly, Christian replied, "That's not it at all. I guess I just assumed you'd go for the city. That's where all the big restaurants are."

"Yeah, and all the competition. Don't get me wrong, there are a lot of great restaurants out on the island, but I think I want to do something a little bit different this time around."

"Wow, this is brand-new information. And you're going to do it with both places or just Montauk?"

"Just Montauk. The Florida place is going to be like my other three—same design and menu, so it's a no-brainer. It makes life a little easier and I know that whole plan works. It's going to be in Orlando in the heart of all the theme parks, so it'll draw crowds no matter what." Then he paused. "But I'm not sure that's where my heart is for any more of them."

"Seriously? What brought that on?"

"I don't know. Something Mom said to me not too long ago keeps playing in my head."

"What did she say?"

"She said, 'Remember where you came from, Carter. Not everyone wants to eat a hundred-dollar dinner. There's something to be said for a good, simple meal.' And for some reason, now that's all I can think about. How crazy is that?"

"Doesn't she realize there are more restaurants that cater to the kind of diners who want simple fare than the more upscale ones? Is this going to be something profitable for you? Especially in that location?"

"Yeah, yeah, yeah…I know. I still have to figure it all out. She's been on my case lately in a lot of ways, but that one comment just won't go away."

"Please, Mom's a marshmallow. I'd love to have her on my case rather than Dad any day of the week."

Carter laughed. "Dad giving you trouble again?"

"Again? When has it stopped?" Picking up his mug, he took another sip and said, "Although I did sort of lose my shit on him yesterday."

"Really? What did he say?"

"You mean after telling me I need to treat him with respect?"

Sighing loudly, Carter replied, "What is his deal with that? With you?"

"It's all about appearances and I guess since I'm his only child working for the family business, he expects me to be above reproach."

"Megan works for Montgomerys now too."

"It's not the same. Trust me. And as much as it would have been nice to have some of the pressure off me, there's no way I could have let that happen to her. It wouldn't have been fair."

"So now you're going to play the martyr?"

"Don't be a jackass. That wasn't what I was saying at all."

"Okay, fine. Let's start over. What set Dad off this time?"

"He claims I faked my anxiety attack for attention."

The curse that flew out of Carter's mouth was vicious. "Hang on, he really believes that you got rushed to the hospital just for attention?"

"His attention specifically."

All Christian heard at first was a low growl. "That's crossing a line, Chris. We need to sit him down and confront him."

"We?"

"Yeah. We. All of us. No doubt Megan would join in as well."

"I'm not asking everyone to fight my battles, Carter," Christian said, feeling more defensive than he probably should.

"Dude, we're not fighting your battles. Dad's been hard on all of us at one time or another. We're not kids anymore and it's time we all stood up to him."

"You already did that. It's why you're so damn happy at your job and in your life."

"You think this is happy?" Carter asked sarcastically. "I work my ass off 24-7. I worry all the damn time about keeping up and making sure my restaurants stay a step above the rest."

"Of course you do. You need to stay on top of things so you don't become stagnant or dated."

"No, it's more than that. I'm a little bit more obsessive than your standard business owner because I know if I fail, Dad is going to be all over me. There will be a never-ending round of *I told you so*s followed by reminders of why working in the family business was a guarantee of job security." He huffed out a breath. "I refuse to let that happen. I can't."

Wow. And all this time Christian thought his brother had it easy. It seemed like it was the same family bullshit, just packaged a little differently.

"So what do we do? I don't even know when we'll all be together again. And it would suck to do something like this and incite a fight around the holidays."

"Yeah, I know. Let me think on that."

They both fell silent and Christian looked over at Sophie, who was also still on the phone. She was partially facing him, leaning against the kitchen counter, and he could only hear part of what she was saying.

"Why would anyone even suggest such a thing?" she cried.

Suggest what? he wondered.

"Carter, look...I have to go. Something's come up."

"Please tell me you're not at work on a Saturday morning."

"No, no. I'm at Sophie's and...I have to go."

Something in his tone must have alerted his brother

to the fact that he wasn't joking around. "Everything all right?"

"I'm not sure, but I'll call you tomorrow, okay?"

After he hung up and put his phone away, Christian eased to the corner of the bed, closer to Sophie, and did his best to listen without looking as if he was listening.

"I don't understand why this is all happening now. Why is this suddenly out there in the open for everyone to talk about?"

He seriously wished he could hear what her grandmother was saying.

"There's nothing to think about," Sophie said wearily, taking a sip of her own coffee. "I'll call you tomorrow." She paused. "Love you too."

She hung up her phone, and Christian watched as she closed her eyes. Even from across the room he could feel the tension rolling off her body. Slowly he came to his feet and walked over to her, taking her in his arms and just holding her. If she wanted to talk, he would listen. But if she wasn't ready to, he was totally fine staying like this.

The slight tremble of her body was immediately apparent to him, so he hugged her a little bit tighter, holding his tongue to keep from asking her if she wanted to talk.

"My father wants to see me."

That was quite possibly the last thing he expected her to say. "How...how do you feel about that?"

"Honestly? I don't know." Letting out a long breath, she shook her head. "I mean, why? Why now?"

Her voice rose with each word and she pulled out of his embrace, pacing frantically in the small space.

Reaching for her, he attempted to get her to breathe and relax a bit.

"Soph," he said calmly, "you need to relax."

"How can I?" she cried. "After all this time, he suddenly wants to see me, talk to me...and...and..."

That's when Christian knew she was having a panic attack. He recognized the signs—the heavy breathing, the agitation, and she had most definitely gone pale. Carefully, he led her over to the bed and forced her to sit. Crouching down in front of her, he placed his hands on her knees and encouraged her to take some deep breaths.

"C'mon," he said softly. "Focus on me. Don't think about anything else. I want you to catch your breath."

Her eyes were a little wild as she looked at him. "What am I supposed to do? What am I supposed to say? I—I never thought about this being a thing!"

Christian hadn't given it much thought either until now. No doubt her father was hoping to finally connect with her after all this time, but he had to wonder why Sophie's grandmother had thought it was a good idea to even mention it to her. If she had felt strongly enough about learning the truth that she'd moved a thousand miles away so she wouldn't have to deal with it, why would anyone think suggesting going to see the man who killed her mother was the right thing to do?

Struggling for something to say that would help calm her down, Christian rubbed her legs in slow, rhythmic circles and watched as her breathing returned to normal. It would be ridiculous to ask if she was okay, because he already knew the answer to that.

She wasn't.

Letting out a slow breath, Sophie's eyes locked with his. "What am I supposed to do?"

Shifting so he was sitting beside her on the bed, Christian took one of her hands in his. "That's not something you should decide right now," he said carefully.

Her eyes went wide.

"I know your initial instinct is to say no. Hell no," he added emphatically. "And there's nothing wrong with that."

"But…?"

"But you're a little in shock right now, and I'm saying that no one expects you to know what you're going to do."

"But I do," she said adamantly. "I'm not going to see him." Standing up, she turned to face him. "There's nothing to think about."

Christian came to his feet and offered her a small smile. "Okay."

The look she gave him showed that she didn't know what to think of his response. "I'm serious, Christian. I know some people would say it would be therapeutic or that it's only natural to get some closure, but…but not me."

The slight tremble in her voice told him she wasn't nearly as confident as she was trying to make herself sound.

Without a word, he pulled her in close and wrapped his arms around her again. She melted against him and for several long moments, they stayed like that.

Crisis averted, he thought. At least for now.

"What am I going to do?" she asked, her voice a mere whisper.

This didn't involve him—not really—and it was a

far more complicated situation than he had ever dealt with in his entire life. And it was more complicated than most couples in a new relationship had to deal with. This may be a new relationship, but Christian already knew that she meant more to him than he'd realized. Whatever it was that had initially drawn him to her from the first time he'd seen her on the beach had continued to grow, and now it was more than he'd felt for anyone in a long time.

If ever.

"Christian..."

He cupped her face in his hands. "Whatever you decide, we'll face it together."

Without waiting for her response, he kissed her—slowly, deeply, thoroughly—pouring everything he felt into it. She wrapped herself around him, holding him close in an almost desperate attempt to keep him there.

His heart felt fuller even as it broke for her.

There were certainly a lot of issues he had to deal with where his father was concerned, but they were nothing compared to what Sophie was facing.

But for right now, neither of them had to think about that.

They only had to think about each other.

Scooping her up into his arms, he carried her back to her bed and did his best to clear both their minds.

Chapter 8

If Sophie had to pick a day that seemed to both change and solidify the relationship she and Christian were currently enjoying, it would be the day in her apartment after their argument. Never had she been so thankful for not being alone. If Christian hadn't been there when her grandmother had called, she wasn't sure what she would have done. Even thinking about it now made her a little crazy.

The good that came out of it all, however, was that the day was a turning point for them. They'd settled into a routine where Christian was working regular hours—thirty-five a week—and Sophie was enjoying the freedom of going to new offices every day and meeting new people. That last one was really the biggest perk for her. It hit home just how isolated she'd been feeling since moving to San Diego. Every day was a new adventure for her.

Besides work going well for them both, they had started exploring beyond their immediate neighborhood. At first it was just going out to eat someplace new or to a concert, but then they branched out to taking weekend trips along the California coast, exploring different places and trying new things—they went hang gliding and to wine tastings. They went to Disneyland, where she found out that Christian was really just a big kid at heart. They had laughed more on that day than any other she could remember, and all the while, they continued spending their nights together. Christian stayed at her place more than she'd thought he would, but she was too embarrassed to ask to go to his place, because she didn't want him to think that was the only reason she was with him.

She was happy.

She felt good.

Unfortunately, there was still one dark cloud hanging over her head that kept her in a mild state of turmoil. Most days she was okay with it, then the next she'd work herself up into a frenzy.

Her father.

She no longer felt so sure about her decision not to see him. It was crazy, she knew that, but there was still a part of her that was curious. Seeing him might answer some of the questions swirling around in her head since she'd found out the whole sordid truth about her life.

In keeping with her need to be one hundred percent truthful, she shared her feelings on the subject with Christian—and she had to hand it to him, he never tried to tell her what to do. He would listen patiently while she reasoned things out loud and then would tell her how he would stand with her no matter what she decided.

It was both perfect and frustrating.

As much as Sophie wanted to make her own decisions, in this particular instance she really wished someone would simply tell her what to do!

"You're doing it again."

Startled, she looked up from her salad and found Christian looking at her with amusement. "Um…doing what?"

"You were staring at your plate and frowning," he said mildly. "That tells me that you're thinking too hard about something." He paused. "And if I had to take a guess, I'd say it's about your father."

Damn. Was she that transparent?

Placing her fork on the table, she sighed and looked at him. "Sorry. Sometimes it just creeps up on me and I don't know how to stop it."

Reaching over, Christian took her hand in his. "Sophie, you don't have to apologize for anything. I know this is weighing heavily on you and I wish there was something I could do or say to help you—or at least distract you."

She blushed at the memory of just how he was a master at distracting her when they were alone. He must have read those thoughts, because she heard a low, deep chuckle from him.

"All I'm saying is that I wish this wasn't bothering you so much. I love that we were able to have lunch together today and I hate the thought of you not enjoying yourself because you're in your own head."

There was such a change in him from the first time she'd met him. There was a...mellowness about him that hadn't been there before. Cutting back on his work hours had done wonders for him and it showed in so many ways. He smiled more, he dressed more casually, and he had even grown a beard. It wasn't anything wild, but it looked good on him.

And it felt really good against her skin when he was kissing her or making love to her.

She shook her head to clear it and smiled over at him. "You're right. We're having a good day and a delicious lunch and I should be focusing on that right now." Taking her fork again, she examined her salmon and picked up a small piece. "How do you feel about kite flying?"

He laughed a little heartier this time as he released her hand. "Kite flying? That's a new one."

"Remember when we saw that group of people on the beach Sunday flying them?"

He nodded.

"I've been thinking about them ever since and I thought it could be fun to try it."

Christian took a forkful of his own salmon as he considered her suggestion. "I wouldn't even know where to buy a kite."

"I ordered one online and I'm hoping it's going to be waiting for me when I get home today," she said excitedly. "If it is, I would love to try it out tonight. What do you say? Are you interested?"

"There are some other things I'd planned on us doing tonight," he said with a mischievous grin, "but they can wait until we're done with the kite."

Now she had even more to look forward to!

They finished their lunch and walked back to the office. It was a beautiful day out and they had gotten in the habit of walking more rather than driving to wherever they were going—provided it wasn't too far.

Taking her by the hand, Christian led her into the elevator and as soon as the doors were closed, he backed her up against the wall and kissed her soundly. It was the perfect ending to her break, and there was just enough heat to make her squirm and enough tenderness that she felt loved.

Christian Montgomery had some mad kissing skills and she was happy to be on the receiving end of them.

He lifted his head as the elevator came to a stop. "Wow," she said breathlessly. "That was better than dessert."

"We didn't have dessert," he reminded her playfully.

"It was better than anything we could have had."

They stepped out of the elevator and walked toward the glass doors that led to the company's office suite. Sophie went to turn toward her office, but Christian whispered her name and stopped her. She looked at him quizzically.

"I'm supposed to get an update to my doctor," he said softly. "What do you say we go to your office?"

Sophie knew his physician was still closely monitoring him, but she also knew they had just done that earlier in the week. With a sassy grin, she looked up. "Why Mr. Montgomery, are you asking to play doctor in the middle of the day?"

He grinned back. "Maybe."

Turning, she led the way. "Then far be it from me to argue."

They hadn't gone more than five feet when Erin came walking up, seeming a little tense. "I'm glad you're back," she said.

Christian immediately let go of Sophie's hand and faced his assistant. "Is everything all right?"

Erin looked nervously at Sophie before looking at Christian again. "Um... You have some unexpected company."

Figuring it was a client, Sophie started to move away. "I should probably go."

But Christian wasn't really paying attention. His gaze was still on Erin's. "Who is it?"

"Your parents."

That made Sophie stop in her tracks.

"What?" Christian hissed, and she knew he was deliberately keeping his voice down. "When did they get here and—and why?"

Erin glanced toward his office and then back to him. "They mentioned how they wanted to surprise you and see how you were feeling."

The string of curses that followed were said so quietly that Sophie was certain she was the only one to hear them.

"I'm sorry, Christian," Erin said, taking a step back. "If you want, I can tell them you're not back yet or that you got detained or—"

He held up a hand to stop her. "No. That won't be necessary. I'll be there in a few minutes, okay?"

Nodding, Erin turned back toward his office and once she was out of sight, Christian took Sophie by the hand and led her back to hers.

When they were inside with the door closed, Sophie finally spoke. "Are you all right?"

He paced and raked both hands through his hair. "I hate this. I absolutely hate this!"

Yeah. She could tell. Hell, she could practically feel the frustration vibrating off him. Stepping into his path, she gently grasped him by the biceps. When he looked at her, she offered a small smile. "First, you need to relax," she said carefully. "I know you're upset, but you shouldn't get worked up."

Normally that sort of thing worked on him, but

not this time. Christian stepped out of her grasp as he snapped, "Nothing's going to happen if I get worked up. I haven't had an episode since that day I went to the ER. My blood pressure has been fine and I'm practically the poster boy for good health." He stopped and let out a long breath. "And every once in a while, it's okay to get upset. I'm only human."

She noticed he was trying to control his temper and the tone of his voice.

"Maybe you should—"

"I can't believe they'd do this!" he said, pacing again. "It's like they think I'm a child or—or that I need someone watching over me!" More pacing. "I have tried to put my foot down, but obviously it wasn't enough. Now I'm going to have to go in there and argue and..." Another stream of curses came out and Sophie knew he needed to vent—that these few minutes before he faced his parents were necessary for his own sanity.

And she hated that for him.

"So don't go in there," she said impulsively and held her breath when Christian stopped pacing to stare at her.

"What?"

"Don't go in there," she repeated. "Just...leave. We'll go to the beach and...and...go for a run!"

He looked at her skeptically. "You hate running."

She mildly relaxed. "And you hate to argue with your parents."

He laughed softly and leaned against her desk. "Maybe we won't argue."

She moved over to him until they were practically toe to toe. "Maybe you won't."

His shoulders sagged. "Soph, come on. This isn't helping."

Pressing up against him, Sophie looped her arms around his shoulders and gave him a small smile. "I'm sorry. I don't know what else to say." She kissed him softly on the chin. "Just know that whatever you decide, I'm here for you. If you want to leave, we'll leave. If you want to stay, I'll go in there with you and we'll face them together."

Christian's eyes went wide. "You'd go into my office with me? Why?"

Unable to help herself, Sophie let out a laugh. "Christian, do you remember what you told me about my situation with my father?" When he nodded, she continued. "This is what we do. We support one another. And who knows, maybe my being there will mean things won't get so heated."

She could tell he was considering it.

But ultimately, he turned her down.

Leaning in, Christian captured her lips in a sweet, lingering kiss. When he finally lifted his head, he told her, "Let's say that's plan B, okay?" Then he moved from her embrace. "I need to go in there so I don't prove them right." He sighed. "But be on standby."

With a lopsided grin and a wink, he walked out of the office.

"Extended lunch?"

Fighting the urge to tense up, Christian forced a smile and walked over to kiss his mother on the cheek—ignoring his father's question. "It's good to see you,

Mom," he said softly before moving to take a seat at his desk. Once he was situated, he faced his father. "Dad. Good to see you."

The look on Joseph's face showed that he didn't appreciate Christian's tone.

"What brings you both here?" he asked pleasantly, choosing to focus on his mother. "You didn't mention a trip to California."

"We're going to visit Megan and Alex this weekend and thought we'd take a detour and come check on you," his mother said with a smile. "You know we've been worried about you since your…you know, your episode."

The urge to roll his eyes was strong, but he held it together and never let his smile falter. "I'm feeling much better. I've changed my diet and I'm getting more exercise, and my blood pressure is excellent. I get it checked regularly thanks to your new program, Mom," he added for good measure.

Eliza's face lit up. "Oh, that's wonderful! Who would have known that this program would prove to be such a blessing so soon! And to our own son!" She looked over at Joseph and smiled. "Isn't it wonderful?"

Joseph shrugged, his eyes never leaving Christian. "And what about your work hours? Are you up to speed?"

Ah…so they were going to go there right away, Christian thought miserably.

"I'm working the perfect amount of hours," he answered. Looking at his mother, he asked, "So how long are you here for? Will you be staying with me?"

"Oh, no," Eliza said, but still smiling. "Your father and I are staying at the Marriott. We didn't want to impose."

"It's never an imposition, Mom."

He should burst into flames for that lie.

"Well, considering we didn't call first, I thought it was the best thing to do." She paused. "How about dinner tonight?"

"That sounds great," Christian replied and then decided to poke the bear a little. "Why don't I meet you at the hotel around five? We can have cocktails there and then go to dinner at that seafood place you like so much. I felt bad that I didn't get to take you there when you and Aunt Monica were here."

"Five's a little early, isn't it?" Joseph asked.

Christian looked at his father but held his smile. "Not at all. It will give me time to go home and change first too." Turning back to his mother, he added, "And you'll be happy to know that I'm bringing a date."

Eliza's face lit up like a kid's on Christmas morning. "Really? Who...I mean, you haven't mentioned..." She let out a happy little laugh. "You know what? It doesn't matter! I can't wait to meet her!"

"Actually, Mom, you already have."

Her eyes grew wide. "I have? Who is she?"

"Remember Sophie Bennington? You met her on the beach and told her about the position here?"

She looked confused at first, then instantly pleased. "Really? You're dating Sophie? That's wonderful!"

Christian relayed the story from the day he met Sophie on the beach and how she was here when he had the anxiety attack. "She's the one who was with me in the ER that day and we just hit it off."

"Oh, that's wonderful!"

"I can see why you thought Sophie was perfect for the job. She's amazing."

"I'm so happy! I knew when I met her on the beach that she was special!"

"You're dating an employee?" his father asked with a snort of disgust. He raised a hand to his temple and rubbed it.

"Sophie's not really an employee. We hired the agency she works for and they're the ones who pay her salary. She's here only once a week, and she also works for several other companies in the area. I had no idea corporate nursing was such a big thing!" he said. "The agency she ultimately signed with has more work for her than she ever imagined."

"I know she didn't want to go through an agency," Eliza said. "But I'm glad she finally did. Good for her!" Beside her, Joseph continued to rub his temple. Facing him, she asked, "Are you all right? Should we go back to the hotel?"

Joseph waved her off. "It's nothing," he said gruffly, and Christian noticed that his father's eye was twitching too. No doubt he was freaked out over the news of him and Sophie dating and was trying to hold his tongue.

Rising, Christian walked around his desk. "I hate to be rude, but I do have an appointment this afternoon. Sophie and I will meet you in the hotel bar at five. How does that sound?"

His mother stood and hugged him tightly. "It sounds wonderful!" She kissed him soundly on the cheek. "I'm so happy!"

It felt good to know that he'd done this—he'd done something that brought a smile to his mother's face.

Joseph stood and held out a hand to Christian, who stiffly shook it. "We'll see you later, then."

Without another word, Joseph walked out of the office. When he was out the door, Christian turned to his mother. "You know he's not pleased, right? I don't want any issues tonight. If he's going to be rude to Sophie..."

Placing a hand on her son's arm, Eliza looked worried. "He's had that headache since we got off the plane."

"Mom," Christian began. "Please don't make excuses. We both know why he's behaving that way."

She gave him a sad smile. "I'll talk to him. Don't worry. I don't think he realizes how abrasive he can be at times. I'll remind him to be on his best behavior."

Somehow Christian doubted it would help, but for now he'd humor his mother.

"Thanks, Mom."

He stood in that same spot for a solid minute after his mother left and realized he didn't feel tense.

He didn't even feel angry.

If anything, he felt...hopeful.

"Let's see how long that lasts," he murmured before turning to his desk and getting back to work.

At five minutes to five, Christian took Sophie's hand in his and helped her from the car. He couldn't help but smile as she fidgeted a little with her hair and smoothed her dress. Stepping in close, he said, "Relax. You look beautiful."

She let out a small breath as she looked up at him. "I'm just a little nervous."

"You already met my mother and she is very excited to see you." That put a smile on Sophie's face and he took the moment to start walking toward the hotel entrance. "And she said she was going to speak to my father, so hopefully he'll go easy on both of us."

Beside him, Sophie laughed. "Do you really believe that's going to work?"

Opening the door for her, he replied lightly, "Not a chance."

They walked across the massive lobby and into the hotel bar. Christian scanned the room but didn't spot either of his parents.

"There's an open table right there so they should be able to see us easily," Sophie said, as if reading his mind.

Letting her lead the way, Christian waved to a waitress to let her know they were taking the table. Holding out a chair for Sophie, he glanced at the entrance one more time. Her hand on his almost startled him.

"I think you need to relax too," she said softly. "We'll sit and maybe order drinks—I'm sure you know what your parents like—and they'll be here any minute. Okay?"

When the waitress came over, he did as Sophie suggested and ordered for all of them. Two minutes later, he spotted his parents walking in and instantly stood to greet them. "Mom, you remember Sophie," he said, waiting to introduce her to his father. "Dad, this is Sophie Bennington. Sophie, this is my father, Joseph."

Sophie smiled brightly as she shook his father's hand, but as usual, his father was stiff and only murmured his greeting.

Typical.

Christian motioned for his parents to sit and even held the chair for his mother. "I hope you don't mind, but I ordered our drinks. I know how much you like the Moscato, Mom. And Dad, I ordered you your Glenfiddich."

"Thank you, sweetheart," his mother said before returning her attention to Sophie. Christian was fine with that, as his own attention turned to his father, who was rubbing at his temple again.

"Dad? You still have a headache?" he asked casually, turning only briefly to thank the waitress who was placing their drinks on the table.

"Ish fine," Joseph said curtly.

For a minute, both Christian and Eliza stared at him. *Ish?* Was his father already drunk in preparation for their dinner? Seriously? And drunk enough to slur his words? He shot a glance at his mother, who simply shrugged as if it wasn't a big deal. All that did was make him feel like he had to be even more on his guard. As if the old man wasn't enough of a hard-ass, he had to come to dinner like this? Rage simmered, but he suddenly felt Sophie's hand squeeze his thigh and the look on her face showed that she knew exactly what he was feeling. Her smile went a long way in helping him to calm down.

"So how do you like your job?" Eliza asked with a bright smile. "Christian tells me you signed with an agency as well."

Nodding, Sophie replied, "I love it. I could kick myself for waiting so long to go that route, but at the time I was enjoying finding my way around the city and embracing this new life."

"What was wrong wif your old life?" Joseph asked, and Christian had to give Sophie credit, she didn't even blink an eye at his slurred speech.

"I grew up in a small town in Kansas," she began

with an easy smile, "nothing at all like California. When I moved here, it was because it was time for a change. Small town life is fine, but everyone knows your business and you know theirs. I thought it might be nice to experience something new."

Christian held his breath as he waited for the cross-examination he was certain was coming, but...it didn't. Instead, his father simply nodded and reached for his drink.

Really?

"How many clients do you currently have?" his mother asked after a moment of awkward silence.

"Including Montgomerys, I have eight other companies I visit on a regular basis." She sipped her wine. "I'd like to add more so that I'm working a full forty hours a week, but I'll get there eventually."

"That's fantastic. I'm so pleased for you," Eliza gushed. "And how about the surfing? Any improvements there?"

Both he and Sophie chuckled at the question.

"What? What's so funny about that?" Eliza asked.

Christian started to speak, but Sophie stopped him. "I've come to the conclusion that I'm never going to be a surfer. At least not a good one. When I do it now, it's just for fun and I'm not doing it every day like I used to."

"But you were so enthusiastic!" Eliza said with a hint of disappointment.

"Unfortunately, enthusiasm doesn't equal talent," Sophie joked. "I even tried to get Christian to try it with me."

"Really?" His mother looked at him with excitement. "And how did you do?"

"Worse than Sophie," he said solemnly and then grinned. "But I was okay with that. Once we realized that neither of us had a future in surfing, it opened us up to trying other things." Reaching over, he took Sophie's hand in his. "We've gone to wine tastings and to a couple of plays, we went paragliding, and up to San Francisco to Fisherman's Wharf."

"And Disneyland!" Sophie exclaimed. "I had always wanted to go and Christian took me. It was awesome."

Christian saw his father's eye twitch several times. No doubt this conversation was making him crazy. It was one thing for Christian to cut back on his hours, but quite another for him to be off gallivanting in his free time instead of watching the stock market.

"How exciting for you both!" his mother said, clearly pleased with what she was hearing. "What have you got planned next? A trip to the East Coast, maybe?"

Christian knew what his mother was hinting at, but judging by how awkward this first outing already was, he wasn't quite so anxious to plan more of them with his parents.

"That one hasn't come up," he said diplomatically. "Right now we're enjoying getting to know the state of California. For all the years I've been here, I really haven't seen anything other than San Diego." He kissed Sophie's hand. "Until Sophie showed me how much fun that could be."

"That is wonderful," Eliza said and turned to her husband. "When have we traveled just for fun?"

The question was asked lightly, but Joseph scowled before saying, "Wasche of time."

Unable to help himself, Christian slammed his hand

down on the table. "You know what?" he said, full of frustration. "Not everyone has to live their life for work!"

His father looked up at him and something was—off. Joseph was looking at him, but Christian could tell that he really wasn't focused. And it wasn't because of the alcohol—he'd seen his father after a few drinks. This was different. Very different. He looked at his mother and then at Sophie. She must have seen his concern because her attention immediately went to his father.

"Mr. Montgomery?" she asked softly and waited for him to look at her. Very gently, she took one of Joseph's hands in hers. "How are you feeling?"

Joseph winced at her words as if she'd shouted them, but Sophie's inquiry had been quiet.

"Maybe we should go back to the room," Eliza said, worry lacing her voice. "It's just a migraine. He's been getting them more and more lately and—"

"Mom..."

But Sophie wasn't paying attention to either of them. She was studying his father's face and he watched as she casually took his pulse, then felt his forehead. Her actions didn't surprise him as much as his father's did.

Joseph sat there and let her touch him—in the middle of the hotel bar—without uttering a word of protest. Christian could remember his father losing his patience if his mother so much as wiped a piece of lint from his suit!

For several minutes, Sophie asked his father questions and got him to do simple tasks like follow her finger, squeeze her hand, or even try to hold his hands out. Just when he thought she was done and everything was all right, his father took his drink and it instantly fell from his hand and crashed to the floor.

His mother gasped and immediately called their waitress over, but Christian looked to Sophie.

"I think we need to get him to the hospital," she said in a low voice, for his ears only. "I can't say with any great certainty, but I think he may have had a stroke."

Christian's gut clenched and he quickly came to his feet. Stepping around the table to his father, he placed a hand on his shoulder. "Dad, I think we should go," he said slowly, cautiously.

"He's probably tired," Eliza said nervously as she helped her husband to his feet.

"Mom, we need to get him to the hospital. Something's wrong. Trust me." He met his mother's worried gaze and was relieved when she nodded.

So many times in his life, Christian had hated being compared to his father, but right now, he could honestly say that he knew how Joseph was feeling. With Christian on one side and his mother on the other, they slowly led Joseph from the bar as Sophie ran over to pay their tab. She caught up to them a minute later, walking right past them and out the front door to get the valet to bring the car up. Part of him worried that they should call for an ambulance, but the hospital was five minutes away and he knew he could get them there faster.

It amazed him how calm he felt. He kept up a running dialogue with his parents as they made their way out to the car, but he wasn't sure if it was for their sake or his own.

"I'll sit with him," Sophie said as they helped Joseph into the car.

No one argued.

Pulling away from the hotel, Christian reached for his mother's hand and held it tight as he made the quick drive. Behind him, Sophie was softly talking to his father and he heard the slurred—almost incoherent—responses he was giving her.

That can't be good, he thought.

"I need to call Megan and Carter," Eliza said, and he heard the tremble in her voice. "They should know what's going on."

"Not yet, Mom. Let's get to the hospital and see what the doctors have to say before we get everyone all upset."

She nodded, turning to look at her husband.

"It's going to be okay," he said quietly, giving her hand another squeeze. Although if he were honest, he wasn't quite so sure.

"Here you go, Eliza," Sophie said quietly, handing her a cup of coffee. They'd been at the hospital for over two hours and Joseph was still undergoing testing—they knew no more than they had when they arrived.

"Thank you, dear."

Looking across the room, Sophie saw Christian standing with his back to them and his phone to his ear. No doubt he was finally calling his siblings. He and Eliza had been talking about that before she left to go to the cafeteria for coffee, so she figured they'd come to the decision that it was time to start making calls.

"I hate this," Eliza said, her voice low but firm. "I

understand that they need time to examine him and run tests, but the waiting is awful." She sighed. "I knew something was wrong."

Sophie studied her for a moment. "What do you mean? Earlier? Before you came down to the bar?"

Eliza didn't say anything for a long moment before she shook her head. "Before that. This morning, actually. I almost canceled our flight, but I just figured it was Joseph being Joseph." She let out a mirthless laugh. "My husband never admits to being sick or to feeling any pain. I've watched him work while he had pneumonia or the flu. He used to get migraines and yet he always worked through them. And when he found out—" Stopping abruptly, she shook her head. "But this morning he was different, and I chose to attribute it to the issues he and Christian were having. If I had just canceled the trip..."

Reaching for her hand, Sophie said, "Then you would have been dealing with this back in New York, Eliza. And maybe there would be a little more comfort because you were home and with your own doctors, but this was still going to happen." She could have kicked herself. That wasn't the most encouraging thing to say to someone, was it? "I mean..."

"No, you're right. I would be alone or maybe have some friends with me. At least now I have Christian and you." She gave Sophie a small smile right before her eyes welled with tears. "You knew something was wrong and you acted so quickly. I would have just kept waiting for him to tell me he needed help, and then who knows what would have happened."

"I know what to look for. Although, to be honest, I

wasn't sure at first. Since I'd never met Joseph before, I had no idea if his behavior or speech was normal. And he didn't have the usual symptoms. It wasn't until I saw the look on Christian's face that I knew something was up." She gave Eliza's hand a squeeze. "I'm glad he was agreeable to my helping him."

Eliza sniffled. "He looked scared," she whispered and choked back a sob. "I've never seen him look like that."

Unsure of how to respond, Sophie simply nodded.

"I should call Joseph's personal doctor. He'll need to know about this."

Sophie was about to respond when Christian walked over and crouched down in front of his mother. "Megan's going to fly in tonight and Carter's coming in tomorrow." He looked solemnly at Sophie and then at his mother. "I'll call Uncle William and Uncle Robert next if you want me to."

She looked at him as she cupped his cheek. "Thank you, but...I think I'll make those calls. It will give me something to do."

"Mom, you don't have to. I'm here. I can help."

"I know." Her smile was sad. "But I need to do it or I'll go crazy. Why don't you take Sophie and get something to eat in the cafeteria? Coffee isn't a proper dinner."

"We're fine," Sophie said, "but how about we get you something to eat?" Again, she could have kicked herself for not thinking of it earlier when she went to get coffee.

"I don't think I could eat, but I want the two of you to get something. I'm going to make the calls and hopefully we'll have some answers soon."

"Mom, I don't want to leave you alone here. What if the doctors come out while I'm gone? I think—"

"Christian," Eliza said, sounding stronger than she had in hours. "Go. I will call you if anyone comes out to talk to me and I won't let them say anything until you're back." When he made to argue, she said, "Go."

He gave a curt nod and held his hand out to Sophie.

Together they walked in silence down the long corridor and to the cafeteria. The food selection wasn't great, but they each picked a salad and grabbed a couple of bottles of water. After they paid and sat, Christian made no attempt to eat.

She looked at him sympathetically. "Christian, this could be a long night. You need to eat."

But he shook his head and wouldn't meet her gaze. "I was mocking him."

"What?"

"While we were in the bar and he was rubbing his temple and slurring his words, I thought he was drunk. I was so angry, because I thought he'd come down to meet you that way. I was about to say something to him when you stepped in." He shook his head again. "I'm so ashamed."

"Christian—"

"It's true," he quickly interrupted, finally looking at her. "If something happens to him, that's what I'm going to remember—the fact that he was struggling and suffering from…from a stroke, most likely, and I sat there thinking he was drunk and being pissed at him!" He let out a long breath and raked a hand through his hair. They sat in silence for several long moments before he seemed to calm down. "Do you think that's what it is? A stroke?"

Wordlessly, she nodded.

With a curse, he shifted in his chair. "Is it possible to catch it before it gets worse or does any damage?"

And this was the part she hated. Strokes weren't something to take lightly and there was no way of knowing what lasting effects they might have—which was what she said to him. "The good news is that he was still responsive when we brought him in and he was able to speak. There was no paralysis and no drooping of his face. Those are good signs."

"But…?"

Straightening in her seat, she did her best to sort of detach herself from the situation and speak to Christian as she would any family member of a patient. "Okay, how much do you know about strokes?"

"Honestly? Not much."

"Okay, then let me give you a quick explanation."

He nodded.

Sophie explained to him what happened to the body when a stroke occurred. He asked questions and she answered as best she could. When she was done, Christian let out a slow whoosh of breath and nodded as he took it all in.

"Could it happen again?"

Solemnly, she nodded.

"The good news is that they're going to monitor him, Christian. They'll know when it happens and hopefully treat him before there is any damage. If he were home or asleep and it happened, time would be lost and damage would set in. So for now, the fact that he's here is a good thing."

Sophie looked at their salads. "We should eat. By now your mother is probably done with her calls."

She could tell he was thinking about everything she'd said.

"What time is Megan getting in? Do you want me to pick her up at the airport?"

"No," he said, his voice low and fairly devoid of emotion. "She's going to rent a car so she can get around easier while she's here."

"That makes sense." She took the lid off her salad, opened the dressing, and poured it on. "Will Alex be with her?" Christian smiled at her question. "What? What did I say?"

"You remembered."

She looked at him quizzically. "Remembered what?"

"It's just..." He paused, shaking his head and chuckling. "You remembered my family."

"Of course I remember your family. Why wouldn't I?"

He shrugged and looked away, embarrassed. Opening his own salad, he said, "I guess I can't remember a time when I was involved with someone who took the time to remember things like that."

"Or maybe you didn't share that part of yourself," she said lightly. Reaching out, she took one of his hands. "Either way, I'm thankful you took the time to share with me all about your family."

He let out a small snort. "Right. This must be great for you. First you save me from what we thought was a heart attack and then you help my dad while he's possibly having a stroke. At this rate, I wouldn't blame you if you didn't want to meet any other Montgomerys."

While he was saying it lightly and trying to play it off like it was a joke, she had a feeling there were some real doubts there. "Believe it or not, I feel blessed to have been there for both of those events." He began to protest, but she stopped him. "I know now that you were fine, but I was still glad I was there because that's just one of the things that got us here." She twined their fingers together and smiled. "And I don't mean here at the hospital—although that's true too—but I mean here as in this relationship. I have loved the time we've spent together, learning all about you, and I want to keep learning about you. Do you know what I mean?"

"I do," he said hoarsely. "I'm very thankful for you, Sophie, and I want you to know that I—" He stopped when his phone rang. Frantically, he released her hand and picked up the phone. "Mom?"

And even without listening, she knew they had to get back to the waiting room. Sophie closed up their salads and asked the cashier for a bag to pack it all up in, and then quickly picked up a bottle of water and a prepackaged turkey sandwich for Eliza. By the time she was done, Christian was sliding his phone into his pocket.

"Everything okay?" she asked.

"A nurse let her know someone would be out to talk to us soon, so..."

Sophie packed up the food as he spoke. When she was done, she looked at him and said, "Whatever the news is, we're going to get through it, right?"

He nodded, but he didn't look like he felt too confident about what they were going to find out. And honestly, she wasn't feeling too confident either.

Taking her hand, Christian led her out of the cafeteria and back to the waiting room. They sat on either side of Eliza and simply awaited the news.

It was almost midnight when Christian stood next to his father's hospital bed. So many emotions threatened to overwhelm him, but he did the only thing he could—breathe.

The man, the giant of a man who had made him into the person he was today, suddenly looked small and frail. It scared the hell out of him. His sister took his hand.

"C'mon, we should go," Megan whispered.

"Someone should stay here."

Megan let out a slow breath. "Chris, he's stabilized and sedated and he's going to stay that way until morning. We're no help to anyone if we're exhausted. I'm going to take Mom back to the hotel and stay with her. You and Sophie should go and we'll all meet back here in the morning."

He knew she was right, but it still felt wrong to leave. She gently tugged him away from the bed and reluctantly, he followed her out the door. The sight before him stopped him short—his mother was asleep on the sofa with her head on Sophie's shoulder and it looked as if she was asleep too.

His heart ached.

"I like her," Megan said softly. "I mean, I know I only got to talk to her for maybe ten minutes, but I feel like we'd be friends." She smiled at him.

And he couldn't believe it, but he smiled back. "You will be. Sophie's amazing."

"Good for you." Releasing his hand, Megan walked over to the sofa and carefully woke both women up.

Within minutes they were in the elevator and riding down to the lobby, quietly making plans to meet back there in the morning. He kissed his mother and sister on the cheek and watched as Sophie did the same. It didn't take long for them to get to his car and start the drive home.

Neither spoke.

Christian knew why he wasn't talking—there were too many thoughts in his mind that he was trying to come to grips with. Right now he appreciated Sophie's silence, because…well, he just needed it right now. As usual, she seemed to understand.

He didn't offer to take her home, but instead drove straight to his place. Together they walked inside where he didn't turn on any lights and simply led the way to his bedroom.

And still neither spoke.

Exhaustion—both mental and physical—had him going through the motions of stripping down to his boxers, tossing back the bedding, and sliding in. And Sophie was there right beside him two minutes later after slipping her dress off and grabbing one of his T-shirts to sleep in—a habit she'd taken up that he found adorable.

She pressed up against his side as he wrapped an arm around her to hold her close. Christian was certain he'd be able to close his eyes and instantly fall asleep, but that wasn't the case. He stared up at the ceiling for several minutes before he finally spoke.

"What do you think tomorrow will be like?" he asked, knowing that Sophie was still awake. There was a good chance she'd say something just to make him feel better but he had a feeling her need for honesty would win out.

"I wish I knew," she said after a moment. "They can do all kinds of scans to see if there's any damage to the brain, but until a patient is awake and they're able to evaluate them and speak to them, it's anybody's guess." She paused. "The good news is that he's stable."

It was an incredibly neutral response at best.

"Was it normal for them to sedate him?"

She nodded against his shoulder. "The doctor said your father was getting agitated at one point, so sedating him was really for his benefit." She paused. "There's a good chance that he'll wake up tomorrow, and other than maybe feeling a little weak, he'll be fine. He'll be monitored and put on medication like antiplatelets and anticoagulants and be able to go home in a couple of days." She raised her head and looked at him. "You'll be able to help him, since you recently experienced something similar. You can encourage him on how to eat better and exercise more."

Chuckling, Christian kissed her softly before guiding her head back down to his shoulder. "I can't even imagine anyone convincing Joseph Montgomery to change his life that much."

"He won't have a choice."

"The doctor tonight—Dr. Fordham—he mentioned surgery. So many options were mentioned that my head began to swim. Wouldn't that be dangerous?"

And right then he wanted to curse himself for not speaking up more at the hospital. In truth, three different doctors had come out and talked to them and mentioned multiple scenarios for his father's treatment and recovery, so it had been a lot to take in. Now he wished he'd asked more questions.

"Dr. Fordham said it was a possibility, and again, until they do more tests and your father wakes up, they're not committing to one form of treatment or another. One surgery was minimally invasive while the other was a little more complicated. For now, let's hope that when he wakes up, he's fine and shows no sign of permanent damage."

"I can't even imagine—"

Sophie shifted and placed a finger over his lips. "Shh…don't. Just don't even go there. Not now. Not tonight. Right now, we need to stay optimistic."

He knew she was right. But he also knew it was easier said than done. If there was one thing Christian struggled with, it was shutting his brain off and relaxing. Granted, he'd grown better at the relaxing part since Sophie had come into his life, but just like his mind was normally always on business, right now it was on his father and what tomorrow was going to bring.

Relax, relax, relax…

It took a moment for him to realize that Sophie's hand was gently caressing his chest. That in itself calmed him a bit. He let out a low, long breath and felt some of the tension leave his body.

Then she placed a lingering kiss on his shoulder.

"Mmm…" He made a throaty sound.

She shifted and kissed his chest.

I really do love that, he thought.

One kiss led to another and when he felt her soft tongue flick against his nipple, he practically bucked off of the bed. He hissed and anchored his hand into her hair. "Sophie…"

"Shh," she whispered. He gripped her hair tighter as

she moved over him until she straddled him with her thighs. He was afraid to even think that he was in love with her, but...now wasn't the time to think about that, because with what she was doing to him right now, he could believe it.

He loved what she did to him.

Loved the way she made him feel.

Unable to take it another minute, Christian quickly flipped Sophie over and kissed her deeply, his need for her so great that he growled into her mouth. Her limbs wrapped around him as she gave as good as she was getting, and that right there—her response to him—was something else that he loved.

And for right now, he refused to think beyond that.

For now, he was done thinking.

All he wanted to do was feel.

Chapter 9

"I KNOW I'M NOT A DOCTOR, BUT...THAT WASN'T GOOD, right?"

Christian didn't respond right away and kept walking toward the hospital lounge where everyone was waiting. But his brother's hand on his arm stopped him in his tracks.

"I don't want to discuss this in front of Mom," Carter said firmly but quietly. "Dad wasn't very responsive and it didn't seem like it had anything to do with him being sedated. He was awake but not there."

Raking a hand through his hair, Christian took a few steps away and then returned. "Yeah, that wasn't what I was expecting either." He muttered a curse. "I thought we'd go in there and he'd be...you know, himself."

"Why didn't Mom say anything when she came out? Why wouldn't she warn us?"

He shrugged because he honestly had no idea. His mother had been the first to go in—alone—and when she came out of the room, all she had said was "He looks good." Well, he didn't, Christian thought. He was pale and weak and unlike anything he'd ever seen.

"Uncle William and Uncle Robert are coming in today, right?"

"Yeah, they should be here after lunch," Christian said wearily. "What are we supposed to do? What do we say when we get back to the lounge?" He paused. "And I'm worried about Megan."

"Megan? Why? I would think you'd be more concerned for Mom."

"Mom's been in there and whether she's in denial or something, she seems okay. I think Megan's going to freak out a little when she goes in there."

"So one of us should go in with her," Carter said and then let out a long sigh. "I'll do it. You go and sit with Mom and Sophie and see when we'll get to talk to Dad's doctors."

It seemed like the best way to handle the situation, but it did little to ease Christian's mind. Within minutes Carter and Megan were heading to see Joseph and Christian was sitting on the sofa next to his mother.

"He looked good, didn't he?" Eliza was hopeful.

Christian took his mother's hand in his and gave her a small smile. "Did he talk to you while you were in there?"

She shook her head. "He's just tired. After all, they sedated him, and you know your father never sleeps more than five hours a night. His body doesn't know what to do when it's forced to relax." Pulling her hand carefully from his, she stood. "I'm going to call Monica and make sure their flight is still on time and maybe grab some coffee. I'll return soon."

When he went to stop her and remind her that his aunts and uncles were already in the air and on their way and most likely couldn't get phone calls, Sophie stopped him.

"Let her go," she said softly. "I think she needs time to herself. This is a lot to handle and she hasn't had any time alone since it happened. Either we've been with her or Megan has." She paused. "She'll be all right."

It made sense but still bothered him to watch his mother walk off by herself.

Sophie moved in close beside him on the sofa, resting her head on his shoulder. "I take it your father didn't look like you were expecting."

"How did you know?"

"It was written all over yours and Carter's faces when you came out," she said. "Plus, Megan had gone to the ladies room and while we were alone, your mother admitted it to me."

He muttered a curse. "Any word on when we're going to get to talk to the doctors?"

"At eleven. Dr. Fordham called your mother while you were in with your dad. He said he had rounds to do first and then he'd meet us here."

Nodding, he picked up her hand and kissed it. "I appreciate you being here, but I would understand if you needed to go. I know your hours are a little flexible, but you have clients today."

Lifting her head, she frowned at him. "I called the agency when you were in the shower earlier and told them there was a family emergency and I wouldn't be in today." She paused. "Would you prefer it if I left?"

"What? No," he replied quickly. "That's not it at all. I just know your job is important, and I don't want you to get into any trouble."

Cupping his cheek, she said, "Christian, you're important to me. I want to be here for you and your family. I'll understand if you think I'm overstepping or something or if your family would prefer it to just be them. They don't know me. So if it would be easier—"

He didn't give her a chance to say another word because he silenced her with a kiss. When he lifted his head, he rested his forehead against hers. "I want you here. I know my mother wants you here and my siblings feel the same way."

They sat in silence for several moments until Megan and Carter joined them.

"Where's Mom?" Megan asked.

"She wanted to get coffee and call Aunt Monica."

Megan looked at him curiously. "She knows Aunt Monica's on a plane, right?"

Christian shrugged. "I think she wanted a few minutes to herself."

Christian looked at his watch and calculated how long his mother had been gone. "Maybe we should all go to the cafeteria and get some coffee and join her."

No one argued and they all filed out of the lounge and down the hall. Christian reached for Sophie's hand and kept her close as they walked. They found Eliza in the cafeteria, sitting in the far corner by herself looking sadly out the large glass window.

His brother muttered under his breath about being irresponsible before stalking across the room. Christian was about to follow when Sophie held him back.

"Trust me, she needed the time alone," she assured him. "She'll be happy that you're all here now with her, but those few minutes to herself were important."

"How can you be so sure?"

"Back home, we didn't have a lot of extreme medical

cases, but there were a few times when we dealt with terminal illnesses. Family members were always there asking questions and wanting to help, but after a while some of the spouses just asked for privacy." She paused and looked in the direction of his mother, who was now smiling at something Carter was saying. "We all need a little time to think about what's going on and have a little peace and quiet to let it sink in."

Megan stepped up next to them. "I saw some muffins over in the case that looked fresh." She turned to Sophie. "Want to come with me and pick some out?"

"Ooo, muffins," Sophie said and then looked at him with a smile. "I'll grab you a blueberry one if they have them."

Leaning in, he kissed her and thanked her, watching as she and Megan walked away. Then he looked at his mother and brother, and with a weary sigh, headed toward them.

They stopped talking when he sat down. "What? What's going on?"

"Carter was asking when we should see about flying home so your father could be seen by his own physician."

It was hard not to roll his eyes. "Carter, one thing at a time. We need to get all of the test results and see when it's going to be safest for him to travel." He looked at his mother. "I want you to check out of the hotel and come stay with me. There's no reason for you to stay there by yourself."

"Hey," Carter said. "I'm staying there and so is Megan. She's not alone."

Was everything going to turn into an argument?

"Okay, fine." Then he smiled at his mother. "The offer is there should you want it."

"Thank you, Christian. Right now I'm just trying to take things a little at a time."

"You didn't offer me a place to stay," Carter murmured.

Sighing heavily, Christian looked at his brother. "Yes, I did. When we spoke yesterday, I said you could stay with me and you said you'd let me know. This is the first I'm hearing of you staying at the hotel."

"Boys," Eliza said wearily, "can't this discussion wait?"

They both immediately apologized.

"We've got muffins!" Megan said excitedly as she approached the table. It looked like she and Sophie had bought all of the muffins.

"Did you save any for anyone else?" he teased.

"Ha ha, very funny," she replied as she took a seat to his left, and Sophie sat to his right. While they divvied up muffins and Megan handed out coffees, the conversation was completely neutral. For a few minutes, it was as if life was normal.

He just wished it really was.

Eliza's phone rang and she frowned before answering. They all sat silently while she spoke. "Yes?... When?... Okay, we'll be right there." Sliding her phone into her purse, she stood. "Dr. Fordham wants to see us now." She looked nervously at them and took a steadying breath. "I don't know if I'm ready for this."

They all stood and huddled around her as Megan cleared the table. Sophie stopped her. "You all go on ahead. I've got this."

"Sophie, it's not a big deal," Megan countered. "Let me help."

But again, Sophie stopped her. "You guys need to hear what Dr. Fordham has to say. I'll be five minutes behind you. Go." It was said lightly and with a smile, and as his mother and siblings thanked her and walked away, Christian turned and kissed her quickly on the lips.

"Thank you."

She gave him a gentle nudge. "Go. I'll be there soon."

He hated leaving her there, but he was anxious to hear what Dr. Fordham was going to say. With one long look at her, he gave her a small smile and quickly took off after his family.

As they made their way back to the lounge, no one spoke. No doubt they were all lost in their own thoughts about the news they were going to hear. And right now, Christian had no idea what he was expecting. If he hadn't seen his father already, he would have said he was expecting a positive report, but being that he had seen him…

They were about to turn the corner that would lead to the lounge when his mother stopped.

"Mom?" he asked. "Are you okay?"

She sounded shaky as she turned and faced the three of them. "What if it's bad news? What if something's really wrong?"

"Mom," Megan began softly, "something is already wrong. Now we need to find out what happens from here."

"But that's just it," Eliza cried, her eyes going a little wide and wild. "What if there's more to it? What if it's something he can't recover from? I don't know what I'll do! I don't know how we'll handle it! What if—"

Carter grabbed her and wrapped her in his arms and did his best to soothe her. "It's going to be all right, Mom," he said calmly. "We're all here for you and it's going to be all right."

Christian wished he could sound so confident.

Or feel it even remotely.

"Whatever happens, Mom," Christian forced himself to say, "we'll get through it together."

And they walked into the lounge and collectively held their breaths.

Sophie didn't follow right away.

She got a bag to wrap up all of the food, then threw away the coffees and trash and sat for a moment. She'd meant what she said earlier about Eliza needing the time to herself, because that's what she needed right now.

Earlier, she had declined going in to see Joseph because she didn't want to take that time away from his family. She didn't know him and he didn't know her, so there was no reason to make him feel like he was on display for strangers. He was already dealing with that from the hospital staff.

Right now, she felt helpless. There wasn't anything she could do or say that was going to help the situation. She could listen, but that was starting to frustrate her. And as much as she wished she could tell the doctors she was a nurse and try to get some inside information, that didn't seem like something she should do. Not that anyone had asked her to, but… Okay, it was her own curiosity that was getting the better of her.

Sophie enjoyed helping others and right now she'd give anything to be able to help the Montgomerys and put their minds at ease about all that was going on with Joseph.

But she couldn't.

No doubt Dr. Fordham was explaining what the tests had shown and the damage they'd found to Joseph's brain. And then she knew that she needed to be with Christian—and not because she was a nurse who would be able to explain things to them or offer an opinion—but because she cared about him and wanted to be there to support him.

Grabbing her purse and the bag of food, she headed to the lounge. The closer she got to it, the more commotion she heard. There were alarms beeping, she could hear people scurrying around, and it made her heart ache. Somewhere, a patient was in crisis. Hurrying, she wanted to make sure she wasn't in anyone's way as she continued on to the lounge.

Turning the corner, she came to a stop as she saw Christian standing in the doorway and behind him, Megan hugging Eliza.

Oh no.

He caught sight of her and she could see the distress written all over his face. She raced over to him. "What happened?"

For a moment, he seemed too stunned to speak. "I…we…we don't know. We heard all kinds of beeping and alarms and a nurse came and called for Dr. Fordham."

Sophie looked over her shoulder and down the hall. "Maybe it's not—"

"It is," he said grimly. "I saw the team of people going into his room."

Gripping his hand, she squeezed it and walked into the lounge, putting her bags down before going over to hug Eliza.

The wait seemed endless. Christian eventually sat, but no one was speaking. So many questions raced through her mind—how much had Dr. Fordham told them before getting called away? Had they had a chance to even hear everything they needed to hear? How long were they supposed to sit here and wait before someone came in and talked to them?

Another fifteen minutes went by before Dr. Fordham returned.

His cautious look didn't give her much hope.

"We believe Joseph's had another stroke—this one worse than yesterday's. We're taking him for a CT scan and then for surgery."

"Surgery?" Eliza cried. "Why? Why would you need to do that?"

He spoke for several minutes about everything that could have happened in Joseph's brain in technical terms. Then he switched gears and tried to explain it in a way they'd understand. "There's pressure on the brain right now—which is what I started talking to you about earlier. And right before this stroke happened, the nurse who was taking his vitals said he was agitated and started grabbing his head." He paused. "There is a real possibility that this is a hemorrhagic stroke, and we need to treat it and relieve the pressure immediately."

They all started to ask questions, but he stopped them.

"That's all I can tell you right now. Until I see the scans, there's nothing I can say with any certainty." His look was grim as he added, "I'll send someone to give you updates when we have them." And then he was gone.

Eliza was crying, Carter was pacing, and Christian was sitting stiffly beside her. Sophie had no idea what to do or say.

A hemorrhagic stroke was not a good thing. Not that any stroke was a good thing, but this was particularly bad. Up to half of all people with an intracerebral hemorrhage died. Many within the first two days. For those who survived a brain hemorrhage, recovery was slow. Only a small percentage of people were able to recover complete or near-complete functioning within thirty days of the stroke.

Sophie hated that she knew those statistics. It wasn't the kind of information she wanted to share with any of them right now, because no matter how she tried to spin it, the news wasn't good.

"What time are Uncle William and everyone landing?" Carter asked, his voice low and rough.

"Around noon," Christian replied. "They have a car service picking them up and they're coming right here, I believe."

"Someone should call them," Megan said as she fought back tears. "Maybe they landed early. They should know what's going on."

Christian pulled out his phone and walked out of the room, and Sophie felt like she was intruding. She didn't want to be there without him even though she had been before. With this turn of events, she felt like an outsider suddenly.

"Sophie," Eliza said as she tried to compose herself, "did you understand everything Dr. Fordham told us?"

Slowly, she nodded. "I did."

"So what do you—"

"But here's the thing," she quickly interrupted before anyone could ask anything specific. "Until they do a CT scan, no one can say with any great certainty what's happening. For them to know there's a hemorrhage, they need the scan. And there are various degrees of hemorrhaging. The important thing right now is for them to relieve the pressure on his brain."

"So surgery is the only way to do that?" Megan asked.

"I believe so," Sophie said carefully. "I've never dealt directly with a situation like this. I'm only remembering scenarios from my textbooks, so please know I'm not someone with the answers. I can try to explain things, but we need to wait to hear from Joseph's medical team to know for sure what's going on."

Carter gave her a sharp look before leaving the room and Megan murmured about needing to call Alex before she walked over to the other side of the room—effectively leaving Sophie and Eliza alone. She immediately reached for the older woman's hand.

"I'm so sorry. I wish there was more I could say, but I am not an expert on any of this—it's far too serious for me even to be commenting on. I should have just kept my mouth shut."

Eliza wiped a tear away as she shook her head. "Nonsense. Listening to these medical professionals talk is overwhelming. I went to nursing school before I had children, but I don't remember much from it—and certainly nothing on this level." She let out a long breath. "But I'm not foolish enough to not realize how serious this is, and I hate it. I hate that something like this can happen without warning." She held in a sob.

"Eliza," Sophie said softly, "we need to be positive right now. It's going to be a long day and you're going to have to talk to a lot of people and listen to a lot of information that's even more overwhelming."

"I was snipping at him all afternoon," she said after a long moment. "The entire time after we left Christian's office I was nagging him about behaving himself at dinner."

Sophie couldn't help but let out a small chuckle. At Eliza's confused look, she said, "You should talk to Christian. He's struggling with the same thing. And I'm not laughing to make light of it, but it just struck me how similar the two of you are."

That brought a little smile to Eliza's face and for that brief moment, Sophie felt better.

After that, things got hectic. Carter came back into the room, but was talking on the phone to what Sophie assumed was one of his restaurants. He was barking orders about who was in charge and what needed to be done. She wished he would have taken the call in the cafeteria and away from patient rooms.

Next, Megan walked over and announced that Alex would be flying in that evening.

Then there was Christian. He looked a bit haggard and was hanging up when he entered.

"Did you get in touch with anyone?" his mother asked.

"They just landed," he replied. "They're going to

come here after dropping their luggage off at the hotel, but it will be about two hours before they're here."

That didn't sound like much time to Sophie, but no doubt everyone was anxious to be here for Joseph.

Taking a seat beside her, Christian's head fell back and he yawned loudly.

They were in for a long day.

"Walk with me."

Christian looked up and was surprised to see his uncle standing in front of him. Looking around the room, he saw everyone sitting and talking quietly and wondered when he had dozed off.

Slowly, he came to his feet. "Uncle William, when did you get here?"

"Just now. Robert and I came right here and let your aunts go to the hotel and check in. I thought it was important to get here as soon as possible." He motioned to the door. "Come on."

Christian looked over his shoulder as he walked to the door and Sophie gave him a reassuring smile, so he didn't feel bad about leaving her there.

Out in the hall, they began walking toward the cafeteria. "Your mother told me pretty much the same information you gave me on the phone."

"No one new has been by," Christian commented.

"I figured that," William said and then slowed his steps. They were in a stretch of the hallway where there weren't any patient rooms. He stopped and leaned against the wall. "How are you doing, Christian?"

"Honestly? I'm… I don't know. This all seems so

surreal. I mean one minute we were out having drinks, and the next…" He let his words die off.

William reached out and placed a hand on his shoulder. "We just have to pray for the best."

Christian knew it was the proper thing to say, but right now he wanted to vent and yell and—dammit, he was tired of trying to think and be upbeat.

"You're scowling pretty fiercely," his uncle stated mildly and then looked around. "Follow me."

They walked down the hall and into a stairwell, then to the ground level. It wasn't until they were outside that Christian felt like he could breathe.

"Okay, now let it out," William said.

"Excuse me?"

"You heard me. Let it out."

For years everyone had talked about how intuitive his uncle could be, but this was the first time he was experiencing it firsthand. "I don't know what you mean."

His uncle frowned. "You know, you're one of the most intelligent members of this family—and that's really saying something," he said. "Don't insult us both by playing dumb. You're angry. You're impatient. And in typical Montgomery fashion, you want answers and you want people to fall in line with what you want."

"That's not—"

"That's exactly it," his uncle snapped. "You know what? I'm angry at your father!"

Christian knew his eyes nearly bugged out of his head. "What?"

Nodding, William went on. "That's right. I am! For years I've tried talking to him about taking better care of himself. His blood pressure was sky-high, he didn't exercise, he never relaxed! He spent every waking moment in that office or talking on the phone for business, and for what?"

It was weird to hear someone else—other than Carter and Megan—saying these things.

"I love my brother," William said with a bit more calmness. "But maybe this all could have been avoided if he'd just listened! I have been trying for our whole lives to get him to try doing things another way, but he's always been stubborn." He snorted with disgust. "Of course, it didn't help that he refused to do things simply because I was the one to suggest them."

"What does that mean?"

"It means that your father and I have had a difficult relationship our entire lives. With me being older, he always thought I was trying to tell him what to do." Then he let out a low chuckle. "Which I usually was, but it was for his own good!"

Christian couldn't help but laugh a little too. "Dad never listens to anyone."

"Your father always felt like he lived in my shadow. Our parents always compared us and because I tended to live by the 'go big or go home' motto, it meant that he had to work that much harder to compete. But here's the thing—I never wanted that. I didn't do things so my brothers would have to keep up. I did them because I liked them."

"Then how did you all end up working together? I would think that you'd all do your own thing."

"Christian, you know this story by now. I started Montgomerys and when I wanted to expand, the first people I approached were my brothers. They were the best and the smartest businessmen I knew." He smiled. "And we did one hell of a job working together."

"Then how do you know Dad still felt that way?"

"Because he made it clear," William stated bluntly. "We'd talk about it all the time. One minute he'd be praising me on a job well done and the next he'd make a snarky comment about how I thought he'd never be able to beat me. It's exhausting."

"Tell me about it."

"But you? He is so damn proud of you."

Christian almost choked at those words. "Excuse me?"

William nodded. "It's true. He bragged all the time about every single deal you made, every new client you signed. I'm telling you, Robert and I used to roll our eyes a little bit because your father was such a braggart."

"But…that's not possible," Christian argued. "He was constantly riding my ass and never once did he tell me that I was doing anything right! He'd criticize and tell me how I should have done things differently. Better! So…you're wrong. Or you're saying things to make me feel better."

William studied him.

"And you know what? I don't deserve to feel better!" Christian shouted as he paced. "My relationship with my father is hopeless! While he was sitting there having a damn stroke, I thought he was drunk and I was cursing him in my head. That's the relationship we have. He accused me of faking my trip to the hospital as a way of shirking my responsibilities, and I was ignoring what was happening to him!"

His heart was racing like mad as he stopped speaking.

Hands on his hips, Christian tilted his head and looked up at the sky.

"I had no idea," William said solemnly. "I guess I saw how the two of you were always a little tense around one another, but I attributed that to the fact that you were maybe talking business or that you had the same drive to succeed as he did."

Christian let out another long breath. "There was never an option, Uncle William. I had to succeed. I had to work hard." He paused. "I never got the chance to choose what I wanted to do with my life."

Shame washed over him again. His father was inside fighting for his life and here he was speaking ill of him. What kind of son did that make him? Which was what he asked his uncle.

"I think what you're feeling right now is not only natural but expected. Just because someone is ill doesn't mean we forget their faults. At least, that's how I look at it." Turning, William sat on one of the benches next to the entrance. "The important thing to remember, Christian, is that we're all human. We all have our faults. No one is perfect."

"You don't understand—"

"I'm not excusing my brother's behavior, trust me. But you need to know there's a lot of history behind his behavior. I'm just sorry your relationship suffered because of it. If I'd known…"

"It would have driven even more of a wedge between the two of you," Christian said sadly, sitting on the bench beside his uncle. "I don't know how to feel right now. I'm angry at myself, I'm angry at him. I feel guilty that I never seemed to measure up."

"But you did," William reminded him.

Shaking his head, Christian said, "I didn't. He said all those great things to you to make himself look better. To brag to you that he had a son who was maybe doing better than your sons." He shrugged. "But all he told me was how much of a disappointment I was."

William patted Christian's knee. "And when he wakes up and gets better, this is something we'll all have to talk about. You know his recovery will be long and we're all going to be spending a lot of time with him. Maybe the two of you will finally clear the air and have the relationship you always wanted."

It sounded so easy.

Too easy.

And right now, it seemed like too much to ask for. So rather than keep harping on the whole thing, he opted to change the subject. "Are you staying at the Marriott too?"

"Yes. We thought it best so we can be there with Eliza." He looked at his watch. "Your aunts should be here soon. I think they'll be a great distraction for your mother."

"She's been holding herself together better than I expected. Of course it helped that Megan came in last night and stayed with her and now Carter's here too."

"And then there's your Sophie."

At the mention of her name, Christian smiled.

"Beautiful girl," William commented. "And from what I've heard, she's been a great help during this whole thing. A nurse! What luck, huh? First for you and now with Joseph." He laughed softly. "She certainly came into the family at the right time."

"I'm not so sure about that. I'm afraid that she's going to run for the hills because we're too much work."

"Nonsense," William said. "Monica raved about her when she came home from visiting with you. That girl is a natural caregiver and I think she enjoys being able to help out where she's needed. And it's not like she's had to step up and actually be a caretaker to you—or Joseph. It's been a case of being in the right place at the right time."

"Maybe."

"Definitely." He pulled his phone from his pocket and swiped the screen. "Your aunts are on the way. If you don't mind sitting with me for a little longer, I'd like to wait here for them."

"Sure," he said with a small smile.

William looked him over. "You're a good son, Christian. And you're a gifted businessman. And more than that, you're a good nephew. Never forget that."

While the words were meant to soothe and compliment, Christian couldn't help but wish they had come from his father.

So this is what a large family is like…

The Montgomerys had taken over one corner of the cafeteria and she was surprised at how much everyone talked and laughed and how even during this emotional time, they were able to carry on like this.

Her whole life it had just been her and her nana and the few relatives they had—most of whom were older than Sophie. And she could never remember a time when there were this many of them together being so chatty.

Joseph was out of surgery, but it hadn't gone well. He'd crashed twice on the operating table and right now it was touch-and-go. Eliza had opted to get the news alone—with only William and Robert with her. That had caused Christian, Carter, and Megan to get upset. And when the elder Montgomerys had come back out looking grim, they'd only given the bare minimum of information.

Sophie had to admit that she was mildly intrigued and felt like there was something no one wanted to talk about.

Curious.

What she was discovering about this family was that Uncle William was a charmer, where Uncle Robert was much more reserved. It was almost hard to believe they were brothers except that they looked so much alike. Janice Montgomery was very sweet and had been doting on Eliza since she arrived. Sophie felt drawn to her because she appreciated Janice's giving nature. And Monica had taken her seat next to Eliza and kept her hand in hers since the moment she sat down. Sophie warmly recalled watching the two of them laughing on the beach the morning they'd met, and it was sweet to see that there was such a deep bond there.

Megan was already someone Sophie knew was going to be a great friend. She wished they had met under different circumstances, but they were already talking about things they'd like to do together once Joseph was out of the woods and recovering. Sophie couldn't wait to meet Alex—Megan's fiancé, who was really her husband since they had secretly eloped. She'd been warned not to bring that up in front of the rest of the relatives. Alex was arriving later on in the day.

Next to her, Robert asked Christian if he wanted Ryder to come and help out at the office. She held her breath waiting to hear his response, because she knew that was a sore spot back when Christian had to take time off after his anxiety attack.

"That would be great, Uncle Robert. If Ryder doesn't mind, I would appreciate the help."

Color her surprised.

Robert stood and walked away to make the call, and Sophie turned her attention to Uncle William sharing a story about when he and his brothers were younger and starting their business.

She couldn't help but smile. This whole dynamic was new to her and she was enjoying observing everyone, learning the different personalities and hearing their stories. It would be great to hear more about Christian and what his life was like growing up—something light and fun that didn't focus on the stress he'd felt at the hands of his father.

He was holding her hand with a serene smile on his face as he listened to his uncle talk, and she wished she knew what was going on in his mind. Was he putting on a good show for his family and secretly obsessing about work? At that moment, Christian turned his head and looked at her. He was smiling but it didn't quite reach his eyes. Unable to help herself she smoothed a hand along the side of his face.

"How are you doing?" she asked softly.

Shrugging, he said, "As good as can be expected. I

hate waiting. I wish we knew more, and I'm still annoyed that my mother didn't let us hear what Dr. Fordham had to say."

"I know you're anxious, but you have to know that she's not even aware of which way is up right now. Since your uncles are here, maybe she thought it best if they went with her. They *are* his brothers."

"And we're his children," he said with a hint of annoyance before instantly apologizing. "Sorry. I shouldn't be taking this out on you, love."

Before she could say anything, Megan slid closer and leaned in. "I need to get some air. I'm getting a little stir crazy."

"Aren't you the one who used to live in your cubicle eighteen hours a day?" Christian teased.

She gave him a bland look. "Not in a very long time. Alex has gotten me all...you know, outdoorsy. Now I find that I like being outside more than I ever have in my life."

Christian chuckled. "Outdoorsy? Really?"

Holding up a hand, she ignored him and looked at Sophie. "Come on. Walk outside with me for a little bit? Please?"

How could she possibly say no? Squeezing Christian's hand, she gave him a sweet smile. "I'm outdoorsy too. Kindred spirits here." Then she laughed and kissed him on the cheek. "Be back in a bit."

It wasn't until they were alone and leaving the cafeteria that Megan spoke.

"Okay, I have to ask this—but don't be afraid to tell me no and I swear I won't be offended."

"Um... Okay."

They stopped just outside of the cafeteria doors. "Someone crashing twice on the operating table isn't a good sign, is it? I mean, that's really bad."

Damn. "Megan, without having heard what the doctor said, I don't want to speculate. I don't want to speak out of turn or…or…"

Sighing loudly, Megan slouched against the wall. "I know. I know. Sorry. I shouldn't have even asked."

"It's okay, and for what it's worth, I get it. I'd want someone to tell me too."

With a weak smile, Megan pushed away from the wall and continued to walk in silence until they were outside. There was a small park next to the hospital and that's where they decided to head.

"It's so weird," Megan said, sitting down on a swing. Sophie took the one next to her. "I've always thought of my father as infallible. He's always been this giant of a man and although he's always been a bit of a tyrant, I never imagined something like this happening." She paused. "I guess it's hard to imagine anything happening to our parents, right?"

A knot of dread formed in Sophie's belly. This was so not a discussion she wanted to be a part of. Instead of answering, she made a noncommittal sound.

"I'm trying to imagine what will happen when he wakes up and what his recovery will be like," Megan continued, unaware of the distress Sophie was feeling. "If he has to go into a rehabilitation facility, he'll hate it. I know a lot of times there's paralysis involved after a stroke and he'll give any therapist hell." Then she laughed softly and faced Sophie. "Alex is a physical therapist and I don't think there'd be any way I'd be able to convince him to take my dad on as a client."

Sophie laughed with her but still said nothing.

"But I'll feel better talking to him about Dad's treatment. We'll know if something is working or if there are other options to try." She sighed. "Either way, I think it's going to be a long road to recovery and I hate it for him."

After several moments of silence, Megan studied Sophie. "You're being very quiet. Am I talking too much? Are you tired of hearing about my dad? I know you don't even know him, and hell, you and Christian haven't been dating all that long, so this is an awkward situation for you to be in, right?"

"No," she quickly assured. "That's not it at all. It seemed like you needed to talk, so I was letting you."

The look Megan gave her showed she didn't quite believe her, but she didn't say it. Instead, she changed the subject. "So you got my stuffy, uptight brother to break out a bit, huh?"

That made Sophie laugh. "I'd like to think Christian is enjoying himself, but it's all so new. I can't help but wonder how long it will be before he starts feeling the pressure to work more."

Megan groaned. "Unfortunately, I think this whole situation with my dad may cause him to regress. But don't let it happen! You have to promise me that you'll force him to stay on this course and not live at the office."

"That's really kind of out of my hands, but—"

Megan swung toward her and grabbed the chain holding Sophie's swing. "No, you need to promise me on this. I can see what a difference you've made in his life, and I know if I was here visiting under different circumstances, we'd be out having a great time! I know my brother and I know how he thinks. My father has thrown plenty of guilt on him and I know that's got to be playing on his mind right now, but we can't let that happen."

"Megan…"

Megan swung away. "Just—just at least promise that you'll try." She looked at her pleadingly. "Please."

Nodding, Sophie said, "I'll try."

They swung back and forth a few more times. "We should probably get back in there. I'm afraid to stay away for too long."

"I'm sure if they got any updates, someone would have called or texted you." Standing, she waited for Megan to do the same and was surprised when Megan grabbed her and hugged her.

"Thank you."

"For what?"

"For listening," Megan said as she pulled back. "I know there's my whole family in there and we've been doing nothing but talking, but…it's all superficial talking. Everyone's trying to keep Mom's spirits up and I think that's great. But eventually we're going to have to talk about what's going on."

"Well, until we know for sure what's going on, it's all just speculation. I think once your father comes out of recovery and the doctors can do more scans and tests, the real conversations will begin."

"I guess you're right." They started to walk back to the hospital. "So what about you?"

Sophie looked at her oddly. "What about me?"

"What's your family like? Do you have any siblings?"

"Oh…um…" She was saved from answering when they ran into Carter out on the sidewalk.

"Is everything all right?" Megan asked.

He looked tense and angry and didn't say anything at first—almost as if he was surprised to see them both there.

"Is it Dad? Is there an update? Is he awake?" When he still didn't say anything, Megan grabbed him by the shoulders and shook him. "Dammit, Carter! What's going on?"

"Mom dropped a bombshell and I had to get out of there," he said with a huff, stepping out of her grasp.

"What? What did she say?"

"Apparently, Dad's been sick for a while. Cancer." He stopped and cursed, pacing a few steps away and then back again. "*Cancer!* And no one thought to say anything!"

"How? Why?"

"And he's got a DNR that was suspended during the surgery, but now that he's out, it's back in play! I mean…this is crazy!"

All Sophie could think about was getting to Christian and with a muttered "excuse me," she went in search of him.

It was late—well after midnight—and Christian couldn't sleep. The day had been beyond exhausting, and as much as he tried to hold it together for his mother's sake, he wasn't very successful.

Once his father had been moved to ICU, the doctors all confirmed that it would be best to go home for the night. Everyone had gone to the hotel and had dinner together, but Christian was done with playing nice and being social. He was tired, he was angry—even more so after his mother's big cancer reveal—and all he'd wanted was to go home and be alone.

Well, not entirely alone.

He wanted Sophie with him.

They'd stopped at her apartment, where she'd grabbed a change of clothes and picked up her car and then followed him back to his house. Once there, they'd gone for a long walk on the beach. Honestly, he wanted to get back in the car and just drive, and keep driving until they were far away from home and his family and everything he was dealing with. Running away had never been his style—except for the London incident—but right now it was looking mighty appealing.

The walk had done a lot to calm him down. Not once did either of them bring up the current situation and instead talked about neutral topics, even started making plans for what they wanted to explore and experience next.

Hot air balloons in Napa.

Go figure.

The look of pure delight on Sophie's face when he agreed to go was quite possibly the greatest thing ever. He loved being able to make her laugh and smile and knew she probably hadn't had a whole lot to laugh and smile about in her life. And that had him thinking about her—really thinking about her. Before this crisis with his family hit, she was dealing with one of her own. The two situations weren't anything alike and yet…there was one similarity.

Their fathers.

Right now, knowing that his father was in grave condition, Christian couldn't help but think of all the things he wished were different—the questions he had, now that he knew more from his uncle. Once Joseph was well enough to talk, that was something they were going to do. They were both getting older and life was too short to keep living with such animosity. The air needed to be cleared and their relationship still had a chance to be fixed.

But what about Sophie's?

In the beginning, she'd been fairly adamant about not seeing her father—she didn't *want* to see him. Then she started questioning that decision and wondering if maybe she should go just for her own peace of mind and to finally get the answers that she wanted. She'd waffled, and still hadn't made a decision.

Sighing, he shifted and hugged her closer. She was sound asleep and had been for well over an hour. After their walk, they'd come inside and had some popcorn and wine while they watched some TV before coming up to bed. Sophie read for a while; Christian had his laptop and had checked emails and read some of the news in hopes of putting himself to sleep.

Nothing had worked.

So now what? Count sheep?

Another sigh.

His phone was on the nightstand and he thought about texting his brother. Things had grown tense earlier in the day and they hadn't had a chance to sit and talk alone like Carter and Megan had. And the only reason he knew they had was because Sophie had told him when she'd come in after their walk. Now he wanted to talk, but he didn't want to wake her up.

Waking his brother up wasn't a concern.

He eyed his phone again and groaned. He was comfortable, somewhat relaxed, and the thought of getting up wasn't as appealing as he thought it would be. Beside him, Sophie snuggled closer and sighed softly. Unable to help himself, he kissed the top of her head and she hummed in her sleep. He loved the sounds she made. He loved the feel of her. Hell, he loved her. And if his life wasn't such a colossal mess right now, he'd totally wake her up and tell her.

Soon.

Things would return to normal soon and then he would do it.

Making that one little decision seemed to relax him more than he'd thought it would. Settling into his pillow a little deeper, he gave Sophie a gentle hug and one more kiss.

Talking to Carter could wait until the morning. Closing his eyes, Christian yawned and finally let himself fall asleep.

Only to be woken up an hour later by the ringing of his phone. Groggy, he reached for it without being able to open his eyes enough to see on the screen who was calling.

"H'lo?" he said, his voice a gruff whisper.

"Chris...we need to get to the hospital." It was Carter.

"What happened?" he asked, instantly awake.

"He's gone."

Chapter 10

"MAY YOU BE AT EASE. MAY YOU BE FREE FROM suffering. May you be healed. May you know joy and lightness of being. May you dwell in comfort and compassion. May you be a source of comfort and compassion for all whom you meet. Go in peace." The minister looked out at the group of people surrounding Joseph Montgomery's casket and said, "Amen."

All around, Christian heard people say "Amen" before coming forward to offer their condolences. They were graveside at the same cemetery in upstate New York where his grandparents were buried, and just like then, it was a cold, gray day.

It had been seven days since he'd received the phone call from his brother, and for most of that time he'd felt like he was simply walking around in a daze. He didn't remember much about the drive to the hospital—Sophie had taken him. The days that followed were sort of a blur because there were so many details to deal with. The logistics of getting his father back to New York to be buried turned out to be more of a nightmare than he had thought possible.

He stood stiffly, staring at the casket that was going to be lowered into the ground once they were all gone, and felt numb. How did this happen? And why now? Why, when there had finally been a chance that they could have talked and maybe worked through their issues, did this have to happen?

So many people came over and shook his hand or hugged him while they shared a kind word about his father, and all he could do was nod. He was certain that later on he wouldn't even be able to remember who had been here or who he'd spoken to. Faces blurred together and their words all sounded the same.

Before he knew it, the funeral director was ushering the immediate family back to the limos to take them home to his parents' house. But Christian didn't move.

"Chris?"

He turned and looked at his brother. "I need some time."

"Mom wants to get back to the house. We can't keep the car here for much longer."

And while he knew that made sense, it still angered him. Wasn't he allowed to grieve as well? Wasn't he entitled to take an extra minute or two to say goodbye?

When he still didn't move, Carter walked closer and let out a huff of annoyance. "Let me make sure Mom's okay and then I'll come back for you."

He nodded. "Thanks."

"It's going to be about an hour. You sure you want to do this?"

"I need to." Then he turned and looked toward the line of cars. "Where's Sophie?"

"She's in the car with Mom, Megan, and Alex. Do you want me to ask her to stay with you?"

"No. Just…just tell her I'll be back at the house later." Then he turned to the casket that was strewn with flowers and swallowed the lump in his throat.

Carter's hand clasped him on the shoulder and squeezed. "I'll be back as soon as I can."

Christian waited until he couldn't hear any more cars and the air around him was still. There were chairs set up from the service, but he opted to stand, hands clasped in front of him.

"I know you never liked the phrase, but right now it's the only one I can think of—it's not fair. Things were coming to a head. I know that. But now we'll never know how it would have worked out." He paused and forced himself to breathe through the emotions that were threatening to overwhelm him.

"I did everything you ever asked of me. I studied hard, worked hard, and tried to be everything I could to make you proud. But it was never enough." His voice cracked and he felt the sting of tears, and even that made him angry. "Do you see what you've created here? What you've done? A normal son should be able to stand here and openly grieve for his father and yet I'm standing here fighting with myself and my emotions because you always said that crying made you weak. Well, I'm not weak!" he called out. "I have never been weak and I resent that you made me feel that way!"

A car drove down the small road that went through the middle of the cemetery and he waited until it was out of sight before he continued.

"I'm good at what I do, and on top of that, I'm a good person. Just once, I wish you would have acknowledged that and told me you were proud of me. I hated hearing Uncle William say you bragged about me, because I know exactly why you did it—it wasn't to praise me, it was for yourself, to make you look good."

Sighing loudly, he finally sat down on one of the chairs. Resting his elbows on his knees, he sank his fingers into his hair. When he looked at the casket, he knew he was never going to get answers. He was never going to know why Joseph Montgomery had chosen to put so much pressure on his oldest son or if there was ever anything Christian could have done to earn his praise or approval.

"It's like you got the last word without saying a thing," he said quietly. "I hate that our last conversation was spent picking at one another. I hate that you didn't get to see how happy I am and what a great girl Sophie is." Then he let out a mirthless laugh. "And it doesn't matter that she works at Montgomerys part time, Dad. She's amazing. She's caring and funny and kind... Honestly, I don't feel like I even deserve her. But you know what? For some reason, she cares about me and it feels so damn good to have her in my life. Her lightness and her honesty and...she gives me hope."

A cool wind blew and he shivered. Maybe waiting an hour wasn't the smartest thing to do, but he had needed this time. There were so many things he'd never have the chance to say, so many issues left unresolved. It was funny how he'd always thought there'd be more time—had actually felt optimistic about it while his father had been in the hospital—and now he knew with great finality that there wasn't.

Now he had to worry about how his mother was doing and remember not to let so much time pass between the times they spoke. He'd make sure he called his siblings more and took an active interest in their lives. There were cousins to reach out to and keep in touch with, friends that he'd been meaning to call. The list was endless, and right now it was starting to feel like a daunting task. On top of all that, he had to work. Needed to work.

Who was going to run his father's office? Who was going to handle his affairs? Who was going to help his mother sort through it all? Granted, it didn't all have to fall on Christian's shoulders, but a fair amount of it would.

And here he was.

Taking on the bulk of it in his own head before anyone had even said a word.

"Do you realize how neurotic you've made me?" he asked out loud, glaring at the casket. "I swear, it's like I have no idea how to just sit and relax without worrying about stuff that I think you'll judge me on! Even from the grave I know you'll be doing it!"

And he was back on his feet.

But one look at the large display of floral arrangements—particularly the one at the head of the casket that read Rest in Peace—and all the fight went out of him.

"You're lucky," he grumbled. "You do get to rest in peace now, while I'll spend the rest of my life wondering what it was that I did so wrong." Walking around the casket, he looked at all of the flowers, read each of the cards attached to them, and when he was done, he sat down and waited for his brother to return.

Christian had no idea how long he sat there, but the sun was going down and the temperature felt like it had dropped significantly when he spotted Carter's rental car pulling in. He didn't move, but stayed where he was, slouched in the chair, arms folded, staring at the intricate design on the side of the casket.

A few minutes later, Carter was beside him, mimicking the pose. "Feel any better?"

"Nope."

They were silent for a moment. "I thought I'd feel different."

Christian turned his head and looked at Carter. "What do you mean?"

"I thought I'd be relieved—like all the years of him bitching at everything and being a damn know-it-all on every topic would finally be over and we'd all be able to breathe easily." He paused. "But it's not like that. It's—it's worse."

"Tell me about it."

His brother looked at him and shook his head. "Sorry. Who am I to be saying anything. He was hardest on you, and no doubt a lot of shit's going to get dumped on you now."

He shrugged. "That's what I figure too. And I'm already dreading it."

"Damn."

"Yup."

More silence.

"How was Mom when you got home? Is she okay?" Christian asked.

"There were so many people there, so it was a good distraction. There's a ton of food, and I think for now she's got enough to keep her busy. I think tonight will be rough and the next few days. After that? It's anyone's guess."

And still more silence.

"What about Sophie?" He muttered a curse. "I shouldn't have left her like that."

"Relax. Last I checked, Sophie was sitting in the family room with all of our cousins' wives and Megan. And before you ask, she was smiling and holding her own, so you don't have anything to worry about."

That didn't make him feel better.

But it didn't make him jump up and go either.

Finally, Carter nudged him in the shoulder. "I don't know about you, but I'm freezing. I'm not used to these cold temperatures anymore."

"I thought you were building one of your restaurants here in New York."

"I am, but the majority of mine are in warmer climates." He shrugged. "And besides, nothing's written in concrete. After this chilly reminder, I may change my plans."

And right then and there, it was the perfect distraction—something to talk about that wasn't about death and unwanted responsibilities. For a little while, it would be nice to talk about what was going on in his brother's life and put his own life and worries on hold.

"Is it wrong that I think this is completely weird?"

Sophie couldn't help but giggle. They'd been joking about it for three nights—how they were sleeping in his childhood room, his childhood bed. It was a full-sized one, so it was definitely cozy, but the room still looked like a teenage boy lived there.

A scholarly teenage boy.

There were trophies on the shelves, a collection of

science fiction novels, and multiple model airplanes. There wasn't a trace of anything silly or frivolous, and that made her a little sad. Before she could think on that thought any further, Christian tugged her close under the blankets and gave her a loud, smacking kiss on the top of her head.

"I'm sorry I left you alone today," he said quietly.

They'd been over this at least a dozen times already. She understood what he needed to do, and really, she was fine hanging out with his family. The more Montgomerys she met, the more she found to love.

Apparently, the news of Christian having a girlfriend was a big deal, and they were all curious. Not that Sophie minded talking to them—they weren't looking at her like she was an oddity or talking in a disparaging way against Christian. They were genuinely concerned about him and happy that he was dating someone.

Her.

Just the thought of how they had welcomed her and treated her like she was an old friend or part of the family made her smile.

"The lights may be off, but I swear I can feel you smiling," Christian said. "You think it's funny that we're sleeping in my room, don't you?"

"You know that I do," she teased. "We've already covered that. Multiple times too, might I add."

"Then what are you smiling about?"

She supposed it was odd to be smiling on a day that was filled with sadness, but…

"I was thinking about your family."

He groaned.

Instantly, she leaned up on her elbow so she could at

least try to see him in the dark. "Don't even go there," she said. "Your family has been incredibly sweet and friendly. I have loved getting to know everyone, and today Megan and all of your cousins welcomed me into the fold."

"I hate that I put you in an awkward position," he argued.

"Christian, it's okay. I didn't have a chance to feel even remotely awkward because your sister and your mother were busy introducing me to people. I'm telling you, it reminded me a little bit of the socials we used to have at church. By the end of any event, there were no strangers. Everyone knew everyone."

"You're far too forgiving," he said, pulling her down to rest her head on his shoulder. She loved when he did that.

"Can I ask you something?"

"Sure," he replied and then yawned.

"Did it help?"

"Did what help?"

"Staying at the cemetery. I mean, I figured you wanted to be there to maybe make sure everything was done properly by the funeral home."

He let out a long breath. "That wasn't why I stayed."

"Then why would you...?"

"I had some things I wanted to say and for some reason, I felt like I needed to do it before he was...you know...in the ground."

"Oh, Christian." She hugged him tight and her heart ached for him. "I had no idea."

"I never imagined my father dying so young. So soon." He paused. "For that short time he was in the hospital, I kept telling myself that when he got better, we'd clear the air and have the relationship I always wanted to have. It was right there within my grasp and then…it wasn't."

Tears stung her eyes and as much as she willed them not to fall, they still did.

"I stood there and just…talked. Well, at one point I yelled, but I had so much I needed to say. Not that I was going to get any answers."

"I know how much you wanted that—the reconciliation. I hate that you'll never get the chance."

"It's not even reconciliation. I think I would have been happy just finding out…why. Why was he so hard on me? Why wasn't anything I ever did enough?"

They both lay silently until Sophie felt him relax and his breathing slowed and evened out. She knew he hadn't been sleeping well—and not nearly enough. With any luck, he'd finally let himself sleep tonight.

She snuggled closer and relaxed, closing her eyes. She was almost asleep when he whispered, "Don't wait, Sophie. If you have the chance to get your answers, you should do it."

There wasn't a doubt in her mind what he was referring to.

"Right now, I would kill for just one hour. Hell, five minutes more to just…say what I needed to say, ask the questions I needed to ask. And now I'll never have the chance."

"Christian, it's not the same."

He was quiet for a moment and she thought he was through—that he understood what she meant.

"Don't you want to know why?" he asked after a

minute. "It's not going to change anything, I know that, but can you honestly say that you're going to be fine for the rest of your life without ever knowing why he did what he did? What went wrong? And if he regrets it? Does he ever think about you and wonder if you're okay?"

Those were all the things she wanted to know.

And so much more.

It wasn't as easy as just deciding to go talk to the man. There were so many things she needed to take into consideration for her own sanity and right now was not the time to get into it. It was late, she was tired, and she knew that Christian needed to sleep.

Placing a soft kiss on his chest, she said, "We'll talk about this tomorrow. Get some rest."

And this time when she closed her eyes, she said a silent prayer that he'd be willing to drop the subject.

The next time she opened her eyes, the sun was up, and she was alone in the bed. Rolling over, Sophie looked at the bedside clock and saw it was after nine. Wow, she must have been more tired than she thought. She had to wonder how early Christian got up.

"Not going to worry about that right now," she said as she stretched. Reaching over to the table on her side of the bed, Sophie picked up her phone and fluffed her pillows. Relaxing, she pulled up her nana's phone number and hit Send.

"There's my girl," Nana said when she answered the phone. "How are you doing? How's Christian?"

Sophie had kept Nana up-to-date on what was going on and was surprised at how compassionate she was being. Before Joseph's death, she had been feeling a little less than friendly toward Christian and their relationship, but something about him losing his father caused Nana to soften toward him. Whatever the reason, Sophie would take it. It made their conversations a lot less snarky.

"Yesterday was sad," she began. "The service was beautiful and there were so many people who came to pay their respects."

"That's nice. I'm sure his wife was comforted by all of her friends and family."

"She seemed to be, but she's got a lot to deal with now that the funeral is over. It's not any of my business, but I know she's worried about whether or not she wants to stay here or sell the house and move closer to one of her kids."

"Doesn't she have any family there in New York?"

"I think so, but she seems to be leaning toward wanting to be near either Christian or Megan."

"Isn't there another son? Charles? Carl? Something like that?"

Sophie chuckled. "Carter. But he travels a lot. He doesn't have a home base, so to speak."

"Well, that's just sad."

It was too much to think about right now. "So what about you? What are you up to today?"

With one of her famous weary sighs, Nana replied, "You know, nothing much. There isn't a whole lot for an old lady to do. I'll probably go sit in the park and feed the birds. Or maybe I can stay home and refold all of the towels. You know how messy they can get."

Rolling her eyes, Sophie got a little more comfortable in the bed. "Towels can be unruly," she teased. "Good for you for looking out for that."

"Oh, you're no fun."

"You realize these theatrics don't work, right? I know darn well that you're more than likely going to go to the senior center for mahjong today. And if it isn't that, you'll do chair yoga. You've never fed the birds and you fold your towels with military precision, so knock it off," she said with a laugh.

"Fine." Nana paused. "When do you head back to San Diego?"

"Later today. I couldn't take any more time off."

"Is Christian flying home with you?"

"No, he can't. He needs to stay here and help his mother with some things. He's going to take me to the airport after lunch. My flight is at three."

"I don't like the idea of you flying alone," Nana said, and Sophie could hear the disapproval in her voice.

"I'll be fine. And I'm not completely going it alone. Christian's brother-in-law is flying out today too, so we'll have each other to hang out with at the airport, at least."

"Promise you'll call me as soon as you land and then again when you get home so I know you arrived safely."

Unable to help herself, she smiled. "I will. I promise."

They talked about Sophie's job and about all of the Montgomerys she'd met before hanging up. Just as she was kicking the blankets off, Christian walked into the room carrying a cup of coffee.

"Hey," she said as she stood. "Good morning."

He kissed her slowly and thoroughly before handing her the mug. "Good morning. Did you sleep okay?"

She took a sip of her coffee and nodded. "I did. How about you? You were up early?"

"Not too early. It was about eight when I slid from the bed. I wanted a little time to talk to my mother before everyone got up. Neither Carter nor Megan are particularly morning people, so I figured as long as I got up before them, I'd be okay."

"And did you? Talk to your mom, I mean."

"A little. She was tired and seemed distracted. I didn't want to bombard her with a lot of questions quite so early in the morning. Uncle William and Uncle Robert are coming over later today to help me go over some things."

"Oh, well…I don't want to interrupt that, so if you need to stay and meet with them, Megan can drive us to the airport. It's not a big deal."

Carefully, Christian took the mug from her hand and put it on the nightstand and then cupped her face in his hands. "Sophie Bennington, when are you going to realize that you are not a bother, you're not interrupting, and that you're not in the way? Everyone knows I'm taking you to the airport today."

"And Alex…"

He chuckled. "And Alex." Then he placed a light kiss on the tip of her nose. "We don't have a formal schedule here and there's nothing that we're going to look at today that can't wait for me to get back."

"I know, but I'm sure you're anxious."

One strong finger pressed against her lips. "You are not talking me out of this. As it is, I hate that you're leaving without me. I understand why, but I don't like it. As of right now, I don't even know when I'll be back." Sighing, he rested his forehead against hers. "I'm going to miss you."

"I'm going to miss you too. But we're going to talk

every day and I promise to check on your place when I go surfing."

Another soft chuckle. "So you're going back to that since I'm not there to bother you, huh?"

She laughed with him. "You never bothered me. But I need to have something to do to keep me from going crazy without you."

He groaned and captured her lips with his. The kiss was carnal, and if they weren't in his parents' home, in his childhood room, she'd totally drag him onto the bed and make good on everything that kiss promised. But this wasn't the time or the place for that. When they broke apart, they were breathless.

"Well, if that doesn't motivate me to hurry through all this legal stuff, nothing will."

Sophie playfully swatted him away and turned to pick up her coffee. "Anyway, I'll check on your place for you and collect the mail if you want."

"I'll give you a key," he said casually, walking over to his luggage.

"You don't have to do that, Christian. I can just take the mail home with me." Then she stopped. "Wait, didn't you have the mail stopped? I thought you mentioned doing that before we left to come here."

"Oh yeah," he said distractedly. "I think I did." He pulled out his keys, took one off the ring, and handed it to her.

"That won't be necessary," she said, taking a sip of her coffee. "There isn't any need for me to go inside." She put the mug down and walked over to her own suitcase and began pulling out clean clothes. When she turned, Christian was right behind her. "Oh!"

Gently, he grasped her shoulders. "I want you to have the key, Sophie. I want you to feel free to go in and check on things. Hell, stay there if you want, or put your stuff in there while you surf, and park your car there if it makes things easier."

Cupping his cheek, she smiled. Then she got up on her tiptoes and kissed him. "You're very sweet, but I'm fine doing things the way I always do. The locker at the surf shop is just fine."

He huffed. "Why is it such a big deal for you to accept the key?"

"Why is it such a big deal for me to take it?" she countered. And with a sassy grin, she all but skipped away and went into the attached bathroom and shut the door.

Four days later, Christian was packing his suitcase when his mother came into the room. Looking over his shoulder at her, he smiled.

"You sure you don't want me to drive you to the airport?"

He declined, zipping up the case. "You know New York airports can be a nightmare with traffic. I have a service picking me up."

"I appreciate you staying as long as you did," Eliza said as she moved into the room and sat on the bed.

He was the last one to leave. Carter left the day after Sophie, and Megan had left yesterday. Uncle William and Aunt Monica went home in between, and Uncle Robert and Aunt Janice lived only an hour away.

"And I'll be back next month for the reading of the

will. I hate that all of this gets dragged out. It would have been easier if it all could have been done this week." And honestly, he didn't mean to gripe about it; it would have been easier while they were all there. Scanning the room to make sure he had everything, he caught sight of the sad look on his mother's face.

"I can stay if you need me to," he said softly, sitting beside her. "Or you can come home with me and get away for a while." Wrapping an arm around her, he hugged her close.

"You're very sweet and I appreciate the offer, but this is going to be my new normal," she said, and he didn't miss the catch in her voice. "There are things I need to do, and to be honest, I'm looking forward to having some time alone. I haven't had that in over a week."

He nodded in understanding, remembering Sophie's words from that day in the hospital not so long ago. "Just know that you are welcome anytime." He kissed her cheek and stood.

Eliza stood and looked around the room. "You know, it's funny, I never considered giving any of your rooms a makeover. There was always something comforting about keeping them all the same as when you kids were younger. But after watching you come here with Sophie, and Megan with Alex, I think maybe it's time to consider doing that."

"Mom, that's not something for you to worry about right now. The rooms are fine the way they are."

Shrugging, she walked around the room—touching shelves, stopping to read plaques. "I'm not worrying, Christian, I'm thinking out loud. It might be nice to have a project to keep me busy."

He wasn't going to argue or mention how much work she had ahead of her with all of the legal aspects of getting his father's estate in order. He was thankful they had a family lawyer to take care of it and the fact that both his uncles were willing to help out so Christian could get home and back to his own office.

And Sophie.

It amazed him how much he missed her. They talked every night, and it bothered the hell out of him that she wouldn't take the key to his place. The thought of going home and having her there waiting for him had sounded wonderful in his own head, but after forcing her to talk about it, he realized she didn't feel comfortable being there without him.

In his mind, he imagined giving her the key, her being there waiting for him when he got home, and then convincing her to give up her tiny apartment in town. He hated the place—it was small and cramped, and she slept on a sofa bed. She deserved so much more than that. He wanted to give her so much more than that.

Unfortunately, life was going to be a little crazy in the foreseeable future. He'd been away from the office for nearly two weeks and he needed to get caught up. Then there were things with his father's estate that would require his attention, and he had to talk to his siblings about how they were all going to pitch in and help his mother.

His head started to hurt just thinking of it all.

And even though he shouldn't let it, he knew this was an opportunity not to let his father down. So he'd take care of his mother in any way he possibly could.

He'd make sure the office here in New York was run properly and all of his father's final wishes were carried out.

No matter how long it took.

~

Climbing from the car, Christian thanked the driver and accepted his suitcase. Looking up at his house, he was sorry that he hadn't told Sophie the truth about when he was coming home.

He wanted to surprise her.

Every night when they'd talked, she'd told him about going surfing. She'd even finally taken Randy up on his offer for more lessons. So tonight, Christian planned to surprise her out on the beach.

Rushing into the house, he knew she'd be out there within the next thirty minutes. It wasn't like he had a lot to do—he wasn't picking up his mail until tomorrow, so there wasn't anything for him to sort through—but he needed to get changed and open up the house to air it out. When he opened the doors that led out to the deck, he inhaled deeply and smiled.

Stepping out farther onto the deck, he scanned the crowd on the beach. It was lighter than usual but he was able to spot both Surfer Dude and Older Surfer Dude. Ollie was coming out of the ocean, and Christian couldn't help but scowl. It had been ages since he'd seen the guy, but just a glimpse of him reminded Christian of how mean he'd been to Sophie and...well, he still wanted to punch the guy over it.

"Nope, not gonna ruin my mood," he said lightly and turned to walk back into the house. He turned on lights, opened windows, and within minutes the sounds and smell of the ocean were filling the place.

In his bedroom, he put his suitcase in the closet and vowed to deal with it and the laundry tomorrow, before stripping down to his boxers and looking for a pair of shorts. Grabbing a T-shirt as well, he was about to walk into the bathroom when he heard a sound downstairs. It was possible the wind had maybe blown something over, but he also heard a muttered curse.

He cautiously walked across the room. The only thing he could think of was that someone had entered the house. Seriously? Just because the doors were open didn't give someone—a stranger!—the right to just walk in! Mildly pissed, he pulled his shorts on and slowly crept from the room and down the hall. He was about to turn the corner toward the living room when someone screamed right before something hit him in the face.

"*Bollocks!*" He stumbled back a foot or two from the impact.

"Oh my goodness! Christian! What are you doing here?"

Rubbing his nose where the throw pillow had hit him, he grinned at her. "I should be asking you the same question."

"I saw the doors open and you didn't say you were coming home, so I thought something was up!" She placed her hand over her heart. "You scared the heck out of me!"

His eyes went wide. "*I* scared *you*?" Then he started to laugh and pulled her into his arms, kissing her soundly. "And what were you planning to do, love, if I was a burglar?"

She squirmed to get out of his arms, but he wouldn't allow it. "I—I don't know," she said with a hint of defiance, but she was grinning. "I thought I was protecting your house."

"So you were trying to save me, do I have that right?"

"Well, now I wish I hadn't," she said, effectively pulling out of his embrace. Stepping a few feet away, she turned on him. "Why didn't you tell me you were coming home?"

She looked utterly stunning and it was the wrong time to think about seducing her—especially since she seemed to be quite peeved with him at the moment—but her hair was in wild disarray, her cheeks were flushed, and her breath was still a little ragged. Add to that the clingy top and bikini bottoms, and he was a goner.

Slowly, he stalked toward her. "I wanted to surprise you," he said, his voice low and a little rough.

Her brilliant green eyes sparkled.

"My plan was to go down to the beach and come upon you when you came out of the water. I was planning it all day."

Her beautiful mouth formed a perfect "o."

Now they were toe to toe. "Tomorrow, I'm heading in to the office and it's going to take some time to get caught up. I wanted this one night to be just for us—with me surprising you and pleasuring you because I missed you so damn much."

Then he was done talking and it appeared that Sophie was one hundred percent on board. She leaped into his arms and wrapped her legs around his waist even as he reached for her. She kissed him like her life depended on it and Christian awkwardly made his way to the back doors to close them, and then considered his options.

The bedroom was too far away.

The sofa looked like a beacon of light so that's where he went, where he lay her down and where he loved her until neither could remember their own names.

He'd missed the feel of her skin.

Craved the sweet scent that belonged only to her.

Every touch, every moan made him want more. He stripped her out of the top and the skimpy bikini bottoms as his mouth feasted on all of the skin he exposed. It was wild and intense and all he could think of was taking her, claiming her, hearing her cry out his name.

Her legs wrapped tightly around him, keeping him close—not that there was much of a chance of him moving away. If anything, Christian was desperate to be as close to her as humanly possible.

And as Sophie's nails scraped along his spine, he was pretty sure he'd achieved that goal.

Much later, while sharing Chinese takeout on the deck, Christian felt more relaxed than he had in...well, forever. Sophie was talking about the new company she was working with and how they had a childcare center for their employees to bring their children. She was going to see about the possibility of working with the children as well as the parents. Christian didn't think it would be possible—too much liability and a chance of people taking advantage of the free service their employer was providing and using it for sick visits instead of going to their own doctors, but he kept that to himself.

He loved listening to her talk about her day, her life, her plans. She was so damn optimistic about everything she did and he wanted more of that in his life. Needed it!

"Of course, Nana then accused me of looking to get sick by being around a bunch of kids," she said with a laugh.

"How is your nana doing? Have you talked to her about coming to visit yet?"

She shook her head. "I'm still trying to get my schedule under control. And I'd want to be able to take time off to show her around."

That one statement left him feeling guilty. She had taken a week off to be with him and his family, and because of that, she couldn't take time off to be with hers. He silently cursed himself and wished there was something he could do to help her.

"If you plan it right, you can use your days at Montgomerys and take them off. With pay, of course," he added with a wink. "Then you'd have some time during the week to be with her, plus the weekend."

Putting her carton of lo mein on the table, she stared at him with a frown. "Christian, first of all, I don't get paid days off. You know that. And I don't want you trying to add that because we're dating. That's not right."

"Sophie..."

"And while I appreciate what you're trying to do, I'll make it work out when the time is right. I'm not ready for Nana to come here and..." She paused and sighed loudly. "I think I'm going to see her soon."

This was brand-new information.

"Really?" He placed his own carton of food on the table and eyed her warily. "When did you decide this?"

"I…I've been thinking about it for a while, but after spending so much time with your family, I realized how much I missed mine. There's nowhere near as many of us, but…I've never been gone for this long without seeing them."

"I see."

There was more to this. He knew that. But he wasn't going to push.

"I'd only go for a long weekend. Nothing extended or anything."

"Will you see your father?"

So much for not pushing.

Her eyes went wide. "I…I haven't decided."

"O-kay…"

"I'm just afraid to make the wrong decision." She picked up her lo mein and went back to eating, so he figured they'd said enough on the subject for tonight. He didn't want their first night home together to be filled with arguments or awkward conversations, so he'd let it go for now.

Again.

"So tell me more about the surfing lessons," he said casually, effectively changing the subject and lightening the mood. "You think I should look into taking some?"

And just like that her face transformed into the beautiful and happy one he loved to look at. Maneuvering his chopsticks, he listened to her talk, and while she didn't come right out and say it, he knew she was gracefully trying to tell him to find another hobby.

No argument there.

They talked about the people on the beach—she'd made friends with two older women who were learning to surf, as well as a teenage boy and his mom, whom the boy was trying to teach.

"I'm not trying to brag or anything, but now I'm like the head cheerleader for all the new people," she said with a sassy grin. "I may not have a lot of surfing talent, but I can sure as heck cheer people on."

Yes, she could, he thought.

Sophie had always considered herself a low-maintenance kind of girl—especially when she was someone's girlfriend. She wasn't clingy, she didn't nag, and for the most part, she could go with the flow.

Only…this flow sucked.

It was a Friday night and Christian had been home for three weeks and she could count on one hand the number of times she had actually seen him. She saw him when she had her days at Montgomerys, but the most time he'd spent with her were rushed lunches.

And she'd just about had enough.

They were supposed to go to dinner tonight. It was his idea, and he had been apologizing left and right about all of the hours he was putting in at the office. At first she was understanding. Then she got mildly annoyed. But now? When he was an hour late? She was supremely ticked off.

At first, Sophie was sympathetic. Christian wasn't handling his father's death well at all, and it always came back to the same thing—he felt cheated. Cheated that he never got the answers on why his father had treated him the way he did. Cheated because he had finally been ready to work on their relationship. The list seemed to grow with each passing day, and as much as she tried to be optimistic and encourage him to move past this, she was out of cheers.

And patience.

Glancing at her phone, she noted he was now an hour and fifteen minutes late. Her fingers hovered over the screen as she considered calling him, but decided against it. She looked at her freshly painted nails and smoothed her free hand over her gauzy skirt, deciding that she wasn't just going to sit here and wait or call and listen to him make excuses.

She was going to the office to confront him and hopefully snap him out of this destructive pattern of behavior. She cared too much about him to let him stay in this downward spiral and she refused to let their relationship become a casualty of it.

Jumping up, she grabbed her purse and keys and stormed out the door.

Traffic was a bit of an issue, but she eventually pulled into the parking lot of Montgomerys and let out a small huff. The only other car in the lot was Christian's.

Muttering a couple of choice swear words, Sophie climbed from the car and entered the building using her employee passkey. Up the elevator she went and as soon as the doors opened on Christian's floor, she had a head full of steam and was ready to unleash on him.

Until she saw him.

His door was open and he was bent over the desk.

Asleep.

This certainly took some of the wind out of her sails. But not for long.

Walking into his office, she took note of the containers from lunch in the trash can, along with numerous empty water bottles and a half-empty cup of coffee. None of this was good for him—and it had nothing to do with his health scare. This wasn't a way for anyone to live, and as a healthcare professional, she was concerned, but as his girlfriend, she was incredibly sad.

When she reached him, Sophie gently shook his shoulder and whispered his name. It took several attempts before he raised his head. When his eyes focused on her, she knew the instant he realized what had happened.

"Dammit," he muttered and swiped a hand over his face. "I'm so sorry. What time is it?"

"Almost nine," she said quietly.

He looked around in confusion—as if she couldn't possibly be telling him the truth—before he stood and stretched. "Why didn't you call me?" He yawned loudly and reached for the cup of coffee, drank some, and then grimaced.

"Because this has gone on long enough," she said with a little snap in her voice. Christian's eyes went a little wide at her tone. "You're killing yourself, Christian. Do you realize that? Look around you! This isn't how you're supposed to be living!"

Raking a hand through his hair, he came out from behind his desk. "You don't understand."

"Yes, I do! You're working yourself to death to try to gain some kind of approval that is never going to come!" As soon as the words were out of her mouth she regretted them. This wasn't who she was. She wasn't confrontational—at least, she didn't like to be. The last time she had been was when she'd found out the truth about her parents and—

She gasped and cursed him.

To say he looked confused was an understatement.

"I can't keep doing this with you, Christian," she said after a moment.

"Doing what?" Now he was the one with a snap in his voice.

"This. Watching you kill yourself while I'm home alone waiting and wondering when I'm going to see you! This isn't who we are!"

Taking a step toward her, he yelled, "Who we are? Do you realize that this is who I was before I met you? This is my life, Sophie!" He paced a few feet away before turning toward her again. "I thought I could change! I thought I could live more like you, but you know what? I can't! This is who I am, and if you can't deal with it, then..." His words trailed off.

Her heart was racing like mad because she hadn't quite expected this response from him. The old Sophie would have turned and run, but right now, she relished the idea of fighting with him.

For him.

"Here's the thing, Christian," she fired back, surprised at her bravery. "I don't think this is who you are! I think you're letting someone else's expectations define you, and you know what? There's no reason for it! It doesn't matter if you work twenty-four hours a day, seven days a week, it's not going to change anything."

His blue eyes blazed with fury. "You have no idea!"

"The only difference it's going to make is that you will have wasted your life!" she cried. "You're wasting your life because of someone else's twisted views on your work ethic. Don't you see that by continuing on this path, he wins?"

For a moment he only stared at her. "This is all I know how to be!"

"Then you're not trying hard enough!" she argued. "The only one keeping you here in this box is you."

"No, it's not! My whole life, I did what I was supposed to—what my father expected of me. And I don't know why—why it was so important for me to do it. So I'm working and doing everything he asked for and I keep hoping that someday, I'll know why! Maybe when his will is read or—or if I talk to my uncles or some of his colleagues..."

"Christian, do you even hear yourself? This is crazy! You can crunch figures and manage stock portfolios all day long. They're not going to tell you why your father was such a tyrant to you!"

"Look, you don't understand because your job isn't like mine. It's complicated and requires a lot of dedication. I don't get to pick and choose my hours or flit around socializing like you do."

It was quite possibly one of the biggest insults she'd ever received.

"I don't have to work in corporate finance to see what's going on." She waited for him to respond, but he didn't. "So because I took control of my life and my career," she said calmly, hating the tremor in her voice, "you think that I don't understand."

"You ran, Sophie," he said stiffly. "It's not exactly the same thing."

She was wrong.

That was the biggest insult.

They were at a standoff, and she lost track of how long they spent facing one another without saying a word.

Then...she was done. She didn't fight like this, and she didn't want to. Maybe she was running, but at least she was running from things and situations that were ruining her life, not staying in them like he was so obviously willing to do.

"You know what? I guess I can't deal with who you are. The man I thought I was in love with doesn't exist." She took a steadying breath. "I want a life, Christian. I want to know I'm with a man who is willing to put in the effort, and for a while, that was you. But now I see that you're not capable of change—of being the man you were in the weeks before your father died. And that makes me sad for you."

"Sophie..." he said wearily, but he didn't move. He looked tired and disheveled, and as much as her heart ached for him and all he was dealing with, she simply couldn't continue to help him if he wouldn't help himself.

"You put so much pressure on yourself and I refuse to add to it. So...I'm going to go."

He sighed. "Why don't we go to dinner tomorrow?" he suggested.

Shaking her head, she felt the first sting of tears and willed them not to fall. "I don't think that's a good idea." Another step back. "I don't think we should see each other anymore."

This time he did move, but she held up a hand to stop him.

"I can't stand by and watch this." She shook her head again because she couldn't finish, she was too close to tears. "Goodbye, Christian."

And when she ran from the room, he didn't follow. Somewhere in the back of her mind, she'd thought he would—that he'd try to reason with her and tell her she was being crazy. But he didn't. And that just proved how little she meant to him. She had been a diversion, a distraction, a way to kill time while he tried to make some changes in his life—changes she'd been positive he wanted to make.

Clearly, she was wrong.

His obsession with his job and his father were... crazy! With Joseph gone, there could never be a satisfying conclusion—no answers, no pat on the back or congratulations for a job well done.

Once she was in her car, she stared up at the building with an overwhelming sense of sadness. She had wanted so desperately to have a life with him—to keep having their weekend adventures, and staying up and talking to him, laughing with him, loving him. But she had fooled herself.

Christian was searching for answers he was never going to find. That time was gone.

As she made her way home, she realized that seeing what this situation was doing to him was something she needed to learn from.

She could have her answers. True, she might not like them, and once she had them, she might wish she hadn't. But she'd have closure.

She'd have her peace.

And right now, that's what she wanted almost more than anything.

Almost.

Chapter 11

"Humph. Like father, like son."

Looking up, Christian was surprised to see Uncle William standing in the doorway. Quickly glancing at his calendar, he searched to see if he had somehow forgotten his uncle was coming to see him. Standing, he smiled. "Uncle William? I wasn't expecting you, was I?"

With a laugh, William walked into the office and shook Christian's hand. "No, no, I wasn't on your schedule, but I was doing some business in Oceanside and decided to stop in and see if you were free for lunch."

Lunch? Is it lunchtime already? he wondered.

His uncle was walking around the office making small, noncommittal sounds, but Christian knew his mind was going a million miles an hour. He caught a glimpse of the pile of clothes in the corner and looked at Christian. "So…are you living here now? Because if you are, I'm going to have to insist that we officially give all of your father's things to you to make the transformation complete."

"Excuse me?"

Pulling up a chair, William sat and gave his nephew a patient smile. "What is going on? I thought you were through with this whole workaholic phase. And I would have thought after losing your father, you would have felt freed."

"Freed?" he asked incredulously. "How can I possibly be freed?" He took a moment to catch his breath, but it was like he had no choice except to unload all of his anger and frustration. "It's like I can't move past it! Every day I keep thinking I'll talk to someone who has some insight, or I'll become enlightened by doing the job he loved so damn much, and I keep looking and hoping and…and…"

"Okay, okay," William replied soothingly. "So you're spiraling here, and that worries me." He looked over his shoulder toward the door. "Let me go and see if Sophie's here. Maybe she can—"

"She's not," he said miserably.

"Oh. Okay. Would you like me to call her?"

God, yes!

But he shook his head. "It won't matter. She's not… I mean, we're not…*shit*." He collapsed in his chair and closed his eyes, hating that anyone was witnessing this breakdown he was obviously having.

Then he waited for the lecture he was certain would come.

And waited.

And waited.

Finally, he opened his eyes and looked at his uncle, who was still sitting in his seat with that same smile—just waiting him out.

"Your father knew he was dying," William said. His words were neutral—as if they weren't talking about someone they knew. "Three months ago, he found out about the cancer. Prostate. He didn't tell your mother at first, but he told me and Robert. It was already at stage four and he declined any treatment."

Christian quickly did the math. "So that wasn't long before..."

"For years, I tried talking to him about taking better care of himself, but as I shared with you at the hospital that day, he didn't like taking advice from me." There was no malice there, just a statement of fact. "The thing is, Christian, you're looking at a future you can avoid."

He looked at his uncle curiously. "What does that mean?"

Another serene smile. "It means you don't have to walk the path my brother laid for you. For all the things he swore he was doing right, in the end it hurt him. And his family." He studied Christian for a moment. "When you were a little under two years old and your mother was pregnant with Carter, she left him."

Eyes wide, he asked, "What? Why?"

"Your mother was tired of living alone raising a toddler with another child on the way." He shrugged. "She came and stayed with us in North Carolina for about a month."

"A month? Seriously?"

William nodded.

"So...what happened? What made her go back?"

"Well, your father let her stay and cool down for about a week—at least, that's how he reasoned it. Then they started talking on the phone and he agreed to go for couples counseling and to cut back on his hours, effective immediately."

"But...?"

William chuckled. "That lasted all of three days. He was supposed to fly down to spend the weekend with her so they could talk face-to-face and he canceled at the last minute."

"Sounds about right."

"Naturally, things got tenser and tenser, until your mother refused to take any of his calls. Back then there weren't cell phones, so your father was calling the house and it was up to me and your aunt to deal with him."

Christian let out a mirthless laugh. "He must have hated that."

"Oh, he did. He did."

"Obviously, something must have happened, because I never remember them living apart."

"One night when your father called, I was the one to answer. I lit into him something fierce. It was a risk, because I knew how much he hated listening to me, but there were things that had to be said. I told him he better get his ass to North Carolina and man up!" He chuckled again. "He sputtered and carried on that it was none of my business, and I let him talk until he had nothing left to say. Then I told him I expected to see him on my doorstep the next day or I was giving Eliza the name of a good divorce attorney."

Christian could only imagine how his father must have looked at that ultimatum.

"And did he? Was he there?"

William grinned like the Cheshire cat. "The next part, we owe to you."

"Me?"

"Your father showed up the next evening and you were playing with Lucas. Like I said, you were barely two and you followed my boys around and pretty much let them do all the talking for you. I think they overwhelmed you because they were so loud and rambunctious, but you were also a very aware little boy."

"And...?"

"Your father and I were sitting in the den talking—your mother wasn't ready to talk to him yet—and you came into the room with a toy truck to show it to me. Your father...well, let's just say he was pretty devastated."

"Because I showed you a truck?" Christian asked, confused.

William shook his head. "Because you didn't acknowledge him and called *me* 'Daddy.'"

There wasn't a doubt in his mind that his eyes were bugged out and his jaw might very well be on the floor.

"I knew you only called me that because that's what you kept hearing my boys call me, but your father didn't see it that way."

"Is that—do you think that's why...?"

His uncle's face softened and then grew sad. "Oh, Christian, no. That's not it at all, and that's not why I told you this story."

"Then why?"

"That moment I just described to you was the opportunity for your father to change course—to forge a new path and make things right for his family."

"But he didn't."

"Believe it or not, he tried. I know he did." He paused. "But your father wanted success more. Success in the business world. Success and praise from his peers."

"I don't know why my mother stayed. No one deserves that. She could have been happier with someone else," Christian stated, feeling a new layer of resentment toward his father.

"I can't speak for your mother, all I can say is that

you kids are her life. She did what she could to give you a good upbringing and—"

"By staying with a man who didn't want to be a father?" Christian cried out.

"And," William went on, "she did the best she could. Over the years, your father mellowed, but by the time he realized that he had this amazing family, the damage was done."

Leaning back in his chair, Christian blew out a breath.

"You may not believe it, but he went to London to save you."

Snapping forward in his seat, Christian's jaw dropped. "Save me? Save me from what?"

"People knew about what that girl was doing behind your back. They talk, gossip spreads..." He raised his hands helplessly. "I don't condone it, but it happens. He went to London to try to get you out of a bad relationship."

"No," he argued. "He went there to try to control yet another aspect of my life."

"Your father always had the worst delivery," William said with a sigh. "I hate speaking ill of the dead, but there it is. Joseph was my brother and no matter what, I loved him. But he didn't always have a lot of tact." He leaned forward in his seat. "What you need to remember, Christian, was that his heart was in the right place."

"I don't think so." The snort of derision said anything else he might add.

"After that, he just sort of gave up. He knew he'd blown it, and...he figured too many years had gone by with him being a lousy role model."

There was a good chance his uncle was telling the truth, but more than likely, he was trying to plant a good memory in Christian's head.

They sat quietly for a minute. "Learn from his mistakes, Christian," William said solemnly. "Don't give your life to a job. Go out and find a beautiful girl who makes you laugh and makes you smile, make a family with her. Make a life with her!"

A few weeks ago, Christian had thought he was on that path.

But not anymore.

His uncle stood and walked over to the wall of windows that looked down on the city. "Somewhere out there, there's the perfect girl for you. She could be walking around the city streets on her way to lunch, or she could be on her way to Kansas, who knows?" He looked over at Christian with a sly smile.

"Yeah, she mentioned something about going to see her grandmother," Christian said. "But I didn't know when that was happening."

"It's happening now," William said firmly, turning to fully face him. "I recommended Sophie for a corporate nursing position with a friend of mine. That's the business I had up in Oceanside. Your aunt called her and found out she wouldn't be available for the next week because she was going to Kansas."

Just thinking about Sophie and her going back to her hometown made his gut clench. He knew how much she didn't want to go, so he had to wonder if she had decided whether or not to see her father.

He'd never know.

He'd blown it and now he had no right to ask how she

was or if she was okay, and he had to hope she didn't get hurt.

"So how about lunch? I remember there being this fantastic Mexican restaurant not too far from here. You interested?"

"I'm not hungry," he murmured. He couldn't get the image of Sophie all alone out of his head.

"Well, I guess I've taken up enough of your time," William said, clasping Christian's shoulder. He turned to walk away and then stopped. "Oh, I almost forgot." He pulled out a thick envelope, which he held out to Christian. "Answers," was all he said before walking out of the office.

Christian immediately opened the envelope and read the words at the top of the first page—*Last Will and Testament for Joseph Martin Montgomery*.

It was terrifying—more terrifying than moving herself to a place sight unseen. But as Sophie stood in the baggage claim area of the Wichita airport, she second-guessed this trip.

When she'd told Nana of her decision to come and see her father, it had led to an argument. The thing that bothered her the most was how all along Nana had said it was her decision to make, and yet when she did, Nana disapproved. How was that logical? Ultimately, Sophie decided that she was done looking to other people for approval and had to stop worrying about their feelings getting hurt. It had become more and more obvious that no one took her feelings into consideration, so why was she overly concerned with theirs?

It took an hour from the time she retrieved her suitcase and picked up her rental car to when she finally pulled away from the airport. The town where the correctional facility was located was only forty miles from the airport, and she had made reservations at one of the two hotels near it. It certainly wasn't a tourist destination, but she wasn't really interested in sightseeing.

Just thinking about all the things she wanted to ask and say was enough to have her heart racing. She couldn't imagine how she was going to feel when she checked in to see her father on Saturday. That was two days away. Well, a day and a half now.

Still, it was a lot of free time to do nothing but think and obsess about how it was all going to go.

One of the things that had added to the argument she had with Nana had been that she'd asked for a picture of her parents. All of her life, she'd only seen pictures of her mother, with Nana saying she never could find any pictures of her father or that he didn't like having his picture taken. When Sophie had decided to make the trip, she felt like she needed a visual of the man she was going to meet—even if it was seriously outdated.

That had sparked a dialogue that quickly escalated, with Nana accusing her of betraying her mother by going to see her father. And if Sophie were honest, that was one of the things she struggled with the most. Hearing Nana say it made it worse, and yet…this was still something she needed to do. Watching Christian struggle in his grief with all of the unanswered questions he had was the deciding factor. There was no way she wanted to live with that hanging over her head for the rest of her life.

So here she was. Driving down I-35 and hoping that after this weekend, she'd finally be able to move on and come to grips with her past.

And her future without Christian.

"Geez, any more depressing topics to think about, Soph?" she murmured.

Hoping to clear her mind, she turned on the radio and instantly groaned. Adele was singing about lost love. "Next!" she called out, changing the station and landing on Sam Smith's "Stay with Me." "Ugh, next." After that it seemed every channel was playing sad Ed Sheeran songs.

Switching off the radio, she sighed. Now what?

The silence was maddening, and she couldn't wait to get to her hotel and get something to eat. "Probably should have grabbed at least a snack at the airport. Brilliant, Sophie."

And there was her new focus for the rest of the drive—her poor decisions and what she was going to eat.

Which, really, could be one and the same right now.

Thirty minutes later, she was checked in and placing her suitcase on the luggage rack. She'd booked a suite, but it was a typical chain hotel, so basically all that meant was she had all the usual amenities plus a small sofa and coffee table. They called it a living room—she wasn't sure she'd go that far.

Either way, she was here and ready to grab some food. Sitting on the sofa, she reached for the folder that told her what was close by and cringed when so many of them required getting in the car. With no other choice, she picked up her purse and headed out.

It didn't take long for her to find a burger place

where she went through the drive-thru, got her order, and returned to the room. Setting up at the coffee table, she spread out her meal and reached for her laptop.

She checked her emails, caught up on the national news, and pulled up the information on the facility she'd be visiting on Saturday. There were a lot of steps she'd had to follow in order to visit, and even though she'd gone to the website multiple times, she couldn't help but read it all again to confirm that everything was in order.

More scrolling, more reading… Her eyes were starting to cross and when her phone rang, she let out a small yelp and then laughed as "Nana's on the phone… Nana's calling you" rang out. She instantly answered.

"Hi," she said nervously.

"Are you there? Did you really fly in?" Nana said instead of a greeting.

Resting against the sofa cushions, Sophie let out a small laugh. "Yes, I'm here and I'm checked in at the hotel."

"I don't know why you went there so dang early. You could have come here."

"Nana, the last time we spoke, things did not end well. I thought it best if I came here first," she explained. "I know you don't agree with what I'm doing, and I know if I had come to you, you would have spent the entire time I was there trying to talk me out of this."

Silence.

Sophie waited a moment before speaking again. "I'm not looking for your approval on this. I needed to do this for me."

"You have no idea what it feels like," Nana said, her

voice thick with emotion. “That man took my baby from me. You can’t imagine the pain of burying your own child, Sophie, and I hope you never do. I’ve had a lot of years to come to grips with Laura being gone, but… it never goes away.”

“Nana…”

“Even though I spent almost your entire life not talking about it—the truth about what happened—I felt her loss every single day. Every time I watched you laugh and smile, I thought of her because you look so alike. And now with you going there…the pain feels fresh. Raw.”

“I didn’t mean for it to be this way,” Sophie said quietly. “This was something I felt I had to do—for me. And I’m sorry that by doing so, I’m hurting you.” She paused. “But if I didn’t do it—if I didn’t come here—then I was going to spend the rest of my life agonizing over it. Can you understand that?”

“What do you think is going to happen when you go there? What can that man possibly say that is going to bring you peace? Have you thought about that?”

“Of course I have! I’ve run every scenario in my head, but until I go there and confront him, I have no idea what’s going to happen!”

“Why would you open yourself up to that, Sophie? What good can come of this? He can’t bring your mother back! He ruined so many lives and he doesn’t deserve the opportunity to see you or get to know you! Your mother will never get that chance!”

And they were back to the heated words.

“We’ll never agree on this. It doesn’t matter how much we talk about it, it’s never going to happen,” she said wearily, her eyes closing as she tried to calm herself.

"I need to understand..."

And that's when Sophie told her about Christian and his father—their turbulent relationship and how Christian had struggled since his father's death. "He's obsessed with what he should have said or what he wished he would have asked his father. Everything he does is in search of an answer and you know what? He'll never get that. That chance is gone. But I still have that chance!"

On the other end of the phone, Nana sighed. "The only difference is that Christian might have had a chance of resolving his issues with his father, and now he'll never know. But for you, there won't be any resolution. Nothing he says can undo what he did."

"And I know that," she replied with frustration. "And maybe I need to go there and tell him how awful he is, or...or...how much he missed out on because of what he did! Maybe he knows that already or maybe he doesn't, but you're never going to understand, and I don't have to justify it to you or to anyone. I'm here and I'm doing it and that's it!"

At that, they both fell silent.

And she hated it—hated that this would always be between them.

But then again, it already was—not this exact situation with Sophie going to meet her father, but the way Nana had lied to her for her entire life about her parents.

"Do you remember when you begged me to understand why you kept the truth about my parents a secret?" she asked warily.

"I do," Nana replied sadly.

"That's what I'm doing here. I need you to understand."

"But you didn't," Nana argued. "You were upset and you were hell on wheels to live with until you left town—mad at me and everyone you knew. How is that understanding?"

Unfortunately, she had a point.

Letting out a long breath, Sophie stood and walked over to the window, looking down at the parking lot.

"So where do we go from here? I'm mad at you, you're mad at me, and you know what? We're all each other has! And yes, I was mad, and I didn't understand why you did what you did, but I'm trying. I really am. In a perfect world, things would be different, and we wouldn't be having this conversation because my mother would still be alive!"

And more silence.

After what seemed like forever, Sophie heard Nana let out a shaky breath. "Sophie, there is nothing in the world you can do that would make me stop loving you. And you're right, I have to accept that you have to do this. I don't have to like it, but I can accept it. All I ask is…is don't tell me about it. I don't want to hear anything that man has to say or any excuses he tries to give you or any more of his lies." A small sob escaped before she could continue. "I know you're not going there in hopes of being his friend or to give him the opportunity to be your daddy, but…I need you to know that I can't go there again. I can't give him that kind of power in my head or my heart again."

Now Sophie was openly weeping. Nodding, she swiped at her tears. "I understand. And I promise, after Saturday, we will never talk about this again."

"Okay then."

They talked about her flight, her long ordeal at the car rental counter, and about her hotel room. They even made tentative plans for Sophie to drive out to see her on Sunday, but they both agreed to wait and see how she felt after her trip to the prison.

When she hung up the phone, she was emotionally drained. Crawling onto the bed, she wished she wasn't alone—that someone was there with her to hold her and tell her it was going to be all right.

And as she curled into the fetal position and more tears fell, she wished that someone was Christian Montgomery.

"I don't understand. What's happening right now?"

With a grin, Christian chuckled and tossed the last of his paperwork into the basket on his desk. "I'm taking some time off," he said to Erin, who looked utterly confused. "David Marcum is going to take over my clients, Matt Bladen is his backup. All of my clients have been notified."

"But—but I didn't talk to any of them," she said, slowly sitting in one of the chairs by Christian's desk. "How…? When…?"

"I made all the calls personally." He shut his desk drawer and locked it, pocketing the key. "I explained to all of them about losing my father and how I needed the time away to deal with my grief. Luckily, everyone was very understanding, and then I had David call and do a follow-up with them. It worked out quite well."

"So…but where are you going? How long will you be gone?"

Shrugging, he took his phone off its charger and slid it into his pocket before wrapping up the charger and placing it in his briefcase. "I'm not sure. I haven't worked it all out yet."

"Oh. Okay," she said slowly, still watching him warily.

A light knock on the door had them both turning. "Uncle William! I'm glad you were still in town. Come on in."

Christian had to hold in the laughter, because his uncle was looking at him as if he were crazy—pretty much just like Erin was. Which reminded him…

"Erin, everything you need is in the email I sent you. David has all of the information that he needs and I think we're in good shape." He winked at her. "And don't worry. It's all going to be fine."

She didn't look one hundred percent convinced, but she stood and gave him a weak smile before greeting his uncle on her way out.

Once they were alone, he caught his uncle's wary expression. "Please, have a seat," he said, motioning to the chair Erin had vacated.

"Everything all right, Christian?"

Leaning on the edge of his desk, he grinned. "I'm not sure. But… I'm hopeful."

William's expression narrowed. "Oh?"

Reaching behind him, Christian picked up the lone envelope on his desk and handed it to his uncle.

William accepted it and looked at it briefly. "What's this?"

"Answers I realized I don't need."

And just like that, his uncle's face lit up. "Is that right?"

Nodding, he couldn't help but smile. "True story."

Sliding the envelope into his coat pocket, William shifted in his seat, a smile of his own on his face. "What changed your mind? Did you read it all?"

He shook his head. "No. I stared at that cover letter for about an hour and never looked any further. I know that you and Uncle Robert are handling all of the business stuff, and as for any inheritance that may be left, I'll wait until I hear from Dad's lawyer. Other than that, there's nothing else I need to know."

"But...but you said... When I was here yesterday, you were going on about—"

Christian held up a hand to stop him. "I know. I sat here for a long time and thought about everything you said and I realized you were right. I am the one in control of my life. My destiny. There was nothing on any piece of paper that was going to change that."

"Well, you don't know that for sure. For all you know, your father left you a hefty inheritance that could change your life!"

He shrugged. "If he did, I'm sure I'll hear about it eventually." Moving away from the desk, he stepped around it to pick up his briefcase, jacket, and keys. "All I know is that the answers I want—really want—weren't in that envelope."

"Really? And where are they?"

Christian grinned. "I believe they're in Kansas, and that's where I'm going to find them."

Jumping to his feet, William walked over and hugged him. "Splendid! When are you leaving? What can I do to help? Do you need a ride to the airport?"

"Actually, I was hoping we could grab some lunch first."

Once more, his uncle's face beamed with pure delight. He wrapped an arm around Christian's shoulder and led them both toward the door. "I always said you were a smart boy, Christian. I'm so glad you proved me right."

Laughing, they walked out of the office and Christian shut the door behind him, and not once did he bother to look back.

From now on, he was only looking forward.

It was a little after five on Friday when Christian pulled up in front of the hotel. Finding Sophie hadn't been nearly as hard as he'd originally thought it would be. After talking to Patricia in Human Resources and getting Sophie's nana's phone number, everything had fallen into place.

Ida Colby was a bit of a pistol, but once she'd spoken her mind on how much he'd broken her granddaughter's heart, Christian had assured her that he was willing to do whatever it took to win her back.

Now he had a new best friend.

Climbing from the car, he scanned the parking lot and realized he had no idea what car Sophie was driving or if she was even here right now. Maybe she'd gone out to get something to eat or went shopping or...he had no idea. It was a small town and from what he could see, there wasn't much to do.

He hadn't gone more than two steps when the automatic doors slid open and she walked out.

And took his breath away—she looked as beautiful as ever, but sad. Her hair was long and loose, she had on a pair of faded blue jeans, a black sweater, and black boots. Gone was his California surfer girl and in her place was her beautiful Midwestern twin.

They both had his heart.

He stood still and waited for her to notice him. When she did, she nearly tripped over her own two feet. They were no more than ten feet apart and he was scared to move any closer. Her face was unreadable—for all of his pep talks to himself on the flight here, he suddenly had no idea what to do or say.

Sliding his hands into the front pockets of his jeans, he finally said, "Hi."

"Hi."

He took one step closer. "How are you?"

Without moving, she said, "Fine."

For the past few months, he'd seen Sophie laughing, smiling, yelling, and crying, but right now, he had no idea what she was thinking or feeling. So he took another step closer and saw and heard the hitch in her breath.

Okay, so she wasn't as unaffected as he'd thought.

"So...um, I was wondering if I could take you to dinner?"

Smooth, idiot. Real smooth. Way to remind her of the last thing you majorly screwed up!

Emerald eyes widened briefly before narrowing. "Really? You came all the way to Kansas to ask me to dinner? Seriously?"

Another step and now he could smell her perfume.

"Well, that wasn't my *only* reason for coming to Kansas, but I figured it was a good place to start." He gave her a lopsided grin in hopes of getting her to smile, but she didn't. And that's when he thought,

To hell with it and closed the distance between them. "Talk to me. Please."

"And say what?" she asked, not meeting his eyes now.

"Yell at me, scream at me, tell me I'm the world's biggest jerk, but please talk to me," he begged as he boldly reached out and took one of her hands in his. She didn't immediately pull it away, so he took that as a good sign.

For a moment, she looked like she was going to say something—her stance changed, her lips moved, but ultimately, she stayed silent.

Cupping her cheek with his free hand, he whispered, "Please."

A ragged breath was her first response. "I've already yelled, screamed, and cried, Christian." Then she looked up and her green eyes shone with unshed tears. "You hurt me. No, wait—you devastated me. I deserved more than that from you. With everything we shared together, I deserved more than being cast aside while you spent day after day killing yourself in the office."

"I know," he said lowly, gruffly. "I don't have an excuse, Sophie, and I'm not going to stand here and make one up."

"I was there for you at your lowest point, I was there with you while you tried to figure out how to finally live the life you wanted, and I was there with you when you cried over losing your father. And at a time when you should have been talking to me, you pulled away. I'm not talking about going out on dates, I'm talking about having a conversation because you were overwhelmed with grief. I shared with you the most horrific details of my life—I laid myself bare to you and you wouldn't do the same for me."

"Sophie..."

But she pulled her hand free and moved away. "We were in two different relationships. I saw a future for us and...and...I don't know what you saw. All I know is it seemed pretty easy for you to walk away from it."

"It wasn't," he gently argued. "I let my grief and fear paralyze me and I know I should have gone after you that night—I cursed myself for not doing it. But ultimately, I thought I was doing the right thing. My life was a mess and you had enough on your plate without having to deal with any more from me. As it is, I have enough guilt over the fact that you got roped into dealing with both my medical problems and then Dad's."

She laughed softly. "I didn't get roped in, Christian. It's my job, it's what I do—what I love to do! Don't you know that I was happy I was there with you that day? Not that I was happy that you were sick, but that I was there to help you. And it was the same with your father." She then stepped forward and touched his hand. "I wish I could have done more."

In that moment, he thought they were going to be okay. She wasn't moving away from him and she wasn't telling him to get lost, so he figured they'd crossed their first hurdle.

"The thing is," she said, interrupting his thoughts, "this is all too much for me to deal with right now. I mean, you know why I'm here in Kansas and I'm already a bit of a wreck over the whole thing, so..."

Man, he was really bad at reading situations.

"I understand how you feel," he said quickly,

scrambling for a way to keep talking to her. "But if you're not able to forgive me or—or you don't want to talk about giving me a second chance..."

"Do you want a second chance?" she asked cautiously.

"More than anything."

"Wow," she said with a sigh.

And he didn't take that as a good sign.

Taking her hand in his again, he gave it a gentle squeeze. "So here's the thing—I don't want to add to the stress of this weekend, but let me be here for you. As a friend. You shouldn't be here alone, and I want you to know that you don't have to deal with this all on your own."

The tears were back in her eyes. "Christian..."

"I promise I won't pressure you for more than you're willing to give," he said, his tone soft. "At one time, we were friends, Sophie. Back in the beginning when we'd go surfing or jogging."

"I hated the jogging," she reminded him.

"And because you were being a good friend, you put up with it," he teased, squeezing her hand again. "We don't have to go jogging right now, just to get something to eat. I want to hear about how you're doing and how you're feeling about this visit."

Her shoulders sagged a little and her voice was small. "I'm scared."

Unable to help himself, he pulled her into his embrace. She didn't fight him and he simply relished the feel of her in his arms. Kissing the top of her head, he said, "I know. But I'm here for you. Talk to me." He rubbed his hand up and down her back and felt her relax against him.

"This doesn't feel like a friendly hug," she murmured.

But he wasn't deterred. "Then I guess you're hugging the wrong people." When she whispered his name in protest, he pulled back a little. "Come on, love. Let's go grab something to eat and talk, okay?"

"I don't know…"

He moved away and did his best to reassure her of his motives. "Look, I get why you're wary, but I'm here and I'm not leaving. I reserved a room here and I'm staying until Tuesday."

"But…I'm staying until Tuesday," she said, confused.

With a small grin, he said, "I know."

"What about work?" she asked. "How come you're suddenly able to be away? Is it because it's just a long weekend?"

He shrugged. "For now."

"For now?" she repeated. "What does that mean?"

"It means come to dinner with me and I'll tell you all about it."

The look on her face told him she was considering it—and trying to think of a way out at the same time. Yeah, her face was that expressive, and he'd spent a lot of time studying it.

"I passed a diner about a mile up the road and you know they probably make some great burgers and milkshakes," he taunted, knowing the nurse side of her would freak out that he was looking to eat junk food. Then he shrugged. "I guess I could always go alone and find out. Oh, and I bet they serve those giant onion rings too!"

"Christian Montgomery, don't you dare go eat a meal like that! Do you have any idea how high the fat content in that would be? After all your hard work to try and eat healthier, you'd undo it all in one meal!" she cried.

With a satisfied smile, he leaned in close to her. "Then I guess you need to come to dinner with me and make sure I behave."

With a grimace, she said, "I fell right into that one, didn't I?"

Firmly clasping her hand in his, he led her over to his car. "You certainly did." He winked. "And I couldn't be happier."

It was after nine and they were standing in the lobby while Christian checked in. Sophie waited, her mind utterly confused.

He was here.

He was beyond charming.

And it felt like the most natural thing in the world to be with him.

So why was she letting him get a room of his own?

When she had stepped out of the hotel earlier and seen him standing there, she'd thought she was imagining him—especially after thinking about how much she'd wished he was there with her the night before. They had a great dinner together where they talked and laughed, and there wasn't one romantic thing about it—it was like he promised. Two friends going out to eat.

Dammit.

"I'm on the fifth floor," he said as he walked over. "What about you?"

"Oh...um, fifth," she said, still trying to wrap her

brain around the fact that he was here and not coming to her room with her.

It felt weird and all kinds of wrong.

Christian turned and started toward the elevators and Sophie followed, listening to him talk about how exhausting traveling was—even when it was a short distance—and how much he hoped the room was quiet because he never slept well when he was away from home…all kinds of trivial stuff that friends and acquaintances might talk about.

They got into the elevator and she seriously considered pushing him against the wall and kissing him senseless. She could do that, right? There was nothing wrong with the woman being the one to make the first move. Over the course of their relationship, she'd done that on more than one occasion. So why couldn't she?

Ding!

The doors swooshed open and in the blink of an eye, Christian stepped out and was looking from side to side to get his bearings.

She'd missed her chance.

Following behind him, she asked, "What room are you in?"

"Five ten," he said and began walking in that direction. "And where are you?"

"Five fifteen." Okay, so at least they were both going in the same direction and it wouldn't be awkward for her to have to turn and walk away.

At the door to his room, he slid the keycard in and opened the door, placing his suitcase in the doorway to hold it open. He gave her a small smile. "What time are you heading out in the morning?"

Heading out? Wait…what?

Then she remembered.

"Oh, uh… I was thinking around ten. I was going to have breakfast first. It's only a fifteen-minute drive, but there's a lot of security to get through and…I don't know…that's when I thought I'd go."

"How about I meet you downstairs at nine?"

"Um, sure. Yeah. That's great. And then I'll go and I can text you when I'm on my way back."

His brow furrowed as he looked at her. "Sophie, I thought you understood—I want to go with you." He reached for her hand. "I didn't want you to have to go alone." Before she had a chance to respond, he gently tugged on her hand and led her into his room.

It was a king suite like hers and she wondered if he was actually cringing at the thought of staying there. This was a small town and they didn't have any five-star luxury hotels—she highly doubted Christian had ever stayed in a place like this.

"I bet you're sorry you came here, huh?" she couldn't help but ask.

He turned and looked at her oddly. "Why would you say that?"

"Christian, look at this place." She motioned at the room. "When was the last time you stayed in a hotel like this? I mean, there's no way you could have ever."

Releasing her hand, he gave her a light tap on the tip of her nose. "I think you believe I'm a snob." Then he laughed softly. "I'll admit, it's been a while, but there's nothing wrong with the hotel. It's clean, the room is big, and as long as I have a blanket and a pillow, I'll be fine." Then he stepped farther into the room and stretched. "I've been sleeping at my desk for far too long—especially lately—so this will be downright decadent for me."

At dinner, she'd noticed how tired he looked, but now after hearing him talk about how he'd been sleeping, she could tell.

"Then you should get some sleep," she said quietly. "And as for tomorrow, I appreciate that you want to go with me, but the truth is you can't."

"What do you mean?"

"I mean there was a ton of paperwork I had to fill out to get this visit approved and there's no way for you to secure that on such short notice. So it's really a moot point."

"Then I'll drive you there. I'll wait in the car and be there so you don't have to do anything except...I don't even know what I'm trying to say here," he said with a nervous laugh.

"I don't want you to feel like you have to go to the... well, you know. It's bad enough that it's where I have to go. You shouldn't feel obligated to go there too. It means a lot to me that you're here for me to talk to. I was feeling very alone, and the fact that you flew here so I didn't have to be..."

He was right in front of her before she knew it, her face gently cupped in his hands. "Obligation has nothing to do with any of this, love. Don't you know that? I'm here for you because I want to be. You mean everything to me, Sophie. I know we still have a lot of issues to work through, but if you'll give me a chance..."

Everything in her was telling her to scream "Yes!" But her emotions were all over the place right now and she could only deal with one thing at a time.

"I need some time, Christian," she said honestly. "I've had to deal with so much in the past year and so much of that was based in anger. What happened between us broke my heart." She took a moment to compose herself, otherwise she'd break down in tears. "I—I'll see you in the morning."

She saw the disappointment and sadness on his face, and she was feeling those same things herself. But staying with him tonight wasn't going to do anything but blur lines and confuse her. She didn't want to be seduced with just their bodies.

Although that would be a fantastic distraction right now, it wasn't the right thing to do.

"I'll see you at breakfast" was all she said before walking out of the room.

Sleep eluded her all night. She'd tossed and turned, but no matter how hard she tried, her mind wouldn't shut down.

And none of it had to do with Christian, but about meeting her father.

She'd risen and was showered and dressed by six thirty and was contemplating going down to breakfast and leaving before Christian got her. Then she realized how rude that would be and did her best to try to distract herself.

Sitting on the small sofa, she pulled out the tote bag she had packed to bring with her to the prison. In it were some small photo albums she had put together to show to her father—snippets of her life so he could essentially get to know her in this one brief visit. The thing was, she had no idea why that was so important. What difference was his knowing anything about her going to make? For him or for her? Their time was limited and she couldn't imagine wanting to come back here.

Pulling out one of the albums, she slowly flipped through the pages and smiled. There were pictures from each of her birthdays, her first day of school, all of the usual milestones in a child's life.

He'd missed all of that.

Her hands trembled as she slowly closed the book and slid it back into the bag.

Maybe this was a mistake. Maybe Nana was right and she should let this be. If she was this emotional and fragile just from looking at some pictures, how was she going to be able to be in a room with this man who was a stranger to her? Would she be able to look at him and see him as her father, or would she only see a murderer?

A soft knock on her door startled her.

Taking a steadying breath, she walked over and looked through the peephole to see Christian.

She opened the door and looked at him quizzically.

"I had a feeling you'd be up already," he said sheepishly. "I thought I'd come and see how you were doing and if you maybe wanted to get an earlier start."

She smiled gratefully and motioned for him to come in. He spotted the bag sitting on the coffee table and looked over at her. "What's this?"

"I...I brought some photo albums with me. I don't know why. I guess it seemed like the thing to do. It's not like he has any clue about my life or anything, so I thought having some visuals would help." She knew she was stammering and then waited for him to tell her it was a crazy idea.

Instead, he sat on the sofa and looked at her expectantly. "May I?"

"Um...sure." She sat quietly beside him while he pulled the first book out of the bag. It held baby pictures—pictures that were taken when her parents were alive. For the life of her, she had no idea why she had brought that one with her. Thinking about it now, she'd probably leave it behind. No need to point out the obvious.

"Look at how adorable you were," he said with a grin, turning pages.

"All babies are adorable," she countered.

But Christian shook his head. "I don't think so. But you were—with your bright eyes, and always smiling." Then he turned his gaze up to her. "Beautiful then, and beautiful now."

Sophie could feel herself blush but didn't say anything as she watched him continue going through the book. When he was done, he pulled out the next one. That was the one she had been looking at before he showed up.

"There are a lot of awkward years in this one that will have you reconsidering how adorable I was," she teased. But as Christian turned the pages, he found something incredibly sweet to say about each and every picture, and that had her heart skipping a beat. When he stopped on a picture of her at thirteen wearing braces and a cast on her arm, she looked at him blandly. "You cannot possibly find something nice to say about this one. I was chubby as well as being a klutz."

He studied the picture for several long moments and shrugged. "I still only see you—same amazing smile, same spunky personality." Then he chuckled. "And I love the hot-pink cast. Totally you."

It was hopeless.

He was hopeless.

Either way, she relaxed and talked with him until he had gone through all of the pictures. When he slid the final one into the bag, he said, "Thank you."

"For what?"

"I learned more about you in the past hour than I did in the past several months. I like that."

Playfully, she nudged him with her shoulder. "I don't think you learned that much. They were just some pictures."

But he wasn't smiling. His face was one of thoughtful consideration. "Every picture told a story—one that you shared with me. And for that, I'm thankful."

Letting out a long, low breath, she tried to calm her heart rate. Christian Montgomery had a way of making her feel things she'd never felt before and it was clear that he still could. At any other time, she'd enjoy it. But right now, she had something that had to be dealt with before she could move on.

Standing up, she looked at him. "How about that breakfast?"

Chapter 12

Christian watched as Sophie walked into the massive penitentiary and he had never felt so helpless in his entire life. That morning, she had kept up a brave front—all through the time in her room and then through breakfast—but as soon as they had gotten into his car, she had gone quiet.

He couldn't imagine what was going on in her head—how confused and conflicted she must be feeling. There wasn't anything he could do or say to help her through it, so instead, he made small talk about the weather, a funny story on the news about a pregnant giraffe, and his thoughts on the hotel. The whole time he talked, she would occasionally smile, but for the most part she was quiet.

The drive was short and he almost wished it had been longer so she could have more time to prepare herself. When they got through the gate and parked, he'd looked at her and said, "It's not too late to change your mind. If you want to leave, just say the word and we'll go." And for a solid minute, he waited, thinking she was going to ask him to take her back to the hotel. But she'd surprised him and reached for the door handle. He'd stopped her with a hand on her arm and said, "I'll be right here waiting for you. It doesn't matter if you stay ten minutes or ten hours. I'll be here."

Swallowing hard, he stared at the building. Since the moment he'd met her, Christian had known that Sophie was quite possibly the bravest person he'd ever met. She wasn't afraid of a challenge, and even though he knew he had accused her of running, the truth was she hadn't. She'd merely taken the opportunity to remove herself from an atmosphere that wasn't good for her.

She was brave and smart and kind, and if he were in her shoes, he didn't think he'd be able to do this—to go into a massively imposing prison to meet the person who had essentially ruined her life.

All his life Christian had looked at his situation with his father as being so horrible and so complicated, but it was nothing compared to what Sophie had to deal with. Where he had been afraid to confront his father even while in the comfort of their family home, Sophie had gone to Kansas to confront her father behind bars.

Yeah, she definitely had him beat in bravery.

It killed him that he couldn't be in there with her. Although, if he thought about it logically, he knew it was probably for the best. She was nervous enough about doing this and the last thing she needed was an audience.

But damn if he didn't want to be there to hold her hand and give her the strength she needed. And as soon as this day was over, he was determined to do whatever it took to win her love.

Clarity about his life had hit him hard this week. That brief visit from his uncle had caused him to sit back and think about life in a way he had refused to do. It didn't matter that a lot of what Uncle William said was on track with what so many others had been saying to him for weeks—years, if he were honest. But on that day, for some reason, he had finally been willing to listen.

And learn.

Having his father's will in his hands meant he'd get some of his superficial questions answered, but was there more? Was there maybe a letter from his father or something else that would shine a light on why their relationship had been what it was for his whole life?

He'd sat at his desk until well after midnight with that stack of papers folded up beside him. Fear had kept him from reading them. What if it was only a will? What if there was no letter or anything personal from his father? He knew the disappointment and anger would be back tenfold. He thought of calling Carter or Megan to see if they'd gotten their copy of the will, but he didn't act on it.

The thing was, it didn't matter what it said. It didn't matter what his father left him. Christian was wealthy in his own right—he'd worked hard, invested well, and lived within his means. That last part was primarily because he hadn't done much living. And he was done with that—done with the days of working eighteen hours and going home alone. This sabbatical he was taking didn't have an end date—he was waiting to talk to Sophie about that. But when all was said and done, he wanted to have someone to come home to, someone to travel with, someone to laugh with. Someone to love.

And the only person who he wanted all of that with was Sophie.

The decision to put the will back in the envelope without reading it had been hard—but not as hard as he would have thought. If anything, once he decided, he felt relief. A tidal wave of it. And that's when he knew he had the greatest answer of them all.

The only approval he needed was his own.

And right now, he approved of being here for Sophie.

Before they had left the hotel, Christian had packed a satchel that contained his iPad and some snacks. Taking it from the back seat, he pulled out the tablet and a bottle of water, moved the driver's seat back and tried to get comfortable. It was tempting to open the *Wall Street Journal* app, but instead, he opted for solitaire.

And he settled in to wait for his girl.

It was quite possibly the most depressing place she had ever been.

Looking around the waiting room where she had been directed, Sophie felt nothing but a sense of sadness. Everyone in the room looked somber and it was hard to imagine what it must be like for some of these people to come back time and time again to visit their loved ones, knowing that this was the only place they could see them.

A group of people came through one of the secured doors. Sophie imagined they were through with their visit and no doubt anxious to leave. None smiled. If anything, they looked tired. There was a young woman with a toddler, two twentysomething men, and an older couple. They looked the weariest, and Sophie almost got up to hug them because they looked like they needed it.

"Sophie Bennington?" an officer called out. As she stood, her gut clenched and her head spun. This was it. She was really doing this.

Walking over, she did everything she was instructed to do—went through another round of security and was finally led into a large, loud room that was designated for visiting the inmates. There were dozens of tables and chairs and as she was led to one of them, the guard explained to her that she was not allowed to sit beside her father, she had to sit across from him, and someone would be standing there monitoring their conversation the entire time. It wasn't a surprise and yet…it still felt awkward knowing that their every word was going to be witnessed.

Too late to change that.

Before she knew it, another guard was walking toward her with an inmate, and she quickly turned and held her breath.

Derek Bennington was tall and lanky and nothing at all like what she'd expected. His head was shaved but he had some scruffiness on his jaw. The prison-orange jumpsuit was almost blindingly bright, and when he looked at her, she saw the same wariness she knew was on her own face.

The guard stepped back, but neither of them moved.

"Hi," she finally forced herself to say.

A bashful smile played on his face. "Hi." His voice was low—barely a whisper. He had a kind face—especially his eyes—and it was hard in that moment to wrap her brain around the fact of who he really was.

Clearing her throat, she pulled out a chair and sat, waiting for him to do the same.

"I…um… I couldn't believe it when I heard you agreed to see me," he said, his eyes scanning her face as if memorizing it. Then he let out a low chuckle. "I'm so nervous. I didn't think I would be, but I'm…I'm shaking."

And for some reason, that broke the ice. Maybe because she appreciated his honesty.

And that, in turn, gave her the confidence to stay where she was and talk to him.

"Me too," she admitted. "I wasn't sure I could do this—come here and meet you—but...I knew I needed to."

He didn't say anything, just nodded.

"I only found out about...well, the truth about..." Damn. There was no way not to talk about the elephant in the room.

"I know," he said quickly, putting her out of her misery of trying to find the right thing to say. "Back then, we all decided it would be best if you thought... or that you didn't know..." He let out another nervous laugh. "This is a lot harder than I thought it would be."

Tears stung her eyes and her throat burned as she nodded. "I know."

"I—I'm not going to sit here and waste what little time we have with making excuses," he began after a moment. "I know what I did and there isn't a day that goes by that I don't regret it and wish that I could change it, but I can't." His voice hitched. "All I know is that I'm so glad that you're here and—"

"Please don't," she quickly interrupted, openly sobbing.

And in that moment, all of her questions why, all of the things she thought she wanted to know, suddenly didn't seem so important. Instead, she reached into her bag—and noticed that the guard instantly stepped in close—and pulled out a photo album. She held it up for the guard to inspect and smiled when he handed it back to her.

"I wasn't sure what was going to happen when I came

here today," she said, her voice strengthening with each word. "But it was important for me to show you that...I had a good life. Nana made sure of it."

The look of devastation on his face spoke volumes, but it didn't deter her. Sliding her chair closer to him, she opened the book. The first picture was from her third birthday—her first without her parents. And just as she had done with Christian earlier, she shared a small story or a memory for each picture. It amazed her that they were sitting like this—so civil—when there was such a horrific history. But today she chose not to focus on that. For this one day, she was going to be a girl meeting her father.

Just as she had earlier, she talked her way through each of the photo albums. There were people in them who he remembered, and Sophie took the time to give him an update on them. Then she told him about her life, her job, and how she was currently living in California. He asked so many questions and seemed almost desperate for them to keep talking.

But eventually, they ran out of things to say—things that were normal, things that didn't hurt. Clearing the table, she placed the last album back into her bag. Then they both became quiet. Contemplative.

This is it, she thought. *I came and I faced my fears and...I need to say goodbye.*

Looking at him and then the clock on the wall, she gave him a sad smile. "I should go."

He looked at her, his expression one of great sadness. "It feels like you just got here."

She knew what he meant. It felt like that for her too. Standing, she picked up her bag.

He stood and faced her.

In the time they'd been in the room together, he hadn't touched her and right now, he looked like he very much wanted to.

"There's nothing I can say that can convey how sorry I am," he said gruffly. "You may not believe this, but I always thought of you and loved you. And I'm so honored that you came here today and let me get to know you."

And then she started to cry, couldn't even stop the tears if she wanted to. Because this was their beginning and their end. There wasn't going to be a next time. Her whole life and their whole relationship had been developed and summed up in a matter of hours.

"I hate this," she finally choked out. "I didn't expect… I didn't think I'd feel this."

He nodded, tears in his own eyes. "You gave me the greatest gift in the world today—one I didn't deserve." Then, slowly, he reached out and touched her hand. Without hesitation, she clasped it. The gratitude on his face for that one simple gesture spoke volumes. The moment was over quickly as a guard stepped forward.

"So what"—she cleared her throat—"what happens now?"

"Now I go back to my cell and I think about this day—which to me has been the most perfect day I could have ever imagined." His expression was one of sad acceptance. "Thank you for being willing to come. I know it wasn't easy for you, and to be honest, I don't expect you to come back. This isn't a place I want you to ever have to see again."

"But…"

There were suddenly so many things she wanted to

say, but he motioned to the guard that he was ready. At the door, he turned and smiled at her. "Do great things, Sophie. I love you."

And then he was gone.

Unable to do anything more than sink into a chair, she took several minutes to pull herself together. Luckily, the guard didn't rush her; if anything, he looked at her sympathetically. When she finally felt ready to move, she rose and nodded at him before heading toward the exit.

The walk out of the facility was drastically shorter since she didn't have to be screened, and when she stepped outside, she breathed in the fresh air. Remembering she was supposed to text Christian when she was coming out, she cursed and opted to walk over to the car and risk scaring the heck out of him.

But he saw her first and was standing beside the car. As soon as she got close, he opened his arms and she readily stepped into them.

There were no words.

It was pure coincidence that Christian happened to look toward the building to see Sophie standing on the sidewalk staring up at the sky. And as she got closer, he could see that she'd been crying and he'd done the only thing he could—hold her.

She trembled against him as a fresh wave of tears came.

And he held her.

She burrowed in as close as she could to him.

And still he held her.

And he was going to keep holding her until she felt strong enough to move. It didn't matter how much time it took, he was there to give her exactly what she needed. His heart ached for her and he wondered what exactly had gone on inside the prison. Was she crying because it was horrible? Was her father mean or hateful toward her? There were so many possible scenarios—all of which he'd been thinking about while trying to distract himself with games of solitaire—but he wasn't going to ask her about it. He was going to wait until she was ready to talk.

The sky was a little overcast, and it wasn't until the wind picked up that he realized there was a good chance it was going to rain. But that didn't matter. He'd stand here and get soaked if that's what she wanted.

There was a strange sound he could faintly hear, and when Sophie pulled back a little and apologized, he wasn't sure for what.

"That was my stomach," she said ruefully. "I guess that cup of yogurt and granola wasn't enough this morning."

Unable to help it, he laughed. Keeping one arm around her, he led her to the passenger side of the car. "Then let's get you something to eat." She nodded in agreement and slid into the car. When he was seated beside her, he asked, "How about the diner again? Their food was pretty good and it had more of a variety than any place else we've seen around town."

"I guess," she murmured.

They pulled out of the penitentiary parking lot and out onto the highway before she spoke again.

"You know what I wish?" She was looking out the window and her voice was soft and a little wistful.

"No, what, love?"

"I wish we were back home and eating Chinese food out on your deck. That would be so good right now."

He heard the longing in her voice and wished like hell that he could do that for her. "We could go to the hotel and pack and find a flight home and be there in time for dinner," he suggested. "What do you say?"

When she looked at him, there was so much sadness there and it was killing him. "I say I don't have it in me right now. It sounds exhausting. Delicious, but exhausting."

They drove in silence for a few minutes and he racked his brain to try to remember if they had passed any Chinese restaurants on their way out of town, but for the life of him, he couldn't. But now he was determined. Reaching for his phone, he quickly swiped the screen and pulled up the app he needed and asked, "Chinese food restaurants near my location," and waited. Five restaurants came up and he held the screen for Sophie to see. "It won't be out on the deck, but it's the best I can do."

Some of the sadness faded away and she took the phone from him to pull up the directions to the one with the highest rating. "I think we'll have to go in and order. By the time we pull up the menu and consider our options, we'll be there."

"That's fine with me," he agreed and sure enough, ten minutes later, they were there.

It was amazing what a little distraction could do. As they shared the menu and discussed what they were going to order, Sophie seemed way more relaxed than before. He ordered her a soda to tide her over until they got to the hotel, and they spent the time they had to wait comparing this tiny hole-in-the-wall place to their favorite Chinese restaurants.

"You know we should have zero expectations going into this, right?" he teased.

"Weren't you the one telling me that you're not a snob?"

"Maybe."

"Because that statement, Mr. Montgomery, sounded a wee bit snobbish."

The look of pure mirth on her face pleased him so much that he figured he'd run with this topic to keep her smiling.

"I mean, I was tempted to order a vegetarian dish, because I have a feeling the meat and fish are going to be iffy." Then he shrugged. "But I figured if I got food poisoning, I have a nurse with me, so..."

She laughed out loud. "No one's going to get food poisoning! And you need to keep it down or they'll hear you!"

Another shrug. "So...what? I'll get less squirrel in my moo shu pork?"

This time she fought back the laugh and leaned in close. "You didn't order the moo shu pork, so don't even."

He was trying to think of a witty comeback, but their order was ready and he was anxious to get them back to the hotel so Sophie could relax and eat.

Even if the food was iffy.

Back at the hotel, they opted to go to Sophie's room—mainly because he figured she'd want to change and freshen up.

No way was he going to argue with that.

As he'd figured, the first thing she did was excuse

herself after grabbing a change of clothes from her suitcase. While she was out of the room, he set up their food on the coffee table and opened their drinks. When she stepped out of the bathroom, she looked like her old self—hair in a ponytail, no makeup, yoga pants and a T-shirt.

His beautiful girl.

"I am starving," she said as she walked over to sit on the sofa. She looked at the array of food they'd ordered—dumplings, crab rangoon, shrimp lo mein, beef and broccoli, and General Tso's chicken—and grinned. "It all looks good, right?"

He felt bad for teasing earlier. "It does. And it smells great." In that, he wasn't lying, but he still wasn't so sure it was going to be all that tasty. "So…dig in."

With each thing they tasted, they commented on and compared it to their usual choices. Christian had to admit that he was pleasantly surprised, and it didn't take long for them to both lean back on the sofa, completely full.

"I think I ate too much," Sophie commented, her hand on her belly.

"Does that mean I can eat your fortune cookie?"

Eyes closed, she swatted at him playfully. "I didn't say I'd never eat again, I just meant that right now I am full."

"Is that a yes or a no on the cookie?"

Turning her head toward him, she opened her eyes and smiled. And she kept looking at him, studying him until he was ready to squirm under her scrutiny. "What?"

"I wished for you," she whispered, taking his hand in hers.

"You did?" he asked quietly.

Nodding, she said, "I did."

"When?"

"The day I got here. I was all alone here in my room and all I could think of was how I wished you were here with me."

"All you had to do was call, Sophie, and I would have come."

She made a face that told him she didn't believe him and he realized that, considering how they'd left things that day in his office, his statement wasn't quite believable to her.

"I know that sounds crazy, considering…"

"Considering what a jerk you were to me?"

"Um…yeah."

"It's okay, Christian," she said, squeezing his hand. "You were going through a lot and it was just bad timing for us."

Twisting in his spot so he could face her, he told her about his uncle's visit. He hadn't gotten that far into the story when she stopped him.

"How is your mother doing? I'm so sorry, I should have asked about that sooner, shouldn't I?"

Leave it to Sophie to be thinking about others even when she had her own struggles. By now, he thought she would have at least alluded to how things had gone at the prison, but it was clear she still wasn't ready to talk, and he wasn't going to push.

So he updated her on how his mother was holding up and then returned to his story about his visit with Uncle William and his father's will.

"And you just gave it back to him? Without reading it?"

He nodded.

"But...why?"

"Because you inspired me," he said simply.

"What?"

"It's true. Everything you said—hell, everything everyone said—finally sank in. Nothing was going to change the past. I needed to let that go."

"There could have been an apology in there!" she said incredulously, eyes wide.

He shrugged. "And maybe someday I'll find out, but right now, I don't need it." Unable to resist the urge any longer, he moved in close to her and gently grasped her shoulders. "I look at you and all that you've overcome and the way you handle things, and I'm in awe of you."

Those green eyes got incredibly wider. "Me?" she squeaked.

"Sophie Bennington, you are the most incredible person I've ever known. You've been faced with things no one should have to and yet you still have a smile on your face and you encourage everyone around you. You're the reason I want to be a better man." He scanned her face—from the emerald eyes, the freckles on the bridge of her nose, to the full, soft lips—and he fell utterly and completely in love with her right then and there.

"There was nothing in that will that I needed, because all I need is you," he finished.

Her soft gasp and look of wonder were her only response at first. "I...I don't know what to say."

It was a good thing Christian had more.

"I got a little lost there for a while," he admitted honestly. "I was so caught up in my anger and grief that I lost track of what was important—all of the things you'd taught me. And I am so sorry for the things I said to you and for taking you for granted. I promise you—right here, right now—that it will never happen again. That person? The one I was when we first met? He's gone, and I don't ever want him to come back."

Sophie caressed his cheek, and he closed his eyes and savored her touch. "Christian, I think we both said some things we shouldn't have, and I'm sorry if I pushed—"

He immediately placed a finger over her lips to stop her. "You have nothing to be sorry for. Nothing." Then he paused. "Although there was something you said that day that I think you need to explain."

Pulling away, she looked at him in confusion. "Oh… um…okay."

"You said I was the man you *thought* you were in love with," he stated quietly. "And I need to know if—if maybe there's a chance that I could be the man you *know* you're in love with. Because I love you, Sophie. I am so in love with you and missed you so much, and if I ruined this for us…"

She opened her mouth to speak, but he quickly stopped her again.

"I swore I wasn't going to pressure you and I don't want you saying anything because you think you have to. I guess I just needed to know there's a chance for us." It was his turn to caress her cheek. "From the moment I saw you, you gave me hope and something to look forward to. And when we met, it was like I was able to see the possibilities of what my life could be." He smiled. "The first time we kissed, it was everything I ever wanted." He rested his forehead against hers. "I love you, Sophie."

Then he waited.

He'd interrupted her twice, but he was so anxious to tell her how he felt that he couldn't hold back. Now that he had, he hoped she'd tell him how she felt—and he prayed it was the same for her.

Slowly, she moved away from him, her expression grim. "Christian, I think you should know...I was wrong that day. I lied."

With those two little words, he lost hope.

The look of devastation on Christian's face made her heart ache. But she knew if they were going to try to move forward, he deserved to know the truth.

He stood and walked over to the window before she had a chance to explain. Following him, she stood—staring at his back—and let the rest come out.

"Christian, I fell a little in love with you the night you came down to save me on the beach. When you walked away that night, all I thought was how I wished a man like you would want a girl like me." She stopped and swallowed hard when he didn't turn around. "I fell a little more in love with you the day of your anxiety attack."

Then he did turn around and looked at her like she was crazy.

"You were vulnerable and scared and—believe it or not—it was all of the silly and random conversations we had in between all the tests that showed me how funny you could be. The way you talked to the nurses and all the lab techs who poked and prodded you showed me how kind you could be."

Now he looked a little more relaxed.

"I fell a little in lust with you the day I showed up at your house and you were just wearing a pair of shorts," she added bashfully. "I had never seen a more perfect male specimen and I was quite literally tongue-tied."

When he moved closer, she laid it all out on the table for him. "But I fell in love with you the day you let me shower at your house after I had my meltdown. A lot of guys would have taken advantage of a woman in that situation, but you took care of me—putting my needs first." She shrugged. "That sealed the deal for me. So you see, when I said that I thought I was in love with you, I was lying, because I was already one hundred percent completely in love. And no amount of bad behavior was going to change that."

"So you're saying..."

"I'm saying I love you too, Christian Montgomery. And I—"

She never got to finish, because he closed the distance between them and crushed his lips to hers. It felt so good, so right, and as she held him close, Sophie knew there was no place else in the world she'd rather be right now.

Together they maneuvered away from the window and across the room until they were next to the bed. Christian raised his head, breathless, and looked at her face in complete wonder. "I've missed you so much."

"I missed you too." Her hand pressed against his abs and then up his chest. "And right now, I need you."

No further explanation was needed.

Slowly, reverently, he undressed her.

Sweetly, softly, he kissed her.

Sophie lay on the bed as Christian stripped down to his briefs and then he was beside her.

"You know we don't have to do this right now. I'd be happy to keep holding you."

But she shook her head. "It's been forever since we made love, and right now, that's what I want."

His smile was incredibly sexy as he leaned in and murmured against her lips, "Then that's what you shall have."

His kiss was fierce and wild and exactly what Sophie had been hoping for. Wrapping herself around him, she pulled him in as close as she could, relishing the feel of him. It had been too long and she was nearly frantic with need for him.

When he broke the kiss, one hand cupped her breast. "I wanted to go slow with you, but I don't know if I can."

"I don't want slow," she said boldly. "Right now, I need…I want…" Her hips lifted as she rubbed against him, showing him exactly what she wanted.

A low rumble of laughter came out of him and he met her heated gaze. "Patience."

"Later. I'll have patience later, I promise." She moaned as his fingers played with her nipple. Her back arched, her lips parted. "Christian…please…"

And that he did.

Over and over.

"Thank you."

Behind her, Christian chuckled as he hugged her close and kissed her shoulder. "You're quite welcome."

Snickering, she elbowed him in the ribs. "That's not what I meant."

"Oh…well, you can see why I'd be confused. We just had…I mean, wow…and…"

Rolling over to face him, she instantly sobered. "Thank you for not pushing me to talk earlier today. I was freaked out and confused, and I appreciated you understanding that and giving me enough time and distraction to feel better."

Kissing her forehead, he said, "I knew you'd talk about it when you were ready." Pulling back, he looked at her. "And that doesn't have to be today or tomorrow or ever. All I need to know is that you're okay."

"I am," she said, "or at least I think I am." When he didn't question or comment, she snuggled in closer and placed a light kiss on his chest. "Can I ask you something?"

"Anything."

"How did you know where to find me?"

He laughed again. "I had a long conversation with your grandmother."

"You did? When?" Her mind raced and she had to wonder why Nana hadn't mentioned that to her when they had spoken on the phone. "Did she know you were coming here?"

"Oh, yeah," he said with amusement. "After she laid into me about my bad behavior toward you, I explained that I wanted to come to you and make things right. I think if I hadn't said I wanted to come here, she would have bought me a plane ticket."

That sounded like Nana. "She's feisty, all right. But I hope she didn't pressure you or guilt you into coming."

He groaned. “I don’t know how many times I can say this—I wanted to be here with you. If I hadn’t gotten the information from her, I would have kept searching. I already knew you were coming to Kansas thanks to Uncle William and Aunt Monica.”

“Oh, I had forgotten about that.”

“And considering how we’d left things, I didn’t think you’d accept my calls, so I went to Patricia and got your employee file and called Ida.”

She laughed. “I can only imagine how shocked she was to hear from you.”

“I think she was glad I called so she could tell me off. I’m a little scared to meet her now.” He said it lightly, but Sophie heard the uncertainty in his voice.

“I had thought about going to see her before flying home,” she began cautiously, “so maybe you could come with me? I promise to reel her in if she gets a little out of hand.”

“Now you’re making me feel like some sort of a wuss,” he teased. “I shouldn’t be afraid of meeting an old woman, right?”

“I don’t know, Nana’s intimidating when she wants to be. You’re going to have to dazzle her to win her over.”

He laughed again. “Dazzle? Am I supposed to bring her flowers? Chocolates?”

“Yes to both,” Sophie agreed. “She loves dark chocolate and anything with cherries or coconut.”

“And her favorite flower?”

“She’s a roses girl all the way.”

“Done.” They grew quiet for a minute before he asked, “And you? What’s your favorite flower?”

"Hmm...good question. I think I would have to say sunflowers."

"Seriously? Those big giant yellow flowers?"

She nodded. "Yup. They're very cheery!"

"Not very romantic."

"So you're planning on romancing Nana with the roses?"

Making a face, he replied, "No. But I was talking about you."

"You romance me just by being yourself." The look he gave her showed how little he believed her, and she started to laugh. "It's true! Every time you tried surfing with me and all of our little weekend trips and the way you held my hand on Space Mountain... Those things were way more romantic than any bouquet could be."

"Well, when you put it like that..."

Relaxing against him with her head on his chest, Sophie enjoyed the quiet—the soft beating of his heart under her ear, the sound of his breathing. It soothed her. Christian gently played with her hair and they were both content to lie there tangled together.

It didn't take long for her eyes to feel heavy and the need to sleep take over. Considering she hadn't slept at all the night before, it wasn't surprising. She felt Christian place a kiss on her temple as her eyes closed.

The next time they opened, the room was dark. She went to sit up, but Christian was still wrapped around her. Slowly, she lifted her head and spotted the bedside clock—it was almost eight. Her stomach growled and she heard Christian chuckle.

"That's twice today that your stomach has loudly demanded attention," he teased, rolling away from her.

"And it's about time, because mine's been talking for an hour." Switching on a lamp, he got dressed. Once his jeans were on, he faced her. "Do you want me to go and pick up food and bring it back, or are you up to going out?"

The thought of staying in was extremely appealing. She knew she looked like a wreck right now without even looking in the mirror. "Um…"

Christian leaned down and gave her a loud, smacking kiss on the lips before straightening. "Takeout it is."

"No," she said and yawned. "I should get up and go out. Just give me a few minutes to get ready."

But he was already fully dressed and cleaning up their lunch mess, which they'd neglected earlier. "How about this," he said as he tossed the containers in the trash. "How about you stay here and shower and relax, and I'll go and pick up a pizza? You've had a rough day and there's no reason you should have to go out."

A shower sounded wonderful, and even though she felt bad about sending him out, she reluctantly agreed.

As soon as he was out the door, Sophie climbed from the bed and padded to the bathroom. When she saw her reflection, she knew staying in was the right option. And once she stood under the hot, steamy shower spray, it was confirmed even more. A low moan escaped as the water washed over her.

Taking her time, Sophie washed and conditioned her hair while thinking about her time with her father. It didn't matter how much she had thought about or planned, what had transpired wasn't like anything she had expected. While she wouldn't say it was great or a pleasant experience, it was…it was…damn. She wasn't sure what she would call it. All she knew was that in her heart, she felt peace. She'd met the father she never knew and managed to open and close that chapter of her life.

She rinsed her hair, grabbed her body wash, and finished getting clean before shutting off the water. There was no telling how long Christian would be gone, but she wanted to at least be out of the shower and dressed by the time he got back.

Wrapping her hair in a towel, she dried off and went into the suite. Picking up her clothes from earlier, she slid them back on. A look at the clock showed Christian had been gone for a little over twenty minutes, so she went back into the bathroom to brush her teeth and put some moisturizer on her face. Her hair was a lost cause—it would take too long to dry it and she just didn't have the energy.

With nothing else to do, she straightened up the bed and texted Christian to pick up extra drinks so she could keep some in her mini fridge for later. She smiled when he immediately texted back asking if she wanted dessert.

"Like that should even be a question?" she laughed as she texted him back with a simple Duh.

With her phone still in her hand, there was a moment of dread when she realized that as much as Nana had asked her not to talk about it, there was a part of her that felt like she needed to call her and let her know she was okay. Because no matter what, her grandmother was very protective of her and while she might not want to know the details of what had transpired today, her interest in Sophie's well-being would be her main concern.

Before she had a chance to second-guess herself, she pulled up Nana's number and hit Call.

"Hello?" Nana said hesitantly.

"Hey, Nana," Sophie said with equal hesitation. "How are you?"

"I'm good. How—how are you? Are you all right?"

"I am. I really am. And I know we talked and you didn't want to know about this, but I wanted you to know that I love you, that I was thinking of you and that...I'm okay."

"Did Christian get there?"

Smiling, she said, "He did. That was quite the surprise. I was shocked when he told me the two of you had talked."

"Well, I didn't want to like him—and I told him how much I disapproved of his behavior. But then I figured he was grieving and I forgave him."

She chuckled. "Oh, you did, did you?"

"It was the least I could do. Seeing that he's in love with you and wanted to do right by you, I thought it best if I gave him a chance." She paused. "He better not make me regret it."

She laughed harder, remembering Christian's concerns earlier. "Trust me, he wouldn't dare." And when Nana laughed with her, Sophie felt like everything was going to be okay. They had crossed this hurdle and it hadn't been easy. But from here on out, she knew there wasn't anything they couldn't overcome together.

"So the two of you are going to come and visit me before you head back to California, right?"

"Well, that was...unexpected."

"I'll say."

"I don't know what I was thinking, but…that wasn't it."

"Yup."

Christian stood with Sophie at his side in the Wichita airport after having just put her nana on a flight to Miami with two of her best friends. Well, they had put her in the TSA line and watched them walk through before waving goodbye. They were going on a ten-day cruise—compliments of Christian. Getting the three of them to the airport had been a little like herding cats.

Apparently, Ida and her friends had never flown anywhere before.

Something Christian should have considered before offering to send them on this spur of the moment trip.

Sophie hugged him tightly before stepping back. "Thank you for doing that for her. You have no idea how much it meant."

"I think I have an idea."

She swatted his arm. "Come on. Let's go grab something to eat before we check in for our flight. I don't know about you, but I'm ready to go home."

He'd been ready for days. What should have been only two days with Ida had turned into five. Five torturous days where he was forced to sleep on the sofa because Ida didn't believe in an unmarried couple sleeping together under her roof. When he said he'd stay at a hotel, she argued that no grandson of hers—apparently not only were they best friends, but family now—was going to stay at a hotel when she had a perfectly fine couch.

There had been nothing *perfectly* or *fine* about it.

He'd already called and made an appointment with a chiropractor for when he got home to San Diego.

Together they walked across the terminal to the small café that was the only dining option before security. It didn't offer a whole lot, but it was a place to sit and relax while they had a couple of hours to kill. Nana's flight was scheduled to leave three hours before theirs, but it was easier for them to return their rental cars and hang around the airport rather than leave and come back.

"You know, you've been kind of vague about when you're returning to work," Sophie commented as she picked off a piece of her blueberry muffin. "I've got to go to work on Monday, but I'm looking forward to it. I'm ready for it."

Christian made a small sound but continued to read the science fiction book he'd downloaded this morning to his tablet.

Beside him, she huffed and pulled a magazine out of her bag. Slamming it down on the table, she flipped it open and turned the pages as loudly as she possibly could.

It was kind of adorable.

"It's a shame you have to start so soon," he said vaguely.

"Really? How come?"

He shrugged. "Just a short time to get settled before heading back to the grind."

"Oh."

He read quietly. "Of course, if you didn't have to go back to work right away, I would have suggested that we change flights right now and maybe go someplace fun." It was difficult to keep his eyes on his tablet and not gauge her response, but he was having a little too much fun trying to act casual. "I'm hoping to go and see my mother. Carter's thinking of opening a place out on Long Island, and I thought maybe staying a couple of nights in Manhattan could be interesting." Then he looked at her with a serene smile. "But that's just me."

"Wait, wait, wait," she said, tossing her magazine and muffin aside. "You're telling me that you've already taken a week off, away from the office, and you're considering taking a few more days?"

Looking at the tablet screen, he said, "No. That's not what I'm saying at all."

She growled. Seriously growled.

Switching off the iPad, he twisted in his seat to look at her head on. "I never said a few more days. Come to think of it, I never gave a timeline for it."

"Christian," she whined.

"Here's the thing, love. I'm taking a leave of absence from Montgomerys. I have no set time that I have to be back. I've got a brilliant team working for me and I'm finally allowing them to work. Now, the way I see it, you can come with me and make sure I don't revert to my previous evil ways, or I'll be left to fend for myself and who knows how that will go. I may end up working for Uncle Robert or filling in at my father's office until they decide on who they're going to promote." He sighed dramatically. "I might even end up working for Carter."

"Carter?" she cried. "Why would you even think that?"

Another shrug. "I might get roped into helping him with finances and making sure his portfolio is healthy. His new place is possibly going to be out on the far end of Long Island—Montauk, I believe—and who knows? Word may get around of what I'm doing for Carter and the next thing you know, I'm opening a Montgomerys branch in Montauk. And why, you ask?"

"Well, I didn't really—"

"All because I was left to fend for myself rather than having the woman I love there to protect and save me." He shook his head and pouted. "It's a shame, really. We never even gave ourselves a chance."

Now it was her turn to sigh dramatically even as she fought not to laugh. "Are you through?"

"Quite."

She eyed him suspiciously for a moment. "You realize this is way out of my comfort zone, right?"

"I'm aware."

"I'm out of clean clothes and…and…nothing I have with me is nice enough for running around New York!" she said, smiling.

"Completely aware of that as well."

"This is crazy! We can't just do something like that!"

"Darling, New York City is the city that never sleeps. We can get off the plane and go shop. Or we can go to our hotel and get the necessities from their boutique, and shop tomorrow."

"Boutique? Hotels don't have boutiques," she said in confusion.

"Well, not the ones like we stayed at over the weekend, but the kind I plan on taking you to? Um, yeah. Boutiques."

Her eyes went wide and she laughed nervously. "We can't…I mean, we shouldn't…"

"Why not?"

"I have a job, Christian! I've already taken more time off than is considered professional. If I take more time off, I won't have a job!"

That thought had crossed his mind, but if there was

one thing he knew about Sophie, it was that she wouldn't be idle long. If she did happen to lose this job, she'd find another one. He'd make sure of it.

"Then we'll find you another one," he said simply. He looked at his watch and grinned. "Tick tock—we can sit here and read for another two and a half hours, or we can walk over to that counter right there and change our travel plans. What do you say, Sophie?"

She looked at him, then over toward the ticket counter, and then back again. The indecision was easy to see and he really thought she was going to turn him down. Her work ethic was strong and no doubt she was feeling obligated to get back to work. He understood it—admired it even—but right now he wanted her to shuck all of her responsibilities along with him and go on this tiny adventure. He wouldn't beg or try to convince her. He'd laid out his case and given her the options. The rest was up to her.

"You know I'll want to go to the Empire State Building, right?" she asked, gathering her things and putting them in her carry-on.

"And you know I'm going to want to eat some food from the street vendors."

"Ugh. How many times do we have to talk about eating healthy?" she huffed. "You have no idea how clean those vendors are or how long the food has been out!"

"What about the Statue of Liberty?" he asked, trying to distract her. "Do you feel strongly about seeing it?"

She was on to him; the side-eye she was giving him confirmed it. "I wouldn't mind seeing it, and maybe a Broadway show. Do you think we could do that? Oh!

And can we shop at Macy's at Herald Square? I watch the Thanksgiving parade every year and always wanted to shop there!"

"I think that can be arranged." Pulling her in close, he kissed her soundly. "I love you, and whatever it is you want to do, we'll do it."

"You're going to spoil me," she said shyly, hooking her arm through his as they made their way across the gate area to the ticket counter.

"Get used to it, love. I'm going to be doing that for a very long time."

With a sweet smile, she shrugged dramatically. "Well…if I have to!"

Epilogue

Six months later…

THE SUN WAS SHINING, THE SKY WAS BLUE, AND AS CHRISTIAN stood outside their private bungalow at the Four Seasons Hualalai, he couldn't help but smile. His feet were in the sand and he had the perfect view of the beach and the waves crashing on the shore.

"Paradise," he murmured, sipping his coffee.

And really, right now they had been in desperate need of a little paradise. After their fateful trip to Kansas, they had gone to New York and spent ten days seeing the sights in Manhattan, visiting his mother, and hanging out on the east end of Long Island with Carter. Their mother had talked him into doing a cookbook for some charity she was a volunteer with. Not wanting to upset her, Carter had agreed, but he was not happy about it. Christian was just glad that his mom's attention was focused on Carter for now, even though he had been calling Christian to grouse about it daily.

Then there'd been Sophie's family.

And not just Nana.

A month after they had gone back to San Diego, Sophie had finally broached the subject of meeting her other grandparents. Of course Ida had been upset and that had caused another month of arguing and his poor girl trying to please everyone before taking her own feelings into consideration. Eventually, they had resolved it, and Sophie had contacted Darren and Judie Bennington.

His head was still spinning from that visit.

Not only had they been thrilled to see Sophie, but they had gone overboard and bought her enough presents to make up for the last twenty-plus years.

They'd had to rent a truck to get it all to Cali.

And then waiting for them at home was Ida. Sophie had convinced her to come and visit after her cruise, and since then, she'd decided to make San Diego her part-time home.

With them.

To say that they needed this vacation was an understatement.

Growing up, the Montgomerys had always been close, but not live-in-your-house-with-you close. It had taken some getting used to, and he missed having the spontaneity to come home and make love to Sophie wherever and whenever he wanted—because Ida had some serious ninja skills and had snuck up on them one time too many—but she'd be heading back to Kansas soon.

Of that, Christian was certain.

He scanned the beach in hopes of spotting Sophie. She had left earlier so she could get in a little surfing before the beach got too crowded. He had to remind her that they were at an exclusive resort and the beach here would never get crowded, but she had insisted on going early.

For three days they had played tourists, taking in all of the amazing offerings of the resort. They'd played a round of golf—which Sophie almost instantly declared she was not a fan of. Then they had gone for scuba lessons—something they'd both enjoyed—and even went canoeing.

Their bungalow was very secluded and included not only an oceanfront view but their own hammock right on the beach. Butler service allowed them to have food brought right out to the beach and their privacy was guaranteed.

Which he hoped was true, because they'd done quite a few things out on the beach that really should have been done indoors! They'd laughed afterward at how bold they were being, but he couldn't really say that he had any regrets. He'd do each and every one of those sexy things with Sophie again in a heartbeat.

Speaking of…

He finally spotted her coming out of the water with her board under her arm. She had on a tiny blue bikini—no wetsuits this time—and she looked like a goddess. Placing his mug on one of the small tables on their deck, he slowly made his way toward her, waving to get her attention.

Smiling, she dropped the board and untethered it from her ankle before picking up her pace to meet him halfway.

"Good morning, beautiful," he said, kissing her. "How's the surfing here? Any different from home?"

"Nope. I stink here too," she replied sassily. "The water is so amazing and I'm having fun, but I think it's time to let this hobby go."

"Never," he teased. "You'll get it eventually."

Frowning, she gave his shoulder a playful shove. "Did you order breakfast yet? I'm hungry."

He looked past her briefly and then met her curious gaze. "I hadn't ordered yet. I wasn't feeling well. That's why I came out here to get you."

"Oh no! What's wrong?" She instantly morphed into nurse-mode and started asking a bunch of questions and feeling his forehead. "I bet it was that fish last night. You thought it tasted funny. Do you think it may be food poisoning?"

He shook his head. "No, it's not that. I'm just…I'm a little shaky and my heart is racing, but my chest feels tight."

"We need to get you back to the bungalow so I can call a doctor." She went to lead him up the sand, but he stopped her. "Christian, this is serious. We need to get you looked at."

Taking her hand, he tugged her close and placed it over his heart. "Do you feel that?"

Standing very still, Sophie pressed her hand firmly over his heart. "Christian…"

"Sophie Bennington, my heart belongs to you. You were the one who taught me how to live, how to feel, how to love. The only reason my heart is racing right now is because I'm standing here ready to take on another adventure with you." He dropped to one knee. "You've given me everything I ever could have hoped for and so much more. You make me smile. You give me joy. And every day I have with you is like getting the greatest gift in the world. You are my world, and I would be honored if you would be my wife."

"Oh my goodness," she gasped, her eyes going wide and bright with tears.

Reaching into his pocket, Christian pulled out the

ring he'd had designed especially for her. The princess-cut diamond was one that he knew she loved and that was all he'd had to go on. By the look on her face, he'd made the right choice.

Slowly, he slid the ring onto her finger. And it fit perfectly.

Just like her and the way she fit into his life.

"Will you marry me?" he asked.

Her smile was beyond radiant, but then turned a little impish. She looked at the ring and then at him before letting out a dramatic sigh. "I guess I have to now."

Christian came to his feet. "You guess?"

She looked at her hand again. "You clearly need someone to look after you, and now that this ring is on my finger, you're stuck with me."

He knew she was teasing—at least, he thought she was teasing—but then she pretty much jumped into his arms and he held her tight as they laughed.

This was how their life was going to be—crazy and unpredictable, and filled with love and laughter.

And Christian wouldn't have it any other way.

Read on for a sneak peek at the next book in the Shaughnessy Brothers series

SEVERAL THINGS HIT BOBBY HANNIGAN AT ONCE.

First, his head was pounding.

Next, this wasn't his bed.

And finally, he was going to smash whatever was making that beeping noise.

Prying his eyes open, he was surprised to find it took a minute to bring everything into focus. His gaze slowly scanned the room—dim lighting, white walls. Then he looked down and noticed the white bedding.

What the…?

The beeping was coming from someplace behind him but he didn't have the energy to move his head to see what it was.

Now panic started to set in.

As things finally came into focus, he groaned, and then he knew—he just knew—he was dead.

He groaned again and slammed his eyes shut.

This isn't happening…this isn't happening…

"Bobby?"

Opening his eyes again, he sighed with resignation. "I'm dead, aren't I?"

A low, deep laugh was the first response. "Hardly. Although, you did scare the crap out of everyone." A pause. "Wait, why would you think you're dead?"

"That's the only explanation for waking up to your ugly face."

Quinn Shaughnessy didn't look offended. Nothing seemed to offend the arrogant SOB.

Stepping closer to the bed, Quinn kept a serene grin on his face. "Yeah, well, I drew the short straw."

"What?" Bobby asked, hating how much effort it took to get the word out.

"It means your parents went back to the hotel to sleep and I volunteered to stay here with you."

"Where's Anna? Shouldn't my sister be here instead of you?" Yeah, he knew he was sounding a bit ungrateful, and Quinn *was* his brother-in-law, but he wished it was Anna—or anyone else—with him instead.

"Dude, she's eight months pregnant and practically on bed rest. There was no way she could have made the drive and stayed up all night. She's pissed off that she's not here, believe me, but between needing to take it easy, and Kaitlyn and Brian—"

"Maybe you should get off my sister and give her a break," Bobby said, but there was no heat behind his words. He didn't have it in him. If anything, he was breathless. "Stop at three, okay?"

Quinn laughed again. "Your sister says the same thing and then—"

"Ugh, stop. Let's just leave it there, okay?"

They were both silent, and as much as Bobby hated asking anything of Quinn, waiting around for answers wasn't an option.

"So, uh...have you talked to any doctors?" he asked warily.

The fact that Quinn looked as uncomfortable as Bobby felt was not encouraging.

"Look, um... Maybe we should wait for him to come in. It's still early and—"

"Damn it, Quinn!" Bobby snapped and winced. Everything hurt, and as much as he wanted to reach out and strangle his former foe, he didn't have the energy.

With a loud sigh, Quinn stepped closer to the bed, raking a hand through his dark blond hair. "Do you remember anything about what happened yesterday?"

The searing pain in his shoulder was a pretty good reminder. "I walked in on an armed robbery," he said slowly, racking his brain to remember what had happened. "I was off duty... I stopped at the convenience store to get gas and went in to grab a soda and..." Then he looked up at Quinn helplessly. "I tried to reason with them, I really did, but..."

"I know, man. I know," Quinn said quietly. "You were lucky. This could have been a lot worse."

"I don't see how."

He noticed his brother-in-law was avoiding eye contact.

"Quinn?"

"Bobby, why don't you wait and talk to the doctors? And your parents and the police chief. I'm sure they'll be able to answer all your questions better than I could."

That was the thing: there wasn't a doubt in Bobby's

mind that all those people would sit here and explain everything in a very reasonable manner. Right now, however, he wanted someone to just…be honest with him. His parents would try to play down his injuries, a doctor would be way too clinical, and his boss would be more than a little detached. He'd never thought there would come a time when he would want to receive news of any kind from Quinn Shaughnessy, but right now, he did.

Taking a steadying breath, Bobby let it out slowly. "How long have we known each other?"

A mirthless laugh came out before Quinn could stop it. "Too long."

"Dude, we've known each other for almost thirty years. Most of that time, I've wanted to punch you in the face."

"Hey!"

"And each and every one of those times were because you said what was on your mind and didn't care whose feelings you hurt."

"Bobby…"

Doing his best to sit up in the bed, he looked at Quinn pleadingly. "Right now, I need you to pretend you're not married to my sister, we're not family, and that we still pretty much despise one another."

No response.

"You owe me," he said, his tone serious.

"Owe you?"

Nodding, Bobby said, "Remember the car?"

"That was like…what, twenty years ago?"

"Doesn't change the fact that I never called in the favor."

For a minute, Quinn could only stare at him as if he was crazy. "That's not possible. In twenty years, I'm sure I've done you at least one favor."

"I asked you to leave my sister alone, and you didn't."

"Not the same," Quinn argued. "And that wasn't a favor."

"You didn't help me move."

"You didn't ask!" A smile crossed Quinn's face. "I let you stay with us when you come to town to visit, so technically—"

"Still not a favor, dumbass. We're family. That doesn't count."

Quinn muttered a curse.

"I'm serious, Quinn. I need to know what I'm dealing with and I know you aren't going to sugarcoat this. I don't want to be blindsided when the doctor comes in."

Looking over his shoulder toward the door, Quinn let out a long huff of frustration before facing Bobby again. "Okay, look," he began quietly. "You took a bullet to the shoulder."

"That much I assumed."

"Yeah, well…it wasn't exactly a clean shot."

"Meaning what?"

Quinn sighed loudly. "I really think you should wait and hear this from the doctor. Maybe I misunderstood what he said or maybe there are more test results, or—"

"Quinn!" he snapped.

"You lost a lot of blood," Quinn replied reluctantly. "They had to give you, like, three pints of blood in the ER." He paused. "And there's damage. Possibly permanent. They won't know for sure how extensive until the swelling from the surgery goes down. It's your left arm, so I know that has to work in your favor because—"

"Because I'm a righty," Bobby finished, but it did little to comfort him. "What kind of damage are we talking about?"

"Nerve damage," Quinn said grimly. "Some bone was fractured, nicked an artery and the nerves. If nothing else, you've got a long recovery ahead of you."

Bobby let it all sink in. A long recovery meant time off from the force. Permanent damage could mean the end of his career. He couldn't allow himself to think about that yet.

"How many casualties?" he asked quietly.

"Four."

Cursing, he pounded his fist against the mattress.

"I'm sorry, Bobby. I really am," Quinn said after a minute. "You want me to go and find a doctor? A nurse? You want me to call your folks? Their hotel is right across the street."

"No. It's okay. I just… I need to process all of this. There weren't a lot of people in the store, but they were all young and—"

"Don't, okay? Just…don't. Try not to think about it. You need to focus on you right now, and figuring out what happens from here."

"Yeah. Easier said than done."

They both fell silent. Though Bobby wanted more information, his brother-in-law wasn't a doctor and he didn't want to hear it from Quinn. The information he'd relayed already didn't even scratch the surface.

As if sensing he needed time to think, Quinn went and sat down in the lone chair in the room without saying a word. Bobby had no idea what time it was, except that it was early in the morning. Now that he was a little more awake, he realized how uncomfortable he was—not only his shoulder, which was throbbing, but his whole body hurt. His head was pounding and his throat was dry.

The last thing he wanted—ever—was to have to rely on anyone to help him. He enjoyed being the type of man who could take care of himself. Granted, he'd lived close to his family up until a couple of years ago, but ever since moving away, Bobby found he enjoyed being on his own. Not that he didn't love his family, but he had an independence now that he'd never had before. And on top of that, he simply didn't like asking for help. He wanted to be the one helping others.

Still, these were extenuating circumstances, right?

Clearing his throat and wincing at how sore it was, he said, "Um… Is there anything to drink? Some water or something?"

"Yeah. Sure." Quinn was instantly on his feet and pouring him some water from the small pitcher on the table. Bobby thanked him and slowly sipped from the cup. His hand was shaking and he felt weaker than he would have thought possible. Quinn helped him, and neither said a word about how awkward it was.

When he was done, Quinn put the cup back on the table and sat down again. Several minutes passed until Bobby couldn't take the silence any longer.

"You know, in that moment, when I knew what was coming, it felt like everything moved in slow motion."

Quinn listened but said nothing.

"I remember thinking there had to be something I

could do, something I could say, that would change the outcome. I wanted to stop anyone else from getting hurt." He paused. "But then someone made a break for the door and the guy—the gunman—he just...he freaked."

And just like that, Bobby could hear the shots, the screams. He could hear the glass breaking, the crying... and then the searing pain. Reaching up with his good hand, he carefully touched the bandage and immediately winced.

Not a good sign.

"I've been a cop for almost fifteen years," he went on. "I've been punched, I've been kicked..." He stopped and let out a bitter laugh. "I've even been spat on, but I never thought I'd be here." Then he looked at Quinn and let out another laugh. "Or that you'd be the one with me."

"Yeah, well..."

"I appreciate the fact that you are," he said solemnly. "For real. I think if I had woken up and it had been my folks standing there, they would have freaked me out. My mom would be crying and my dad would be trying to keep her calm."

Quinn stood and came back to the side of the bed.

"And if it were Anna, she would probably punch me in my good shoulder and yell at me for scaring her."

Quinn smiled. "That's my girl."

"So, I guess what I'm trying to say is, I'm...thankful. For you, you know, being here."

Quinn looked as uncomfortable as Bobby felt at the admission. Luckily, they were saved from having to say anything else when a nurse walked in to get his vitals. Window blinds were opened and he had a feeling quiet time was officially over.

After that, everything seemed to move at warp speed. People kept coming into the room to check on him, examine him, change out his IV, replace bandages—there was a steady stream of them until he thought his head would spin. The only problem was that none of them were his doctor. Every time he asked a question, he was told a doctor would be in to see him shortly.

It was maddening.

By the time a doctor came in, all Bobby wanted to do was take a nap.

"Officer Hannigan, I'm Dr. McIntyre," the sixty-something man said as he walked into the room. "How are you feeling?"

"Like I've been shot," Bobby said flatly.

"That's because you were," the doctor replied levelly, studying Bobby's chart. He was quiet for a few moments before he put the chart down and faced Bobby, his expression serious. For the next five minutes he explained in very dry, medical terms all that had happened to Bobby's shoulder and what had been done to repair the damage. He talked in a way that Bobby had a hard time following. Why didn't doctors learn to speak in layman's terms?

"So?" Bobby asked after he took a minute to let it all sink in. "What am I looking at here?"

"A long recovery."

Later that night, even once Bobby was alone in his room, sleep seemed impossible.

Nerve damage…

Loss of motor function…

Three months of rehabilitation...

None of it sat well with him. According to the doctor and just about everyone else who had come to see him today, it was still too early to tell what the final outcome would look like. Only one thing stood out to him—he wasn't going to be returning to active duty any time soon.

If ever.

Don't go there, he warned himself. But it was hard not to.

This was the first time today he'd had the chance to really think about the future. After Dr. McIntyre had left, the room had filled with people—friends, family, coworkers. Half of the police department had come to see him, his parents had sat by his side all day, and his phone had rung constantly with well wishes from just about everyone he knew. It had been a great distraction, but now he was left with a whole lot of silence and his own wild imagination.

What if he couldn't use his left arm again? What if he only got partial range back? He wouldn't be able to return to the force. He'd have to retire, and he was too damn young for that. What the hell was he supposed to do if that happened? Being a cop was all he'd ever wanted. He'd worked for that to the exclusion of all else—even avoiding long-term relationships because he didn't want the distraction. So where did it leave him?

Alone.

Completely alone.

He looked up at the bundle of balloons tied to the corner of his bed. His mother had brought them with her this morning as a way of cheering him up. Right. Because a dozen mylar balloons fixed things when you'd been shot and were facing the possibility of your career being over.

Not her fault, he reminded himself. She was doing what she always did—her best to make her family feel better. It wasn't her fault that there wasn't anything she could do. No number of balloons or flowers or freshly baked cookies were going to help.

Although right about now he'd kill for a batch of something sweet.

Grimacing, he did his best to get comfortable. He was a stomach sleeper and having to sleep sitting up wasn't helping at all. That and the pain.

Earlier, a nurse had come in and offered him something to help him sleep. He'd turned that down. She'd offered him a lot of things, actually, all of which he'd declined.

It wasn't anything new. Bobby wasn't arrogant, but he knew women found him attractive. And for some reason, a man in uniform was like catnip to some of them. And now it looked like he could add "injured cop out of uniform" to the list.

Great.

He sighed and shifted a little in the confines of the hospital bed, wishing like hell he could be at home recovering in his own space. It didn't look like that was going to happen any time soon. He'd be here getting poked and prodded for at least another couple of days, and then what? He wouldn't have to live at a rehab facility, but he was going to need some help since he wouldn't be able to drive or do a whole lot for himself.

Earlier, his folks had offered to come and stay with him until he got settled. He'd turned them down. His condo was a small two-bedroom and he knew it wouldn't take long before the walls started to close in on him. Then they'd offered to have him come and stay with them while they looked into rehab places back home. That one held a little more merit. Not that he was looking to move back in with his parents, but they had a lot more space and a lot more distractions. He wouldn't feel like he was under the microscope all the time.

It was a lot to think about. Maybe he was getting too far ahead of himself.

Or not. After all, what if Dr. McIntyre came in tomorrow and said he could be released to go home? Maybe he'd only need to come in once a week until he was healed and then he'd get a recommendation for rehab. Hell, if that happened, he'd jump at it and pay for his parents to stay at the hotel for a couple more days until he got settled. His mom would protest, but Dad would side with him.

Feeling a little more relaxed, Bobby let out a slow breath and allowed himself to close his eyes. He'd give anything to go back in time and stop all of the things that had happened—not just to him, but to the other victims. Knowing that he couldn't didn't make him feel any better.

Maybe he should have accepted that pill to help him sleep.

Muttering a curse, he reached for the call button and loathed himself for it. He didn't want to be weak. He didn't want to ask for help.

But more than that, he didn't want to be alone with his thoughts anymore.

"This is great, isn't it?"

A shrug was the only response.

"C'mon, admit it. This place is really cool. We're going to have so much fun! We can go to the park, and to the beach, and we have all summer to check everything out!"

Another shrug.

Teagan Shaughnessy looked at her five-year-old son standing in their new front yard and held in a sigh. Lucas was not thrilled with their cross-country move. He'd made that point abundantly clear all through the long drive. Luckily, her parents had joined them them, and the whole group had caravanned from Colorado to the Carolina coast, doing their best to make an adventure of it.

Unfortunately, Lucas wasn't feeling very adventurous.

She knew it was temporary. His moods often were. But just this once, she wished his mood would lighten up sooner rather than later. This move was a big deal for her too. She'd done her fair share of moving all over the country thanks to growing up as an Army brat, and once she'd left home, all she'd wanted was a place to call her own for good. Somewhere she could settle in and call it a day.

But life had made other plans.

"It's hot here," Lucas stated, interrupting her thoughts.

True enough. It was a definite change in climate from Colorado, but she was determined to make him believe it was all for the best.

Even as she felt herself sweating more than she had in a long time.

"Let's go inside where there's air-conditioning and unpack some of your toys. What do you say?"

"I want to go home," he pouted, his little arms crossing over his chest.

As much as she wanted to be angry and demand that he stop being difficult, Teagan did her best to stay calm. It would be great if she had some help—someone other than her parents—but that wasn't going to happen. Lucas's father had been killed in combat before Lucas was born, and it had always been just the two of them. Sometimes—like now—she really resented it.

"Lucas, we promised Meema and Pops we'd meet them for dinner. And that's not going to happen if we don't get some work done around here," she said, calmly but firmly.

"Fine," he said with a loud, dramatic sigh before dragging himself into the house.

They worked together—she used that phrase loosely—for two hours. Lucas had to be coached and directed every step of the way. Teagan knew she'd get much more done alone, but her parents were doing their own share of unpacking and couldn't babysit. For now, she had to do her best to make this a game and try not to cringe at how long it was taking to get even simple things done.

"Can I play one of my games now?" Lucas asked, standing beside her. They finally had his room almost completely set up and normally she wouldn't want him playing video games on a weekday, but these were extenuating circumstances.

"Sure," she said with a smile. "You worked really hard and I'm very proud of you!"

He beamed at her praise. "Does that mean I can have a snack too?"

There wasn't much to choose from, and she glanced toward the kitchen. "Um… I think we have some cookies somewhere…"

"I know where!" he yelled as he took off toward the kitchen.

The house was a small, temporary rental, just a two-bedroom, one-and-a-half-bath bungalow with an open floor plan. Even so, she was truly grateful. The house had been one of the signs that this move was meant to be. Two months ago, her parents had brought her out to visit her uncle and cousins, and they had all fallen in love with the town. It wasn't as if they hadn't been here before, but it had been over a dozen years since their last visit.

Back then, she had often asked why they couldn't live at the beach all the time like her cousins did. But the answer she'd always gotten was that the military was her father's life—like it or not. After a while, she'd stopped asking. So this time, when the opportunity had come to make the trip again, Teagan had been super excited. It had been great to reconnect with everyone, and it was amazing how much the family had grown. Her head was still spinning from trying to remember all the new names. That was something she was going to have to get better at now that she would be seeing them on a regular basis.

The house had come on top of the joy of reconnection, a rental property owned by her cousin Quinn's wife, Anna. Part of Teagan felt a little guilty because of the great deal they'd given her, but she'd graciously accepted their offer and promised to take care of the place as if it were her own. Her parents had found something just as nice a little closer to the beach, thanks to Uncle Ian. Her mother was so excited.

And then there was her job. Back in Colorado, she

had been temping as a guidance counselor for elementary schools. There weren't any openings for her to have a permanent position like she wanted, but she filled in where she could. Once she had mentioned what she did for a living to her cousin Aidan's wife, Zoe, she suddenly had a list of people she could contact here in their new school district. Zoe was an interior designer who was very active in the community and seemed to know everyone. Talk about luck—within a week, she had several interviews over the phone and had secured a position!

Everything had fallen into place.

It had all happened so quickly, but Teagan supposed it was better than dragging it out. Her position wouldn't start until the middle of August and it was only the first week of June now, so she had the entire summer ahead of her to settle in and prepare herself. She'd considered getting a part-time job somewhere to help recover the cost of the move but wasn't sure if she should. Not that she wouldn't be able to find one—not with so many Shaughnessys in town with businesses of their own—but because Lucas maybe needed her attention more than they needed the cash right now.

The thought of her cousins made her smile. It had been so long since she'd had more than her parents around. Sure, she had friends and coworkers she adored, but there was something to be said for finally having the kind of big family she'd always longed for. Being an only child and constantly moving wherever the U.S. Army stationed them meant she hadn't had the chance to make and keep friends for long. And while Teagan had sworn she'd never move again, this time would definitely be her last.

Until she had to move out of the rental.

Don't think about that now! she admonished herself.

Looking around, she saw Lucas had indeed found the cookies and was happily settled in front of the television playing one of his favorite games. A small sigh of relief came out before she could stop it. If nothing went wrong, she could have a solid hour to put some work into getting her own room unpacked before meeting her parents for dinner. They'd already received multiple invitations from her uncle and cousins, but until she was settled in, she needed as few distractions as possible.

While reconnecting with her cousins was certainly a perk, she hoped she'd make some friends on her own too. No need to be the clingy relative who'd moved to town.

Unfortunately, no distractions meant having time in her own head for worried thoughts of all that could go wrong with this move.

"Nothing's gone wrong so far," she said to herself. "Stop looking for trouble."

Easier said than done.

While she was used to moving around, Lucas wasn't. Though Teagan knew her son would adjust, there had been a certain comfort for them both in living in Colorado. Probably because it was where he'd been born and she had her own circle of friends she was going to miss.

Ugh, that was a depressing thought for sure.

Pushing her worries aside, she unpacked three boxes of clothes and hung them up before moving on to getting the bathroom unpacked and set up.

"Mom!" Lucas called out. "Is it time to see Meema and Pops? I'm hungry!"

Hungry? Already? But when she looked at the clock,

she saw it was definitely close to dinner. Where had the time gone?

"Give me fifteen minutes to freshen up and we'll go, okay?"

"Aww, Mom," he whined, but that was the norm. Lucas hated waiting on anything.

A shower would have been nice, but she'd have to get by with a quick change of clothes and running a brush through her hair.

That was, until she looked in the mirror.

There was no hope. She was sweaty, her makeup—the little she usually wore—was already smeared beyond repair, and her hair was…well, it wasn't pretty.

"No problem. Three-minute showers are fun," she murmured as she turned the water on.

Five minutes later, Teagan felt marginally better.

And clean.

Moving as quickly as possible, she dried off and pulled on clean clothes. With her hair wrapped up turban-style in a towel, she walked out into the living room. "Almost ready!"

Lucas looked over his shoulder at her and groaned. "We're never going to eat dinner."

"Yes, we will," she promised, grabbing her purse from the kitchen island. That was the last place she had stuffed her makeup bag. "We'll be in the car in ten minutes!" As she ran back to the bathroom, she heard her son's cry of disbelief.

And as it turned out, he was right.

It took her fifteen minutes because her hair wasn't cooperating. Though it was a little longer than she normally wore it, even at shoulder length it seemed to take forever to dry. She made a mental note to look for a hair salon. At the very least she was going to need a good cut and style before starting her new job.

When Teagan walked back into the living room, Lucas had the television off and was waiting by the door. She grabbed her purse, keys, and phone and bent down to give him a loud, smacking kiss on the cheek.

"You took forever."

"I know, bud. Sorry." She ran a hand over his dark hair. "And you will be rewarded for your patience."

His big brown eyes widened. "I will?"

She nodded. "An ice cream cone as big as your head for dessert tonight. How does that sound?"

"Yay!" he yelled as he ran out the door and to their car.

Later that night, after Lucas was finally asleep, Teagan lay in bed staring at the ceiling. Her mind raced.

That had been one heck of a curveball her parents had thrown her at dinner. They were leaving on a two-week cruise next week! At first she had been certain she'd misheard them. After all, they had just moved across the country. Why would they be going on a vacation right away? And worse, how were she and Lucas supposed to settle in without them?

Which is exactly what she'd asked, and as she lay there in the dark, she still couldn't believe the response she'd gotten.

"We thought it best to do this now," her mother said. Catherine Shaughnessy was the best mom a girl could ask for—loving, sweet, and very level-headed.

Right now, Teagan hated that last one the most.

"But…why? We just got here. You can see how hard Lucas is taking the move," Teagan had argued. Fortunately—or maybe it had been planned—her dad had taken her son out on the pier so he hadn't heard any of the conversation.

With a patient smile, her mother responded, "That's why we thought it best, Teagan. You and Lucas need to settle in together and figure out how to make this move work for the two of you. With your father retiring, we're looking forward to traveling that isn't about work. You understand, right?"

Sadly, she did. It didn't make her feel any better about it, but she understood.

"Why didn't you say anything sooner?"

"There was so much going on and we didn't want to add to your stress. The subject came up when we were here in April. Ian and Martha mentioned they were going on this cruise with some friends and I mentioned that your father and I had never gone on one. Next thing I know, they extended the invitation. Your father was very excited about it." She smiled. "He's worked so hard his whole life, it's nice to see him looking so relaxed."

"I know, I know. And now I feel like a selfish brat because I'm just thinking about myself."

Reaching across the table, Catherine took Teagan's hand in hers. "You're the least selfish person I know, Teagan. And your concern isn't for yourself, it's about Lucas."

"It's the same thing, Mom."

"No, it's not. You've always put Lucas first, and it's a wonderful quality. And you know how close Lucas and your father are, so you're afraid Lucas is going to be devastated that we're gone."

"I've relied on the two of you too much," she admitted in a low voice. "Lucas isn't a baby anymore. It's time for us to let the two of you have a life."

"The two of you *are* our life." Catherine smiled. "We aren't going on the cruise to get away from you. We're just looking to do a little something for us. Something fun."

"And you deserve it. You really do."

"Plus, it's a chance for us to make some new friends," her mother went on. "You remember Jack and Mary Hannigan, don't you? They're Anna's parents, and they still live next door to Ian and Martha." When Teagan nodded, she said, "They're going as well."

"I'm sure you're all going to have a great time. And after this move, I'm sure you're ready to relax a bit."

"Oh, believe me, we are. But we're not the only ones who need a little bit of rest and relaxation. From what I hear, the others are looking to get away just as much."

"What do you mean?"

"Well, Quinn and Anna just had their third baby last month."

Oh, right. Teagan remembered her mom talking about that, but with everything else going on, it hadn't really stuck in her mind. "That's great. What did they have again?"

"A little girl," Catherine said wistfully. "They named her Bailey."

"That's sweet."

"Anyway, Ian and Martha have been helping with Quinn and Anna's two little ones for a while, because

Anna was on bed rest for the last month of her pregnancy. And then with the birth of the baby..."

"What about her folks? They're nearby—couldn't they have helped out?"

"Their older son was shot last month. He's a police officer in Myrtle Beach."

"Oh my goodness!" Teagan gasped. "How awful!"

"They say he's doing well, and getting better every day. He was shot in the shoulder and has some nerve damage, but he's recovering."

"Well, that's a good thing."

Catherine nodded and then laughed softly.

"What? What's so funny?"

Her mother waved her off but then said, "They claim he's fussier and more demanding than the new baby!"

"Mom, that's terrible! The man was shot!"

"I know, I know. He's just incredibly grumpy and Mary said he was a lousy patient. So believe me when I say they're looking forward to getting away for a little while."

"Just like you are," Teagan added. "I really am excited for you."

Now as she was looking back, Teagan realized she was both excited and not, all at the same time.

How messed up was that?

The good news was there were plenty of things she and Lucas could do to entertain themselves while her parents were away. Like she'd told him earlier that day, they could go to the beach, the park, and generally explore their new town. There were plenty of cousins for him to play with now and she hoped—in time, maybe once school started—he'd make some friends on his own. They'd scout out the local library and see if there were any kids' programs there, or maybe even some local day camps.

Tons of options.

For Lucas.

It was a lot easier to make friends when you were five, she thought. Making new friends at twenty-seven? Not quite as easy.

Not that she was shying away from it, but...

Yeah, okay. If she had the choice, she'd avoid it altogether. She was the new kid all over again. You'd think she'd be used to it after so many years of constantly starting over, but the thought of trying now was simply exhausting.

Ironic, considering how physically exhausted she was right now and yet she couldn't seem to fall asleep.

Kicking off the blankets, Teagan climbed from the bed and went out to the kitchen to grab a glass of water. Standing in the dark, she wondered what she could possibly do to fall asleep.

"Try not thinking about sleep," she murmured. "That should help."

Easier said than done.

A box sat where she'd plunked it on the kitchen table—books and photo albums. She reached in and pulled out the photo album that was on top and took it back to her room, quietly closing the door behind her.

About the Author

Samantha Chase is a *New York Times* and *USA Today* bestseller of contemporary romance. She released her debut novel in 2011 and currently has more than forty titles under her belt! When she's not working on a new story, she spends her time reading romances, playing way too many games of Scrabble or Solitaire on Facebook, wearing a tiara while playing with her sassy pug, Maylene...oh, and spending time with her husband of twenty-five years and their two sons in North Carolina.

Also by Samantha Chase

The Montgomery Brothers
Wait for Me / Trust in Me
Stay with Me / More of Me
Return to You
Meant for You
I'll Be There
Until There Was Us

The Shaughnessy Brothers
Made for Us
Love Walks In
Always My Girl
This Is Our Song
A Sky Full of Stars
Holiday Spice
Until I Loved You

Shaughnessy Brothers: Band on the Run
One More Kiss
One More Promise
One More Moment

Holiday Romance
The Christmas Cottage / Ever After
Mistletoe Between Friends / The Snowflake Inn

Novellas Now in Print
The Baby Arrangement / Baby, I'm Yours / Baby, Be Mine
In the Eye of the Storm / Catering to the CEO
Exclusive / A Touch of Heaven

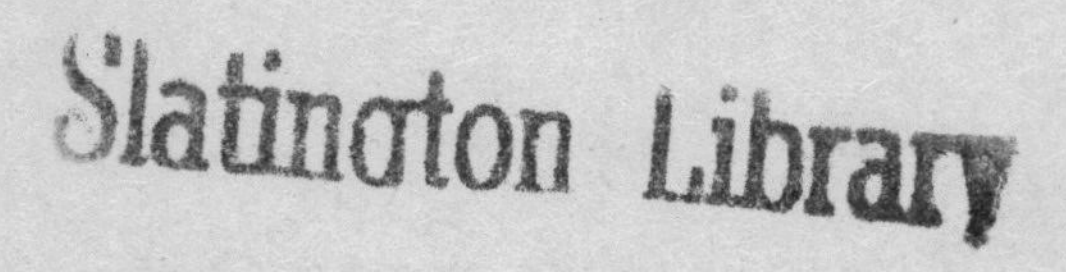